Bang scythe[...] legs out from under him

Bolan rose to one knee, swung up both .45s and emptied them into the remaining enemy gunner. He dropped his left-hand gun and clawed for his last magazine. The two surviving bikers tore away.

The soldier got to his feet and lurched into the street. The biker he had shot was crawling away. Most people didn't crawl away with three .45's in their back. That told Bolan the guy was wearing body armor.

The Executioner searched for his team. Kaino was helping Svarzkova to her feet and weeping from the CS stench she gave off. Bang had reloaded and was covering Bolan, who could barely hear his own voice as he shouted, "Banger, we're taking this guy with us! Get the car. We're out of here!"

Don Pendleton's Mack Bolan®

State of War

A GOLD EAGLE BOOK FROM

WORLDWIDE®

TORONTO • NEW YORK • LONDON
AMSTERDAM • PARIS • SYDNEY • HAMBURG
STOCKHOLM • ATHENS • TOKYO • MILAN
MADRID • WARSAW • BUDAPEST • AUCKLAND

Recycling programs
for this product may
not exist in your area.

First edition December 2012

ISBN-13: 978-0-373-61557-5

Special thanks and acknowledgment to
Chuck Rogers for his contribution to this work.

STATE OF WAR

Printed in U.S.A.

Junk is the ideal product… The ultimate merchandise. No sales talk necessary. The client will crawl through sewer and beg to buy.

—William S. Burroughs

There's a new drug on the scene, one that consumes the addict's flesh from within. What kind of madness is this? We must drive the people who promote this horror back to the sewers they emerged from. Permanently.

—Mack Bolan

CHAPTER ONE

Mack Bolan, aka the Executioner, slid into the unmarked car and stuck out his hand. "Evening, Master Sergeant." Miami-Dade Police Master Sergeant Gadiel Kaino could have been Bill Cosby's younger, bigger, redheaded brother who had been a prizefighter but let himself go. The Puerto Rican cop shook Bolan's hand. "Call me Kaino."

"Call me Cooper."

"You sure you want to do this? They eat white men alive where you want to go, and they'll eat me for aiding and abetting."

Bolan had done his research. Kaino had a large reputation in the Miami Metropolitan Area for breaking rules, stepping on toes and being one of the toughest cops in the county. Bolan noted the small tattoo of a heart with a scrolling *N* inside it on the flesh between his right thumb and forefinger. Kaino had been a member of the Puerto Rican Netas gang in his youth. "I'm down if you are."

Kaino was down. He stepped on the gas and the eighties-vintage Crown Victoria rumbled forward. Bolan could feel the tightness of the suspension as Kaino took them into the bowels of the Metro. Kaino was clearly wary of Bolan. "Justice Department Observation Liaison Officer?"

Bolan grinned. "That would be me."

"You aren't Marshals Service."

"No, but I know some good marshals."

"Yeah, me, too." Kaino's eyes narrowed. "You sure as hell aren't a lawyer."

"No."

"Homeland Security?"

"Nope."

Master Sergeant Kaino had come up through Miami-Dade during the explosion of cocaine and the war on drugs of the 1980s. He gave Bolan a disparaging look. "Tell me you aren't CIA."

"I'm not CIA," Bolan confirmed.

"Okay, so, not to be a dick or anything…"

"But…?"

"Who the fuck are you?"

Bolan looked at the ID badge hanging over his chest. "I'm a Justice Department Observation Liaison Officer."

Kaino made a noise. "That's messed up."

"Yeah, they're usually a little more creative."

"I hope you brought some heavy iron, man. Where we're going isn't good."

Bolan glanced at his bulging gear bag in the back. "The hugest."

Miami-Dade sweltered in the summer heat, and they instantly lost the breeze off the ocean as Kaino took them inland. The neighborhoods went from bad to worse to urban war zone. Groups of people on porches and street corners gave the Crown Vic very hard looks. Bolan noted a number of the hard cases gave Kaino wary nods of recognition and respect. A small minority waved. On a corner a pair of prostitutes dressed like aerobics instructors shrieked happily as they rolled by. "*Hola,* Kaino!" "Looking good, *Papi!*"

"*Hola,* Allana!" Kaino called. "And not as good as you, Bebe!"

Allana and Bebe fired off a string of sexually challenging remarks in Puerto Rican Spanish that Bolan wasn't quite sure he wanted to understand. "Kaino, those girls are dudes."

Kaino regarded Bolan with great seriousness. "I have a broad spectrum of support in the Miami-Dade Latino community."

"Broad-spectrum support is good," Bolan acknowledged.

Kaino pulled into what could only be described as urban Armageddon. A lonely gas station sat in the island of glare from the lights over its pumps. Most of the streetlights on the block around it had been shot out. Nearly all the telephone lines had shoes tied together thrown across them. Gang graffiti was everywhere.

Bolan regarded the little old-fashioned filling station with interest. "Interesting."

"You ain't seen nothin' yet."

The soldier grabbed his gear bag, and Kaino led him around back. There was little to see other than a weed-choked lot and some warped and ancient picnic benches. Someone had smashed off the doorknob to the men's room. Someone else had painted an X-rated fever dream of an Aztec priestess on the door. Even Bolan had to admit it was a triumph. It was such a work of art that no one had tagged it. He noted the security camera over the door hung by wires like a half-decapitated chicken. Kaino drew a pair of four-inch Smith & Wesson revolvers. Bolan carried a .50-caliber Desert Eagle in one hand and a Beretta 93-R machine pistol in the other.

Kaino regarded Bolan's steel. "Jesus! You weren't kidding!"

Bolan shrugged.

Kaino kicked the door. "Miami-Dade!"

The men's room was empty.

Bolan mentally cataloged the wall-to-wall, ceiling-to-ceiling gang graffiti covering the bathroom. It appeared that Los Zetas, the Gulf Cartel and Mara Salvatrucha-13 all claimed this men's room. Given the acts of gastrointestinal Armageddon covering the floor and the facilities, it appeared that none of the gangs felt compelled to take responsibility for the state of hygiene and maintenance of their claimed territory. Bolan gave Kaino a wry look. "The Netas don't seem very well represented in this establishment, Kaino."

"La Asociación del Ñeta is a cultural organization, Cooper." Kaino scowled. "And if we were in charge of this lavatory, people would be wiping their asses with toilet paper rather than the walls."

"You know, I like the way you said that with a straight face. That was good."

Kaino smiled despite himself. He looked around the lavatory measuringly. "But you're right. The Netas aren't well represented. Back in the day the Netas ran the prisons in Florida. Only the Aryans and the Latin Kings dared to give us any static on the inside. On the outside the Colombians ran the drugs and everyone fought for their business. Mexicans were mules for the Colombians. Mexico was just a transshipment point. And El Salvador?" Kaino scoffed. "A mud puddle where they ate guinea pigs. A Central American tragedy you heard about in the news. Now the Mexicans run everything. The Mexican cartels are the alpha predators now. They're expanding south as well as north. And MS-13 is like a bunch of pit bulls roaming the streets, animals, biting everything that moves, and moving in on whatever they can move in on."

Bolan was intimately aware of the ebb and flow of gang structure in the Americas. He had spilled blood fighting it. Kaino had obviously lived it, survived it, threaded the eye of the needle and come out a lawman. "Hard times for the old association these days?"

"We aren't what we were. Netas are still strong on the inside, but out on the streets?" Kaino slowly shook his head. "MS-13 is pushing my people, and they push hard."

"So why did you bring me to this shithole again?"

"Oh, this is a happening nightspot around here."

"I can imagine."

"No, it is. It's the only gas station for blocks around. The rest all closed their doors. Every gangster's whip needs gas, and no one wants to start a war over this station and see it close."

Bolan ran his eyes over the mystery stains streaking the walls. "Like the *Highlander,* holy ground."

"That was a good show." Kaino pointed to the wall over the sinks. All the mirrors had been ripped out, and the wall there was an almost Jackson Pollockian fusion of gangland graffiti tags piled one over the other in such profusion that it was a startlingly profound work of art unto itself. "That's the message board. That paint has to be at least an inch thick by now."

"The gangs leave each other messages here."

"Hey, man, during the cold war even Washington and Moscow had a red phone. Sometimes you have to talk."

"People come here, check the latest messages and word spreads out," Bolan concluded.

"That's it exactly, you saw those benches outside? Sometimes the gangs come here when they need to have an actual parley."

"So if this is holy ground, how come we have to walk heeled with big steel?"

"Because around here I'm considered dangerous big game," Kaino told him. "And you? Well, let me tell you something Mr. Blue-Eyed Devil, you would be a genuine trophy. Get it?"

"More than you'll ever know."

"You're scaring the shit out of me. I'm really wondering what I'm getting into."

Bolan nodded. "I get that a lot."

"I just bet you do."

Bolan shrugged. "Want to see something cool?"

"Oh, I can't wait."

The soldier reached into his bag and took out a couple of cans of spray paint.

"No!" Kaino was appalled. "Oh, hell no!"

Bolan had run missions in Mexico and El Salvador. On several occasions he had run roughshod over the organized crime affiliates using the name El Hombre. He wondered if anyone in Florida would have heard of the moniker, and whether it would send any reverberations in the right directions. Bolan had practiced his painting skills before he had come to Florida. He did a credible job of painting *El Hombre* in bloated, amoebalike letters along with the date and the symbols that said El Hombre was now taking ownership of this men's room. Bolan finished with a flourish of his own design.

Kaino's jaw dropped. "Mother of God..."

"You like?"

"You just signed your death warrant," Kaino stated.

"Fourth one I signed today."

Kaino's face went blank. "What?"

"Oh, I painted similar tags in Zeta, Gulf and MS-13 territory earlier."

"Why...you..." A stream of Puerto Rican invectives poured forth from the master sergeant.

"I didn't tag any Neta territory."

"You fuckin better not have, *ese,* or I'll kill you myself. Not that I need to, because you just killed us both." Kaino eyed Bolan scathingly. "You already knew about this place, didn't you?"

"Knew about it, but I appreciate the guided tour, and the sitrep from a veteran on the ground." Bolan checked his watch. "They should be coming soon."

"And that's another thing. What do you think is going to happen when the Zetas, Gulf and MS-13 all roll up on this little slice of heaven at the same time?"

"Tension, apprehension and dissension?" Bolan suggested.

Kaino was so upset he forgot he was holding revolvers in both hands as he waved his arms up and down in outrage. "It'll be fucking World War III! And you started it!"

"It'll be Armageddon, but a focused Armageddon."

"Oh, and how are you going to focus three rival gangs?"

"We're going to make them focus on us."

Kaino simply stared. Bolan's phone rang. "Hold on, I need to take this." He checked the caller icon and answered. "What've we got, Bear?"

Aaron "the Bear" Kurtzman's voice came across the line from the Computer Room at Stony Man Farm in Virginia. "We have multiple vehicles converging on the filling station from all directions."

"Give me visual."

A mile up in space a National Security Agency satellite peered down at Kaino's corner of Florida and sent its feed to Bolan's phone. The soldier saw the grid of streets that framed the neighborhood in greens and grays. Well over a dozen automobiles were converging on the station. He held out the phone so Kaino could see. "They're coming."

Kaino blinked. "You have a helicopter watching us?"

"Satellite."

"You have a satellite."

Bolan grinned. "Cool, isn't it?"

THE EXECUTIONER unzipped his bag and pulled out what appeared to be a pair of assault rifles on steroids.

"Jesus!"

"AA-12 semiautomatic shotgun." Bolan slapped in a massive drum magazine and racked the action. "I know, you've never fired one before. So a buddy of mine installed a laser sight." He squeezed the grip and a red dot appeared on the closest stall.

"So we're just going to hose down Zetas, Gulfs and the

MS-13 boys in a premeditated and, may I say, arranged act of mass murder?"

"Your weapon holds twenty-four rounds. That drum is loaded with tear gas." Bolan pulled out a gas mask with night-vision goggles and an armored vest in the master sergeant's size. He pulled out a second drum. "This one is loaded with rubber buckshot. Keep your shots low."

Kaino stared at the weapon as if Bolan had handed him a two-headed baby.

"Come on," Bolan cajoled. "You used to be Neta, tell me you're not down with laying a little less-than-lethal hurt on these *vato* interlopers."

A slow smile spread across Kaino's face. "You know, this is almost like a wet dream, but I like my job. Plus, can I tell you something, just between you and me?"

"Shoot."

"I don't like lifting weights or having sex with men, and that's all there is to do in prison."

"Sorry, almost forgot," Bolan pulled a business card from his shirt pocket. "Here."

Kaino's face went slack. Bolan geared up. The cop slowly shook his head. "That is the Seal of the President of the United States."

Bolan slapped the Velcro tabs on his armor shut. "Yeah."

"So you like, carry around presidential pardons in your pocket?"

"No, but I will take full responsibility for anything that happens here tonight, you were never here, and if for any reason someone disputes that, that is the phone number they can call and complain to."

"Dude, who are you?"

"Gear up or scoot. Clock is ticking."

Kaino geared up. "Well, seeing as how you are a guest of the Miami-Dade Police Department I would be derelict in my duty if I abandoned you to your folly."

"I like your attitude, Kaino. You've used night vision before?"

"Nothing as cool as this, and never fitted to a gas mask."

Bolan adjusted the mask to Kaino's face and locked the night-vision in place. The soldier assembled his own unit. Kurtzman's voice spoke on speaker. "Hostiles arriving on site."

"Copy that, Bear." Bolan pulled his mask down over his face. "On my mark."

"Copy that, Striker. On your mark."

Bolan heard vehicles screeching up to the gas station. Angry voices called back and forth in Spanish as more gangsters arrived by the second. Bolan walked out and strode around the station. Low-riders, SUVs, vans and pickups filled the parking lot. Gangsters shouted, swore and pointed angry fingers. The name El Hombre flew back and forth. Kaino was right, these weren't upper echelon cartel men, they were gangbangers, and they were strangely reluctant to start shooting here at the one place they all respected.

"Kill the lights," Bolan ordered.

"Denying your area power grid access…now."

Gangsters of various stripes shouted in alarm as the street went dark. Bolan clapped the master sergeant on the shoulder. "Lay down the law, Kaino."

The cop began to fire.

The gas rounds thudded from the barrel of the big 12-gauge in slow, methodical fire. They didn't have a huge payload but Kaino had a lot of them. Bolan poured fire in on top of his partner's, arcing high for a two-tiered barrage.

"Shoot and scoot, Kaino. They can't see you but they can see your muzzle-blast."

Pistols popped in answer from among the cars. Bolan and Kaino moved and dropped gas into the milling gangsters without mercy. The return fire came ever more sporadically.

Bolan popped his drum, slipped in a specific 5-round clip and stalked toward the gas cloud.

"Cover me, Kaino."

Kaino slapped in a fresh drum as Bolan strode up to an SUV and fired.

The Dragon's Tongue ammo sent a one-hundred-foot jet of flame playing over the vehicle. The effect lasted less than a second. Any exposed person in the path of the flame would be badly burned. Gangsters choking on tear gas screamed at the effect. The driver slammed his vehicle into Reverse and rammed the vehicle behind him. Bolan hosed down two more vehicles and sent tongues of fire into the lanes between the clusters of gangs. Gangsters ran in all directions.

Kaino's mask smothered the sound of his laughter to the general public, but Bolan heard it loud and clear as the master sergeant sent out clouds of rubber buckshot at calf level and swept his former opponents from back in the day off their feet. Bolan reloaded and flamed another five vehicles.

The rout was total.

Rubber screamed on asphalt as smoking rides peeled to get out of the gas and flamethrower effect. Bolan took the loudspeaker out of his bag and connected it to the mike in his mask.

Bolan's voice boomed like God on High. "I am El Hombre! The gas station is mine! Miami-Dade is mine! I'm coming for all of you!"

He watched with mild satisfaction as the remaining gangsters ran, limped or crawled out of the war zone.

CHAPTER TWO

Miami-Dade Safehouse

"Did you have fun?" Aaron Kurtzman asked.

Bolan glanced at the *Miami Herald*. The morning headline read Gang War Erupts! In a smaller font the side story talked about a "Disturbing new twist in the ongoing turf battles. Police tactics purported used in battle." Bolan turned to Kaino. "Did you have fun?"

"Oh, big fun." Kaino held his hands three feet apart. "Huge."

"Yeah, I guess we had fun, Bear."

"Speaking of fun." Kaino glanced at the laptop he'd been issued. He was speaking to someone named Bear, but his video window was blank. Kaino was a trained investigator, and he could tell by facial cuts that the man across the table from him was looking at a face. Kaino spoke to the Bear. "Your man here told me he would prefer it if I didn't contact my department unless it was an emergency or to request resources."

"That would be preferable," Kurtzman agreed. "What's on your mind?"

"Last night was fun, but what's my status now?"

"As of now you are on an open-ended, paid, consulting leave of absence."

"Never heard of such a thing."

Bolan held up his Justice Department Observation Liaison Officer badge. "Want one?"

"Nah, open-ended paid consulting leave is good. So what's next?"

"That depends on you."

"Me?" Kaino threw back his head and laughed. "Dude! You just kicked the Zetas', Gulf Coast's and MS-13's asses all at the same time. You're El Hombre! King of the street, and may I add proud new absentee owner of a gas station! Dude, I just walk in your shadow and I'm thankful for the slot."

"Didn't know you were a poet, Kaino."

"Puerto Ricans," Kaino acknowledged. "We're poetic people. So what can I do for you, El Hombre?"

"We've been picking up some real strange chatter. That led us to the Miami-Dade area."

"Chatter?" Kaino queried.

"Yeah."

"Like intelligence communications and satellites and shit like that?"

"And shit like that," Bolan confirmed.

Kaino shrugged. "Oh."

"Oh what?"

"I thought you were here about *cocodrilo*."

"Crocodile?" Bolan queried.

"Well, yeah. Oh, and by the way, just so you know, Cocosino will be coming for both our asses after your little stunt last night."

"Killer croc? Isn't that a Batman villain?"

"Well, yes and no. I assure you Cocosino is real, and we have a trail of bodies to prove it."

"You're saying you have a supervillain straight out of a comic book in Miami-Dade?"

"We have a killer for hire straight out of your worst nightmare. A guy who doesn't care. An enforcer. A guy who everyone's afraid of. And you wrote your name on a wall. I really hope you understand the implications of that. Cocosino will be coming." Kaino gave Bolan a very shrewd look. "But that's not why you're here, you're here because…?"

"What's *cocodrilo?*"

Kurtzman spoke triumphantly across the link. "Spanish from the Russian, *krokodil,* and that's our link!"

"What does this crocodile stuff mean, Bear?"

"It's bad."

Kaino nodded. *"Muy malo."*

"*Krokodil* is Russian for crocodile," Kurtzman said.

"I picked up on that."

"*Krokodil* is a new designer drug. It's a desomorphine, or morphine derivative."

"A heroin substitute," Bolan stated.

"Right." Kurtzman clicked a key and a window of text appeared on Bolan's and Kaino's laptops.

"The main ingredient is codeine," Kurtzman informed them. "In the U.S. codeine is a controlled substance, but in Russia codeine is widely available as an over-the-counter drug."

In Bolan's experience what was readily available in Russia over the counter, much less under it, was appalling. A frown passed over the soldier's face. "Most heroin addicts I've met would consider codeine a pretty piss-poor substitute for heroin."

"It's what they mix it with."

"Like what?"

"Try gasoline, paint thinner, iodine, hydrochloric acid, even red phosphorus."

"Bear, I've had Russians throw red phosphorus at me in anger. Now you're saying they're injecting it?"

"According to reports, the high is similar to heroin— a whole lot rougher, but if you're a degenerate heroin addict, *krokodil* will get the job done, and it's about ten times cheaper. The other benefit is, given the ingredients, you don't need a friendly heroin dealer. You can get all the ingredients and cook it up on your own."

"Should I even ask about the side effects?"

"The side effects are how *krokodil* gets its name." Kurtzman hit a key. "Hold on to your breakfast."

Bolan stared long and hard at the jpeg. He could tell it was a human ankle because two hands pulling down a sock framed it. Where the flesh wasn't gray it was green. In between the blotches of necrotic color, the skin rose and cracked like a lizard's scales. Bolan easily identified several suppurating injection sites. "This isn't good."

"It gets worse. A heroin high can last four to eight hours. *Krokodil* lasts for about ninety minutes, and by all accounts the withdrawal symptoms are obscene. Once you're hooked on *krokodil* you need to hit three to four times per day. All you live for is to cook it or score it. According to the Russian medical service, once you start taking *krokodil* your life expectancy is a year or less. It's the cell death and scaling that give the drug its name, and those scales eventually rot off. I'm reading accounts here of advanced users being found still alive but with their bones showing. In Russia they call it the drug that eats the junkie, literally and figuratively. It is the absolutely lowest form of addiction I have ever heard of."

"And now it's here in Miami-Dade."

Kaino spoke quietly. "I've seen it. Smelled it, too. Any lab cooking the *cocodrilo* smells to the skies of iodine. So do the cooks. Most of the cooks are junkies themselves. Sometimes they pour the iodine into their wounds as remedial first aid. Sometimes they drink it. There's some misguided mythology that drinking what they're cooking with will make them stronger."

Bolan had found himself drinking potassium iodide on several occasions; however, that had usually been after exposure to spent nuclear material. "So, the skin is rotting off their bones but they have very healthy thyroid glands."

Kurtzman smiled bleakly. "That's about it."

"So now that El Hombre is here to save us, what are we going to do?" Kaino interjected.

"Russian chatter brought me, but it was tied up with the gang situation here in Miami-Dade. That's why I asked for your help. Speaking of which, what are you willing to do, Master Sergeant?"

"After last night?" Kaino sighed, and not unhappily. "I'm looking forward to exploring the envelope of my first open-ended, paid, consulting leave of absence for the health and safety of the greater Miami-Dade metropolitan area."

"Glad to hear that, Kaino."

"So what are we going to do?"

"Well, I've got Russians chattering about gangs. You've got gangs spilling Russian filth on your streets. I think we should go talk to some Russians."

"JUST SO YOU KNOW," Kaino warned, "the Russian mafia isn't one of my areas of expertise."

Bolan sat in Kaino's unmarked car and watched the back door of Papi's Tea Room through binoculars. "It's one of mine."

"You've been staring at that door for five minutes." Kaino regarded Bolan dryly. "Has it done anything yet?"

"No, but it's not happy."

"The door isn't happy?" Kaino queried.

"No."

"It's not a happy door."

"No, someone violated it," Bolan said.

"It's a violated, unhappy door?"

"Yeah."

"How do you know?"

"Look closer."

Kaino squinted into his binoculars. "Well, it is a filthy door covered with graffiti."

"Look at the hinges and the knob," Bolan suggested.

Kaino looked, then slowly smiled. The steel security door was filthy, old, weathered and well covered with spray paint. The hinges were brand-new. So was the knob, and the metal around them was dented and blackened. Whoever had rehung the door had taken a pretty cavalier attitude toward his job. "Someone took a Masterkey to that door."

Bolan nodded. A Masterkey was usually a 12-gauge shotgun loaded with sand or some kind of granulated composite designed to slam off door hinges and locks. The soldier shook his head at the door. "You know, if you're not going to do a job right, you just shouldn't do it at all."

"My mother always said that."

"My mother always said everyone deserves a second chance."

"A second chance to do what?" Kaino asked.

From the bag between his knees Bolan removed a Remington 870MCS shotgun with a fourteen-inch barrel and a pistol grip. "To hang a door correctly."

"Now, that's not the kind of shotgun a good, God-fearing Justice Department Observation Liaison Officer should carry."

Bolan slid two metal-cased shells into the shotgun and put three yellow plastics in behind them to bat cleanup.

Kaino slid from behind the wheel and pulled his revolvers.

The men walked nonchalantly down the alley. It was midday but Russian rap music made the poorly hung door vibrate. Bolan pointed the brutally shortened 870 at the top hinge and the laser sight in the grip put a red dot on it.

"So," Kaino inquired, "you're just going to light up that howitzer and announce—" The shotgun made a dull slap-click noise and the hinge twisted and broke as though hit by an iron fist. Kaino stood staring. "You have a silenced shotgun."

"No, it's the round that's silent. The gunpowder hits a piston inside the shell and the piston rams the breaching load out of the shell down the barrel. The piston jams in the shell mouth so the entire detonation is contained inside the shell."

"Very James Bond."

Bolan's weapon slap-clicked and the bottom hinge smeared away under the breaching round's blow. He shucked in two more yellow rounds. "You want to go first?"

"Oh, no, you're a guest." Kaino generously waved his guns at the door for Bolan to take point. "By all means."

Bolan kicked the door.

The music hit them like a wall. The bass *thud-thud-thudded* loud enough to rattle bones while someone snarled in Russian, undoubtedly about how bad he was and how many women he had. Bolan moved down the narrow hallway, passing a kitchen with notices that it had been closed by order of the health department. Bolan and Kaino peered through the windows in the double doors that led into the main tearoom.

The place looked like a cross between a shooting gallery and a strip joint. If any tea had ever been served here, the patrons had probably smoked it. Kaino made a disgusted noise. "Well now, that's just sad."

Bolan nodded at the tableau in front of them. "Tragic."

Nikita "Papi" Popov sat at a table flanked by two of his goons. In Russian parlance the goons were typical Russian "hammerheads," big men, probably former military with mixed martial arts physiques filling out their designer tracksuits. The man on Popov's left had the typical stubble hair cut. Popov's right-hand goon bore a startling resemblance to a six-foot-six Jesus.

No one at the table was happy.

Indeed, all three mobsters appeared to have been beaten into pulps. They were well bandaged. Popov's right-hand man had his right arm in a sling. The left-hand goon's head was wrapped like a mummy. Popov appeared to have gotten the worst of it. He sat shirtless with his ribs taped and his left arm in a sling. Contusions grossly contorted the Russian prison gang tattoos covering Popov's skin.

In typical Russian mobster fashion they sat grim-faced, drinking vodka and staring into the middle distance. The sea of bottles on the table indicated they had been at it for a while.

"Those sure are some sulky Russians," Kaino observed.

"I'd go so far as to say morally devastated."

"Morally devastated. I like that."

"Let's see if moral devastation has put them in the mood to talk," Bolan said. "You take Bullethead and I'll take J-man."

Bolan and Kaino strode through the doors. Between the pounding music, the pounding of vodka and the Russians' pounded state of being it took them far too many moments to notice.

The soldier shouted over what he could only loosely describe as music. "Mr. Popov! We need to talk!"

"Shit! Fuck!" Popov went apoplectic. "Kill them!"

The goons rose and kicked back their chairs. Bolan and Kaino closed the distance. The Jesus-looking hammerhead tried to go for the gun under his jacket. Bolan put the ruby dot of the Masterkey's laser sight on J-man's slung right arm and fired. The Russian screamed and dropped to his knees as his already injured wing took a 12-gauge rubber baton round.

Kaino snapped his revolvers forward with practiced ease. He rammed the muzzle of his left-hand gun into the Russian's solar plexus like a fencer, then clouted the Russian behind the ear with the butt of his right. The Russian mobster went boneless across the table and slid to the floor in a cascade of vodka bottles. "There goes my pension..." Kaino muttered.

Bolan put a riot round into the stereo and the Russian rap ceased in a shower of sparks. He shook his head at Popov's state of affairs. "So, besides me, who could have done this to you?"

"Fuck you!"

Bolan pumped his shotgun's action and the laser designated Popov's sling. Popov screamed. "No! For fuck's sake! Please!"

"For the duration of this conversation I would advise you not to make me ask you anything twice."

Popov stared sulkily at the tabletop.

"Tell your boys to resume their seats."

Popov snarled. J-man sat back in his chair cradling his arm. Bullethead managed to scrape himself off the floor and did the same.

Kaino tsked as he confiscated their pistols. "Someone messed these boys up but good."

Bolan nodded. The Russians had been systematically worked over, severely, and by pros. The soldier's instincts told him that the beat down hadn't been punishment or a warning. Popov and his men had been interrogated. "You seen the like around here?"

Kaino eyed the collection of contusions and broken bones with a professional eye. He lifted his chin at the bloody bandages. "Not in a long time. Let's take a look at the wounds."

Bolan ripped a dressing off the top of Popov's shoulder, which elicited a shriek. Bolan's eyes narrowed at a very nasty, ragged laceration across the Russian's medial deltoid. The wound looked as though an animal might have made it. Kaino let out a long breath between his teeth and nodded. "Yeah."

"Blackjack?" Bolan suggested.

"Close. I'd say a flat, beavertail slapjack sap with a coil spring in the handle, lead- and clay-loaded. A snap of the wrist will break bones. You swing side-on—" Kaino nodded at the Russian's wound "—they'll cut right through flesh. Jeez, there was an old-timer on the force when I first came out of the academy. He could put his halfway through the Miami phone book with a good windup."

"Miami-Dade doesn't use saps anymore, do they?"

"Nope." The master sergeant sighed wistfully as he gazed

backward into a bright, shining, never-to-return time in Florida law enforcement. "Banned them years ago."

"Someone worked over our Russians."

"Someone beat them like rugs."

"Popov," Bolan asked, "who did this to you?"

Popov clenched his teeth. Bolan calculated the look in the Russian gangster's eyes. There seemed to be a genuine battle raging in Popov's guts as to whom he was more afraid of, the warrior in front of him or the interrogators who had left him and his men in this sorry state. Popov was a genuine tough guy, but Bolan was beginning to think that whoever had interrogated Popov had gotten what they wanted out of him. Bolan smiled coldly. He wasn't a torturer, but he had no qualms about letting his enemies think that he was.

"Popov, I'm going to start by dropping a hammer on every injury you already have, and then I'm going to start inflicting new ones. Who did this?"

Sweat broke out on Popov's bruised brow. He hissed a single word through his teeth. "Zetas!"

"Well, just, shit," Kaino opined.

Bolan weighed the Russian's response. Zetas weren't good. None of the Mexican cartels and their gangs were good news, but the Zetas had originally been Mexican Special Forces soldiers who had received special training by the U.S. Army Rangers at Fort Benning. Many of the Mexican soldiers had finally thrown up their hands and gone to work for the Gulf Coast Cartel as muscle. In the end the Zetas had gone independent and were now at war with their former Gulf Coast employers.

"We're out of here."

"That's it?"

"That's it, unless you want to add something?"

"As a matter of fact I do." Popov gasped as Kaino ground the barrel of one of his revolvers into the gangster's injured arm and pressed the other between Popov's eyes. "Stop calling yourself *Papi*. That's Puerto Rican. We own that, and you don't have privileges."

Popov glowered.

Kaino ground the muzzles of his pistols in Popov like he was drilling for oil. "Say it!"

"I am no longer to be calling myself *Papi!* You own that! I do not have privileges!"

Kaino holstered his guns. "Smart boy."

CHAPTER THREE

Safehouse

Bolan gazed long and hard at his files. *Krokodil* was just about the worst thing he had ever come across. He had seen the results of weaponized flesh-eating bacteria, but he had never seen that kind of damage self-inflicted. Bolan shook his head and clicked out of the horrific catalog of flesh eaten down to the dermis and bones showing through suppurating muscle tissue. Bolan had dedicated himself to a War Everlasting against organized human evil. He would be damned if he let this drug get a foothold in the United States. Bolan couldn't bring himself to hate the junkies, the cooks or even the dealers. From all his research, when it came to *krokodil* they were all one and the same. They lived to fix until they died looking like extras in a zombie film, but some organization had introduced this filth into Florida.

Bolan intended to introduce himself to those individuals directly.

Kaino sat cleaning and oiling his twin .357s. Had the revolvers not been finished a lustrous gunmetal blue they would have sparkled. "You're not buying the Zeta shit."

"According to my source, they seem to have the most reliable supply of crocodile here in the metropolitan area."

"That jibes with what I know, as well, but I stand by my statement. You're not buying the Zetas roughing up Popov and his playmates."

"No, if the Zetas had paid a visit to the Tea Room there

would have been a bloodbath, and assuming they came out on top, their method of inquiry would have included lopping off limbs and heads. For that matter, most of the original Zetas who were Special Forces operators are dead. Those who are still around are the equivalent of generals in the cartel. They don't do field ops anymore, and they sure as hell don't leave Mexico. On top of that, I'm thinking Masterkeying a door is a little bit above the brains and pay grade of their local street gang affiliates here in Florida. Popov and his pals got worked by pros, like you and me, and they were deliberately left alive."

"You think they're under observation," Kaino stated.

"I wouldn't be surprised."

"You think we got observed going in?"

"Wouldn't surprise me at all," Bolan said.

"Great, we've been made."

"You worried about getting slap-jacked the same way?"

"Hell no." Kaino grinned and reached into the bag he had taken from his apartment. He pulled out a twelve inch beavertail sap that was scuffed from long use, dry from long storage but shined with recent buffing. "I'm looking forward to meeting the competition."

"I thought you said Miami-Dade banned those."

"I'm on an open-ended, paid, consulting leave of absence. I'm interpreting that to mean I have a great deal of leeway in my operational and equipment requirement paradigms.

"So, you want to drop in on Los Zetas, anyway?"

"I think we'll start with the local affiliates and work our way up the food chain. I'm looking at you for a place to start."

"Oh, I got a place we can start." Kaino slapped the sap into his palm.

BOLAN EYED THE DRUG fortress. It was an old, brick, two-story business building that had once housed an accounting firm. The windows were now barred and boarded. The front door was shiny stainless steel with a security camera above it, and a requisite oversize gangbanger stood in front mad-dogging anyone who walked by. The street was busy, but the locals made an extra effort to cross the street and not walk by. "Who lives here again?"

"A Zeta asshole named Salami." Kaino handed Bolan a file.

Walter "Salami" Salemo had hair halfway down his back, wore a big white pirate shirt and stared into the mug shot camera with brown-eyed earnestness. The Salami looked like he should have been playing The Beatles' "Rocky Raccoon" on a twelve-string guitar in a coffee bar someplace instead of being one of Miami-Dade's most notorious meth distribu-tors. According to the file, Salami had recently moved into moving crocodile.

Kaino waved his hand impatiently at the photo. "Yeah, yeah, yeah, I know, but don't let the noble-faired, long-haired, leaping-gnome look fool you. This guy Salami is a total dick." Kaino poked a puckered scar on his chin Bolan had assumed was from his boxing career. "I got the scars to prove it. This guy will fool you. He nearly took my head off a few years back. Practices capoeira and shit."

Bolan duly noted Salami's martial arts background and raised an eyebrow at the man's résumé. "Argentine?"

"The South Americans love coming to Florida."

"Don't I know it," Bolan replied.

"So, you kicked the shit out of three gangs last night. You kicked the crap out of the Russians this morning. What's on the agenda for the afternoon? You going to walk up to the door and start kicking the crap out of Salami and his people?"

"That was my first plan of attack. You got a better one?" the soldier asked.

"Listen, no one respects how you roll more than me."

"Glad to hear that."

"But sooner or later this 'biggest dick on the block' routine of yours is going to get us in some real trouble."

"Well, all right, then. Wait until I've breached the door."

"Your funeral."

"Not if you can help it, Kaino."

"Here we go again…"

Bolan took the baseball out of the box he had received by courier and slid out of the car. He set the modified Pittsburg Pirates cap on his head and walked across the street toward Salami's fortress of narcatude. He wore earth sandals, cargo shorts and a Hawaiian shirt. By his own admission Bolan looked like a total rube. The gangbanger watching the door was built like a sumo wrestler. His tracksuit was blinding white and he had an Army Ranger high and tight haircut. Zeta tattoos covered his throat. Bolan walked up and gave the door guard a happy wave. "Howdy!"

"Basta, gringo."

Bolan tilted his head like a dog hearing a sound it didn't recognize. "What?"

The doorman gave Bolan a pitying look. "Fuck off."

Bolan stared at the door guard like he might start crying. "But…I…"

"Madre de Dios…" The gangbanger rolled his eyes. "Fuck off."

Bolan dropped to one knee and drove his fist three inches below the gangbanger's belt line.

The fat man slowly sagged as his bladder hemorrhaged. "Oh, God…"

Bolan's uppercut ripped the guard into unconsciousness. The soldier took out his Beretta 93-R. He gave the security camera the middle finger and then gave it a 3-round burst. The security camera burst apart. Bolan took a moment to take an indelible marker out of his pocket and wrote "El Hombre" on the fatman's forehead.

Kaino shouted in Bolan's earpiece. "You sick fuck!"

"Bank on it, Kaino."

Dim sounds of consternation occurred behind the security door. Bolan pushed a thumbnail-size lozenge of plastic explosive into the lock and jammed a detonator pin into the mix. He took out his phone and hit an app.

"Fire in the hole!" Bolan pressed the icon and a fat chunk of fire left the doorknob in ruins. He pulled the pin on a grenade. "Any time, Kaino."

Bolan kicked the door. Rage-faced gangbangers pulling guns confronted him. Rage turned to horror as the grenade clattered to the floor at their feet. The soldier waved and stepped back outside around the doorway. The sting-ball grenade detonated to the screams of the blunt-trauma beaten. He pulled the pin on a flash-bang and tossed it in. The foyer flashed with several thousand candlepowers of light and an Olympian thunder crack of sound.

Bolan stepped inside.

The sensory overloaded gangbangers were barely aware as Bolan put the mark of El Hombre on their foreheads. Kaino charged in with guns drawn and took in the scene. "You fascinate me."

Bolan moved toward the stairs. The charging Zeta thugs had been stupid enough to leave the steel security gate to the stair open behind them. Bolan shouted up the stairs. "Yo! Ham-slice! Let's talk!"

A torrent of Spanish insults echoed down the stairs. Bolan lobbed a sting-ball grenade up to the second-story landing. He stepped back as the cloud of rubber buckshot partially expanded back down the stairs. Bolan followed it with a flash-bang and the stairwell turned into the Norse god Thor's personal thunder tunnel. "On my six, Kaino."

Bolan took the steps three at a time.

A gunman crawled across the floor, blind and stunned, with his AK abandoned. Bolan gave him a lash across the left kidney with the slide of his Beretta to keep him honest and moved toward Salami's inner sanctum. Kaino reached the second floor and kept his weapons trained behind them.

"Kaino," Bolan called. "Give me a quick sweep."

Kaino swept the stripped offices. "Empty!" He gave the steel door at the end of the hall a significant look. "They've gone all safety room on us. Probably calling in reinforcements."

Bolan concurred and walked up to the steel door.

"What are you going to do?"

Bolan dramatically pulled out a short cylinder of flexible charge and made a fist. He put the cylinder between his middle and ring fingers and held it up to the security camera like a high explosive middle finger.

"Here we go…" Kaino muttered.

Bolan gave the hapless video device a 3-round burst from the Beretta, pressed the adhesive side of the explosive against the door lock and stuck in the detonator pin. "Fire in the hole."

Bolan pressed the app on his phone and flexible charge cut a blackened crescent around the lock. The crack of the HE died as the soldier came to a decision. "Kaino, I need Salami alive. I'm going to try to take him. If it all goes to shit, you do what you have to do."

Kaino gave Bolan a hard look. "All right."

The soldier ejected his magazine of hollowpoint bullets and slapped in twenty-one rounds of less lethal ammo. In Bolan's experience rubber bullets had a pretty dismal track record unless they came in shotgun slug sizes or buckshot-size swarms. At 21 grains, the 9 mms Bolan was loading were basically like hitting someone with a Gummi bear that had been on the shelf a few months too long. Of course they were coming in at 800 feet per second and the Beretta 93-R did have the advantage of pumping them out in 3-round bursts.

Bolan kicked the door and stepped aside.

A double-barrel went off like dynamite and two ARs

burned their magazines in seconds and pinged open on empty.

The soldier stepped in.

A Zeta gangbanger screamed and charged, wielding his spent rifle by the barrel like a club. Bolan gave him three bursts from the Beretta and dropped him clutching his ribs. Another gangbanger stared stupidly with his sawed-off shotgun broken open, trying to pluck out the smoking shells. Two bursts or rubber bullets below the belt buckle left the gangster sagging and wetting himself.

Kaino came through the door.

Salami literally cartwheeled at Bolan, who put a burst into his ribs. Salami's foot scythed the Beretta out of Bolan's hands. The soldier ducked the ensuing heel kick by a hair and backpedaled.

It had been a long time since someone had tried to kick a gun out of Bolan's hand, and the last would-be Bruce Lee who had tried it had received lead for his trouble. Salami grinned and slowly began to dance from side to side to Brazilian rhythms only he could hear. By the size of the man's pupils Bolan suspected Salami was drugged up and feeling no pain. "How do you like that, *ese?*"

He shot a smug grin at the cop. "Hey, Kaino! How's your chin?"

Kaino cocked his revolvers.

Salami howled in most likely meth-fueled glee. "Gonna do your little gringo friend like I did you, Kaino! Except worse!"

"Yo! Hombre!" Kaino leveled his weapons. "Let me grease this Falkland Island craving little prick once and for all!"

Salami shrieked in nationalistic outrage. "That's the Islas Malvinas!"

Bolan watched Salami's feet. "We came here to talk."

Salami turned purple as he danced. "Talk? Fuck talk! Go ahead! Go for your second gun! You watch what happens!

You want a talk with me, you gotta earn it! Show me something, *puto!*"

Bolan held up his hands in peace. "I told you I came to talk."

"¡Maricón!" Salami spun into another blur and his heel scythed for Bolan's temple. The soldier snatched off his cap by the bill and slapped it into the oncoming foot. Salami screamed as his talus bone cracked. His spinning kick turned into a spinout and he hit the floor in an ugly pinwheel of limbs. He screamed again as Bolan whipped his hat against his elbow.

Kaino stared in wonderment. "What the fuck?"

Bolan tossed Kaino his Pirates cap. Kaino caught it on the muzzle of his left-hand gun. He fondled the cap with his right trigger finger and stopped as he found the packet of impact material sewn high inside the brow. "What the hell?"

"Slap cap."

Kaino grinned from ear to ear. "Oh, I gotta have one! Tell me they make these in Miami Heat!"

Bolan kept his eyes on the crying, cracked-ankle-hugging Salami on the floor and recovered his Beretta. "That can be arranged."

Kaino sailed the cap back at Bolan. "Sweet!"

Bolan caught it and sat on his heels beside the gangbanger. "So, Baloney? Braunschweiger? Headcheese? What was your processed meat name again?"

"Fuck you!"

Bolan cocked back the cap in his hand.

"No more hat!"

"How much hat you receive is up to you, Summer Sausage."

"I want my lawyer…" Salami mewled.

"No lawyers here. Just you, me, Kaino and God."

"Oh, God…"

"And God's busy. So he sent me," Bolan said.

"Who are you!"

"You tell me."

Salami gulped, shuddered and went from pale to green with the telltale nausea of broken bones.

"Don't you puke on my shoes," Bolan warned. "Now, who am I?"

"You're El Hombre…" Salami whispered.

"That's right. So I have one question for you. Who's supplying you with codeine?"

Salami blinked. "What?"

"*Cocodrilo*'s main ingredient is codeine. Codeine is a controlled substance that requires a physician's prescription to obtain and a pharmaceutical lab to manufacture. *Cocodrilo* needs codeine in bulk for production. Tell me who's supplying it and I'll leave you alone."

"I don't know!"

"What do you mean, you don't know?" Bolan asked.

"I mean I don't know!"

Bolan packed the brim of his cap into his palm several times for emphasis. "Last chance, Lunch Meat."

"No one! I mean I don't know!"

"You don't cook it?" Bolan asked.

"No way, man!"

Bolan frowned.

"Man, only the junkies cook it! And they're ripping off drugstores and burglarizing their grandma's medicine cabinets and shit! We get it prepackaged!"

Bolan regarded the hobbled, panic-attacking drug dealer at his feet for long moments.

Kaino waved his revolvers. "You believe this shit?"

"Do you?"

"Well, that is the thing," Kaino admitted. "The labs we've found aren't set up for distribution. Just junkies cooking themselves to death and anyone who can pay. There's too much product and not enough producers. Give him the hat again. Just to verify."

Salami shrieked and clutched his ankle and elbow. "No more hat!"

"All right, then one last question." Bolan leaned in close. "Who distributes to you?"

Salami shuddered. "Oh, God..."

CHAPTER FOUR

Safehouse

"So it's a shell game." Kaino bit off half a Cuban sandwich of his own making and chewed meditatively. "And the game is where's the codeine at."

Bolan also ate a sandwich, and cleaned his Beretta on the kitchen table. Rubber bullets made for interesting bore cleaning. "That seems to be the size of it. I just can't see any underground local manufacturer."

"What about a mainstream manufacturer?" Kaino suggested. "Keeping double books and diverting the goods to the streets."

"I have people on that angle, but it's not my first guess."

"You think the Russians are smuggling it in?"

Bolan had been giving that a lot of thought. "Hard to imagine the Russian mafia smuggling codeine across the Atlantic just so local croc-heads can cook it at pocket change prices. Hard to see the profit margin being worth it, much less the logistics of the endeavor."

"You think it's someplace a lot closer to home."

"Whoever is doing this is doing it through the Latino gangs in Florida. That's our connection until something better pops up. We pound them until something breaks open."

"Listen, man, I do admire your style."

"Thanks. But?"

"I mean, I love hammering the bad guys with the semi-auto Pez dispensers."

"Who doesn't?"

Kaino laughed. "Yeah, but all the pencil erasers at hostile velocity, flash-bangs and tear gas in the world aren't going to break this organization. This can't last. We're about to take it up to distributor level. Man, I just don't how much longer your less-than-lethal approach is going to work."

"I agree. We keep playing it like this, the bad guys are going to start thinking we get squeamish at the sight of blood. Assuming his people haven't already beheaded him, Salami is most likely going to snort himself a sinus load of chemical courage, lose his fear of the hat and want some payback."

"And, so?"

"The fact is, Kaino, we're going to be drenched in blood and bodies before this one is over. Like up to our eyeballs. What do you say?"

"Well, since you ask, I say let's kick this pig and when it's over the Pink Champale is on you."

"Pink Champale?"

"What's the matter, El Hombre, you afraid to see how the other half lives?"

Bolan had drunk everything from cobra venom sacs swimming in cognac in an opium den in Vietnam to fermented mare's milk in a yurt in Mongolia. He was afraid that Pink Champale might just test him. "Done."

"Well, now we're cooking with gas!"

"Any other concerns?"

"Well, you're El Hombre, international ass-kicker of mystery, and you might as well have dropped in from Mars. I suspect you'll drop off the planet again with equal facility. But me? Everybody knows me, and everybody knows where I live. You know what I'm saying?"

Bolan nodded. "You're worried about your family."

"Yeah, I am."

"Maybe you should call them."

Kaino frowned. "Yeah, maybe I should." He took out his

cell and punched a preset number. A smile broke out across his face at the sound of his wife's voice. "*Che, mi amor.* How are you and the kids?" The master sergeant's face slowly went blank as his wife spoke to him. "You're on a plane?" Kaino listened for long moments. He took a deep breath and let it out. "I love you, Marisol. Send me a postcard when you can." Kaino cut the connection. "You son of a bitch."

Bolan stared at Kaino speculatively. "You're not going to start crying, are you?"

"My Marisol, she told me she couldn't call me, and was told not to tell me where she and the kids are headed."

"I don't know where they're headed, either, Kaino, and if this goes bad and we're on the bad end of the blackjacks, then that's for the best. Should the absolute worst happen on this one, your family will be taken care of regardless. I can tell you a gal I know picked out someplace very nice for them. In the Caribbean, all-inclusive and all expenses paid. I know your family is worried about you, but what I can tell you is this. In a few hours they'll be worried about you in a tropical paradise."

Bolan's computer beeped. "What's that?" Kaino asked.

The soldier frowned as his laptop's screen flicked into the security suite screen. It was almost redundant in this modern age, but someone had cut the landline to the safehouse. "Kaino, try to call anybody on your phone."

Kaino hit Redial to his wife and scowled. "I got nothing. I'm talking zero bars."

"Jamming cell phones seems a little out of Salami's pay grade."

"Yeah, him and the next few Zetas up the food pyramid, as well. What do you think?"

"You're about to get your bloodbath, Kaino. Gear up."

Kaino checked the loads in both of his revolvers and picked up one of the semiauto shotguns. He clapped in a drum with a piece of red tape on it that meant it was loaded with lead. Bolan took up an MP-5/10 submachine gun. It looked like a Heckler & Koch that had been going to the gym. Bolan was operating on urban, U.S. soil. He wanted knockdown power without tearing up the neighborhood. The "10" stood for 10 mm and his weapon was loaded with subsonic, truncated cone, flathead bullets. Every light in the house went out as someone cut the power.

Window glass shattered as bullets tracked in a blind search-and-destroy swath through the room. "Shit!"

Bolan racked the bolt on his weapon. "Here they come."

The front door flew off its hinges beneath a hostile boot. Bolan and Kaino both closed their eyes and stuck their fingers in their ears as the flash-bang wired to the door went off. Bolan moved at a crouch to the hallway with Kaino on his six. The lead invader had stepped directly into the flash-bang's audio-visual assault. The attacker didn't fall, but he shook his head to clear it. That bespoke some training. Bolan aimed down the hall and put three rounds into the man's chest. The fact that he didn't fall signaled body armor. Bolan raised his aim and put a bullet through the shadowy figure's head.

The soldier hit the tactical light attached to his weapon and let the next man in have 7,000 candela on strobe function. In the pulsing light show Bolan saw a man in a coverall, armor and night-vision gear. As the gunner shot high and wide, the Executioner put a bullet between the lenses of the man's solarized NVGs.

Suddenly everything was silent.

Dogs began barking and the distant sounds of an alarm began to manifest themselves on the street outside. Thunder clapped as the flash-bang wired to the kitchen door went off. The enemy played it smart and didn't immediately rush in. Bolan took the opportunity to dive through the bedroom door and roll up with his weapon leveled. Outside a man shouted, "Go! Go! Go!"

The interior walls of the old bungalow were 1970s construction and might as well have been paper-thin. Bolan had taken note of where the kitchen door would be in relation to the bedroom wall. He deliberately burned the remaining twenty-five rounds in his magazine on full-auto through the bedroom wall and into the kitchen behind. Men screamed as Bolan vectored his bullets in below the waist.

The soldier slapped in a fresh magazine and slammed the bolt home. "Kaino!"

The master sergeant didn't have to be told twice. Kaino entered the kitchen with his semiautomatic shotgun booming on rapid fire. Bolan took Kaino's six and knocked down the next two men who came through the front door with head shots.

Everything went quiet again.

Bolan spoke softly. "Kaino?"

"I have four men down in the kitchen."

"I have four down in the hall."

"You figure a pair of two-man teams, front and back?"

"Plus the sniper, and command and control should be very nearby if not on the scene."

"I want that sniper's ass."

Bolan eyed the master sergeant's crouching bulk in the gloom. "You hit?"

"No, but my sandwich press is." Kaino growled.

The soldier moved silently to the kitchen entry. He stared at Kaino's perforated kitchen appliance lying among the broken glass and shattered crockery. Kaino wasn't exaggerating. His sandwich press would never panini again. "Bastards," Bolan agreed. "Let's take them."

"I'm figuring it has to be the roof catty-corner across the street. It's the only two-story on the block and it has a For Sale sign."

Bolan's sniper instincts told him Kaino was most likely right.

"So do we play it?" Kaino asked.

"You could stick your head out."

"And you'll pop whoever blows my head off?" Kaino said.

"Yeah."

Kaino shook his head and racked his bolt on a fresh drum. "Cover me."

"Go."

Kaino burst through the kitchen door and out into the street. His shotgun roared as he put blasts of buckshot through the facing windows. Bolan followed, scanning with his optic. He caught no movement on the roof or in any of the windows. Lights suddenly blazed on the side driveway, and a van barreled onto the street. Kaino put three rounds into the grille but round-lead buck wasn't stopping the oncoming vehicle.

"Kaino!" Bolan shouted.

The cop's shotgun racked open on empty. The van plowed straight for Kaino. The master sergeant dropped his shotgun on its sling and slapped leather for his six-guns. The twin, four-inch Smiths rolled in his hands in rapid double-action fire. Glass geysered from the windshield as round after round of .357 Magnum hollowpoints punched through. Bolan had no kill shot with Kaino standing in the headlights. He flicked his weapon to full-auto and put a burst into the rear driver's-side tire. The tire exploded and the van fishtailed wildly past Kaino and stopped hard against a telephone pole.

"You all right?" Bolan called.

Kaino's hands shook slightly as he fished a pair of speed-loaders out of his pockets. "Reloading!"

"Covering!" Bolan scanned the street as Kaino approached the van. He peered in the driver's window and went around to the passenger's side. He opened the door and a body slid out. "Clear!"

Bolan kept his eyes peeled as he trotted over. Kaino had laid down some serious carnage. The driver looked as only a human could who had taken several .357 rounds to the face. Only his seat belt kept the dead assassin upright. There was no one else inside the vehicle. In the back of the van were a pair of chairs and surveillance equipment. Bolan walked around the steaming grille and joined Kaino, who stood over the expired sniper. A great deal of the assassin's blood was coagulating all over an FN P90 personal defensive weapon. The sixteen-inch long civilian barrel, the sound suppressor mounted on the muzzle and the electro-optical sight gave the personal defensive weapon a distinctly offensive weapon aura.

"Did he say anything?"

"Yeah, he mumbled some kind of Euro-trash nonsense, but then he had the bad taste to go all ambient temperature on me." Kaino shook his head disgustedly as the bloody froth bubbles from his victim's chest wounds and mouth slowly subsided. "You want to try CPR? You go right ahead."

"What kind of Euro-trash babble?"

"I don't know!" Nearly being van-rammed seemed to have rattled the master sergeant. "I can tell you it sure as hell wasn't Spanish!"

"Did it sound Russian?"

"Well, what does Russian sound like?"

Bolan slowly enunciated a choice phrase he had learned in Moscow that would have raised Kaino's eyebrow. "Did it sound anything like that?"

"No, and don't think I don't know you said something totally suck-ass, either!"

"Italian? French?" Bolan tried. "Scandinavian?"

"Oh, and like I know how to pick those out of a dying hit man Euro-trash crowd!" Kaino frowned mightily. "And I know you can, but I'm just Miami-Dade master sergeant who works for a living. I'm not an international man of mystery."

"You notice anything interesting, Kaino?"

"Yeah, these guys aren't local." Kaino spit off to one side. "They aren't even Latino. They're pros, and I'm definitely thinking we got made coming out of Papi's Tea Room."

CHAPTER FIVE

Kaino took in the gleaming, efficient and tasteful Federal Bureau of Investigation surroundings. "Swanky."

"Heads up," Bolan advised. The FBI special agent striding down the hallway toward them wore a very purposeful expression her face. It was a pleasing face to look upon. She was African American, but her face bespoke far more of Africa than America and her skin was very dark. She managed to be petite and leggy at the same time, and the cut of her relaxed hair and her navy pantsuit and the true gray of her blouse and shoes showed her off to maximum effect.

"Nice," Kaino opined.

Bolan agreed wholeheartedly. He put on his most amiable game face and held out his hand. "Special Agent."

Despite the special agent's diminutive stature, she had a grip like a clam. "Sophina Savacool."

"Cooper," Bolan said. "And this is—"

Special Agent Savacool had a smile that could light up an FBI foyer and did. Though at the moment it was tinged with a little bit of bemusement. "Oh, I assure you, Mr. Cooper, Master Sergeant Gadiel Kaino's reputation precedes him."

Kaino's massive mitt engulfed the special agent's. "My pleasure, Agent Savacool. In all my years in law enforcement this is my first visit to the FBI Miami office. Thank you for seeing us."

Agent Savacool's bemusement turned up a charming

notch. "Oh, I was the one told to see you, but then again, when legends of Miami law enforcement, and—" Savacool ran her eye up and down Bolan "—a mystery man go on a midnight rampage in the city streets, it's funny how I end up being the one sent to the meet and greet. At least the call said it was you. Is there a reason I shouldn't run you both in by the way?"

Bolan put on his most winning smile. "I mean absolutely no disrespect, Special Agent, but running me in would be… how can I put it? Problematic for you. And Kaino's with me."

"Oh, I got the memo." Savacool's bemused smile turned into a genuine smirk. "And I have never seen a government memo shorter, more distinct, much less more anomalous."

"Savacool?" Kaino frowned. "Is that like Mandinka or something?"

"German Dutch," the agent replied.

Kaino scowled. "What's a soul sister like you doing with a name like that?"

Savacool frowned at Kaino and jerked her head at Bolan. "What's a pulsating piece of Puerto Rican pulchritude like you doing working for the man?"

"Well…because…" Kaino grinned. "He's the man!"

Savacool stared up at Bolan and her eyes went predatory as she did some math. "Well, bless my soul! El Hombre, in the flesh, and in my foyer. You know, there is a fascinating file I read about a guy with that handle. Seems he's torn up the streets of our southern neighbor and ripped the cartels a new rectum on more than one occasion."

Bolan had dealt with more federal agents than he'd had hot dinners. Far too many when they were exposed to him went straight into bureaucratic bluster mode. Bolan gave Savacool full marks. She was absolutely charming while she was trying to figure him out, and was waiting to have all the facts before she ripped his throat out. "Special Agent Savacool, I—"

"Call me Sophie—my friends do." The special agent handed Bolan her business card.

Bolan grinned. "Sophie? I had to pull a lot of strings to make sure that FBI forensics got the bodies from the shoot-out last night, and Master Sergeant Kaino lost some genuine cred with his own people for going along with it."

Savacool nodded without an ounce of commitment. "I feel you."

"I know the circumstances are highly unusual, but I need a complete rundown on the suspects."

"They're like you, mysterious. But follow me."

Savacool led them down a series of hallways. Kaino whispered low at Bolan's side. "What's pulchritude?"

"It means the she thinks you're a fine figure of man, Kaino."

Kaino puffed up with pride. "I am that."

FBI personnel congregating in the hallways regarded Bolan and Kaino with grave suspicion and barely constrained disapproval. A few shot Savacool sympathetic looks. Word had spread. The woman led Bolan and Kaino into an empty conference room. The soldier and the cop took seats at a long table while Savacool cued up the flat screen on the wall and a laptop. "These are your playmates." Autopsy photos of ten men in various states of ventilation appeared on the screen. "Your assailants' fingerprints appear in none of our available databases. All of them were armed with sound-suppressed FN P90 Personal Defensive weapons. One of the weapons had been modified for sharpshooting. Their clothing, NVG and body armor were off the rack and second- or thirdhand. We're working on it, but the equipment has a very sophisticated level of sterility. I wouldn't get your hopes up."

Savacool gave Bolan and Kaino a look. "I don't suppose either of you have anything that might shed a light on things?"

"Kaino got a few words out of the sharpshooter just before he expired. He thought he said something in a European language. We've ruled out Spanish, and he didn't think it was Russian, which leads me to exclude any of the Slavic language groups."

Kaino nodded. "Yeah, what Cooper said."

"That is of interest. We're checking dental records, but none of them match anything in our databases, either. However the driver of the van was a light-skinned black, and he had two fillings, both resin composites."

Kaino gave Bolan a searching look.

"A lot of the European countries have banned silver amalgam fillings," Bolan explained. "The United States and Russia haven't. Silver amalgam is one of the cheapest routes to go with dental fillings, and soldiers don't usually spend a lot of money on cosmetic surgery or trying to go green. It goes a long way toward your Euro-trash merc theory, which by the way I agree with."

Kaino just stared. "Man, who the hell are you?"

Savacool pointed her finger at Kaino. "I'm glad you asked that question first."

"Oh, it isn't the first time I've asked, and I don't think it's going to be the last."

Bolan stayed on subject. "I gather we have nothing on the van?"

"Reported stolen two days ago, and the surveillance gear and electronics inside had the model numbers and identifiers scrubbed. The mounting screws and the holes for the equipment are shiny-new. I suspect this entire operation against you was mounted within the last forty-eight hours and was pro all the way. And now that we have established that you're El Hombre—" Savacool rolled her eyes "—it starts to make one hell of whole lot more sense."

"Can you give me anything?"

"Well, you two seem to have a habit of shooting people in the face, but we ran your sharpshooter through the facial recognition software and looked for a match in the database. Interpol gave us this image—it's a 75 percent likelihood of a match."

A grainy security camera picture dated over a year ago showed a blurred image of what might have been the sharpshooter. He was snarling and had to have whipped his head. Bolan stared long and hard at the crystal-clear picture of the weapon in his hand and spitting brass in what looked to be a very posh living room. "SIG SG 551 short assault rifle. Swiss."

Savacool glanced at her file on the desk. "Wow…you are good."

"It's an awfully swanky piece," Bolan admitted. "Where was the picture taken?"

"In Mexico, during the assassination of Christo Bruno."

Bolan searched his mental files. "He was Gulf Coast, wasn't he?"

"Bruno was actually the head of the Gulf Coast's armed, or La Resistencia wing. The attack on his hacienda in Matamoros last year was positively surgical. He had a heavy security presence on the premises and they along with Bruno and every other person present, including women and children and the hired help were gunned down. The forensic evidence the *federales* shared with us imply that the attackers took no losses. In fact the Mexican State police in Tamaulipas did a lot of angry muttering about suspecting it was Navy SEALs or Delta Force."

Kaino leaned back in his chair. "If Bruno had his place wired, how come only one pic?"

Bolan eyed the shooter up on the screen. "The attackers knew where the security cameras were. The shooter must have been forced past that camera during the firefight, or he hadn't knocked it out yet." Bolan turned to Savacool. "I gather the house was stripped of security?"

"All the security systems were destroyed. Bruno reached

his safe room, but they breached it with explosives and gutted its security suite. We have this pic because Bruno's security system had a wireless backup and transmitted to an outside data storage facility."

"There was nothing from any of the other cameras?"

"Oh, there was plenty. Pictures of the grounds and perimeter. All show everything right as rain until they suddenly start going dead. The outside cameras were taken out with precision rifle fire."

"The attackers didn't leave anything behind at all?" Kaino asked.

"The only things they left behind were bullets and bodies. They even took the time to clean up their spent brass."

"I'm going to need everything you have on this Bruno character and what he was up to for the year before his killing."

Savacool held out a blue flash drive with the FBI logo on it. "I figured you might say that. It also has contact information for Mexican officials pertinent to the investigation. The drive also contains everything Forensics has so far on your boys down in the morgue."

"Thanks, I appreciate that."

"So what are you going to do now, Mr. Cooper?"

"Oh, I don't know, just be myself."

Kaino snorted in amusement.

Savacool was not amused. "You know you can't just run around pulling a *Terminator* in the streets of Miami."

Bolan shrugged. "I needed a few ass-kickings to start busting things open."

"You do realize, Mr. Cooper, that the FBI doesn't usually think in terms of ass-kickings to bust things open?"

"Yeah, but admit it, you wish they did."

"Mr. Cooper, from what I've read, I will freely admit that it would be more fun than a barrel of monkeys to roll with you, throwing local, state and federal law out the window and laying down the hurt on the bad guys." She shot Kaino a look. "And apparently armed with a 'get out of jail free' card issued from God on High to boot. But you have to understand, you—"

Bolan made his decision. "You want to?"

Savacool's face went uncharacteristically blank. "Do I want to what?"

"Would you like to roll with me, Special Agent Savacool?"

"You have got to be kidding."

"I can arrange it—" Bolan snapped his fingers "—like that."

"I'm on an open-ended, paid, consulting leave of absence," Kaino confirmed. "It's been pretty educational."

Savacool just stared.

"Sophie," Bolan asked, "do you speak Spanish?"

"Spanish, French, Russian and I'm currently taking courses in Arabic at the Miami University Middletown campus."

"Oh, she's good." Kaino nodded happily. "Dude, we totally want her on the team. Sophie, you want to join the home team?"

"The winning team?" Bolan added.

"I…" Savacool was literally at a loss for words. "I'd have to take that up with my superiors."

Bolan took out a blank business card and wrote two phone numbers on it. "You can direct any questions you may have to the top number."

Savacool took the card. She was FBI and she knew the Washington, D.C., 202 area code on the first one like an old friend. "And the bottom one?"

"You can call me anytime."

Savacool nodded, then she stood and left the conference room.

Kaino nodded judiciously. "She likes you."

Bolan took the flash drive and plugged it into his phone. "Who doesn't?"

"Salami?" Kaino suggested.

"He just doesn't know me well enough yet." Bolan's phone peeped at him. The Farm's own cybernetic wunderkind, Akira Tokaido, had developed the phone's security suite personally, and Tokaido's security applications examined the flash drive for bugs, malware or any kind of FBI shenanigans and proclaimed the files were clean. Bolan hit Send and the info went straight to Kurtzman back in the Computer Room in Virginia. "Let's go."

Kaino fell into formation with Bolan. They were a pair of large and dangerous-looking men, and FBI personnel unconsciously moved to get out of their way.

Kaino sighed as they reached the foyer and his FBI adventure came to a close. "You think Savacool will join the winning team?"

"Definitely."

The Miami afternoon heat hit them like a wall as they stepped out of the FBI office and crossed the parking lot. "What now?" Kaino asked.

"I have people processing the information Agent Savacool gave us. They'll contact me when they have anything useful." Bolan glanced up at the sun and knew it was about noon. "You know a good place to eat?"

"I know a place in Little San Juan that makes goat stew like murder, man."

"On me."

"Cool."

They stopped in front of Bolan's ride. The shiny black Signature L Lincoln Town Car had been violated. Bolan took in the almost childlike graffito of a crocodile painted in electric-pink spray paint across his hood. Kaino spit in disgust. Some genuine dread crept into his voice. "I told you he'd be coming for you."

The noontime, midsummer Miami air was brutally hot, heavy and still. Bolan sniffed it. "You smell that?"

Kaino's nose wrinkled and his face made a fist of disgust. "Yeah, I smell it, and I told you! Didn't I?"

Bolan slowly nodded. "You did." Bolan tasted the turgid, humid air again—the two entwined scents were unmistakable. One was the acrid, burned metal by way of nail-polish remover smell of iodine.

The other was the stench of rotting flesh.

Bolan punched in Savacool's business card number from memory. She answered on the first ring, and had apparently memorized Bolan's number, as well. "What's happening, Cooper?"

"I'm going to need your parking-lot surveillance video, specifically the south side, from within the last forty-five minutes."

"I have been told to give you my full cooperation. However my superiors have been adamant that I report all contacts with you."

"I feel you," Bolan replied.

Savacool snorted. "Please state the nature of your emergency, Mr. Cooper."

"Cocosino just tagged my ride."

Every ounce of fun dropped from Savacool's voice. "Oh my God…"

CHAPTER SIX

Little San Juan, Miami

The goat stew was excellent, and the restaurant's little patio was shady and cool, but only Bolan seemed to be truly enjoying it. Kaino and Savacool regarded Bolan gravely over their plates. The agent shook her head. "I'll give you credit, Cooper. You know how to pick your friends, but you sure know how to make some serious enemies."

Bolan sopped up goat gravy with an immense chunk of Puerto Rican water bread. "They're complementary talents."

"Well, I have to give you this, too. You gave Miami law enforcement our first picture of Cocosino."

Bolan watched the FBI security camera footage again on his phone. The video clip wasn't much to go on. A man in filthy black jeans, filthy black combat boots and a filthy black hoodie with a baseball cap underneath that hid his face had walked up, tagged Bolan's Town Car and walked away. Gloves and a black bandanna and dark glasses completed his camouflage. It was of interest that Cocosino had violated Bolan's car in broad daylight in an FBI parking lot. "You don't mess with a man's ride."

"That's just wrong," Kaino agreed.

Bolan watched the video again. The FBI had a swell suite of cameras covering all the angles. "I'm figuring five-seven? He couldn't be more than 150 pounds dripping wet."

"We ran identification software on the tape. The computer puts him at about those measurements."

Kaino sipped his coffee with little pleasure. "Don't be fooled by his size. That junkie piece of shit has left a trail of bodies across Miami."

Bolan wasn't selling the killer short. He had found out long ago that it wasn't the size of the dog in the fight but the size of the fight in the dog. Worst of all was one with the gift of emptiness. A killer who didn't care was as dangerous as they came.

"Sophie, you say he does most of his damage with a machete?"

"That's his preferred MO," Savacool confirmed. "But he's also made some serious mayhem with a .44 Magnum when he's had multiple targets."

"Does he take heads?"

"You'd think he would," Kaino muttered. "That's real popular with the Mexican cartels these days, but no, our boy prefers to chop his victims beyond recognition. Even without the stench, everyone recognizes a Cocosino crime scene. What I want to know is, how does he pull his vanishing act looking and smelling like that?"

"Probably goes back and lies in his grave until the next job comes along," Savacool said. "Man's a goddamn ghoul if you ask me."

"You're not far off the mark," Bolan said. "This guy doesn't go out. He doesn't have friends. Wherever he's holed up is most likely not much more than a hole. Cocosino only lives for three things—to kill, get paid for it and fix. He most likely has a handler who transports him and brings him food, drugs and jobs."

"And who the hell would handle a zombie like him?" Kaino asked.

"Someone just like him, but can still pass for human at first glance."

"Jesus," Savacool said. "That's the most horrible life I can imagine."

Bolan nodded. He and Kaino had smelled Cocosino, and if the assassin was really was addicted to *krokodil,* then some part of him probably relished the idea of being killed and ending his suffering. Savacool was also right about another thing. After a year of *krokodil* addiction and paying for it with murder, Cocosino was now more ghoul than man in more ways than one.

Now Bolan and Kaino were his prime targets.

"What now?" Kaino inquired. "The safehouse is trashed and definitely not safe. Unless you want to go back and let them take another swing at us."

"I doubt they'd try it again, particularly since they saw us visit the FBI office. Then again, our enemies don't know where we are at the moment, and I want to keep it that way. I have my people working up the info Sophie was kind enough to give us. I want to take the files on the Zetas you have and the info we got out of Salami and work up our next plan of attack. Like you said last night, we're taking this up to the distributor level."

"Ass-kickings to bust things loose?" Savacool mused.

"I offered you a spot on the team. First string."

"We'll get to that in a minute. The good news is I think I may be in a position to help you on the safehouse front. You have Cocosino after you, and he is as gutter level as it gets. On top of that you were attacked by some kind of very professional international hit squad. Whoever is pulling all this together has a pretty extensive reach." Savacool grinned. "But I doubt they know about my great-aunt's place in the suburbs."

Kaino smiled happily. "She's on the team!"

"Actually, after the tagging in the parking lot my superiors have ordered me to, and I quote, 'wear you two like underwear.' I'm your babysitter in Miami as of now and for the duration." Savacool gave Bolan a very frank look. "Mr. Cooper, that was one fascinating phone number you gave us, I must admit. The Miami office's cooperation with you has been given a very high sense of urgency. But I expect you to be honest with me at all times. You don't pull any more James Bond shit without telling me first. We may have to cooperate with you, but that cooperation could quickly become…how shall I put it? Less than enthusiastic?"

"Agent Savacool, I understand the position of you and your office completely. I can't tell you who I am or reveal most of my sources. But I can tell you this. We're on the same team. You're at every meeting. Your input on investigation and strategy is not only welcomed but encouraged. I have no authority over you. My only requirement is that in a combat situation you let me lead, and I say that simply because I have the most experience at it. The second you can't hang with me or my methods, you can walk and report me to your superiors, no hard feelings."

"He gave me the same deal," Kaino affirmed.

"You know, I thought for sure you were going to get mad."

"He doesn't get mad." Kaino resumed attacking his goat stew with gusto. "He gets all spooky and shit, and then he goes all Action Jackson."

Bolan smiled. That was one way of putting it.

Savacool wrote an address on a napkin. "It's on the edge of the Everglades. The roads get a little twisty and dark, but most map apps can find it."

Kaino looked up from his plate. "You're not coming with us?"

"I need to report in, and pick up a few things. I'll meet up with you tonight." Savacool turned to leave. "The key is under the gnome."

Bolan and Kaino watched Savacool walk to her car. Kaino frowned. Bolan frowned in return. "I thought you liked her."

"I do."

"Then what up?"

Kaino was doing some kind of Puerto Rican mathematics as he watched Savacool's chiseled calves. "She's awfully damn skinny."

"So?"

"So we're spending the night."

"And?"

Despite having mostly demolished a heaping plate of goat stew, the master sergeant's right hand reflexively went to his belly. "You think she can cook?"

Miami Beach

SALAMI POPPED MORE painkillers, washed them down with half a glass of wine and tried not to vomit at the stench pervading his beach house retreat. It radiated off the visitors sitting on his couch. Through his haze of pain, he was thinking he would have to have the sofa disinfected. He might just have to have the whole house fumigated. He might just have to move.

Salami's guest of honor hid his features under a hoodie, hat, sunglasses and a bandanna. A woman who looked like a Latina vampire-stripper who had been buried alive for a hundred years sat beside him. From what little Salami had gleaned, she was Cocosino's "handler," and few steps farther from the grave than he was. She wore a black turtleneck sweater despite the heat.

Salami tossed back the rest of his glass and poured himself another. "So, you saw him? You saw El Hombre?"

The wraparound dark glasses focused on the amber prescription bottle on the coffee table. Cocosino's voice was a tuberculotic rasp. "What's that? Percocet?"

"Yeah, doctor's orders."

A horrible sound came out from under the bandanna that Salami realized was laughter. "I got something that will make you feel a lot better."

Salami cringed in horror. "No, man, I'm good. El Hombre? You saw him?"

"Saw him. Tagged him. I like him."

"You like him?"

"You know, people think I'm just a degenerate junkie."

Salami withheld comment.

"And I am a degenerate junkie, but I am not just a degenerate junkie."

The gangbanger wanted more wine and drugs, but he didn't want to appear weak. "Oh?"

"I think about things. I have lots of time to think. I've read the newspapers. I watch TV and heard what they're saying on the street. I've listened to what you and others have told me."

"Yeah?"

"There's an El Hombre who's rampaged through Mexico on several occasions."

"I've heard that."

Cocosino cocked his masked, rotting head in question. "Did you know the first time I fixed on *krokodil,* I bought it from you?"

Salami flinched so hard it hurt his cracked joints.

"Anyway, this El Hombre, I think he has a real problem with shedding innocent blood. He's got a code. I watched him and Master Sergeant Kaino. It's like some bad buddy movie. They have a code."

"So what are you saying?"

"So I want to give them a surprise. Something they're not going to like. Something they have no answer for."

"Yeah?"

Cocosino turned his mummy-wrapped head. "Delilah."

Delilah leaned forward, and the stench coming off her was unbearable. She slid a piece of paper across the coffee table. Salami stared at the laundry list. *"¡Madre de Dios!"*

"It's not too much to ask," Cocosino rasped. "Considering."

"Okay, give me a day or two and—"

"I need it by tonight."

Salami nearly strangled on his wine. "And what are you going to do with all this shit?"

"I'm going to give El Hombre something that will haunt his dreams, even if he survives it."

"And how are you going to find him again?"

"There's something in the paint I tagged his car with. Something that satellites can see and people can't."

Salami stared at the rotting killer on his couch. "You have a satellite watching El Hombre?"

Delilah smiled and spoke for the first time.

"No, but someone else who wants him dead does."

West Miami

THE KEY WAS UNDER the gnome.

Special Agent Savacool could cook. Kaino happily held out his plate for a second chicken-fried steak. "You know, I really like breakfast for dinner."

"Most men do," Savacool agreed. She seemed to appreciate men with hearty appetites. Her great-aunt's abode was a solid, brick house of Shaker-style built in the housing boom after World War II. Savacool had kept with the clean simple lines of the builder but added all modern appurtenances. The river was close by. A pleasing breeze blew off it and Savacool had opened up the house to receive it. The houses on the winding lane were few and far apart, and none had fences. The streetlights were few, ancient and dim. Spanish moss hung from the huge live oaks in swaths of Southern Gothic glory.

Savacool smiled as Bolan finished his meal. "You like fried steak?"

"Haven't had one since the last time I was in Argentina."

Savacool cocked her head. "How do they do it?"

"Well, there's no gravy or biscuits. They fry it in oil and squeeze lemons on it. Usually have French fries on the side."

Savacool made a noise. "Savages."

"They'll put fried eggs on top if you ask."

"Well, at least that's progress."

Kaino suddenly snapped his head up. "You smell that?"

Bolan snuffed the air. "What?"

Savacool's face contracted in disgust. "Oh, yeah, I was in New York in 2010 for the blooming of the corpse flower. It just about knocked me off my feet. Nice nose, Kaino."

"I'm a gourmet and a gourmand, man. My nose takes me where I need to go." Kaino pulled one of his .357s.

Bolan caught the sent of rotting mammal on the breeze and what lay beneath it. He rose and pulled his Beretta. "Iodine. Cocosino is here."

Kaino took out his second .357. "Go for the head. Nothing else will stop him."

"No." It sickened Bolan to say it, but Cocosino was one of their few active leads. "Take his legs off if you can. I want him alive, and if he really is a *krokodil* addict, twenty-four hours without a fix will leave him willing to tell us anything we want to know."

Savacool pulled her .40-caliber FBI-issue Glock and checked the load by reflex. "Hardcore, Cooper."

Bolan took in the architecture. "Fuse box in the basement?"

"Yes."

"Let's kill the lights before he does and call 9-1-1." Bolan sniffed the air again. The stench was becoming more powerful. It was unfortunate that all the windows and doors were open. "Be careful coming back up. If he's close enough to smell, he'll be in the house in moments."

Savacool ran at a crouch to kill the lights. Bolan and Kaino stayed low and reached into their gear bags.

Kaino sniffed the air and nearly gagged. "Jesus, it smells like a dead wildebeest rotting on the savannah!"

"Didn't know you were a poet, Kaino."

"Yeah, well, you know." Kaino pulled his NVG on top of his head and nearly gagged again.

Bolan had been exposed to dead bodies that ranged from fresh to mummified and every shade in between. It had long ago lost any power over his nose or his stomach. But Kaino was right. The stench was so strong it was almost anomalous.

The lights cut out. Bolan and Kaino pulled down their NVGs. A second later the agent's voice spoke softly at the top of the stairs. "Savacool."

"Clear."

Savacool crouched beside the kitchen island cradling an M-4 carbine.

Bolan tapped an icon on his phone. "Bear, I need satellite on my position, stat."

"I thought you'd gone dark on the Savacool family estate?"

"Stat, Bear."

"One second. Checking available satellites. Have one with window. Nonessential shore surveillance. Assuming priority…now." Kurtzman's voice rose in instant alarm. "Striker! Be advised! You are surrounded!"

"Show me." Bolan's screen filled with an overhead thermal image of Great-Aunt Savacool's manse. It was surrounded by what looked like between thirty and forty individuals. They formed an arc, cutting off the house from the road. The river behind blocked any escape out the back.

Bolan's eyes narrowed. "Show me my car."

The satellite zoomed on the hood of the Town Car. Cocosino's crocodile graffito glowed like a neon sign. Kaino glowered beneath his goggles. "Jesus, when Cocosino tagged your car, Coop, he really tagged your car."

Savacool risked a peek over the kitchen island and out the window. She didn't have any NVGs, but it was a clear night. The ancient and poorly dispersed streetlights threw small islands of yellow light. The huge, spreading live oaks threw pools of blackness. She popped down grimacing in the dark of the kitchen. "It's like *Night of the Living Dead* out there."

Bolan rose and took a quick look. In his NVGs the world was lit in green and gray. Savacool wasn't far off the mark. Dozens of figures were literally shambling toward the house. However, the walking dead didn't usually carry bats, knives and other improvised hand weapons. They also didn't usually have a universal uniform of a black hoodie.

Even for Bolan the smell was starting to become overpowering.

Savacool clicked off the safety on her carbine.

Bolan shook his head. "No."

Savacool was appalled. "No? What do you mean, no?"

"They're junkies."

Kaino quietly exploded. "So fucking what? I'm with Cool! We cut our way to the car and—"

Glass shattered outside and fire spread across the hood of Bolan's ride.

"Oh, that's just grand!" Kaino snarled.

Bolan read his opponent's mind. "He wants us to start shooting."

"I want to start shooting!"

"These people are *krokodil* junkies. I suspect he gave them all a nice fat fix hours ago and bused them in while they were flying high. Now they're coming down and they're hurting for it, and the price of free fixes for life is our heads."

Savacool's voice was quiet but firm. "Cooper, that is the sickest thing I have ever heard, and I feel for those poor souls outside, but I am not going to be dragged down and torn apart by rotting junkies."

Another Molotov looped through the air. It fell just short of the porch and broke on the flagstones.

Kaino spoke through clenched teeth. "Coop, they're going to burn us out!"

"Cocosino wants a massacre, and while it's going on he's waiting to take his shot."

Savacool gave Bolan a desperate plan. "Tell me you have a plan."

"I do."

"What's that?"

"I'm going out there."

The FBI agent and the Miami-Dade master sergeant spoke in unison. "What the fuck!"

"Cool, you're going onto the porch with your rifle. Cocosino is camouflaged, just another skell in an army of them. When he takes his shot at me, you take him down. Kaino, you're going to defend the porch. I suspect some of these guys are going to get past me."

"And if I'm not allowed to shoot, how am I supposed to do that?"

"Unless someone shoots at you, you're doing it with your fists."

"Jesus!"

"We're out of time." Bolan shrugged into his vest. He wished he had a full raid suit of rip stop material gloves and a helmet. He belted his Beretta to his thigh and cinched the retaining strap so it couldn't be taken from him in a clinch. "Let's go."

Bolan strode out the front door and marched down the steps.

One of the junkies in the oncoming crowd screamed. "Get him!" He let loose with a tee-ball. The hate stick revolved through the air. Bolan turned his body slightly to avoid it and marched straight up to the hater. Up close the soldier saw sunken eyes and cheeks. He sent his fist crashing into the emaciated face. The junkie flew back five feet and fell like a broken scarecrow. Several junkies moaned. Others clutched themselves more tightly than their weapons. Many were already shivering from withdrawal. Bolan cracked his knuckles and regarded the crowd by the light of his burning Lincoln. "Who's next?"

Fear rippled through the swaying crowd and fought addiction on nearly equal terms.

"Kill him!" a woman in the crowd shrieked like a harpy. "Kill him and we get all we want!"

The cry was like the crack of a whip. Addiction won the battle. The junkies released their individual fears and gave themselves over to their need. "Kill him!"

The crowd surged.

"Get out of there!" Kaino roared.

Bolan waded in. His fists became battering rams, his fingertips spears and the edges of his hands blunt axes. The soldier went for disabling strikes. He kept his kicks low so he couldn't be taken off his feet, breaking clavicles and jaws. When he threw a kick, a junkie lost a knee or an ankle. Bolan didn't whirl like a dervish. He moved through the crowd like a juggernaut. The attackers were weak, malnourished and, by the smell, carrying soon-to-be lethally infected wounds. They had two advantages, and those were numbers and abject desperation that had turned into bloodlust.

A rock thudded into Bolan's left shoulder. A bandaged hand missing a finger clawed across the lenses of Bolan's NVGs and left a swathe of rotting infection across them. Bolan grabbed the stick-thin wrist and shattered the elbow behind it. He ripped the half pound of contaminated gear from his head and threw it into a screaming face.

"Kill him! Kill him!"

Bolan felt his gorge rise, and not just from the stench of rotting flesh. This might well have been the worst attack anyone ever had ever perpetrated on him. Cocosino had recruited an army of rotting junkies willing to kill and burn for one more fix and bused them into West Miami. Given what Bolan knew about *krokodil* addiction, killing them might have been a kindness.

A .44 Magnum gun went off like a bomb in the crowd, and Bolan staggered as he took a sledgehammer blow low in his left floating ribs.

"Kill him!"

"Cooper!"

An emaciated arm wrapped around Bolan's throat and squeezed with chemically fueled strength. The *krokodil* zombies were only a few steps away from the living dead. They could hardly feel pain beyond the agony of their addiction, but they still had to breathe. Bolan rammed his elbow into his assailant's guts. Fetid breath blasted out of degraded lungs. The grip around Bolan's neck loosened and he took a step forward to give himself room. He swung again backward, and this time snapped his arm straight. The Executioner's fist slammed up into his assailant's groin. It was the one place where no drug could make a man invulnerable. The croc-zombie slimed off Bolan's back vomiting. The soldier suddenly had a few feet of breathing room.

A figure indistinguishable from the other ghouls raised a gleaming stainless-steel revolver. The .44 Magnum gun went off like a cannon and hit Bolan in the chest like a thunderbolt. A junkie ghoul-girl stepped in the way, and Cocosino's second shot blew through her body and hit Bolan a second time right over the solar plexus.

Savacool's rifle fired three times rapidly in return and tore dirt where Cocosino had been standing. She screamed over the sound. "Cooper! Cooper!" The creatures of the chemical apocalypse responded with everything from shrieks to moans, but all said the same thing.

"Kill him! Kill him!"

Bolan staggered. He couldn't tell if his armor had held and couldn't get any air into his lungs. Three junkies converged on him, and Bolan's limbs responded too slowly to stop them. The iodine and death stench was overpowering as they swarmed him. Another arm snaked around Bolan's neck. A ten-inch boning knife chopped into the degraded armor covering Bolan's chest. A fist crashed into his jaw. Bolan shot out his hand and seized the throat of the knife-wielder. With her hood fallen back, she was little more than a halo of wild hair and stark bones. The soldier's fingers sank into the suppurating wounds where she had been injecting into her neck. Two more croc-zombies hit the pile of horror, and Bolan found himself in a rugby scrum of the living waiting to be dead.

A girl grabbed his arm in spindly hands. A palpable cloud of corruption exhaled out of the dying junkie's mouth and broken and rotting teeth sank into Bolan's biceps. Another set of teeth sank into his thigh. The knife chopped into the soldier's chest again, and this time he felt the cold burn as it slid home and the hideous grating on bone as it jammed between his ribs. Another fist hit him in the face and more hands grabbed at his legs.

The paean of dead junkies walking was almost a moan of benediction.

"Kill him! Kill him!"

The knife ripped free from Bolan's ribs and the skeletal, witch-thing wielding it pulled back for another stab. A small revolver popped from one side, and Bolan took three more in the chest. He dropped to one knee as a starving, rotting junkie chop-blocked him in the back of his legs. Bolan felt tooth stumps scrape against the back of his neck as suppurating limbs smothered him.

The ghouls were dragging him down.

Bolan roared like the apex predator he was and erupted upward.

The knife-wielder shrieked and took her blade overhead in both hands for the kill shot. Bolan snapped his head forward in a butt. The junkie would most likely not even register a smashed septum or cracked cheekbone. Bolan went skull to skull. Purple pinpricks danced around his vision, but his would-be butcher dropped like a bullock in the slaughter shoot.

The Executioner risked multiple concussions and snapped his head backward into the face of a junkie biting at his nape. He felt a jaw break and that gave him just enough room to rip his arm free from the ghoul eating his biceps. He gave the withered, rotting girl an elbow that sent teeth flying and eyes rolling. The addict chewing on his leg took a knife hand to the temple and went boneless. The chop-blocker was still on hands and knees, and Bolan drove his heel into the top of the addict's right hand and shattered it.

A Goth-looking junkie screamed and shoved his revolver forward. "Die! Why don't you die?"

Bolan jerked his head aside as the revolver snapped and spit fire. The hair ripper behind him howled as he took a bullet in the shoulder. The soldier chopped his left hand into the shooter's needle-tracked wrist and the revolver went flying. He took his bit of room and spun, his back fist unhinging the addict's jaw. The drug-addled assassin dropped to his knees. Bolan slammed a knee up into his jaw and sent him into a temporarily blissful sleep.

Savacool's rifle broke into rapid semiauto fire. Bolan heard tires squeal out on the street, but he had no time for it.

Kaino was suddenly beside him and he dropped junkies with Ali-worthy left jabs and Foreman-worthy rights.

The crowd fell back.

Bolan suddenly had space. He stood with his bloodied fists clenched. The mob's moral check returned. The degenerate drug addicts reverberated between the two opposing poles of need and fear, but the battle dynamic in West Miami had changed. The dozen junkie croc-zombies still standing visibly deflated like balloons. Bolan's voice was ice-cold. "Now, which one of you primate, screw heads lit up my ride?"

A frizzy-haired young man with a claw hammer in his

hand dropped his weapon on Savacool's lawn and fell to his knees in supplication. "Please…"

"All of you!" Bolan bellowed. "On your knees! Now!"

The standing junkies knelt. Some moved to hands and knees and others assumed the prone position with obvious practice. Savacool came down the steps with her weapon shouldered.

Bolan looked out onto the road. "He got away?"

"I didn't want to risk firing into the crowd when he fired into you. I got a shot at him when the van screamed up, but I don't know if I hit him. I gave the van the rest of my magazine." Savacool shook her head unhappily. "He got away."

Kaino stared at Bolan in awe. "I have never seen anything like it."

Bolan took in the army of broken, moaning, drug-addicted and rotting humanity littering the field of battle by firelight. "Neither have I."

CHAPTER SEVEN

Mercy Hospital, Miami

The doctor was appalled, both by Bolan's smell and by his condition. She shook her head at the massive, blackening contusions where Bolan's armor had taken .44 Magnum hits and held. "These are firearm-related blunt trauma contusions, Mr. Cooper?"

"Yes, ma'am," Bolan replied.

"That one's a knife?"

"Yes, ma'am."

Dr. Gubatan had already known the answers. She sucked in her breath as she looked at his neck, biceps and thigh. "These are human bite wounds?"

"Yes, ma'am."

"I'm required to inform you that I must report this to the police."

Agent Savacool held up her badge. "It's already been reported to the FBI."

Dr. Gubatan sniffed Bolan again. It was pretty clear it was a smell she had encountered before. "This wouldn't happen to be related to an incident in the West Miami area that is blowing up across all channels?"

"Doctor, I'm afraid I can neither confirm nor deny that."

There were few things E.R. doctors in Miami hadn't seen. Dr. Gubatan was even shorter than Savacool but about five times as wide. She scowled at the FBI ID like it was a personal affront, but her features set into a grimace of concern as she prodded Bolan's blackening biceps. "The bite wounds are already going septic."

Bolan wasn't surprised, but he just didn't have time for hepatitis. Anything even more chilling that a *krokodil* addict's bite might be carrying would just have to be dealt with later. "I'll need a round of full spectrum antibiotics."

"You're telling me." Dr. Gubatan left the room nearly at a sprint while rapidly typing into her tablet. A nurse came in and began cleaning the bites.

"You all right?" Savacool asked.

"I feel like a zombie crawl just stomped a mud hole in me and tried to chew it dry. With a few shootings and stabbings in the mix."

"No, Cooper. You went down in that rotting crowd, and I was too scared to shoot into it. Are you okay?"

"That was bad," Bolan admitted.

Savacool was about an inch from collapsing in tears. "I'm still shaking."

Bolan nodded. "Me, too."

Savacool laughed, but it was laced with tension. "Not you! You're stone cold."

"I shake on the inside. I don't shake on the outside until the job is done." Bolan winked. "And I'm someplace safe with someone I like."

"You know? Speaking as a black female Southern FBI agent—you're the first man of any color or description who ever made sensitive sound cool."

"That's how I roll."

"So how are you?"

"Hungry. Where's Kaino?"

"Well, he went all Muhammad Ali on anything that even came close to the porch. You should have seen it."

"I caught a bit of it. He had my six when it was getting really bad. He was something to see."

"I relieved him of porch patrol and he went to back your

play on the run. I pulled a sweep around the mob and tried to stop the van. Anyway, he busted some knuckles. He's getting his hands taken care of and Miami-Dade pooh-bahs are debriefing him hard."

"How about you?"

"I have been sternly informed to report in first thing in the morning."

Bolan looked at his swollen hands and was reminded of the damage he had wreaked. "How about Cocosino's army?"

Savacool's shoulders twitched in revulsion. "They've been isolated for obvious reasons, but I visited their ward."

Bolan nodded. "Bad?"

"Cooper, you don't want to see these people under bright lights, and I'm not even adding in what you did to them. I still see them when I close my eyes." Tears spilled down Savacool's cheeks. "I know why you did it the way you did, and I respect it. I just don't know if you did them any favors."

"What are you going to do?"

"Well, I already threw up," Savacool said.

"Me, too."

"What I want to do is to go to church. I want to pray for those people, and I shit you not, I wouldn't mind hearing some words of comfort. But I just don't think that's going to happen anytime soon."

"You got a big heart, Cool. But I mean they know about your great-aunt's place, and that means they know about you. You're on the list. I wouldn't go home if I were you, or to any friends or relatives."

"Well, hell, Cooper. Chances are they know we're here. I don't know if any place in Miami is safe, so unless you can requisition a helicopter, get clearance to land on the roof and…" Savacool's voice trailed off. Her bemused disgust look returned. "You're smiling."

Bolan nodded at himself. "Some of this is going to require stitches. Gather up Kaino and meet me on the roof in an hour."

Overtown, Miami

DELILAH TEASED THE BULLET out of Cocosino's back. He never flinched. "You got it out?"

"Yes."

"Rifle or pistol?"

Delilah held up the conical .22-caliber bullet to the single bulb in the room. "Rifle."

"The FBI bitch…"

Delilah tossed the bullet to the filthy basement floor and the surgical tweezers after it. "You want me to sew you up?"

"Hit me."

Delilah took a cooked syringe of *krokodil* and injected it straight into Cocosino's bullet wound. He visibly relaxed as the cocktail of codeine and solvents flooded his veins. Delilah looked at the rotting yet still strangely vital man beneath her and saw her future. There had been a time when he was one of the up-and-coming hot things in South Beach. Model, gigolo, getting acting jobs and working the club circuit. Then addiction had taken him down to the lowest, most execrable possible path a junkie could go. She had followed him down that spiral path. Then *krokodil* had arrived on Miami's shores and taken him from the gutter to hell itself. He had become Cocosino, had become a killer to ensure an endless series of fixes until he could no longer function. Delilah didn't want to think about what was happening to her own body, but she couldn't help smelling it. Cocosino would need a new assistant soon. She pushed the image aside with drug-addled insanity and took a sniff of meth before sewing the bullet wound. "I like this El Hombre."

"I love him. I love everything about him." Cocosino lay motionless as the surgical needle moved through noninfected flesh. "I want him."

"They called."

"What did they say?"

"El Hombre, Agent Savacool and Kaino left the hospital by helicopter. Their whereabouts are currently unknown."

"That's not a problem," Cocosino said.

"We're out of a job."

"Lots of people in Miami-Dade need killing. There are plenty of jobs." Cocosino turned what was left of his face toward Delilah. "And we'll see El Hombre again."

Trump International Beach Resort

"Wow." AGENT SAVACOOL stared out at the Intracoastal Waterway from the twenty-seventh-story balcony.

Kaino looked almost uncomfortable among such luxury. "Jeez, this hotel room is bigger than my house," he said.

Bolan pulled his hand out of the ice bucket and flexed his fingers. "I was told 1,174 square feet."

Kaino's face went flat.

"It is a double suite," Bolan admitted, and it *was* pretty damn swanky. "I've operated in Florida before. I know a few people who owe me a few favors."

Savacool gave Bolan a stare equal to Kaino's. "Donald Trump owes you favors?"

"No, and keep that in mind when you order from room service."

Kaino waved his taped-up hands as he picked up a menu. "Don't worry about that, man. A burger and a beer, and I'll be—" Kaino sat upright in outrage. "A burger costs what! *Madre de dios!*" Kaino lost his English in shock and reverted to the Spanish of his youth.

Bolan turned to Jack Grimaldi. "Thanks for coming on short notice, Jack."

The Stony Man pilot grinned. "When have you ever given me notice, Sarge?"

No one raised an eyebrow at the usage of the word *Sarge*.

"On average?" Bolan conceded. "Never."

"And now he finally starts talking sense."

"I got no notice, either," Kaino concurred.

"Mine was short," Savacool agreed.

Bolan sighed. "Any of you want out?"

"Oh, hell no!" Kaino laughed. "I'm seeing this one through."

"To the end," Savacool agreed.

Grimaldi gave Bolan a droll look. "I gather I'm here for the duration?"

"I'm thinking at least to Mexico. What have you got for me?"

The pilot put a laptop and several files on the dinner table. Bolan's team gathered around. Kurtzman's face appeared in fuzzed-out mode on the screen. "There have been a slew of killings in coastal Tamaulipas that are awfully damn similar to Savacool's boy Christo Bruno's. It looks as if there is a real fight shaping up for Tamaulipas. Someone is pushing hard to move the Gulf Coast off the Gulf Coast or force them to play ball. Of course they're not having it, and the bodies are piling up."

Bolan nodded. "Do we have anything on Salami?"

"An informant told us he's holed up in a bungalow on Miami Beach. We have it under surveillance. You'll also be happy to know that the *krokodil* supply has been seriously disrupted. Word on the street is you just can't get it. Junkies are picked up left and right committing burglaries to try to steal prescription meds to cook with. But that was always your plan, to make a mess and see who comes to clean it up."

"It's one way to get the ball rolling, and we have Cocosino and foreign mystery assassins."

Savacool gave Kaino a glance. "You sure the sniper was speaking Russian?"

"Man, I couldn't swear to it."

Savacool gave Bolan a searching look. "*Krokodil* is a Russian drug. It would make more sense."

"In some ways, but like Kaino and I discussed, it's an awfully long hop from Moscow to Miami to pedal stuff junkies buy with pocket change, and speaking of Russians, when we found Popov he had already had his ass handed to him."

"So you don't think the Russians are involved?"

"I think they're somehow part of the mix and, more important, I think there are players in this game that have yet to reveal themselves."

"So how do you want to play it?"

"I think I want to have another conversation with Salami."

Kaino smiled happily. "Wear a hat!"

"Definitely."

"Oh." Grimaldi reached into his gear bag. "Almost forgot. A friend worked this up for you." He tossed Kaino a Miami Heat cap. It made a strangely meaty thud in the big master sergeant's palm as he caught it. Kaino massaged the impact material in the brim almost erotically and began adjusting the tab in the back for his head. "Sweet!" Kaino settled his cap on his head with a happy sigh. "So why do you want to talk to Salami? He's an asshole. You think he lied to us?"

"No, I think he believed everything he told us when he told it, but I think he may have had some very interesting conversations with some very interesting people since you and I had our powwow with him. Plus, I'm thinking if Savacool can get a line on where he's hiding out, so can the people we're working against."

Grimaldi had seen this more times than he had fingers and toes. "You think he's being watched?"

"I'm counting on it."

"So we're going to pile into a car, drive up to Salami's beach blanket Babylon and see who shoots at us? Again?" Kaino asked.

Bolan shook his head. "Not exactly."

Savacool leaned her elbows on the table, perched her chin in her hands and gave Bolan the big brown eyes. "Do tell."

"You and Kaino are going to pile into a car, loaded for bear, and be ready to hit Salami's place on my signal."

Savacool regarded Bolan with grave suspicion. "And you?"

Bolan looked at Grimaldo. "Did you bring me a jump rig?"

"Did I bring him a jump rig…" the pilot scoffed.

CHAPTER EIGHT

Miami Beach, 10,000 feet

Grimaldi shouted from the cockpit into the helmet com link in Bolan's ear. "Go! Go! Go!"

The soldier stepped out of *Dragonslayer*'s cabin and arched hard as he gave himself to gravity. Miami was a spectacular pool of light below, cut by the dark lines of waterways and counterpointed by the vast darkness of the ocean to the east and the Everglades to the west. The Stony Man pilot spoke in Bolan's earpiece.

"Triangulating target." The helicopter's navigational computer synced with the grid of light below. "Target acquired, illuminating."

The gimbaled infrared laser mounted on the helicopter fired a beam invisible to the human eye. In Bolan's NVGs a bright pulsating spot appeared near the ocean's edge. The spot pulsed on the roof of Salami's beach bungalow.

"Copy that, *Dragonslayer*," Bolan replied. "I have visual." He stretched his arms behind him, turning his body into a streamlined dart aimed for the ocean's edge. He enjoyed several more seconds of free fall and hit his chute as he crossed over the target. The canopy deployed, and Bolan began a tight spiral over Salami's domicile. Out front Bolan could see a pair of men with slung rifles. They were smoking cigarettes, obviously in a low state of alert. Most of the lights in the house were off. The back patio and the beach beyond were dark and appeared empty. Bolan vectored in. The wind off the water was mild and the sand was soft. The soldier flared his chute as the beach rushed up at him and made a textbook landing. "On the ground. Going in."

"Copy that, Sarge. Orbiting your position."

Bolan clicked out of his harness and pulled his stun gun. He silently walked around the house and right up to the thugs lounging against Salami's yellow Corvette. A black SUV sat parked to one side.

"Hey."

The two men started. Bolan shot each one in the chest and held down the trigger. The men grimaced as their limbs contracted with voltage, and they dropped shuddering to the drive. One rifle clattered on the bricks of the drive. Bolan took out his pistol and waited, but no lights came on. He swiftly gagged and hog-tied the two guards and gave each one an El Hombre tattoo on his forehead with a black marker. The soldier took one of the guard's keys, then loaded the men into the back of the SUV. Donning his cap, he let himself into the house.

Salami seemed to have a fetish for black leather furniture. The other thing Bolan noticed was the odor of iodine and rotting flesh. It was very faint, but it was a smell the soldier was becoming very sensitized to. The smell seemed old. Bolan suspected Salami had received a guest in the past day or so. He walked into the living room and took note of an Uzi pistol lying on the kitchen counter. He turned on the TV a little too loud and took a seat in Salami's easy chair. He was soon rewarded with a familiar and irate "What the fuck!" from the master bedroom.

"Manolo! If you are watching jai alai when you should be outside, I'm gonna kill your ass!"

Bolan sat in the shadows and took in the majesty of Salami hobbling down the hallway with a cane, wearing nothing but an air cast, a sling and an electric-green thong. Salami obliviously grabbed the remote off the coffee table and clicked off the TV. "Manolo!"

"Yo, Cold Cut, how's it hanging?"

Salami's eyes popped in stone-cold horror. "Oh… No! No! No!" The drug dealer hobbled desperately toward the Uzi on the counter.

"Don't do it," Bolan advised him.

Salami gave up hobbling. He tossed his cane away and began hopping for all he was worth. Bolan crossed the room in three strides, just as the drug dealer's hand closed on the Uzi's grip. The soldier doffed his cap and cracked the brim across the man's clutching fingers. Salami shrieked as two of them broke. Bolan led the man by his sling to the couch and shoved him down into the leather. He took a seat on the coffee table in front of him.

"We need to talk."

"Um, about what?"

"First off, I let you live. You repaid that kindness by sicking Cocosino on me. I regard that as a genuinely unfriendly action on your part."

"I didn't!"

Bolan leaned in a little closer and sniffed twice. "It sure smells like you did."

"Oh, my God! That motherfucker smells like an open grave! I'm having the whole place fumigated! I…" Salami trailed off under Bolan's tombstone gaze.

"Stay on point, pal."

"Okay! Listen! I didn't sic him on you! He wanted to know about the fight you and I had in my crib!"

"What about it?"

"Like, everything and stuff," Salami said.

"And stuff?"

"Yeah, he was like, thorough."

"And?" Bolan prompted.

"And what?"

"Have I mentioned I don't like asking questions twice?" Bolan drummed his fingers across his cap. "It gets me all hatty and stuff."

Salami's eyes moved toward the ball cap in alarm. "He, like, gave me a shopping list. It was totally freaky. Two shuttle buses. Molotov cocktails. Baseball bats, knives—"

"Guns?"

"That was the weird part, just a couple. Cheap pieces of shit."

Bolan nodded to himself. Cocosino had wanted his horde to have just one or two firearms, just enough to start the slaughter in earnest and leave the blood of dozens of dead junkies on Bolan's hands. "And product?"

"Oh, shit, man, we're talking like a suitcase of it. Like enough to shoot up an army."

Bolan scowled internally in memory of the shambling battle. That was about the size of it. "Tell me about Cocosino."

Salami shuddered. "Man, he was wearing a bandanna and sunglasses, but I'm pretty sure he doesn't have a nose."

"Was anyone with him?"

"Yeah! Yeah! He had this chick with him. Total skank! I mean, she looked like she might have been hot once. I think I might have even seen her on the club scene a while ago, but she looked bad, and she was all covered up despite the heat. You could tell she's probably fixing in every vein in her body. Nice rack, though. If you held your nose you might…" Salami caught Bolan's look. "I'm on point! I'm on point!"

"So, with Cocosino you were just doing as you were told."

"Yeah, man! I was just obeying orders!"

"Who was giving orders?"

Salami got real quiet. Bolan drummed his fingers on his cap again.

"Like, they came from the top!"

"Where's the top?"

Salami began shaking as he began betraying. "Matamoros. That's in—"

"I know where that is." Bolan filed that one away next to his mysterious hit team and surveillance photo of Christo Bruno's assassination. "Los Zetas?"

"Yes."

"Who called you and told you to cooperate with Cocosino?"

"Raulito."

"Raulito who?"

Salami began spilling in earnest. "Raulito Paz! He's the point man for pushing the Gulf Coast out of Tamaulipas! He said he wanted El Hombre done, and done sick. He told me to pull a fade from the scene but be ready to supply whatever was needed on the ground, and be ready to receive Cocosino, like, if need be."

"He say anything about a hit team?"

Salami blinked. "Um…no."

"I had to deal harshly with some serious gunsels the other night in North Miami. You know anything about that?"

"No! I mean, yes! I mean, I heard El Hombre, I mean you, went all hard two nights ago, but no one told me anything about it. I mean, beforehand."

Bolan believed him. "What am I going to do with you, Salami?"

The drug dealer looked like he might start crying. "I think I'm going to throw up."

Between the wine, painkillers, broken bones and betrayal, Bolan wasn't surprised. "Not on me."

Salami made a gagging noise. Bolan scooped up the wastebasket and shoved it in the man's lap. "Make it quick."

Salami retched into the basket. Slowly but surely the man's gastrointestinal convulsions reduced to shudders.

"You done?"

Salami's voice sounded tiny and tinny. "I think so." He raised his head and flopped back.

"Feel better?" Bolan asked.

"A little."

Grimaldi spoke in Bolan's earpiece. "Sarge."

"What's up?"

"I got two individuals, airborne, parachuting into your position. I estimate you got about five minutes before they hit the beach."

"Salami, you expecting the 82nd Airborne?"

"What?"

"Copy that, *Dragonslayer*. Cool, Kaino, be advised I have two potential hostiles parachuting into Salami's residence."

"Copy that, Cooper." It was Savacool's voice. "You want us to come in?"

"Wait on my signal. Be advised when you do I have two separate hostiles down and bound in back of black SUV. Keys are in the ignition."

"Copy that."

Salami blinked. "People are parachuting into my house? What did you do?"

"There is a very low order of probability that anyone has any idea that I'm here, much less would have had the time to mount an airborne operation to do anything about it."

Salami blinked.

Bolan refrained from rolling his eyes. "They're here for you."

"Oh, shit!"

"Oh, shit is right." Bolan walked to the kitchen. He scavenged a roll of tape from a drawer and took up the Uzi pistol. "Hold up your hand," he ordered, returning to the coffee table.

"What?"

Bolan seized Salami's hand. "Be very quiet."

The man gasped as the soldier taped together the drug

dealer's broken little and ring fingers. Bolan checked the loads in the Uzi. Salami's jaw dropped as the Executioner pressed the weapon into his hand.

"This is your one golden opportunity to shoot me, but if you do you're going to have to deal with death from above by yourself, with a cracked elbow and ankle, no Manolo and friend, and God only knows what these guys want to do to you."

The drug dealer stared at the weapon in his hand and then back at Bolan. Despite his present state of moral devastation, Salami was a criminal who had risen through the ranks the hard way, and he saw it.

"When they come for me, you're going to take them down."

"That is the plan."

"Okay." Salami stiffened slightly with resolve. "What do you want me to do?"

"My people will tell me when they're inside the perimeter. They're dropping in. That tells me this is probably a snatch or an interrogation. They probably have a boat somewhere nearby for extraction. When they come through the door, you're going to rip off a burst or two and scream. They'll probably think it was their bad luck that you happened to be awake. If they're like the last bunch, they'll come in hard. That's when I blindside them."

"What about me?"

"What about you?" Bolan asked.

"I mean, after, what about me?"

"If you do this, I'll leave you alone."

"Really?"

"Really, but you're retired. I'll have people keeping tabs on you. You so much as peddle a tube of airplane glue, you'll rue the day."

Salami was just dumb enough to go shifty. "You won't kill me—you have a code."

Bolan leaned in so close Salami had no more couch to re-treat into. "No, I won't kill you. I'll just give you to Raulito, or Cocosino, and if I've killed them already, somewhere be-tween Miami and Mexico City I think I can find someone who would love to find you naked, bound and gagged on their doorstep."

Salami literally squeaked. "I'm retired!"

"Good, now get frosty. When it happens, it's going to happen fast."

Grimaldi spoke on cue. "Sarge! Aggressors are in terminal glide, heading straight for the beach! ETA thirty seconds!"

"Copy that, *Dragonslayer.*" Bolan drew his Beretta. He took his suppressor out and spun it onto the weapon's muzzle. He considered his magazine of less lethal rubber and stayed with lead. "Salami."

"Yeah?"

Bolan nodded at the Uzi in the man's taped hand. "You any good with that?"

Salami looked Bolan straight in the eye. "No."

"Well, ideally, I want at least one alive. They're proba-bly wearing armor. If you have the shot, go low. Reap legs."

"Got it, *hombre.*"

Grimaldi spoke across the link. "Hostiles are on the beach and advancing. Still count two hostiles. Coming straight for the back door. ETA ten seconds."

"Copy that." Bolan nodded at Salami and took a knee in the corner. "Here they come."

Salami limped over to put the kitchen island between him-self and the sliding-glass back door. The door shattered into a thousand pieces as something hit it. "Motherfuckers!" The drug dealer screamed on cue. "Say hello to my little friend!" Contrary to orders, the Uzi pistol in his hand buzz-sawed at head level. The responding flash-bang grenade clattered across the floor. Bolan pulled his hands over his eyes and stuck his thumbs in his ears as it went off. The light, sound and overpressure was enough to topple the half-crippled Salami like a tree. Two goggled and raid-suited men armed with stubby, sound-suppressed weapons swept into the bungalow.

Bolan raised his weapon and touched off two bursts in rapid succession. The assault leader took three rounds through each thigh and took an ugly, limb-folding slide across the hardwood floor. The second man whipped his head around and a burst of subsonic rounds whispered inches over Bolan's head. The soldier put three rounds through the intruder's face. The invader took two steps, tripped over the coffee table and collapsed face-first onto Salami's black leather couch.

Bolan held position as smoke oozed out of his suppressor. "*Dragonslayer,* I have two down. Do you have movement?"

"Negative, Sarge."

"Cool, any movement on the road?"

"Negative, Cooper."

"Cool, I have a hostile down with multiple leg wounds. I need him stabilized and transported stat."

"Striker, I can drop down right now!" Grimaldi shouted.

"Negative, *Dragonslayer.* I do not want our air asset exposed. Cool! Kaino! I need you now!"

"Inbound, Cooper!" Savacool replied. Bolan heard Kaino's modified V-8 engine roar out on the access road.

Grimaldi's voice rose across the link. "I have a boat inbound on your position at high speed! You want me to take him?"

Dragonslayer was in under the radar mode, and could pass for a civilian search and rescue helicopter. A whirlybird enthusiast might wonder at the winch motor pod mounted over both doorways. One was indeed a rescue winch, but if Grimaldi held down the trigger on his joystick, the cellulose cap on the false starboard winch would be blown off as the XM-214 microgun within the winch housing ripped into life at 6,000 rounds per minute. "I can stitch him now."

"Negative!" Bolan ordered. "Do not expose air asset!"

Bolan scanned the man on the couch and the triburst of bullet wounds through his head said he was beyond caring. The point man was groaning, and to his credit was sticking his fingers in the holes in his thighs. "Salami!" Bolan shouted.

"I'm…hurting."

"Get your ass up or I'm leaving you behind!"

Bolan heard tires screech on the brick driveway outside. Kaino shouted over the radio. "We're here! Go! Go! Go! Aw shit! Savacool deploying!"

"Boat is on top of you!" Grimaldi announced, "I can see crew-served weapons on the—" A heavy machine gun hammered into life and stitched the stucco walls of the bungalow in a line from north to south at waist level.

"Engaging!" Savacool shouted across the line.

An automatic rifle began slamming in high-pitched response to the heavy weapon on the boat. Bolan grabbed Salami's cane and hurled it at him. "Go! Get in the SUV!"

"I don't have the keys!"

"It's open! Keys are in the ignition! Go now or not at all!"

Mortality was a good motivator. Salami began hopping at Olympic triple-jump-qualifying levels for the door. Bolan ran up to the living invader on the floor. He punched him dead in the face, then chopped his hand into the side of the intruder's neck to put him limp. Another line of bullets ripped through the living room. Bolan could tell by the sound someone was hitting the bungalow with a .50-caliber weapon. He waited for the burst to subside and threw the invader into a fireman's carry. The heavy bullets were tearing through the house as if it were tissue paper. The soldier's burden was at least two hundred pounds and he was bleeding a river. Below machine-gun thunder the Executioner could hear the boat's engine as it approached at high speed.

Salami burst out the front door, with Bolan right behind him.

Kaino ran up. "You hit?"

"No, but this one has holes in both legs! Get him in the backseat and see if you can stabilize him," Bolan roared over the sound of gunfire. "Cool! We're out of here!"

Agent Savacool came around the corner at the run. Tracers streaked into the chimney she had been using for cover and tore the bricks apart. The crackle of AKs joined the cacophony. "I count six, hitting the beach like D-day!"

Salami's SUV tore away into the night. Bolan jumped behind the wheel of Kaino's Mercury, and the modified V-8 roared into life. Savacool slid into the shotgun position and slammed a fresh magazine into her weapon. Three figures came around the house and Savacool flicked her selector switch to full-auto and let fly. One member of the assault team fell. Bolan put the Merc in Reverse and stomped on the gas. The other two invaders took a knee and returned fire. Bullets walked across the Merc's hood. Three more figures emerged from the other side of the house as the vehicle's tires hit the gravel of the access road. Bolan stomped on the brakes. As the Merc screamed through the 180 degree J-turn, the soldier rammed the car into Drive and stomped on the gas. The Merc lunged like a Thoroughbred out of the gates.

He risked a glance at the rearview. One of the attackers had held up a fist for cease-fire. The assassin, kidnapper or torturer, Bolan wasn't sure which if not all applied, wore a raid suit, armor, goggles and a baklava, but despite that Bolan could easily identify one thing.

The man in command of the assault squad was a woman.

CHAPTER NINE

Eglin Air Force Base

The patient was surly. It had been a bumpy ride getting him to a place on the road where Grimaldi could land *Dragonslayer,* and a bumpier one crossing Florida at high speed. The man lying in medical restraints was big, blond, blue-eyed and a past master at glaring into the middle distance.

"Is it just me?" Kaino pondered. "Or does it look like he's pulling a sulky Russian?"

Bolan smiled and watched the man's face for reaction.

The man in the bed might as well have been carved out of stone.

Bolan turned to the doctor. Dr. Clarke bore a startling resemblance to Jane Goodall except she was six feet tall and usually dealt with sick airmen instead of chimps or surly, shot-up suspected Russians. "So what does his chart say?"

Bolan had dealt with a lot of doctors, military and otherwise who had received bizarre phone calls from on high that they were to cooperate with him in all ways possible while at the same time being totally left in the dark. Clarke was taking it better than most. "Aside from the damage you did to him tonight? I assume the bullets and blunt trauma are all yours."

"Yes, Doctor."

"Well, your playmate has been shot twice before. He has a long, abdominal laceration scar that although it's in the right place looks one hell of a lot more like a knife wound than an appendectomy. He's built like a decathlete. He smokes cigarettes. He has bad teeth and an awful barber, and by all observation his only two modes of communication appear to be glaring and grimacing."

"You don't think he's American?"

"Oh, hell no."

Bolan made his decision. "Can you give me a few minutes to consult with my team?"

Clarke walked away with a sigh. "To be shown all cooperation and courtesy…"

Bolan turned his head just enough so the patient couldn't see him wink at Savacool. "With permission, Special Agent, I would like to speak to the prisoner alone."

"You're not going to mess with his morphine, are you?"

Bolan let his face go dead as he regarded his prisoner. "Special Agent, you need to leave the room, or not the leave the room." Savacool gave the patient a scathing look and left the room. "He's all yours."

The prisoner turned stonier, if that was possible.

As Kaino started to follow Savacool, Bolan said, "Kaino, no one comes in, not even his doctor. No matter what you hear."

Kaino cracked his scarred knuckles. "Done."

The patient turned his head and acknowledged Bolan's existence for the first time. When the soldier stepped next to the bed, the prisoner didn't flinch. Only his eyes changed slightly in a way that told Bolan the man was steeling himself to endure whatever happened.

The big American took off his shirt.

The prisoner's face went from stone to consternation. Bolan raised his arms and turned in a slow circle. "I'm not wearing a wire, I've turned off all my electronic devices." It was an old and often quoted remark by Winston Churchill that Russians were "a puzzle inside a riddle wrapped in an enigma." Bargaining with them was a chess game. They were always circling and looking for the advantage. Bolan had learned long ago that if you wanted to freak out a Russian into spilling something, one way was to kick over the chessboard and reveal everything. They never expected it.

A great deal of the strategy's success or failure depended on how scared of you the Russian in question was or their mission's level of desperation.

"My name's El Hombre. Cocosino crocked-up about forty *krokodil* junkies and sent them at me like an army of the living dead in West Miami. Maybe you heard about it?"

A few of the patient's facial muscles flexed.

Bolan made a show of sniffing the air over the prisoner as he shrugged back into his shirt. "And you smell like you were eating borscht less than a week ago."

The man on the hospital bed flushed against his will. His eyes flared as Bolan pulled up a chair and casually put his boots up on the bed. "Listen, Ivan—" Bolan gave Ivan a solicitous look "—you don't mind if I call you Ivan?"

Ivan scowled mightily.

"If there's anything you want to say, off the record, it's now or not at all. If not, I give you to the FBI, they give you to Homeland Security and God only knows what happens to you after that."

The prisoner locked gazes with Bolan. Neither man flinched. The man on the hospital bed spoke for the first time, and he definitely had a Russian accent. "I know nothing of El Hombre."

"And?"

The prisoner's arms were held by medical restraints, but his wrist turned in the cuff and he pointed a finger at Bolan. "But a man matching your description is known to us. Man matching your method of operation is known to us."

"I get that a lot."

The Russian blinked and regained his composure. "I have recommendation."

"What's that?"

"If you know what is good for you, you will release me to Russian Consulate immediately."

Bolan shrugged. "Sure."

The Russian blinked.

The soldier took his feet off the bed and rose. He clicked on his phone, tapped a security and a tracing app and tossed it onto the Russian's stomach. "You can use mine." He took out his tactical knife and cut the strap holding the Russian's left hand. The man stared at the phone as if it were a snake.

Bolan shook his head. "Like we're not going to trace any call you make on any phone while in our custody anyway?"

The Russian grunted and conceded the point. "I am wishing privacy anyway."

"Sure."

The Russian eyed Bolan with extreme wariness. "Sure?"

"Sure, call your people, have them pick you up. You're going home."

"You let me go? Why?"

"Why not?"

Ivan spent long moments pondering this weird and wonderful conundrum. "You wish me to deliver message."

"Someone brought your Russian *krokodil* shit onto my shore. I'm going to stamp it out. I'm going to stamp out the people who did it. I'm going to burn the entire operation to the ground, and if it leads to the Kremlin, I'm going to burn that down, too. And if 'man matching my description and method of operation' is known to you, then you know I shit you not."

Ivan went stony again.

Bolan took out a blank card and wrote a number on it. "If for any reason you, your government or your team leader would like to talk further about the matter, I can be reached at this number." He tossed the card to the bed.

The Russian looked at the card and looked at the phone. "That is it?"

"No, two more things."

"What are two more things?"

"One, word to the wise, you try to screw with my phone, you'll lose the use of your hand."

The Russian nodded. "And?"

Bolan sniffed the air in the room. "It's pretty clean in here. Tell me you're GRU and not an SVR asshole."

One corner of Ivan's mouth quirked up. The SVR was the Russian ill-concealed attempt to paint a new face on the KGB, and it was their second attempt. GRU was Russian Military Intelligence, and the two agencies despised each other. "I am not SVR asshole."

Bolan nodded. "I know."

"I know you know, and this has been noted in your favor."

Bolan walked out of the room.

"And?" Savacool asked.

"He's calling his people. They're on their way. They'll be diplomats, with immunity. Cut him loose."

Savacool detonated. "What!"

"I got what I wanted. He's not the enemy."

"I shot two of his friends, and Kaino's car is going to need a hell of a lot of work."

"He's GRU, military intelligence. They were there for Salami, same as us and for the same reason, to get information."

"So Russian Military Intelligence has an active paramilitary team operating in the greater Miami-Dade metropolitan area?"

"That's about the size of it," Bolan said.

"And you caught one?"

"Yeah."

Savacool was incensed. "And you're letting him go?"

"Yeah."

Savacool closed her eyes and took a deep breath. "I cannot wait for tomorrow. You know, I've never actually spoken with the director before. He'll undoubtedly be the most august personage to ever tear me a new one. Thanks, Cooper."

"You aren't willing to do what it would require to make the Russian talk. Kaino could do it, but he'd lose his shield. I could do it, but I don't want to. The fact is, we let him and the Russians owe us one, whether they're willing to admit it or not. I give it fifty-fifty it engenders some cooperation, but I think the Russians are here for the same reason we are. They want to eliminate the *krokodil* situation before it spreads. I don't know why, but we're on the same mission."

"Cooper, he's—"

"He's a foreign intelligence agent, engaging in illegal interrogations, attempted kidnappings and running military operations on U.S. soil. He has fired upon U.S. law-enforcement officers and agents. You are a foresworn member of the Federal Bureau of the United States. You say the word and I'll walk back into that room, look Ivan in the eye and say 'Oops, my bad. You're still screwed.' It's your call."

Savacool shook her head angrily. "Damn…"

Bolan nodded. "Good call."

Mercy Hospital, Miami

THE CROC WARD, AS IT was called, consisted of a pair of linked CDC biological hazard containment tents in the back parking lot. The thirty-nine individuals lying in restraints within suffered from a staggering array of infectious diseases that manifested themselves as secondary effects of their *krokodil* addiction. Eight had already died. So far the doctors had performed seven major amputations. Over a hundred pounds of rotting flesh had been excised in last-ditch efforts to stop the spread of infection. Less than half of the patients were expected to leave the tent alive. The doctors and nurses treating the addicts stopped just short of wearing full bio-suits but just about every other safeguard was in place. The pain of *krokodil* withdrawal was so acute that most of the patients were under heavy sedation. All that could be done at this point was to keep them on massive regimens of antibiotics and see who made it.

A doctor and two nurses currently ran the late shift. A uniformed officer sat in the tent's tiny foyer. The cop looked up as a man shambled into the entryway and pulled a bandanna off his face. "Help me…"

"Judas Priest!" The cop recoiled in horror. "Doc! Doc! You gotta get out here right now. We have another—" The cop clawed for his service pistol as the giant, gleaming revolver rose in front of his face. Cocosino squeezed the trigger. The cop's head stopped just short of exploding. Cocosino walked into the ward. The doctor and the two nurses skidded to a halt at the sight of him and his smoking gun. The doctor's eyes flew wide behind his surgical mask. "Listen—"

"On your knees. You and the bitches."

The doctor and the two nurses fell to their knees. One nurse began to cry. The doctor took in the ravaged horror looking down on him. "Son, we can help you."

Cocosino made a gesture encompassing the ward. "Like you're helping them?"

"I expect half to make it through this." The doctor nodded. "And live."

Cocosino smiled. One of the nurses almost threw up at the sight of it. Cocosino gestured at his face. "Like this?"

It occurred to the doctor with absolute clarity that he and his nurses were about to die. He looked Cocosino straight in what was left of the creature's face. "Yes, if you have the balls for it."

Cocosino went rigid. The doctor waited for the bullet. The travesty of what Cocosino called a smile slowly crawled across his suppurating features. "You know, Doc? That's exactly the kind of thing El Hombre would say."

"I like his work," the doctor agreed.

"Love him." Cocosino shot the man in the face. The nurses screamed and lurched to their feet just in time to receive similar .44-caliber cannon shots. The insulated, triple-ply tent material made for excellent soundproofing. Inside the tent it sounded like doomsday. A few of the patients partially surfaced from their anesthetically induced comas and mewled or babbled.

"Delilah, my love!" Cocosino called. Delilah came in from standing guard outside. "Antibiotics, and every drop of propofol in the place."

Delilah went from tray to tray. She made a happy noise and held up a vial. "Medical cocaine!"

"Sweet." Even Cocosino had to admit thirty-nine was a tiring number. He was definitely going to need a pick-me-up on top of a fix after this. Cocosino slid his machete from his pant leg and moved to the closest bed. He took it in both hands and raised it on high. "Give me a count!"

"One!"

"¡En Español, mi amor!"

"¡Uno!"

Cocosino moved to the next bed.

"¡Dos!"

He moved to the third bed. Delilah looked back over her shoulder as she began tagging one tent wall with a croc graffito in hot pink.

"¡Tres!"

Cocosino grunted as he had to take a second swing. So much of his skin was damaged that he no longer sweated correctly, and he felt himself heating up. This was going to take a little longer than he had thought. "Delilah, be a love and turn up the air-conditioning, and bring me some of that coke, would you?"

CHAPTER TEN

FBI safehouse, Miami

"Thirty-nine heads! Have you ever seen such a thing?" Savacool was about to go ballistic. She suddenly gave Bolan a rueful look across the table. "You know, I bet you have."

Bolan eyed the files from the croc-ward massacre. "Thirty-nine is a bit excessive."

"Glad you think so, Cooper."

The safehouse was centrally located in Miami, and Bolan gave it a good 95 percent that the enemy had no idea where they were. He gently rolled his head and flexed his arm and leg. His junkie bites ached, but nothing felt hot and so far he didn't feel sick. Bolan poured himself more coffee and picked up a photo. He frowned at the hot-pink *krokodil* graffito on the tent wall. "Is that the same infrared luminescent paint he marked my Lincoln with?"

Savacool went back into investigator mode. "Yeah, the lab identified it. I guess Cocosino hasn't run out. We had a handwriting analysis expert examine it. It's a pretty crude copy. We don't think Cocosino did it."

"His helper."

"That's my best guess. By the looks of things he was pretty busy."

"Any DNA?"

"Do you realize how much rotting flesh there was lying around after the slaughter? The lab is working with suppurating, infected goo by the bucket!" Savacool made an exasperated noise and visibly hauled on the reins of her emotions. "So what's your take, Cooper? Why do this? Were they his disciples? Does he feel like he owned them? Why take the risk?"

A cold wind blew through Bolan. He knew the answer all too well. "He sent those wretches against me to be slaughtered. I spared them. So he killed them in return. It's a punk card. He wants me to pick it up. He's calling me out."

"God give me strength…"

Bolan changed the subject. "We got anything of note from Salami's house?"

Kaino stepped in from the kitchen with three plates piled high with fried plantains, fried eggs and toast. "A small amount of meth and marijuana—we're assuming its recreational. A couple of illegal firearms and one whole hell of a lot of bullets from the walls. Ballistics makes them AK-74s of some stripe and the .50 cal was Russian, as well. No sign of the intruders except blood."

"Any Salami sightings?"

"Highway Patrol found Salami's SUV by the side of the road just past South Beach. Him and his two boys were long gone. I'm assuming someone picked them up."

"Speaking of pickups, did 'Ivan's' people come for him?"

Savacool chewed and swallowed and nodded in appreciation at Kaino's cooking. "Two cultural attachés and a physician's assistant took him out of Mercy. I passed along your advice not to follow them and strangely enough, the suggestion was accepted."

Bolan steeled himself for another Savacool detonation. "How was your phone conversation with the director?"

"Would you believe my phone has been eerily silent? I'm the one making all the calls, and everyone is giving me everything that I want."

"I would believe it," Bolan said.

"I bet you would."

Kaino spoke around a massive mouthful of plantains. "It's the same for me. But I got a question, Coop."

"Shoot."

"What about Cocosino? Thirty-nine decapitations in one night, plus a doctor and two nurses? That's a record around here."

Bolan turned his gaze on Kaino. "What's your point?"

"Jesus! Don't look at me like that! I'm not blaming you! I'm just asking, what do we do about this asshole? I mean, sure, we can wait another month or two and we can probably just scrape what's left of him up out of some shooting gallery with a spatula, but it seems to me Cocosino is the kind of guy who wants to go out in a blaze of glory. And forty-two dead in one night is a hell of a start."

"You're right, Kaino. He's a situation that needs rectifying."

"Oh, he needs rectalizing, all right. So how do we go about it?"

Bolan had been giving the matter a great deal of thought. "Cool, you want to do something mean?"

"I'm a Christian, Cooper. But right now, I'm dying to do something mean to someone. What do you have in mind?"

Bolan took a piece of paper out of the printer on the sideboard and wrote a note. He signed it "El Hombre" and folded it and handed it to Savacool. "Fax this to the Russian Consulate."

"May I read it first?"

"I wouldn't have it any other way."

Savacool read the note and stopped short of crumpling it in her fist. "God give me strength…"

Kaino stopped eating. "What is it?" Savacool handed over the note. He snapped it open and read it. He expressed admiration rather than outrage. "Okay, Coop. You're the man!"

Savacool stared at Bolan in disbelief. "You want the Russians to hire Cocosino and kill him?"

"You got a problem with that?"

"Personally? No. Professionally…"

Bolan shrugged. "They owe us. He is currently defending the *krokodil* suppliers. I understand Kaino's need to put the psycho down, but it's a distraction from the mission. I don't need the Florida distributors. I need to get to Mexico and hit the Zetas in Tamaulipas. I want Raulito Paz."

Savacool paused midbite. "You're going to go down to Mexico and take on the Zetas by yourself?"

Bolan cocked his head guilessly. "You're not coming with us?"

"I…"

Kaino didn't give it a second thought. "I'm down!"

"You're a good man, Kaino."

"Yeah, but I'm also kind of down with Cool. We got a three-man team versus an entire cartel, and this is gonna be an away game. I'm thinking a guy like you must have some pretty interesting friends."

Bolan smiled. He had some very interesting friends. Unfortunately both Able Team and Phoenix were currently deployed. The soldier opened his laptop and touched an app. Security suites shook hands and Kurtzman appeared on the screen. "What's up?"

"How is the file on Raulito Paz and Los Zetas shaping up?"

"Shaping up well. We're coming up with some pretty actionable intelligence. You won't be walking into Matamoros blind and seeing who takes a swing at you on this one."

"Good to know. Listen. Kaino's down with it. Savacool will have to get permission from her office. Either way I'm going to need some reliable backup."

"All the usual suspects are out and about."

"I know. I think I'm going to need to hire a couple of likely lads, particularly ones who know the lay of the land."

"Private security," Kurtzman surmised.

"Yeah. Which outfit has the highest reputation in Mexico?"

Bolan watched Kurtzman type in info and scan data on several screens. "Seguridad de la Torre seems to have a good reputation."

"Tower Security." Bolan nodded. "I think I've heard of them. Don't they specialize in antikidnapping and kidnap retrieval?"

"They go under VIP protection, but yeah, that's their specialization, and they like to hire bilingual, ex-military Americans. A lot of the kidnapping rings south of the border aren't necessarily cartel. They just pay tribute, and dealing with ex-SEALs and Delta frightens them."

"Have Akira break in to Torres' database and find me at least two guys who meet the mission requirements. Make contact." Bolan checked his watch. "If possible I want a meet and greet by tonight."

"That's awfully tight."

"Tell them they get paid just to show up and hear the pitch, whether they take the job or not. Private contractors are always worried about their next contract and their next paycheck. If they smell money, they'll come."

"All right, I'm on it."

"Thanks, Bear. Tell Jack we'll be at the airport in an hour and set a flight plan for Brownsville, Texas."

Brownsville, Texas

KURTZMAN CAME THROUGH. Two potential recruits walked through the motel door laughing and joking with Grimaldi. The Stony Man pilot had been kind enough to pick up the two men at the border and buy them a steak dinner. Jack Grimaldi was a born schmoozer, and it looked as though he had put the recruits in a good mood.

"Come on in, have a seat." Bolan gestured at the iced

bucket of beers on the table. "Cut the dust." The two men took seats, took beers and eyed Savacool, Kaino and Bolan with open interest. Akira Tokaido, Stony Man Farm's top hacker, had raided the Seguridad de la Torres personnel database, and Bolan already had both men's résumés. He examined the first recruit.

Marvino "Donuts" Donez was ex-federal police for the State of Matamoros and had done a stint in their Fast Reaction Teams. Now he was in the personal protection business. He had quit the force, but there were no blemishes or disciplinary actions on his record.

Bolan got straight to the point. "Why'd you quit the force, Donez?"

The ex-cop had very heavy features and wavy black hair. Donez glowered. He had a border accent but his English was excellent. "You been to Matamoros?"

"Yeah."

"Nuevo Laredo maybe?"

"Yeah."

"You want to be a Mexican cop on the border?"

"No."

"Smart man. Listen, half of my unit, I'm talking top to bottom, were on the take. Like I'm talking if you didn't play ball you didn't just get the shit assignments—when shit happened you couldn't even be sure of getting backup."

"I understand," Bolan said.

"Maybe you do. Anyway, I went into personal protection. Dealing with kidnapping rings is easier than fighting the cartels. The pay isn't bad, I'm still doing some good in the world and I still look at myself in the mirror in the morning."

"Mind if I ask you one more question?"

Donez stiffened. "Sure, you go right ahead."

"How did a Mexican cop end up with a nickname like Donuts?"

Donez smiled despite himself. "I was part of a cross-border antigang task force, working in conjunction with the Brownsville PD. It was three years ago, and I had my first Krispy Kreme. I never looked at a Mexican *dona* or a *churro* again. I swear I can't leave them." Donez got a faraway look in his eyes. "They complete me."

Kaino laughed out loud. "I like him."

So did Bolan. He looked at the other recruit. He was lanky, American and sat sprawled in his chair as if he owned it. John "Jack" Murphy was former Army Rangers and former Special Forces. His file was heavily redacted, but he'd been honorably discharged. He'd drifted around for about six months and then headed south and joined Seguridad de la Torres. The hacked mission profiles and action reports showed the two men had worked together numerous times and worked together well.

"Care to tell me why you left Special Ops, Murph?" Bolan asked.

Murphy reached for another beer. "Honestly, I was sick of the Middle East. Sick of those deserts, sick of those mountains and frankly sick of the people. I missed the ocean. I missed America, and I missed Mexican women."

Donez snorted.

"It's true," Murphy continued. "I learned Spanish at the language school, so on a lark I took a job down here with Donut's outfit. The pay's pretty okay, the girls are pretty and the Gulf is just a stone's throw away. I've had worse guys on my six than Donuts." Murphy shrugged. "Life is good."

"Why not sign on with one of the other big outfits?"

"Dude—" Murphy snorted dismissively "—their work is too much like…work."

Bolan suspected Murphy had a few attitude problems but overall he liked him.

"I'm taking on Los Zetas in Matamoros. You in?"

Murphy shrugged again. "Sure."

Savacool stared in surprise. "That's it? No questions?"

"I'm sure I'll have plenty of questions later. What I need now is to get paid, like a signing bonus. Like yesterday. Besides…" Murphy gave Kaino, Savacool and Bolan a sly look. "He's a cop, she's a Fed, and you? You're plain scary."

"Not bad," Savacool admitted.

"I got a nose for these things. I got a nose for insurgents, bad cops, kidnappers and ambushes. It's a gift, and on top of that I'm good at what I do."

"So why sign up with me now?" Bolan asked. "Just money?"

"I'm writing a memoir, you know."

"I didn't know that," Bolan admitted.

"Oh, yeah. I got the punk kid with Red, White and Blue surging in veins signing up to serve his Uncle Sam opening chapter, then the play the theme from *Rocky* part where I decide to be all that I can be and opt for Ranger training, then deployment and triumph and tragedy fighting the good fight in Iraq chapter. Then I got the joining Special Forces chapter, more training and a whole lot of dwelling on weapons and equipment, for the gun-bunny crowd, then Spec Ops in Afghanistan."

"And then?" Bolan prompted.

"And then I got booze, broads and beaches doing personal protection south of the border. Kidnapping rings, corrupt cops, slinky Mexican MILFs falling out of their cocktail dresses and oil heiresses in distress, which isn't a bad way to wind it up, mind you. But this? Right here?" Murphy circled his finger to encompass everyone in the room. "This pushes me right onto the *New York Times* bestseller list and gets me on FOX and friends."

Bolan nodded. "It's not a bad plan."

"I've spent a lot of time thinking about it," Murphy agreed.

"And I came up with that last part just fifteen seconds ago. I only got one condition."

"And that is?"

"I don't join this man's elite fighting force unless Donuts does, too."

Donez nearly choked on his beer. *"¡Hijo de puta madre!"*

"Aw, c'mon, Donuts. You're sick of babysitting, admit it."

"Murph, I worked real hard to put myself in a place where I don't have to sweat the cartels or my fellow police officers that serve them." Donez gave Bolan a sour look. "Now this blue-eyed, Cro-Magnon son of a bitch wants to pull me back in and go to war with them."

Bolan nodded. "I do."

"Yeah, and what's the pay like?"

"Right now money is a little tight. I can pay you one half of your standard protection rate and I can throw in Murph's signing bonus."

Murphy lost a little of his enthusiasm. "Well now, I can outthink and in a worst-case scenario outshoot any j-hole kidnappers in town. All they got on their side is maybe surprise if I'm hung over that day. But the cartels? They got firepower, resources and half the time half the city on their side. That's hazardous duty pay where I come from."

"I'm hitting a specific drug-dealing arm of the Zetas. There's going to be a lot of money lying around. As long as it doesn't interfere with the mission, you have my permission to rob them blind. To the tune of millions if they're dumb enough to have it lying around in huge piles, which we all know they frequently do. In fact, robbing them blind may become part of the mission."

Murphy and Donez gave each other a look.

Bolan pushed two thick thousand-dollar rolls made up of small bills across the table. "That's for your time, regardless."

Murphy raised his hand. "I'm in! We're in! Donuts! Say

we're in!" He grabbed Donez's shoulders and began shaking him. "Please, please, please, please, please—"

"*¡Maricon!*" Donez snapped his shoulders out of Murphy's grasp and half cocked his hand to hit him.

Murphy nodded triumphantly. "That's means 'were in' in Spanish."

"So, Donuts, you know Matamoros?"

"Like the back of my hand." He scowled.

"Then I need guns."

"What do you mean, you need guns?"

"Me, Kaino, Savacool. No one knows us in Mexico, but our descriptions are known in Florida, and we can't have you two associated with us just yet. So we're all going into Mexico separately and legit. Then we'll meet up at a safehouse in Matamoros. When we get in we're going to need guns pronto."

Donez stared uncomfortably out the window. "Well, that is a conundrum."

"I gather you and Murph are legal to carry in Mexico?"

"Handguns for general carry. If we need something bigger we have to check it out of the Seguridad de la Torres armory—that usually means an Uzi Pro, and Torres has to contact the police and let them know. Raiding the Torres armory would be a really bad idea."

"Conundrum hell." Murphy gave his partner a very hard look. "You know where we have to go."

"Really? Him?"

"Who's him?" Bolan asked.

Donez spoke unhappily. "Morti."

"Savacool, Kaino and I are crossing the border first thing in the morning. We'll get situated. Our cover won't last long, but for the moment Savacool and I are married, and we've hired you two for extra protection."

Murphy waved a beer at the master sergeant. "And who is he supposed to be?"

"He's Kaino, our magical houseboy. Donuts, see if you can set up a meet with Morti for tomorrow afternoon."

CHAPTER ELEVEN

Matamoros, Mexico, warehouse district

Mortimer "Morti" Morelos might as well have had the words "shady Mexican arms dealer" tattooed across his forehead. Short, sweaty and shifty-looking summed Morelos up to a tee. Morelos levered open a long crate and nodded at the contents. *"Bueno."*

"It is not fucking *bueno!*" Kaino waved his arms up and down in outrage at what lay in the straw. "This shit is from World War II!"

Morelos kept a straight face as he answered. "No, the Korean War. Surplus, donated to United Mexican States by the U.S. State Department."

Kaino went apoplectic and began bellowing some very choice things at the man in Puerto Rican Spanish. Morelos regarded Kaino as an insect might regard a washing machine. It was large and it was making noises, but it was without relevance in his existence. Bolan reached down into the straw and took out an M-1 Garand rifle. He turned his cobalt-blue gaze on Morelos and lifted one eyebrow.

Morelos looked at Bolan like a lizard confronted by some new breed of predator it didn't recognize, and the issue of whether it ate lizards or not was in doubt. Morelos's eyes went from reptilian to shifty, and he did some hand waving himself.

"What do you expect, *señor?* You want a brand-new FX-05 Fire Serpent rifle? Only the military gets those! If the army catches you with one, they assume you killed a soldier to get it, and they don't arrest you, *claro?* You want a Heckler & Koch? So does everybody! You want an AK? So does everybody! You want an AR? The line goes around the block!"

Bolan racked the old M-1's action back. He took the light on his keychain and examined the bore. The rifle had seen a lot of hard use, but the bore wasn't bad and the action seemed sound.

Morelos stabbed a finger at the weapon. "That? Nobody wants it. To the army it's obsolete. To the cartels it's old school and uncool. I can't give them away. But you, *señor?* You look like a man of discerning taste. You appreciate craftsmanship."

Bolan raised his eyebrow once more.

Morelos scuttled to another crate and cracked it with his pry-bar. "Here, I know you will appreciate this."

Bolan nodded. "Nice."

Morelos beamed.

The gun smuggler had some reason to. She was a beauty of an M-1D sniper variant. The leather cheek piece had seen better days, but finish and wood-wise the old girl was in better shape than the rifles in the other crate. Bolan racked the action and shouldered the piece. The bore was clean and the optics seemed to be in good shape.

"Um, Cooper?" Savacool asked. The ninety-eight-pound special agent took up a nine-and-a-half-pound rifle and grimaced. "You know I hate to be like, *a girl,* and stuff, but I don't think this is going to work out."

Murphy had no such problems. He raised an M-1, checked the action and sighted down the warehouse happily. "*Gran Torino,* motherfucker. Get off my lawn…"

Kaino began arm waving again. "And how are we supposed to carry this *Saving Private Ryan* shit around in the streets!"

"You got something for the lady, Morti? And something to mollify my friend?"

Morelos looked upon the special agent speculatively. His reptilian eyes displayed a spark of something more than just arms and armament for Special Agent Savacool. "Possibly…"

Savacool scowled. "You say the line for ARs is around the block?"

"Sí, señorita."

"You got any MP-5s?"

Morelos sighed and rolled his eyes. "I wish."

"What do you have?"

"Have you ever fired an Uzi?"

"First automatic weapon I ever fired in training was an Uzi, and like you said, old school. We moved on," Savacool said.

Morelos pulled out what looked like an Uzi except longer and with distinctly odd wooden furniture. "Mendoza!"

"Oh, for God's sake!" Kaino exclaimed. "What is that, Mexican *Untouchables?*"

Bolan admired the bluing of the steel. "Haven't seen one of those in years."

"It's a .38 Super. The *federales* and the army all use 9mms. The cartels want .40s and .45s." Morelos shrugged sadly. "*Mexicanos* no longer about craftsmanship anymore. Much less buying Mexican. Mr. Mendoza? He was—"

"He was a genius," Bolan finished. "A treasure. The Mexican John Browning."

Morelos genuinely sighed. "Like I said, you are man of discernment."

"How many of Mr. Mendoza's masterpieces do you have on hand?"

"Twelve."

"Ammo?"

Morelos shrugged again. "I cannot give it away."

"I'll take all of it. What about the Garands?"

"Crates of it, and perhaps this will interest you." Morelos opened a metal ammunition can filled with loaded Garand 8-round spring clips. He handed one to Bolan. The eight rounds in the bookend-looking spring all had black painted tips.

"Metal piercing," the gun dealer enthused. "And I have incendiary, tracer, you name it. It lies, like the bones of giants, gathering the dust of ages."

"You're a poet, Morti."

"Fine firearms are my passion."

"I want it all."

"Even though I cannot give these fine weapons away, I am loath to give them away, *señor*. If you understand."

"Name a price."

"Twenty thousand, because the *señor* man of taste."

Bolan considered his war chest. He was going to have to take some spoils and plunder from Los Zetas right quick. "Morti, I'm short."

Morelos's eyes went reptilian, and he looked to his two armed men. "I am very sorry to hear that."

"I'm good for what I'm short."

The gun dealer chose his words carefully. "Should you survive whatever it is you are going to attempt, I suspect you would be, but that is the question, isn't it?"

Bolan had arranged for one weapon to be smuggled across the border for him in a diplomatic satchel. He withdrew his pistol and set it on top of a crate.

Sick, glazed longing came into Mortimer Morelos's eyes. "Beretta 93-R machine pistol."

"Yeah."

"You are, what is the American word? Pawning this? It is a rare and beautiful gun, but worth nothing compared to what you are asking in total."

"I'm giving it to you. As a gift. You keep it whether I succeed or not. I have a few spare magazines for it, as well."

Morelos gazed upon the blue steel Italian machine pistol in unadulterated lust. "Not many were made. Few left Italy."

Bolan owned a surprising number of them. "Lost art."

"*Señor?* I believe I am going to do something very foolish." Morelos reached out a trembling hand and touched the slide of the 93-R like a lover.

"Sicko…" Savacool muttered.

Murphy grinned. "It's making me hot!"

"Señor Morelos, I need a safe place for pickup." Bolan wrote a number on a card. "I would appreciate your suggestion as to where we might get in a little target practice."

"It will all be arranged.…" Morelos still hadn't picked up the 93-R. He almost seemed to be waiting for Bolan and his team to leave so he could commit an act of moral outrage with the firearm in private.

Bolan and his team left the warehouse. As one of the three people with a pistol, Donez had been guarding their SUV and standing watch. Donez gave Murphy a wary look. "We got guns?"

"Coop got us guns like you wouldn't believe."

Donez knew Murphy all too well and looked at Bolan. "You got us guns like I won't believe, or I won't believe the guns you got us?"

"Both."

Matamoros safehouse

THE SAFEHOUSE WAS a mud-colored rancho overlooking the mud flats of the Rio Grande as it spread into the alluvial plain that led out of the Gulf. "Eew" was how Savacool had proclaimed it. Bolan liked the little house. It was slightly out of town, and the ancient clay walls were thick and would stop bullets. The rickety little pier gave Bolan access to the water, an escape route, and Kurtzman's files showed that Raulito Paz had a much grander rancho upriver. That put

Bolan in mind of an amphibious assault. There was also a nice flat patch of sand where *Dragonslayer* could put down stat in an emergency.

Grimaldi was currently at Matamoros Airport charming Air Mexicana flight attendants in the captain's lounge.

Bolan was actually considering a combined air and sea assault. Murphy had earned his jump wings as a Ranger. By his own admission he had done nearly nothing out of a helicopter since but he claimed to be ready, willing and able to pull a death from above on Raulito Paz.

The late-afternoon shooting session had gone well. A Garand didn't make for an ideal sniper rifle, but Bolan was confident he could hit a man-size target consistently with the M-1D out to 600 meters. Despite his misgivings and his penchant for shotguns, Kaino proved to be a proficient rifleman. Murphy had developed a love affair with his rifle that Morti Morelos might have envied. Bolan had to admit at Camp Perry with iron sights the ex-Delta might give him a run for his money. Donez, on the other hand, just wasn't going to make marksman in time for the party, but he could hit a two-liter bottle of Fanta at twenty-five yards half the time and that might just be enough.

The Mendoza submachine guns were interesting propositions. They were close to an Uzi at 600 rounds per minute, but the ballistics of the .38 Super ammo they spit out were close to the .357 Magnum, and that turned the weapon into a handful on full-auto. On the flip side, on semiautomatic, the naturally flat-shooting .38 Super ammunition made for more accuracy than was normal in a fifty-year-old automatic weapon. On semiauto at twenty-five meters the entire team could keep the beer cans jumping. Flipping the coin again, a submachine gun firing a round that powerful on full-auto made a hell of a racket.

"I need quiet," Bolan said.

John "Cowboy" Kissinger stared dryly at Bolan across the

laptop link from a workbench in his armory at Stony Man Farm. "Oh, I can forge you five threaded .38 Super barrels with built-in suppressors and get them into your hands by go time. What I won't have time to do is hand load you any subsonic ammo, and from what your boy Morti reports, that is hot-loaded police ammo you got there. It's gotta be going thirteen hundred feet per second plus. There's nothing I can do about the sonic crack and with that kind of muzzle pressure, they'll rip my suppressors to shreds in one or two magazine loads, three tops, and accuracy is going to drop off a cliff seconds after."

"I think if it goes past two magazines, noise starts being the least of my problems."

Kissinger's face went flat. "I just knew you were going to say that."

"Just get them to me ASAP. I'll deal with the rest."

"On it." The window winked out.

Bolan left the study to find Kaino and Murphy cleaning guns. "I have suppressors coming."

Murphy grinned and shot the bolt home on a newly oiled and gleaming Mendoza submachine gun. "Coop? These babies'll rip through a suppressor in about ten seconds."

"That is the rumor," Bolan admitted. "But it'll be a fun ten seconds."

An engine roared out on the river. Bolan scooped up a cleaned, lubed and loaded Mendoza and went out to the back patio. The twenty-two-foot mahogany runabout Donez piloted fit the bill admirably. Bolan suspected the wood was fake, but the jet drive made the little craft very maneuverable, and it might prove very useful in the shallows of the Rio Grande. The twin cockpits had ample space for his five-man team. Donez waved, cut his engines and came to a professionally smooth stop at the pier. Bolan waved back. "Nice!"

"Thanks!"

The soldier walked down to the pier while Donez tied her off. "What'd she cost us?"

"Cost?" Donez rose, wiping his hands. "With the money you gave me? I didn't buy, we leased." Donez shook his head at the Mendoza slung over Bolan's shoulder. "And somehow I think we're going to lose the deposit."

"I'm glad you got something with some horsepower."

"That was slightly selfish on my part."

Bolan had noted the way Donez had handled the motorboat. Bolan saluted. "You just made ship's captain, Captain."

Donez grinned and saluted back. "I took my girl out to see what she could do, and as it so happens I just happened to take a turn up by Raulito Paz's place."

"Figured you might."

"It's not quite a fortress, but he has all the drug lord amenities. I could see from the river the frontage has a high wall. Security cameras and floodlights everywhere. Can't see them, but if he spent that kind of money you know he has motion sensors."

"What about the back?"

"His backyard and the dock have storm fencing, about eight feet tall, topped with razor wire."

"Boats?"

"Three, and two of them are sweet-ass cigarette boats that my girl will not be able to outrun."

"Unless you take them into the puddles."

Donez nodded slyly. "The thought had crossed my mind."

"You got paddles?"

"The dealer looked at me funny, but yeah, four of them, as asked. Paz also has a pontoon boat that could be best described as palatial. I'm not kidding, it has a hot tub."

"Any place to land a chopper?"

"It goes slopey and rough straight down to the water. I haven't seen this exact house but I know the neighborhood—lots of trees, lots of power and telephone lines slung long and low. Murph and I could take the truck and do a drive-by on the frontage if you want, but I think all we're going to see are walls and a security gate."

"No, I don't want the exposure." Bolan checked his watch. "I'm going to have satellite eyes on Paz's place around sunset. Grab some food and a siesta."

A horn honked upslope. Agent Savacool rose through the sunroof of an eighties vintage red Ford Bronco. Bolan had asked her to find a 4x4 to supplement the Jeep Wrangler they had rented at the border. He'd specified something with a sunroof to shoot from and the biggest engine she could get hold of. Bolan waved back. Savacool slid back down and gunned the engine to let Bolan know there was a V-8 under the hood.

Donez waved as Savacool cut the engine. "Looks like you got land, sea and air, *muchacho*. What's the plan?"

"I'm thinking recon tomorrow, mission tomorrow night."

"Day recon?"

"You got the sports equipment I asked for?"

Donez gave Bolan a suspicious look. "Yeah…and?"

Rio Grande

IF AGENT SAVACOOL HADN'T been black her knuckles would have been white. She bobbled in the water and held the handle for dear life. She had spent the past half hour drinking the Rio Grande the hard way. Nonetheless, the FBI agent was ready for another round. "Hit it!" A half dozen of Raulito Paz's gunmen shouted encouragement from Paz's dock. Donez shoved his throttles forward and the runabout surged forward. The rope went taut and Savacool rose on her water skis.

Savacool stood and this time she held it. It wasn't an act. She had just stood on her skis for the first time. Bolan whooped.

The Paz dock erupted into *"¡Arribas!"* and hat throwing. A black woman waterskiing in a bikini was a rarity on

the Rio Grande, and for a moment a half dozen ruthless killers shouted and jumped up and down as though Mexico had
just won the World Cup. Savacool whooped back and stayed
up as the runabout tore upstream. Bolan leaned out over the
stern with his camera to take her picture, except that he had
reversed the digital camera so that it was shooting back over
his shoulder and taking in the Raulito Paz back forty. They
shot upriver past the Paz estate and Donez eased back on
the throttles. Savacool slowed and sank back into the water.
"One more run past the boys?"

"I have it in me!"

"That's my girl!"

"I liked it, so I'm going to let that slide, Cooper!"

Bolan nodded at Donez. "Go."

Donez took the boat in a tight turn and pointed the prow
downriver. The runabout rapidly took up the slack on the
towrope. "Ready?" Bolan called.

"Hit it!"

Donez shoved the throttles forward.

The runabout surged forward and Savacool rose out of
the water in the runabout's wake. Her hair flew behind her
in an ebony mane as they tore downriver. The Paz gunmen
shouted and waved with renewed excitement. Savacool took
one hand off the handle, waved at the killers on the pier and
promptly face-planted into the Rio Grande. The guardsmen
groaned and gasped and even Bolan cringed as Savacool
flopped across the waters like a rug being beaten as she spent
a stubborn second or two not releasing the tow bar. Donez
cut his engines. The boys on the dock cheered as Savacool
bobbed up and shot the thumbs-up. Donez brought the boat
around and Bolan held out a hand to haul the special agent in.

Savacool clasped Bolan's wrist in the climber's handshake
and gave him bedraggled look as he took her aboard. "You
have no idea what this has done to my hair."

"I can see."

"No, I'm talking about the aftereffects. I'm talking aftershocks."

"Some kind of Angela Davis, Black Pantherette, Afro Armageddon kind of thing?"

"I yearn to punch you dead in the face, Cooper."

"I bruise like a peach."

"Well, you do have a charming complexion for a white boy."

"That's white man to you."

Savacool sighed. "Tell me you got what you needed and we're done for the day."

"You did real good, Cool. You stood up and rode the river your first afternoon out, and yeah, we're done."

Savacool shot a smile that lit up the Rio Grande. "Well, all right, then. Let's get the fat lady singing." Savacool stood in the rear cockpit. She tossed her head like a lioness, tore off her top and pumped both fists into the sky in chiseled, water-beaded, ebony glory. "Wooooo-hoo!"

The Paz pier erupted in response.

Bolan reeled in the tow rope. "You're going to be very popular in Mexico."

Savacool spoke over her shoulder as she donned her top and Donez hit the throttles to send the runabout downriver for home. "Popular, hell. You just tell Kaino this girl deserves shrimp and steak."

CHAPTER TWELVE

Matamoros safehouse

"Wow!" Murphy's jaw dropped in awe.

"Not one more word…" Savacool warned.

Murphy stared in mounting awe at the corkscrew curls erupting from Savacool's head. "Wow!"

The woman hauled off and threw a right hook. Murphy had a sixteenth of a second to register shock before Savacool's knuckles skipped straight across his funny bone like a stone. Murphy howled and did a castrated ape dance clutching his elbow.

"Nice Irish jig, white boy," Donez opined.

Murphy snarled as he continued his crushed-nerve Highland fling. "That's white man to you, Donuts!"

Donez jerked his head at Bolan. "That only works with him."

"Asshole!"

"Bank on it."

Kaino threw back his head and laughed as he brought in plates heaped with steaks ranchero with shrimp sides. It was a six-foot-something, 200-pound-plus something, Puerto Rican belly laugh and it was infectious. Everyone joined in, including the elbow-impaired, currently river-dancing Murphy. Bolan let the shenanigans run their course. His team was salty and ready. Kaino was a rock. Savacool was a pro. Donez was local and proved talent. Murphy was a bit of a goof but a likeable goof with Uncle Sam–given abilities.

Bolan would have preferred a few more soldiers, but he had a team of veterans in their professions. They were ready to fight for him. He was ready to lead them from the front, and if he fell he had a good feeling they could finish the mission. They had five suppressed Mendoza submachine gun barrels that had arrived by diplomatic courier. That had been a risk, but Bolan figured any diplomat who cared wouldn't figure out something was amiss much less put it on Raulito Paz's plate until it was far too late.

While Bolan, Savacool and Donez had engaged in aquatic sports, Kaino and Murphy had gone for a drive in the team vehicles. The two men had taken turns driving while the other clandestinely took pictures of Casa de Paz's frontage from the backseat. Added to the satellite shots Kurtzman had sent and the aqua recon on the Paz back forty, they had a pretty complete picture of Paz's place.

Savacool and her African mane took a seat at the strategy table and synced her laptop with everyone else's. Murphy finished shaking out his buzzing arm and raised the big question. "We dropping in, Coop?"

Bolan had been giving that a lot of thought. A combined assault would give them one hell of an edge. At the same time, while Mexico didn't have much of an air defense system, they did monitor air traffic along the border and its air patrol was extensive. Using *Dragonslayer* for airborne assault was a well Bolan didn't want to go to too many times, and he still had a lot of cartel ladder to climb. "I think we're going to paddle in and save the air asset for extraction if things go south."

Murphy almost looked like he might have been relieved.

"Kaino," Bolan asked, "did you get the stuff I asked for?"

"Bolt cutters, kerosene, detergent, Mason jars, rags, torch flame lighters, duct tape, twenty-four feet of surgical tubing, whiskey-tango-foxtrot, yeah. The whole bit. I start mixing Molotovs right after dessert."

"You get the fireworks?"

Kaino gave Bolan a funny look. "Yeah, I got the fireworks."

Savacool shot straight to attention. "Fireworks?"

"Sparklers." Bolan nodded. "The Mexican kind. The good kind."

Savacool's eyes went feral. "Oh, gimme."

Kaino frowned. "What the hell are we going to do with sparklers? Strip naked and distract Paz's *sicarios* with some kind of interpretive rhythmic gymnastics routine?"

"Kaino, I admit that would be something to see," Bolan said.

"You bet your ass it would be something to see. This man mountain has moves like Fred Astaire, El Hombre."

Donez's head snapped around on Bolan. He blinked as wheels visibly turned in his mind. Donez's jaw dropped. *"Madre de Dios."*

Bolan rolled his eyes. "Nice work, Kaino."

Savacool shook her head in disgust. "You want me to hit him, Cooper?"

"It was likely they were going to find out anyway." Bolan gave the master sergeant a frown of his own. "Shocking lapse of security protocols, though."

Kaino looked down and twiddled his thumbs sheepishly.

Murphy's brows bunched. "What?"

Donez slowly pointed an identifying finger at Bolan. "El Hombre."

"It's not polite to point, Donuts."

Donez was too shocked to care. "Man, I should have known. I should have put two and two together. Now it all makes sense."

Murphy frowned. "El Hombre, isn't that that urban legend in Nuevo Laredo about the guy who— Ho-lee-shit!"

Kaino had already had his El Hombre moments firsthand

and in action. "I still want to know what we're going to do with the sparklers."

"Bring them, along with the tape and some scissors, needle-nose pliers."

"And then?"

"Then watch and learn."

Kaino went and fetched a big cardboard box. He dumped a hundred gaily painted boxes of sparklers onto the table. Bolan swiftly assembled fifty sparklers in a bundle. He cut off their sticks and wrapped them tightly in duct tape. Everyone at the table watched in fascination. The soldier took the center sparkler very carefully to avoid a friction ignition and slowly pulled it so it stuck out from the back by about half an inch and then capped both ends with tape. Bolan held up the gray-taped bundle. "That's 2.5 grams of black powder."

"Holy shit!" Murphy enthused. "Homemade flash-bang!"

"We bundle about two-fifty, three hundred, and you're getting close to a stick of dynamite. We're going in by boat, so we've got to keep them dry. Be careful—friction can set these off, and fusing is unreliable. Light it and get rid of it."

Rio Grande

DONEZ CUT THE ENGINE. Bolan and his men broke out the paddles and ushered the runabout into the reeds. The team swiftly changed into their raid suits, which consisted of dark blue cargo shorts, black T-shirts, black do-rags and hiking boots. Bolan, Murphy and Donez applied black grease paint while Kaino and Savacool looked on in mild amusement. Each team member had a messenger bag loaded with two Molotov cocktails, two sparkler bombs and six spare magazines. The Molotovs were wrapped in hand towels so they wouldn't break and the sparkler bombs in plastic wrap to keep them dry. Kaino had acquired a tactical light and a hunting knife for each team member, as well.

The team did an equipment check and each man gave Bolan a nod in the starlight. They broke the paddles out again and pushed out of the reeds. They had traveled upstream and motored past Paz's riverside residence in civilian clothes with beers and music. Bolan had noted two guards on the dock and several figures up on the patio. Now he and his team silently let the current carry them toward their target. They backpaddled at fifty yards from the target and Donez dropped anchor.

Bolan and Murphy slid into the water.

Again they let the current do their work for them. The two men kept just their eyes and noses above water as they breast-stroked toward the dock. At ten yards they dived beneath the surface. The water was inky black, but Bolan had made many such insertions. A part of his mind subconsciously calculated the speed of the river as his fingers touched the mud and rock of the bottom and he kicked hard for the boat dock. He silently counted off seconds.

The current slackened as he got closer to shore. Bolan stopped kicking and stuck out a hand as he let momentum carry him in. His fingers brushed submerged fencing and closed around the links. The links flexed slightly as Murphy found them a second later. Bolan pulled his wire-cutters. His and Murphy's fists bumped at the same link and the two soldiers swiftly began cutting a circle in opposite directions. There was nothing in the blackness other than the sound of the Rio Grande in motion and the rapid snicking sound of the cutters.

Bolan felt his lungs begin to constrict as he reached the bottom of the circle and his and Murphy's shoulders bumped. There was a second's pause as Murphy found Bolan's cuts and made them meet his. The mercenary pulled away the three-foot circle of fencing.

Bolan sheathed his cutters and swam through. He caught the bobbing glow from the lights of the house on the surface above and stayed beneath the dock. Bolan rose beneath the wet wood and squashed the urge to gasp. Murphy's head rose silently and he shot Bolan a grin. Apparently two years of beaches, beer and Mexican women hadn't lost the Delta veteran any of his lung capacity. The two men waited silently. No alarms went off. No floodlights snapped on. The wood creaked overhead as a sentry walked the boards. Bolan heard the chink of a lighter and the dim tones of a smartphone keypad. Rapid Spanish ensued and receded as the sentry walked back toward shore again.

Bolan jerked his head in the gloom.

Murphy's teeth flashed in the dark as he spoke in a voice barely above the lap of the water on the pilings. "He's telling his friend Poti he should have seen the black chick waterskiing this afternoon."

"It was something to see," Bolan agreed.

"You want me to take this clown?"

"I want to talk to him. Give me a diversion." The two men waited as the sentry reached the end of the dock and turned to do another lap. The boards creaked overhead and the sentry did another turn still yapping on his phone.

"He ain't shutting up, Coop."

It was a risk to cut off the conversation, but every second of exposure on the busy river counted. "Go."

The sentry walked down the dock once more. Murphy grabbed the boards above and did a half pull-up. *"Che, chico,"* he said softly. The sentry jumped. Bolan vaulted up onto the opposite side of the dock behind him. Bolan's do-rag came off and he snapped it over the sentry's head and around his throat. Murphy caught the phone as it fell. *"Uno momento."* Murphy ended the call and tossed the phone into the river. Bolan took the sentry to the boards and then rolled off into the water with a small splash. He blew out air and let his weight take the sentry down. Between the strangle and every gasp filling his mouth with river water, the sentry's struggles slowed quickly. Bolan unslung the sentry's AR and let it sink into the mud. He took the sentry back up and broached the surface. *"Silencio."*

"Cabron..." the sentry gasped.

Bolan took his quarry back down and treated him to more oxygen deprivation. The Executioner spent an extra cruel second or two, then kicked up against the muck of the bottom. He snarled into the half-drowned sentry's ear. *"¡Silencio!"*

The sentry whimpered and retched against the fabric wrapped around his throat.

"You speak English?"

The sentry made a feeble noise of assent.

Bolan loosened the strangle. "You want to live?"

The sentry made an attempt to nod in Bolan's grip.

"How many in the house?"

"I don't know!"

"Guess," Bolan demanded.

"Twenty? Twenty-five?"

"Armed?"

"Yes!" the sentry replied.

"Women? Children?"

"No!"

"Twenty-five *sicarios?* No women? No help? No family?"

"The servants were sent home! No women in two days! Señor Paz's family is in Yucatan."

"Why?"

The sentry shook with more than the chill of the water. "They're waiting for you!"

"Paz is inside?"

The gunman whispered his betrayal. "Yes."

Bolan thought he knew the answer, but wanted confirmation. "How does Paz know I'm coming?"

"El Salami, he told them."

Bolan rolled his eyes in the dark. "Salami is inside?"

"Yes!"

"Did Salami tell them or did they beat it out of him?"

"They were pretty mean," the *sicario* conceded. "But he was already in pretty bad shape when they brought him in."

"His ankle and his elbow?" Bolan asked.

"Those were the least of his problems. He looked like it had rained hammers on him or something. It didn't take much to make him talk. When I hit him he— *Ack!*"

Bolan choked the *sicario* out. He gagged him with the do-rag and zip-tied his limp form around a piling.

Murphy hissed in the dark. "It's a fucking trap!"

"One we can choose whether or not to spring. Bring in the team."

Murphy's upside-down head shook once in disgust and disappeared. Bolan heard the man's red-lensed tactical light click three times and the snap of bolt cutters cutting the lock holding the dock gate. Bolan did a pull-up on the boards as the runabout bumped into the pilings and Donez tied off. The team debarked on the dock with their weapons at the ready. Savacool was a flash of teeth in the dark. "What's the scoop, Coop?"

"Paz is inside. So is Salami. It sounds like he's spilled everything he knows and Paz is waiting for El Hombre to make a move."

Kaino grunted unhappily. The Mendoza looked like a toy gun in the big man's hands as he pointed it at the house. "Four to one odds, they have the defensive position, and they're expecting us."

"No, they're not expecting us. They're waiting for us. They've been waiting for nearly three days. I think they're bored out of their minds, and they only have one sentry out on the dock. I think they're expecting trouble in town before the trouble comes here. I think we still have the advantage of full surprise."

"You want to go ahead?" Donez asked.

"Do you?"

Donez cradled his submachine gun and smiled slowly in the dark. "Yeah, kinda."

Bolan glanced toward his one dissenter. "How's your nose, Murph?"

"Twitching," the veteran operator replied. "Something stinks."

Murphy was something of a goof, Bolan thought, but he had kept him and his teammates alive on multiple continents and Bolan respected the man's instincts.

"You want to extract, do another recon tomorrow and re-evaluate? I'm amenable," Bolan said.

"I know you are!" Murphy whispered. It was pretty clear the ex-Delta veteran was conflicted. "And I ain't saying that."

Bolan peered meaningfully at their sodden prisoner below. "You think our boy is lying?"

"No." Murphy grimaced as his intellect and his instinct fought each another. "You owned his narrow ass but good."

"So?"

"So Paz is in there, and we need to take him."

Kaino rumbled low in the murk. "Speaking of narrow asses, I hate to say it, but I think we need to save Salami's."

Savacool peered up at the big man. "I thought you said he gave you that scar on your chin."

"He did, but me and Coop have been using him like a two-dollar ho since all this started. I wouldn't piss on him if he was on fire, if he got busted or taken down dealing, but we visited this on him, and he cooperated."

Bolan nodded. Kaino was a cop who had bent and broken rules in his career, but his personal sense of honor was a thing of iron. "We're all in or nobody's in. Everybody in?"

Everyone nodded.

"By the numbers, just like we planned it."

Bolan's team moved up the dock and spread out in a line up the slope leading to the house. No security lights came on and no alarms rang out.

They flowed over the low adobe wall girding the patio. An Eichler house-worthy wall of glass gave the occupants a view of the Rio Grande and the lights of Brownsville on the northern shore. No one was on the patio. The inside lights were on and men moved back and forth. Some eating, some smoking, some sitting at tables eating or messaging on their phones. Some had rifles and assault rifles slung over their shoulders. Others had pistols tucked in their belts but all were armed. All seemed at a very low state of alert.

"Murph," Bolan whispered. "Give me a rec."

Murphy pulled a fade back into the darkness and moved around both sides of the house peering in windows. Bolan's team waited with nothing but the sound of the river and muted noise of people inside. They tensed at a sudden eruption of noise in the house but it turned out to be cheering. Murphy returned from his sweep. "You got about eight men watching soccer.

"Everyone seems scattered around and pretty goddamned bored, just like you said. I couldn't find Paz, but the drapes on the master bedroom are closed and the windows locked. I couldn't see everywhere but twenty to twenty-five hostiles seems about right."

"Any sign of Salami?"

Murphy made an amused noise. "A beat-up guy is tied to a toilet in a half bath just off the laundry room. You never saw a sorrier son of a bitch. He looks like someone stomped a mud hole in him and walked it dry."

"Like he'd been blackjacked?" Kaino asked.

"Well, Kaino, to my everlasting shame, I've never seen a blackjacking, but if I ever wrote an action novel, Salami looks about like I would describe it."

Savacool sighed with a small modicum of empathy. "So we screwed him, the as yet to be ascertained Euro possibly Russian trash screwed him and now Paz has screwed him. Every side pounds on him to see what comes out of his mouth next."

"I want him alive," Bolan said.

Murphy clearly had another opinion about that but kept it to himself.

"I want Paz alive if possible," Bolan continued. "But if he's salty, don't take any extra risks. Murph, Donuts, I want you to sparkle-stun the master bedroom and insert. Kaino, Cool and I are going straight through the back door. Give me three clicks on your tactical when you're ready. Go on my blast."

"Copy that!" Murphy and Donez scampered off into the dark. Bolan reached into his messenger bag and took out a sparkler bundle. He tore the plastic wrap insulating the makeshift flash-bang and pulled an inch of the center sparkler for a fuse. Three red pulses of light shone briefly at the side of the house.

Bolan spoke softly. "Kaino, I need a hole."

Kaino snagged a two-foot ornamental cactus in a bowling-ball-shaped pot off the barbecue. Bolan held out his pyrotechnic bundle fuse first to Savacool. "Light me."

Savacool pushed the button on her torch lighter. The sparkler fused instantly and began shooting a shower of copper sparks. Bolan nodded at Kaino. "Go!"

The cop took three running steps forward and performed a mighty imitation of a Highland Games stone toss to put the hapless cactus through the sliding-glass door. Glass shattered in a cascade, and the gunmen within shouted in alarm. One gunman dropped as the cactus pot exploded against his head like a ceramic dirt bomb. Bolan sent his improvised explosive device revolving end-over-end through the shattered glass entryway. Gunmen within shouted in alarm at the fountaining pyrotechnic that fell in their midst. One brave soul lunged to grab it and throw it back.

The sparkler bomb detonated with the sound of a giant door slamming and the pulse of golden fire was a joy to behold. The rest of the glass in the door frame blew out, and the drapes promptly caught fire. "Go! Go! Go!" Bolan shouted. His team advanced in full assault. Several weapons opened up inside the house and tore a long, blind burst. Bolan dropped to one knee and fired a quick pair of double taps that dropped the gunmen to the deck. He rose and ran forward as Savacool and Kaino bracketed the broken entry and took down three more shooters. A second clap of thunder rocked the river house from the side. Bedlam was in full effect in Casa de Paz. Glass crunched beneath Bolan's boots. A storm of gunfire erupted out of the kitchen. The man who had tried to throw the sparkler bomb back was a charred and mewling mess.

"Savacool, hit 'em!"

The special agent lit an IED and tomahawked it over the kitchen island the gunmen were using for cover. Bolan, Savacool and Kaino closed their eyes and plugged their ears as the sparkler bomb thundered and pulsed heat outward. The kitchen windows blew out and the kitchen drapes caught fire. Unlike a real flash-bang, which utilized a small charge of explosive composite, Bolan's improvised weapon was using black powder by the handful. Roiling clouds of white smoke and a brimstone stench rolled over Paz's place. One gunman rose swaying and shooting his pistol in all directions. Kaino put three rounds in his chest and put him down. Bolan moved forward. Two more men lay behind the kitchen island with blood from their shattered eardrums leaking between their fingers as they clutched the sides of their heads in agony.

Bolan heaved their weapons out the kitchen window and continued his sweep. The soccer fans erupted out of the den screaming insults and defiance. Bolan dropped to a knee by the entry to the hall and Kaino stepped in to fire above. Murphy threw open the bedroom door and took position to put the crew in a cross fire. The suppressed Mendoza submachine guns turned the hall into a killing box. Four men fell and three fell back into the den screaming imprecations. Murphy shouted over them. "Donuts!"

Donez charged out of the master bedroom with a sparkler bomb held aloft like an Olympic torch and sent it spinning into the den. The bomb went off like a cannon. Kaino and Murphy advanced to the den. The mercenary fired two bursts and Kaino one. "Clear!" the cop called.

Donez nodded at Bolan. "We have Paz!"

"Sit on him! Kaino! Murph! Finish sweeping the house! Cool, get on the roof and keep an eye out!"

Bolan went back into the kitchen and passed through the laundry room. He listened at the bathroom door and could hear Salami sobbing within. "Salami?"

"Yeah?"

"It's El Hombre."

"You're not going to hat me are you?"

"Do you deserve a hatting?" Bolan asked.

"No..." Salami whimpered.

Bolan opened the door. Salami sat in his underwear duct taped to the toilet. He looked like a blood sausage with arms and legs. Most of his skin was covered with contusions. He flinched as Bolan pulled out his hunting knife and cut him free.

"I don't think I can walk," the drug dealer said.

Bolan didn't doubt him. The man had been broken down by professionals and then beaten by amateurs who had made up for their lack of skill with enthusiasm. Salami groaned as the soldier put him in a fireman's carry and took him out. Bolan shouted through the broken kitchen window. "Cool?"

"Clear on the street! Clear on the river!"

Bolan carried Salami into the bedroom and put him on the bed. Four dead men lay on the carpet, and the walls were streaked with black from the sparkler bomb Donez had deployed. Raulito Paz lay hog-tied among his fallen men. Bolan took in the heavy features and the pencil mustache he'd seen in photos. Paz shook like a leaf. Cold sweat oozed out of his pores, and the soldier could smell the fear coming off him over the smell of burned black powder. Something was wrong.

Salami sat on the edge of the bed staring quizzically at Paz through eyes raccooned with bruising. "El Hombre?"

"Yeah?"

"That's not Señor Paz."

Murphy swore a blue streak. "My nose is never wrong! It always knows!"

Kaino scowled. "A double?"

Bolan grimaced. "It's not unheard of."

Savacool shouted down from the roof right on cue. "Cooper! We've got company!"

CHAPTER THIRTEEN

"Ho-lee shit…" Murphy muttered.

Bolan nodded as he, Murphy, Donez and Kaino stood on the firing steps along the inner wall and watched through the razor wire strands as Armageddon came rumbling up the lane on three axles. Bolan mentally shook his head. Holy shit was right.

The behemoth came on like a juggernaut. The soldier had seen a lot of low-intensity conflicts where the belligerents had welded hillbilly armor onto pickup trucks. U.S. soldiers had done it to their Humvees until proper, modular armor suites had been introduced. The thing rumbling down upon them like doomsday was something of higher order. It was something right out of the movie *The Road Warrior*. At one point the leviathan had been a three-axle semi truck. It recently had seen extensive modification and far more than add-on slab armor. A fort of welded steel had been built on top and around the truck including spotlights that could be operated from the inside, firing ports and a bent vee of steel girder on the front for a battering ram.

"Swell." Kaino spit. "They have a narco tank."

Someone had painted the word *Raulito* across the metal slatted grille in electric-green paint. It was the Paz Hammer, and it was coming for them. Donez slapped a fresh magazine into his Mendoza. "They could have twenty men in the back of that thing!"

"So what are you going to do now, Coop?" Murphy enquired dryly. "Throw sparklers at it?"

"Yeah." Bolan sighed. "Something like that. I need all the remaining bombs and the duct tape, now. Kaino, Donez, I need a diversion."

Savacool called from the roof. "Boats on the water, Cooper! Coming from the west at high speed!"

Kaino was appalled as he handed over his sparkler bombs. "A diversion against that?"

"Molotovs, keep it buttoned up, keep it blind and distracted," Bolan ordered. He swiftly began grouping the bundles into the mother of all sparkler bombs. "Murph, get on the roof. Support Savacool, suppressive fire on the river and anyone who jumps out of the tank."

"On it." Murphy dumped his two sparkler bombs and ran across the drive to vault himself onto the roof. "Cool! I'm coming up!"

Kaino and Donez both took a Molotov out of their messenger bags. The Paz estate's wrought-iron gate was locked, but its existence would coincide with the narco tank for about all of a heartbeat. The thick adobe walls framing the gate were another matter. Savacool and Murphy began firing from the roof. The men inside the iron beast couldn't hear the suppressed fire, but they could hear bullets banging off their armor. The thin barrels of half a dozen ARs slid out of the forward firing slits and began returning fire at the house. Bolan finished his tape job. He didn't have the time to unbundle the homemade flash-bangs so he worried he might experience multiple detonations rather than one big bang. It would have to be enough. Bolan was just about out of options.

"Kaino! Donez! Be ready!"

Savacool's voice rose with concern as she called down from the roof. "I count three boats, and they've almost reached the dock!"

"Murph!" Bolan bellowed. "Set fire to the dock!"

He heard a suppressed submachine slapping on full-auto as either Savacool or Murphy burned a magazine into the fuel pump on the dock. A moment later a Mason jar filled with gasoline and detergent spiraled in a beautiful arc over the backyard with a burning rag for a fluttering tail. Bolan turned his eye back on the approaching narco tank. Behind him he heard the whoosh of the gasoline igniting on the dock and then the *crump* as the fuel tank went up. The sky over the river pulsed orange and the breeze off it turned into brief, hot gale.

Donez sighed. "There goes the boat deposit."

"Light 'em up," Bolan ordered.

The narco tank was on them.

Kaino and Donez put fire to rag. Murphy and Savacool had turned their attentions back to the narco tank and pumped fire into it. The iron leviathan hit the gate. Its armor suite was too big to fit through the gate, and the multiton behemoth hit the wall sections framing the gate like a battering ram. Chunks of clay went flying as the top two-thirds of the wall fell, but the adobe security wall was two feet thick and sloped. The foundation held and the narco tank came to a violent stop. Half of the weapons firing from within disappeared. Bolan doubted any of the shooters were wearing seat belts and many had been violently hurled out of position by the impact. Bullets winked along the roof like fireflies as Savacool and Murphy tried to keep the behemoth buttoned up.

"Light him up!" Bolan roared.

Kaino stepped around one side of the crumbling wall and heaved his firebomb straight on. Flame sheeted across the armored section where the driver and his observation slit were located. Gears ground and rubble shifted as the driver rammed the mammoth machine into Reverse to make another run. Donez stepped in and painted the forward firing slits in liquid fire. Kaino lit his second and threw it against the armored slats of the grille, hoping for some fire to seep into the engine block. Donez lit his second and did a credible job of dropping it behind the truck to suppress anyone in the back with wild ideas about deploying. Gun barrels protruded from the flame-engulfed firing slits, but by Bolan's estimation most of them were firing blind. It also seemed no one was in a rush to jump out while the enemy was throwing fire bombs.

Bolan stepped from behind cover and pressed the ignition button on his lighter. "Give me covering fire!"

Every member of Bolan's team turned his or her attention on the narco tank. The sound of their broadside rose from *slap,* to *snap,* to *crack* as their suppressors degraded with every round. The narco tank rolled backward with clay chunks falling off its prow in an avalanche. Fire dripped off it slow-motion sheets. The iron wagon reversed out of the rubble and gave Bolan the opportunity he needed. He touched lighter to sparkler and vaulted forward through the rubble, charging the narco tank with the equivalent of a stick and a half of dynamite erupting like a Roman candle in his hand.

The black iron slab girding the front of the narco tank told Bolan it might well be able to take direct hits from a .50-caliber weapon. Most armored vehicles had thinner armor on the roof, but he knew a skipping, unfocused blast across the top was unlikely to tear the rolling steel open. Bolan had one chance. Narco tanks were designed to intimidate the competition and crush roadblocks. They were urban drug war vehicles. They weren't built for the battlefield, and Bolan was betting the *campesinos* in the machine shop that had designed it had never thought about the vehicle's ability to withstand landmines. The soldier was betting his life they had not thought to armor the monstrosity's underbelly.

Kaino boomed out in alarm. "Throw it!"

Savacool's voice rose to a scream. "Cooper!"

The narco tank driver hit his brakes to make his second run on the gate, but the momentum of the mass of steel he drove still took him several yards backward before it stopped.

That was exactly what Bolan had hoped for. He bowled the world's largest and most likely first antiarmor sparkler bomb beneath the narco tank's flaming front tires.

Murphy roared from the roof of Paz's house. "That's a googly!"

It was the last thing Bolan heard before his bomb detonated. A blast of superheated air slapped him and sat him down. A stick and a half of dynamite wasn't enough to send a rig that was surrounded by steel sky high. It dropped instead as all six wheels blew outward. But Bolan's hunch had been right. The narco tank's underbelly had to have ripped like tissue. Much of the explosion funneled upward and blew out of the firing slits in jets of fire and black smoke.

Bolan suspected the state of the inhabitants was problematic.

He felt Kaino's huge hands yanking him to his feet. The cop was shouting but all Bolan could hear was a high-pitched whining in his ears and possibly angels singing. Bolan instinctively overcame the urge to shout over his deafness. "Kaino, we're out of here."

Bolan took a few steps and felt no vertigo and he negotiated his way back over the wall rubble without mishap. He shouted up at Murphy. "Murph! Grab Salami!" The merc said something Bolan couldn't hear but he jumped off the roof and obeyed his orders. Donez shook the keys to the Land Rover he had liberated from the fake Paz. Bolan nodded. "Grab the fake Paz and get us rolling, Donuts! Cool! Sitrep!"

Savacool might as well have shouted into a wind tunnel.

Kaino clamped a hand on Bolan's shoulder and leaned in. The soldier mostly felt the vibrations of his words rather than heard them as the big man shouted in his ear. "Dock's on fire and the gate still locked! The marine team is looking for a place to land a little downriver! We have maybe two minutes!"

Savacool dangled from the eaves and dropped from the

roof. Murphy and Donez appeared with their charges. Donez tossed Kaino the keys and they piled into the silver Land Rover. Bolan yawned repeatedly as the Rover bucked over the rubble and tore out onto the street.

It had been an interesting evening.

Matamoros safehouse

"PUPILS ARE THE SAME." Savacool's huge brown eyes peered deeply into Bolan's vibrant blues. "None of the wrong liquids running out of the wrong holes." She straightened and handed Bolan back his icepack. "I believe the eyebrows will grow back."

"If I hadn't seen it—" Murphy pulled two beers from the bucket "—I wouldn't believe it."

Donez caught the beer Murphy threw him and regarded Bolan with mild awe. "I saw it and I still don't believe it."

"I believe it." Kaino nodded wisely. "But that's only because you should have seen what I saw in Florida."

Bolan settled back on the couch and perched his icepack on his flash-burned and throbbing head. His ears were still ringing, but he could hear now. "How's Salami?"

Savacool made a face. "I believe you could use the term pathetically grateful at this point. I gave him some painkillers from the med kit. He's not out but he's resting comfortably. I debriefed him a bit on the ride over. They gave him a pretty hard time. He should probably see a doctor. He's peeing blood."

"How about Paz's body double?"

"Scared shitless."

"As he should be." Kaino snagged himself a beer. "Paz has got to know we took his house and you cracked his narco tank like an egg. He's gonna be bugging out."

Bolan knew it all too well. He winced as he rose and spent a moment letting all the pretty colors stop washing across his vision. He walked to the table and tapped an app on his tablet and his security suite connected with the Farm. "Bear, stand by for satellite triangulation."

Kurtzman sounded eager. He hadn't liked the fact that there had been no available satellite for the assault on Paz's riverside house. "We have a window. On it."

Bolan grabbed his sniper rifle and walked into the spare bedroom. Fake Paz was spread-eagled to the bedposts, but someone had put a pillow under his head. "Hey, Faux Paz, You want to live?"

Paz's double regarded Bolan warily.

"I have a headache." Bolan grimaced as he pushed off the Garand's safety and pointed it at the man's face. Fake Paz crushed himself back into the bed as far as his restraints allowed. "The sound of this going off in a closed room is going to ruin my whole night. Listening to you lie to me and then blowing your head off will be even worse. You want to live?"

Fake Paz nodded vigorously.

"You want to walk away free as a bird."

Fake Paz spoke with a heavy border accent. "Free as a bird is good."

"I'll make you a deal. Paz is going down. Most likely tonight. You talk to me straight and I verify it, and I let you walk out of here. Hell, you're his double. You can probably cash in on some of his assets before anyone finds out. Agreed?"

"And if I don't?"

"I'm out of here, but I leave you with Salami, and I loan him my hat."

Fake Paz didn't know what exactly that meant, but he knew it wasn't good as he considered his limited options. "I agree."

Bolan set his tablet on the bedstand. "Where do you think Paz is?"

"If I had to bet, he would be in his house outside town, in the hills. *Casa grande, señor, muy linda,* and a fortress."

"Address."

Fake Paz rattled off the location without a hiccup. Bolan glanced at his tablet on the bedstand. The screen changed to a satellite view that swept earthward as Kurtzman worked. The computer wizard's voice came through the speaker. "I have it, and I have vehicles, moving out in a southwesterly direction."

Bolan glanced at the real-time video of Paz's escape caravan. One large dark vehicle dwarfing the rest of the parade intrigued him. "Get me a close-up on the third vehicle in line."

The image swooped in, and Bolan beheld another narco tank that was the twin of the one he had taken out earlier. It occurred to him he had only three sparkler bombs left, and all the fireworks stands were closed at this time of night. "Bear, track them. We're loading up and going for a second assault tonight."

Kurtzman wasn't shocked. "Tracking, will advise."

"Hey, Faux Paz. Where's your boss heading?"

"If I had to guess, he has a rancho, right on the border with Nuevo Leon."

"Address."

The man told him and Bolan's screen image swooped. An inset window appeared with a road map, and Paz's caravan appeared as a blinking red dot on the road. "It's a straight shot," Kurtzman advised. "And that's the exact direction the vehicles are heading."

Bolan took up his tablet and walked out.

"Che!" Fake Paz shouted. "You said I could walk out of here."

"If I'm alive tomorrow morning, I'll cut you loose. If I'm not, my people will send someone."

The man let loose a torrent of extreme Mexican profanity. Bolan's team looked at him expectantly. "And?" Kaino asked.

"Break out the Garands."

CHAPTER FOURTEEN

Tamaulipas–Nuevo Leon border

Cattle country rolled on ever southward into the purple pre-dawn horizon. Northern Mexico about an hour before sunrise was one of the most beautiful places on earth. Bolan gazed at his target through his binoculars. The glare of the Paz rancho's stalag lights ruined the pastoral Mexican splendor. Paz had put the rancho into lockdown. Ten-foot razor-wire-topped fencing surrounded the rancho. The only thing missing was a guard tower and searchlights combing the skies. The narco tank had disappeared into a warehouse large enough to house a blimp.

Kaino wasn't pleased. "Jesus, Coop! They must have over forty men in there, and that's just the new arrivals! God only knows how many fools were already on point before that, and we're out of sparklers!"

"Actually we have three bundles left, Kaino," Bolan corrected.

Kaino waved his arms in exasperation. "Oh, for— Tell him, Murph!"

Murphy raised one sardonic eyebrow that said he had faced worse odds. Kaino reverted to muttering Puerto Rican potty talk.

Donez was of the same mind as Kaino. "I think there's a lot of them in there, Coop."

"You're just upset about the boat," Bolan chided.

Donez grinned in the gloom. "Man, that was my first jet-drive. I only knew her for a day and a night, but, it was like we loved a lifetime."

"I was fond of him, too," Savacool admitted.

"Boats are she's," Donez stated.

"Says you. I named him *Aqua Thomas*. And I loved him, until Murph barbecued him."

"I hated that boat." Murphy nodded to himself. "Pump jet engines are unnatural. You can't dismember a man with one like you can with an outboard motor. Hell, I'm glad I killed it."

Bolan suppressed a smile. Despite this being the second mission in one night with the odds heavily against them, his team was still cracking wise. Murphy looked out at the rancho with a professional eye. "Coop, they've got a fifty-meter killing zone."

Every tree, shrub and stand of mesquite within fifty meters of the rancho proper had been sawed off a ground level. The rolling Mexican terrain was strewed with rock formations. Raw craters scarred the landscape around the rancho where any rock bigger than a beach ball had been bulldozed up and carted away.

Bolan nodded. "That they do."

Kaino started working himself up again. "Yeah, well? Your answer at Paz's place on the river was fireworks—not that it didn't work, mind you, but I am real curious on how you plan to take out a rancho with seventy-five sparklers."

Bolan shrugged. "Catapult."

Murphy spent a moment dryly examining the scenery immediately around him. "You brought siege engines, did you?"

"I brought Kaino, Donuts and twenty-four feet of surgical tubing."

"Ho-lee shit!" Murphy grinned.

"I want to set fire to the warehouse. I think they might have some interesting stuff stored inside. Possibly flammable. I think it will give the guys inside an imperative, or at least something to do that we can work with. Then we set fire to the rancho. Then we play it by ear."

Murphy was happy. "You know, I did shit like this in high school, at the powder-puff football game. It was with water balloons, and I was dressed like a cheerleader, but this shit could work."

"By my count we should have seven fire bombs left," Bolan calculated.

Bolan's team patted their messenger bags and counted off. "Seven it is," Kaino agreed.

"I want to get within five yards of Paz's kill zone, twenty yards off the approach road. I want a straight shot at the warehouse and rancho proper. Murph, do me a favor."

"What's that, Coop?"

"Open the gas cap on Paz's Land Rover, open up the back and put two of the spare jerry cans in the bed. Open one up and dump it on its side. Open the other but keep it upright and then throw in one of the sparkler bombs and button her up. Rover lights off, engine running."

"This just gets better and better." Murphy rushed off to devise his car bomb.

Bolan took out his double coils of tubing. On the ride out he'd cut a tablet-size square out of one of the messenger bags' dividing panel, punched a hole in each corner of the ripstop fabric with his tactical knife and attached the tubing. Bolan was fairly pleased with his handiwork. "Let's move in."

The Executioner's team moved at a crouch toward Rancho Paz's free fire zone. Bolan took line on the warehouse. He pointed at two spots in the dirt in front of him about four feet apart.

"Kaino, Donuts, stand there and there." Kaino and Donuts gave each other a look and took position. Bolan handed each man two ends of tubing. "Brace yourselves. Hold hard."

The two men gripped the tubing and stood like the two arms of a slingshot. Bolan put one of the Mason jar fire bombs in his sling pocket and started stepping backward. He stopped a moment and eased back. "Both of you, turn about five degrees to your right."

Kaino and Donez shuffled slightly in the dust and rebraced themselves. Bolan began stepping back again, and the tubing went from taut to deeply stretched. He leaned backward to put his body weight into it. Kaino and Donez tensed against the strain. Bolan grimaced with effort and nodded at Savacool. "Light me!"

Savacool thumbed her lighter and the firebomb's rag fuse ignited. Bolan took a moment to bend his knees a bit more to get more elevation and released. It was far from Murphy's dock destroying, perfect spiral on the river, but the firebomb tumbled end over end through space. The warehouse was also a pleasingly large target.

The Molotav crashed along the eaves and smeared fire across the northern roof side.

Savacool cheered quietly. "Woot!"

"Give me another," Bolan directed. Savacool handed him a second bomb. In the glare of the rancho security lights, someone ran outside and stared in shock at the warehouse as fire began to spread across the roof.

"He'll probably see it," Savacool advised.

Two more men ran out of the main ranch house and began pointing stupidly at the warehouse. Bolan stepped back against the elastic strength of the quadruple tubing. "Most likely…" The soldier took the same distance back and bent his knees a few inches more before releasing. The Molotav flew at a higher arc and disappeared from sight as it flew across roof level. The whoosh and glare of fresh fire told him he had hit the warehouse roof dead center. His siege team made pleased noises.

Bolan nodded. "Give me another."

Savacool handed over a third bomb. Bolan took up some slack in the tubing. "Kaino, Donuts, swing with me."

The soldier pulled on the tubes and rotated his human up-rights to bracket the rancho proper. The building was old, and had once been a working ranch. Now it simply ran a few cows as cover for other activities. Bolan suspected the log support beams of the ranch were the same age as the hundred-year-old mud walls and as dry as tinder.

"Brace yourselves." Bolan began stepping backward. He eyed the rancho for a moment with straining arms and let loose. Savacool proved prescient. One of Paz's men spotted the firebomb arcing in and began jumping up and down pointing and screaming like a castrated ape.

All three gunmen took weapons off their shoulders and began spraying bullets into the dark. Bolan's team dropped flat without being ordered and took prone firing positions. The gunmen stared backward as the Molotov hit the roof of the rancho. Bolan unslung his Garand and dropped to one knee. The gunmen returned their attention to firing blindly into the dark. A few bullets cracked and hissed high and wide to either side. The idea that they were standing out in the open under floodlights and their opponents were somewhere out in possibly dark drawing a bead on them never seemed to occur to Paz's men. Bolan peered through his twentieth-century optic and fired three times in as many heartbeats. The three gunmen dropped like dominos.

Donez admired the marksmanship. "Jesus..."

Murphy rolled up Paz's Land Rover in black-out condi-tion. He had smashed out the brake lights. The former Delta Force operative openly wept from the gas fumes within. "I am huffed up, high as a kite and ready to crash this party."

"You know the drill?"

"Roll her at speed at the gate and then ghost ride the whip. You'll most likely do something inflammatory with some of Morti's armor-piercing incendiaries."

Bolan nodded. It wasn't a bad summation. "Get 'em, Murph."

Murphy stuck his head out the window like a dog and wept gasoline-induced tears as he put the pedal to the metal. "Fuck howdy, yeah!"

Bolan took aim at the rancho. "Get ready!"

The Land Rover fishtailed down the access road. In the dust and the glare of rancho lights gas fumes shimmered in Bolan's sight. It might have been the fact that Murphy was Delta Force by way of the U.S. Army Rangers. It might well have been the fact that he was high out of his mind on gasoline fumes, but his insane, Kamikaze by way of crack-head hyena laugh echoed across the pastureland.

"Love that guy." Donez sighed. "I'm gonna miss him."

Gunmen spilled out of the rancho.

Bolan dropped four men with five shots, and his spent spring clip pinged out of the top of his Garand. He thumbed down an 8-round clip of Morti's armor-piercing incendiary ammo and took aim at the Land Rover's tailgate. His voice belted out in command. "Covering fire!"

Kaino's and Donez's rifles cracked in unison. Murphy squirted off one-handed bursts out his window as he rolled on the rancho. Bolan knocked down one cartel gangster and then another. They rushed out of the rancho stupid and trigger heavy. It was exactly what Bolan wanted, but he wondered where the Ranger-trained Zetas or the Euro-trash spec-ops assassins might be. So far it seemed to be spray-and-pray *sicarios* and street muscle.

Chains snapped as Murphy hit the gate. He fishtailed in the dust and then got his front tires pointed back at the rancho. He began to attract bullets from the house. Bolan's rifle drew two green tracer lines across the terrain, and the strobing muzzle-flashes in one of the darkened windows ceased. He whipped his sight back on the Land Rover's tailgate. Murphy ghost rode his whip. He dived out of the driver's seat and rolled behind a stone water trough. Bolan let the Land

Rover travel another ten yards and began methodically drawing tracer lines low through the tailgate.

It was a modest fuel-air bomb by fuel-air bomb standards.

Nevertheless, Rancho la Paz had never seen the like. The Land Rover went up with a tremendous thump and sent an impressive orange-and-black mushroom cloud into the dawn sky. The blast wave knocked down a dozen gunmen. A dozen more scattered in all directions as if it was Judgment Day and they had been found wanting.

A pistol-waving *sicario* burst out the door half strangling a screaming woman in an apron. Bolan thought using the woman who was cooking your breakfast for cover climbed to the rarefied peaks of bad taste. Bolan put his crosshairs on the killer's forehead and sent him on his way. The servant screamed at the spray of blood and bone and ran back in the house.

The Executioner's Garand clacked open and the empty clip pinged out. He shoved in a fresh one and the bolt shot home. Bolan scanned through his scope. There were innocents in the house, and the house was on fire. The assault was about to hit a nasty patch. The question at hand was whether Raulito Paz was the kind of guy to hole up in a safe room or the kind to come out shooting.

The doors of the burning warehouse smashed off their tracks beneath the beak of Paz's narco tank's ram. Someone had spray painted Yunque du Paz across the front. The Paz Anvil was coming. Paz knew exactly where Murphy was, and a machine gun cut loose from one of the narco tank's firing slits. The former Delta operative crouched behind the water trough as dozens of bullets tore into it. He couldn't see Bolan out in the dark but he looked directly at the soldier's position and gave an unmistakable Whiskey-Tango-Foxtrot! gesture.

"Get their attention!" Bolan ordered.

"Good idea…" Savacool muttered. She flicked her selector switch to full-auto and sent thirty rounds ricocheting off the front armor of the narco tank. Kaino and Donez fired as fast as they could pull their triggers. Bolan watched their tracer lines streak into the narco tank. The armor-piercing incendiaries sparked and popped like fireflies against the armor plate. Bolan could see the smoking dents Kaino and Donez's bullets left. The fact was, they weren't penetrating. The narco tank was more tanklike than armored vehicle. It would take a 50-caliber bullet to crack it, and Bolan's team was all out of fifties this morning.

"We aren't cracking this egg!" Kaino snarled.

"Retreat to the vehicles. Take cover behind them," Bolan ordered.

"And when he rolls over them like tin cans?" Kaino inquired.

"He'll have to get past me first, if he does. Scatter. You have four-wheel drive. Go cross-country. That beast is purely a paved road proposition."

"Has to get past you?"

"Go!" Bolan ordered. "And give me some covering fire, and lights when I call for them!"

Kaino, Donez and Savacool ran for the SUVs.

Bolan wound his arm through the M-1's sling and took a stance. The Paz Anvil bore down on him. The Anvil came through the broken gate in the fence and rumbled down the access road. The Executioner suspected Paz and his best men were inside. They intended to roll over anything in their way and roll on to freedom. The Anvil turned into a dark hulking beast as it left the glare of the security lights and the burning ranch buildings behind it. Weapons protruding from the firing slits sent suppressive fire into the dark. Bolan waited a few crucial seconds. "Light him up!"

Kaino and Savacool hit the headlights on the Wrangler and the Bronco and ran for the cover of darkness. Weapons grated in the firing slits and the two vehicles instantly took fire. Bolan was a shadow in the dark off to one side. He put his crosshairs on the driver's viewing slit. He didn't try to keep up with the narrow, bouncing target. He kept his sight on and waited for the slit to bounce up or down into his reticule. Bolan began squeezing off shots on the half second. Sparks screamed as his steel-cored penetrators met inches of steel and failed.

There was no spark on Bolan's fifth shot. The Anvil suddenly slewed wildly on the gravel road. He shucked out of his rifle sling and charged. Ripping a sparkler bundle out of his bag and sticking it in his teeth, the soldier grabbed for his lighter. The narco tank bounced to a halt as the dead man behind the wheel no longer had his foot on the gas. Kaino, Donez and Savacool drilled bullets at the firing slit to try to keep the gunmen within from cutting Bolan in two.

The soldier ran up the bent beak of the battering ram and up the steel vault covering the hood. He pressed the button on his lighter and lit the inch of fuse. Sparks showered. Bolan jammed the bomb into the driver's slit and it stuck, then palmed the bomb as hard as he could. It stuck three-quarters of the way through. Bolan rolled off the hood and covered his ears as the bomb went off.

Fire from all firing slits ceased. The soldier clambered back up on the hood and took a moment to flatten his second bomb as much as he could. He lit it and managed to worm it through the slit, and duck, as it detonated. Powder smoke spewed out of every firing slit. Bolan again took a few seconds and got the third bomb in without a hitch. The narco tank rocked on its chassis, and smoke exploded from every open aperture.

Murphy loped up the road. He kept his submachine gun aimed at the back of the narco tank. Bolan climbed onto the roof and walked to the back. "Kaino! Donez! Come ahead! Savacool! Cover us!" Kaino and Donez ran forward. The rear door of the tank clanged open, and gray smoke roiled out in a brimstone cloud. Several men fell out. They tumbled to the dust, stunned, blinded, deafened and black faced from powder smoke. Murphy and Kaino jumped inside and administered beat downs to anyone who was still moving. They threw beaten and stunned *sicarios* and gunmen onto an ever-increasing pile of Mexican drug muscle.

"Got him!" Kaino shouted. A very bedraggled-looking Raulito Paz found himself bum-rushed onto the pile of his men. Paz let out a feeble yelp as his mostly faceless driver was thrown on top of him.

"Clear!" Murphy called.

Bolan jumped down and eyed his prey. "Murph, put Paz in the back of the Bronco. Have Donez sit on him. You're driving. Kaino, you and Cool are in the Wrangler. Take point. We're out of here in five."

Murphy spit on the moaning and shuddering man pile. "What about them?"

"Leave them."

Kaino gave Bolan a questioning look. "What about you?"

Bolan patted the slab-steel slide of the Anvil. "I'm keeping him."

CHAPTER FIFTEEN

Reynosa, Tamaulipas

The Rio Grande ran brown and slow toward the Gulf. Bolan watched workers roll the Anvil onto the river barge. Despite the fact that it was 10:00 a.m., a card table, two folding chairs and a bucket of beers had magically appeared on the concrete wharf. Morti Morelos sat opposite Bolan and gazed long and lovingly on the rolled steel monstrosity as it belched, jerked and roared its way into its berth. Bolan had driven the Anvil back across the Nuevo Leon border into Tamaulipas without incident and contacted Morelos. The gun dealer had made arrangements and gotten some local cops who owed him to clear a back road. Bolan had taken the steel vault on wheels down the coast to Reynosa. The smell of black powder was still overpowering inside, but the homemade flash-bangs hadn't done much damage to the interior. It was cavernous, capacious and had a World War I trench crawler feel to it. Despite that, whoever had welded everything into place had done a crude, beautiful, "work with what's at hand" job of it.

Much to Murphy's and Donez's gleeful avarice, Paz had packed two suitcases of bug-out money, mostly in U.S. dollars, but there was a significant chunk of change in banded and stacked Mexican pesos along with a shoebox full of Mexican gold coins.

Morelos combed his fingers through his comb-over and shook his head. "I know the man who forged the two vehicles. He does good work."

"That he did."

"You know," Morelos enthused. "I would say I cannot believe you stole Señor Paz's Anvil, but I am afraid I do believe it, and would so even it were not here before my very eyes."

"We're square on the weapons?"

Morelos tapped the bundles of greenbacks. "More than square." He suddenly shot Bolan a wary look and his hand crept protectively toward the Beretta 93-R riding Mexican carry in his waistband. "You do not wish your *pistola* back?"

"Business is business." Bolan smiled amiably and held up his sweating beer. "A gift between friends is forever."

Morelos smiled shyly and clinked bottles. The warrior and the gun dealer drank. Morelos waved his bottle at the Anvil and grew shrewd once more. "Now, *señor,* as to this situation…"

"How much?"

"How much would you charge?" Morelos countered.

"Many thousands," Bolan acknowledged.

"To you? Normally? I would give credit. But you have stolen Raulito's Anvil. And according to rumor, you have blown up the Hammer. He will be very angry. This adds a certain sense of, how shall I say…"

"Raulito Paz currently lives beneath my hand, and at my sufferance."

Morelos did a credible job of not choking on his beer. "I see. Nonetheless, he has superiors who will not be pleased by any of this. I am afraid I will require—"

"Many thousands," Bolan mused. He reached into his bag and pulled out a sack made out of a bandanna Savacool had loaned him. It bulged as if it held a grapefruit. It clinked, jingled and spread out as Bolan put it on the table. "I have a significant amount more of cash since last we spoke, but I think I'm going to need most of it for the next phase of my operation. Would you take this as a down payment?"

Morelos untied the bandanna's corners and watched the gold coins spill across the table.

Bolan nodded. "They weigh a lot, and I can't easily convert them to cash on the fly."

Morti sighed at the thick, gleaming gold coins of his country. "I will indeed accept this, as down payment. Should you live, I will expect the same amount, in gold, on the back end."

"If I'm dead it will take longer, but you'll be paid regardless."

"I believe you."

Bolan decided to take another huge chance with Morelos. Bolan believed he had a good read on the gun dealer, and he thought it was a good chance that it would be life insurance. "Do me one more favor?"

Morelos smiled but his eyes went reptile over his beer. "If it is within my power."

"Scrape that Yunque de Paz shit off my ride."

Morelos grinned and drank beer. "This I can do. *Gratis*."

"Another favor?"

Bolan suspected Morelos would normally become angry at this point, but the man seemed to be in the moment, and eager to hear what would come out of Bolan's mouth next. "What would that be?"

"You know any good graffiti artists?"

Morelos's brows bunched at the odd request. "To be honest, *señor,* most *graffitos* know better than to come near any building I own or am using, but I believe I could find you one. Why?"

Bolan lifted his chin at the Anvil as bargemen chalked the tires and tied tarps over it. "Paint El Hombre on it. Paint it large."

Morelos gagged beer in the back of his throat and snarfed it back up out of his nose. Bolan turned his burning blue gaze on the man. The gun dealer spent several moments recovering himself. He wiped his face with Savacool's bandanna and regarded Bolan with something approximating religious awe. "It will be done, El Hombre."

Safehouse, Matamoros

BOLAN REGARDED Raulito Paz. The man sweated and shook where he sat duct taped to the guest toilet. Powder flash had painted his face a gunmetal blue. Savacool had assured Bolan that both of Paz's eardrums were intact, and he was fit for questioning. Kaino had pulled first guard detail on the prisoner, and he leaned against the bathroom counter glaring at Paz, trying to make him cry. It looked like the master sergeant was getting close. Paz flinched beneath Bolan's red-rimmed, cobalt-blue eyes and what he saw there gave him pause. "Listen, man—"

Bolan cut the drug scum off. "You know who I am?"

Paz couldn't meet Bolan's eyes. According to all intel, Raulito Paz was supposed to be a tough, ruthless son of a bitch. The iron echo-chambering Bolan had given Paz inside the Anvil seemed to have knocked some of the starch out, and the soldier was pretty convinced Paz knew exactly whose hands he was in.

"I'm the man who cracked the Paz Hammer like an egg and stole your Anvil. I also took your house on the river and burned your rancho to the ground. Do you know who I am?"

Paz whispered his answer, as if it was the secret name of God or the Devil and both might be listening. "You're El Hombre…"

"That's right. Do you know what I do for a living?"

Paz searched through his terror for some kind of non-wrath-inducing answer and came up empty.

Bolan was in a helping mood. "I do things, Paz. Like what I have just done to you. The question is, now, what do I do with you?" Paz remained silent. "You know I have your Faux Paz."

Paz blinked.

"Your double—that's how I found you."

Paz flinched.

"I also have Salami, and man, does he want to take a machete to you. You know, both of them pretty much hate you."

Paz stared at the floor.

Bolan had run a quick survey on the men they had unceremoniously poured out of the Anvil while it had aired out. Despite being blind, stunned and stupid and covered in powder smoke, all of them appeared to have been Mexican nationals. "Tell me about the Europeans."

Paz made evasive noises. "Which ones?"

Bolan raised an eyebrow. He was pretty sure Paz wasn't being facetious. "We'll start with the ones who work for you."

"They don't work for me, they were…" Paz trailed off.

"Sent," Bolan concluded. "By who?"

Paz looked down again. "The heads of the cartel."

"The Zetas are hiring foreign mercenaries?"

"Not exactly."

"What, exactly."

"They were sent to Mexico, on…" Paz searched for a word. "Loan."

Kaino glowered. "Shock troops."

Bolan kept his gaze boring into Paz. "Problem solvers."

Paz shivered as the betrayals kept coming out of his mouth. "That is how they were presented to me. You, El Hombre, were a high-priority problem in Florida. Though it was considered risky killing a high-profile cop like Kaino, once he was linked with you it was deemed necessary that anyone who aided El Hombre must pay the price."

"So the mercs sweep in, sweep us up and disappear. No discernable ties to the Zetas, but everybody knows who did it."

"This is the way it was planned, and those were the orders I gave."

"Like you did Bruno Christo?"

Paz flinched and his jaws worked.

Bolan nodded.

"And my family? What were the orders?" Kaino asked.

Paz paled and looked down at his toes.

Kaino cracked his huge, scarred boxer's knuckles. "Can I kill him now?"

"No."

"Can I hit him?" Kaino pressed.

"Maybe in a minute. Paz, you want to live?"

Paz looked up. "I would like that."

"You want me to leave the bathroom and give Kaino fifteen minutes with you?"

"I would not like that."

"Then I need you to answer the next few questions very carefully," Bolan stated.

Paz seemed to collapse into the porcelain he was taped to as he gave himself over to his traitordom. "Ask."

"The mercs, where are they from?"

"I don't know. I only spoke with two of them. One spoke his Spanish with a French accent, I think. The other was black, and his Spanish was so bad I could not tell where he was from, except that he was not American."

"The mercs are on loan from who?" Bolan pressed.

"I don't know, but they were supplied to the cartel."

"Directly to solve problems with establishing *krokodil* in the United States."

"Yes."

"They were sent by the supplier."

"Maybe?"

"Who is the supplier?" Bolan queried.

"I don't know."

"Where are they?"

"I don't know," Paz repeated.

"You received consignment of *krokodil* here?"

"The initial ones, yes."

"They come by truck or plane?"

Paz gazed down miserably. "Boat."

"From where?" Bolan asked.

"I don't know."

"What do you know? Give me something now."

"The men who offloaded the product, they had Central American accents," Paz told him.

"From where?"

"I can't be sure."

Bolan leaned in close. His blue eyes had gone arctic. "You're absolutely sure and I can see it in your eyes. Where?"

Paz shook like a squid. "Guatemala."

Bolan relented slightly. "Who are the other Europeans?"

Paz seemed very glad for a change of subject. "I don't know. No one's seen them. Just the trail they've left."

"Beatings?"

"Bodies," Paz said.

Bolan frowned.

"Beaten bodies! They like, interrogate you and then kill you. It's like they're interrogating and killing their way to the top."

"You realize, Paz, you're lucky I reached you first."

Paz considered this action item and for a moment actually looked grateful. "Thank you?"

Bolan jerked his head at Kaino. "Walk with me. Cool! Watch the prisoner." Paz watched them go sadly. Savacool made a noise from somewhere in the house. Bolan and Kaino walked through the kitchen where Donez was frying chorizos and flipping tortillas. Donez nodded at a couple of coffees he had just brewed. Murphy was currently on the roof. Savacool unslung her Mendoza in passing. Kaino grinned at the special agent. "Like his name, he is meek as a lamb."

Savacool chambered a round as she marched toward the bathroom. "And he shall stay that way."

Bolan paused. "He's talking. Be the good cop. See if you can get him to start babbling up everything he has on Zeta structure and affairs in Florida and Guatemala."

"On it."

Bolan and Kaino took their coffee out onto the back patio. "Murph!" Bolan called. "Status!"

"All clear, Coop!" Murphy called down.

Bolan and Kaino took deck chairs and watched the Rio Grande as they waited for lunch. "What do you think, Kaino?"

"Doesn't add up."

"You're thinking about Papi's Tea Room."

"They didn't kill Popov or his boys. Now Paz says we got the same M.O. except now, if Paz is to be believed, we got cartel bodies piling up the yang."

"Why do you think that would be?"

"Well, I hate to pull the demographic card, Coop, but killing people in the U.S. and killing people in Mexico are two different prospects."

"That's true, but you're not buying that. What else?"

Kaino gave Bolan a hard look. "You already have your own idea."

"Yeah, but I want to hear yours."

Kaino made a noise. "I don't know, maybe because Popov is Russian and sending money home?"

Bolan smiled. "You and me are on the same page."

"We're on the same side. To be on the same page I got to go to spy school, and I'm talking *Mission Impossible* school and shit."

"Those are movies, Kaino. This is the real shit."

Kaino sipped coffee and meditated on the river. "So, Russian GRU international interdiction teams operating in the U.S. and Mexico, and Euro mercs are playing cleanup for the cartels."

"With the North American *krokodil* distribution network as the prize. What's your read on the Guatemala angle?"

"Guatemala? It's lovely, and it's a goddamned hellhole. With the Colombian government raiding everything that moves within their borders, Guatemala has turned into the next major transshipment point for South American drugs." Kaino drained his cup. "But you knew that already."

"Been there once or twice, but not recently."

Kaino went back to meditating upon the waters. "You know, I'm an island boy, and now a confirmed Floridian, but I like this country."

Bolan watched the Rio Grande and thought about his many missions south of it. He considered all of his experiences here good and bad. "I love this place. I want to see Mexico throw off its self-inflicted chains and rise, and El Hombre ride into the sunset."

The soldier's phone vibrated in his pocket. He took it out and found that Kurtzman was calling. "I was just about to contact you. What's up?"

"You need to come back to Florida."

Bolan weighed the reasons that might be. "The Russians want to talk."

"And they'll only talk to you. They asked for you by name."

"I don't remember giving the guy in the hospital my name, just a number."

"Yeah, but he got a real good look at you."

"That's true. What name did they ask for me by?"

"Belasko."

Bolan let out a long breath. It was a cover name he hadn't used in a while, and he considered the Russians who might still be alive who would use it.

"Tell Jack I'll be at the airport in twenty minutes. Kaino, you're with me."

CHAPTER SIXTEEN

Miami, Florida

"Nasty part of town, Coop." Kaino cruised the unmarked Miami-Dade Crown Vic through streets he knew and abhorred. The master sergeant didn't seem to be happy to be home. Bolan understood Kaino's frustration. Home was where the heart was, and his family was in secret protective custody somewhere out in the world. The flight from Matamoros to Miami was a fairly short hop, but it had been made by helicopter and they had been going nonstop with two battles within twenty-four hours. Kaino was a cop rather than a spy or soldier, and things were clearly starting to get to him. Bolan could feel battle fatigue circling, as well.

The master sergeant pulled the car to a stop in front of a tenement. "This is it."

The sun-bleached two-story facade had all broken or boarded-up windows. Kaino gave the horn a swift *rata-tat-tat* with his palm as instructed. Bolan and Kaino watched as skells, junkies and the lowest of low-level prostitutes burst like birds from a building on fire. Kaino laughed low. "Someone of authority is in residence, and we're expected."

Bolan checked the loads in the 93-R that Jack Grimaldi had given to him. "You ready?"

Kaino loosened the .357 Magnum gun in his cross-draw holster and took his second revolver out of the glove compartment and put in his small of the back rig. "How do you want to play it?"

"Bold as brass."

"I hear that."

Bolan and Kaino slid out of the Crown Vic and mounted the sagging steps. "I'll take point," Kaino offered. "I may know someone still in here."

Bolan nodded. "Go."

The soldier and the cop entered the tenement. Not all the tenants had fled. The passed out, the drunk, the tripping and dying littered the halls and rooms with the doors smashed off. They walked down the hall and Bolan's nose wrinkled as he caught the iodine stench of *krokodil* coming from several rooms. "Kaino?"

"Yeah, I smell it. Guns drawn?"

"No, like we own the place."

They came to the end of the hall. The door they faced was fairly new and solid and had probably belonged to the bottom-of-the-heap big man who had run this shooting gallery. If rumors were true, the bridal suite had been appropriated. Bolan knocked three times and the door swung open slightly under his knuckles. "Coming in!"

A woman's voice Bolan recognized called back from within. "Clear!"

He gave the door a slow but firm push to open it all the way.

Bolan beheld a beautiful, six-foot redheaded woman with an eye patch. A pair of Russian hammerheads who appeared to be genuine identical twins bracketed her. All three held silenced micro-Uzi submachine guns. Bolan ignored the bookends for the moment and gazed on a woman out of his past.

Most spy agencies kept a beautiful woman or two on the payroll. Russian Military Intelligence Agent Valentina Svarzkova had come up the hard way through the Russian army, qualifying as a sniper and becoming a first-class field agent. Long ago she had shown up on the U.S. government's doorstep to help deal with a very ugly remnant of the cold war that Bolan thought he had crushed.

Bolan eyed the thin white scar that creased Svarzkova's chin and the ever so slight skewing of her broken nose. In Virginia she had rammed her car head-on into a Jeep full of rocket-armed terrorists and stopped just short of going through the windshield. Later on during that mission she had taken a Russian military entrenching tool halfway through her thigh and had her femoral artery severed. They had operated again later in London, and she had taken two bullets meant for Bolan through her left lung. She had fought beside him in the Congo and had her left eye burned out of her head by a high-frequency antisatellite targeting laser. The standing joke between them whenever they met was wondering what new weird and wonderful trauma would befall her.

Bolan had never seen Svarzkova with red hair before. He noted her right eye was currently green. She was already a tall woman, and the lifts she had in her shoes allowed her to look Bolan in the eye.

The soldier nodded. "Captain."

Kaino took in the Russian agent with appreciation. "You know this one?"

Svarzkova gave Bolan the Russian stone face. "Belasko."

Bolan smiled in memory at the old alias. "It's Cooper now."

Svarzkova's English had always been excellent, but her Russian accent was still clear. "It is Major now."

"Congratulations on your promotion."

"Thank you."

Bolan appraised Svarzkova's muscle. The twins could have been Popov hammerheads except that they were wearing decently tailored tropical wool suits and they held themselves with a cold, angry dignity. Both men had that Russian beard, mustache, head stubble all the same length look. They smelled to high heaven of Russian Special Forces.

"Who're the clones?" Bolan asked.

Svarzkova tilted her head at one and then the other without taking her eye off Bolan. "Igor and Ivan."

Kaino couldn't believe it. "You're shitting me."

Igor spit, fired off a few disgusted remarks in Russian and jerked his head at Bolan. Igor's intention was clear. He was asking permission. Svarzkova shook her head and muttered a few things in the negative.

The Russians never sent agents abroad who didn't speak the language. Bolan knew Svarzkova was pulling the filter routine. He eyed the bulge of a sap in Igor's jacket pocket. "What's his problem?"

"I have told Igor that any attempt to intimidate you would be rash in the extreme, and that you are out of his league, even if his brother Ivan helped him." Svarzkova inclined her head slightly at Kaino in recognition. "And I have reminded him also the master sergeant's reputation is known to us."

Kaino puffed up slightly.

Svarzkova turned her attention back to Bolan and icily radiated the fact that she wasn't pleased to see him again. He ignored the dropping temperature in the room and glanced at the pirate-worthy black eye patch she wore. "No ocular prosthesis?"

"I have several, but I find eye patch conducive to intimidation during interrogation. In former Russian republics, legend of Red Witch with one eye grows, and she is feared."

Bolan nodded. He was currently using an intimidation alias himself.

Bolan grinned at the Russian. "Saw what you did to Popov and his playmates."

A smile ghosted across Svarzkova's face. Food and laying a beat down on the bad guys were neck and neck for the most important things in Svarzkova's life.

"Did you get what you wanted?" Bolan asked.

The smile died on Svarzkova's face. "It would be best

for you to leave. Best if you leave Miami-Dade. Best for the master sergeant to resume his regular duties."

Kaino shook his head. "Mamacita, I was really starting to like you."

Svarzkova tossed her hennaed locks imperiously. "Now you will be suggesting we pool our resources."

Bolan looked long and hard on the Russian agent. They had shared missions, hospital gurneys and on more than one occasion a bed. Something was terribly wrong with the situation, and with her. She didn't want to talk. Svarzkova was on a mission. Bolan's every instinct told him Svarzkova was desperate. He showed her respect by opening the bidding with a right hand lead to the jaw.

"I'm not suggesting anything, Val. I'm telling you. If you continue to operate on U.S. soil without my permission, Kaino and I are going to bum rush you and the twins right off the planet. If that's a problem, let's settle it now."

Svarzkova stiffened. Igor and Ivan snapped their heads toward Svarzkova like exceptionally well-trained attack dogs ready to slip the leash. She shook her head even as she locked gazes with Bolan. "I have instructions not to reengage past liaisons."

"I don't care about your instructions."

Ivan spoke for the first time. "We kill them."

Svarzkova held up a restraining finger. "What must I do to get your permission?"

"Spill," Bolan demanded. "Everything."

"No."

"Then get the hell out of my country and don't come back."

Igor's and Ivan's stubble hair might as well have been nerve endings. You could almost hear their fascia crackling with their need to kill Bolan and Kaino. Svarzkova spoke English for Bolan's benefit. "Very well, we go."

Igor and Ivan looked genuinely crestfallen.

Even Kaino seemed surprised. "You're going to clear out of town? Just like that?"

"We are operating in your motherland. You have too many advantages." She ran her eye up and down Bolan. "And I know this one. We go." Svarzkova lifted an imperious chin at Igor and Ivan, and the twins began gathering up suspicious-looking cases and bags. The Russians were packing light, and Bolan knew they had other operation sites in Miami. Bolan regarded Svarzkova coldly. "Val."

"What?"

"Get out of Kaino's territory. Get out of my country. This is my last warning, out of respect."

Svarzkova's one-eyed gaze went Siberian. "I will see you in Mexico, Cooper."

Bolan had given it fifty-fifty the Russians had a lead on the recent fireworks in Matamoros. Bolan threw the curve ball. "But I'm not going back to Mexico."

Svarzkova stopped. Bolan kept the smile off his face. It was true, she did know him. He knew very well that she knew that even when she had lied about the nature of her missions he had never lied to her. Bolan let her internal battle rage for several moments while she fought to keep from asking where he was going. He moved slowly so as not to get shot and took a pen and a blank card from his pocket. He wrote down a number and handed it to Svarzkova.

"I'll be in Guatemala City. The tamales are fantastic. Call me."

Flight 15, Miami to Guatemala City

KAINO HAD NEVER flown first class before. He swirled his comped rum and Coke and took in the surroundings and the flight attendants in particular. "Posh shit, Coop."

"And?" Bolan asked. He knew Kaino had been waiting hours to detonate.

Kaino growled low and let it boil over. "What the hell, man!"

"What the hell what?"

"Telling that redheaded Russian bitch where we're going."

"Actually she's blonde," Bolan said.

"And how do you know that?"

"I know for a fact the carpet matches the drapes."

Kaino made a pleased noise and painted his own mental picture. He scowled again and got back to business. "Then why the hell did we need to meet if you knew it was going to go to shit?"

"It was always going to go to shit. Her team was already on its way out of Miami. They've been working their way up the food chain, just like us."

"So if they were going to leave anyway, then why take the meet?"

"Val wanted to make sure it was really me."

"And?"

"I let her know it was," Bolan said.

"You really think she's going to meet you in the food square for tamales and make lovey-dovey in Guatemala?"

Bolan smiled in memory and sipped his club soda. "She'll meet me for tamales."

"You sure she won't just shoot you in the head and leave you facedown in your food?"

Bolan had developed a very good read on Valentina Svarzkova over the years. He smiled again. "I give it fifty-fifty."

"And Igor and Ivan? What if the hammerheads throw down on you, as well?"

"Last I saw, you have lightning in both hands, Master Sergeant."

Kaino threw back his rum and Coke. "Well, you are a charming motherfucker. Maybe she'll just go all gushy and give up everything."

"I think she can give up background. I think we're ahead

of the game when it comes to going forward. That's why she'll meet," Bolan said.

"So if we're ahead of the game, why meet? Why give them anything?"

"Why do you think, Kaino?"

Kaino grinned. "Because we're going to war, Igor and Ivan are some serious fucking cannon fodder and you want to see if the new drapes match the carpet."

Bolan reclined his seat and pulled his ball cap low over his eyes. "Nothing gets past you, Kaino."

Guatemala City

THE WEATHER WAS surprisingly mild. Guate, as the capital city was known to the locals, sat at a five-thousand-foot elevation in an inland mountain valley. The late afternoon was positively springlike compared to the swelter of the Mexican and Floridian summer. Despite the clear skies, green surrounding mountains and the mountain breezes they engendered, Bolan knew the city was boiling over. Despite the powder keg they were walking into, Taca Airlines flight attendants and a two-hour power nap had put Kaino in a better mood. He kept up a steady patter with Paco the cabdriver. Puerto Rican Spanish tripped off Kaino's tongue as he effortlessly charmed the man. They'd stopped at a kiosk on the street, and Kaino had bought a carton full of tamales. Ostensibly they were for the team. Bolan suspected Kaino would be licking the sides of the box before they reached the CIA-arranged safehouse.

Kaino leaned back and rubbed his belly happily. "*Madre de Dios,* I have never seen so many kinds."

Bolan grabbed a tamale colorado while the grabbing was good. "The joke goes saying *tamale* in Guatemalan is like saying *snow* in Eskimo."

Paco was pleased and nodded into the rearview mirror. "This is so, *señor*."

The cab pulled up to a very old house in the older part of town in the north. It was small, of Spanish colonial style and to Bolan's satisfaction it included a wall and a little up-stairs balcony overlooking the street. Kaino left his empty tamale carton in the cab and took up his duffel. Bolan tipped Paco well and waited until he had driven away, then tapped a number on the phone. "Donuts, we're here."

"I see you," Donez answered. "Clear, come ahead."

Bolan and Kaino walked through the gate. Donez stepped forward onto the balcony and waved. Murphy lay sacked out in idle glory in a hammock stretched between two flower-ing lemon trees, reading *Soldier of Fortune* magazine. The former Special Ops warrior waved a one-liter bottle of Gua-temalan Gallo beer. "Hey, buddy! Man! Central American beats the Middle East and any fucking 'Stan country you can name!"

"You look comfortable," Bolan observed.

"I just got off guard duty."

"Where's Cool?"

"Cooking, and thank God. You stole Kaino, and I am tired of Donuts' chorizos and beans."

"Tell me you got us guns, Murph."

"Oh, I got guns." Murphy rolled out of his hammock. "The master sergeant is gonna be thrilled."

"No more *Saving Private Ryan* shit," Kaino warned.

"Better."

Murphy gleefully led them inside. Good smells came from the kitchen. "Honey, I'm home!"

"Say that again, sugar man, and you're dead!" Savacool called back.

Murphy led them to four large cardboard boxes marked Live Flowers in Spanish. Bolan reached into the packing and pulled out a Madsen M/50.

"Oh, for—" Kaino was incensed. "Didn't the bad guys use these in *Austin Powers?*"

"No." Bolan shook his head as he checked the action. "Those were Beretta Model 12s."

"Swell."

Bolan opened the square of tube steel that formed the weapon's stock. Everything about the submachine was flat and squared off. He smiled slightly, noting the curved magazine and fatter barrel, pleased to note it was a Brazilian copy of a Madsen M/50. The Brazilians in their wisdom had seen fit to upgrade their firepower by chambering their guns in .45 caliber. For some reason known only to the Brazilians they had given a submachine gun a bayonet lug.

"Tell me we have bayonets."

"We are full-on accessorized, Coop!"

"Nice."

"Ex-Brazilian police issue. Morti was kind enough to give me the phone number of a very understanding Russian import-export individual named Pavel. Pavel says everyone in Guate is buying guns. But just like Matamoros they all want the latest stuff."

"I liked the Mendozas better," Kaino muttered.

Bolan had to admit that next to the beautifully balanced and finished Mexican weapons the Brazilian sheet steel and stamping looked like junk. He unscrewed the barrel nut. The joy of the Danish design was that once you took off the barrel nut the entire weapon butterflied in two. It was just about one of the simplest weapons on earth to both use and maintain.

Murphy held one out like a giant pistol. "It's .45 cal, Kaino."

Bolan took out the barrel. "Brazilian revolutionary Carlos Marighella once said this was the ideal weapon for the urban guerrilla."

"Yeah, Kaino." Murphy grinned. "Your people are all into the urban guerrilla shit."

The master sergeant frowned mightily at the man. Whatever ties Kaino and his family had to Puerto Rican separatists was something he didn't like brought up. "You need to shit can that kind of talk around me, Murph."

Bolan held his barrel up to the light and checked the bore on his weapon. "Save that for the enemy, Murph."

"Copy that." Murphy made an effort at being contrite. "I bought a box of tamales, Kaino. We saved you some."

"Oh!" Despite having eaten almost a carton, Kaino strode toward the kitchen with purpose.

Bolan reassembled his weapon. He could tell that Murphy had already personally cleaned and checked the weapons. "Pistols?"

Murphy lifted his shirt to reveal his weapon. "GI .45s. U.S. government issue, lend lease to Guatemala way back in the last century, and Kaino will have cause to complain. They are old."

"What kind of shape?"

"If you get in a fight in a phone booth, serviceable. I cleaned them up as best I could."

"Tell me you asked your boy Yuri about any Russians running around in Guate."

"I did. He said he hadn't heard anything. I dropped a significant chunk of the coin you gave me on him and the story stayed the same. I told him to let me know if he hears anything. He swears he will, for whatever that's worth."

Bolan nodded. "Nice work, Murph."

"I also contacted a couple of guys I know doing security work in Central America to get the lay of the land and on where and who we want to rain on next."

"And what did your friends say?"

"Well, who are you most excited about taking on first? Los Zetas or MS-13?"

Murphy had named the two most dangerous criminal gangs on earth. "You know any local type locals?"

"Dunno, I can see if I can get a meet with one, but it will be through somebody who knows somebody who knows somebody."

"Do it," Bolan said.

"On it."

Kaino came back with a tamale in each hand. "So what's the plan?"

"Let's go stir up the Mara Salvatrucha boys and see what happens."

CHAPTER SEVENTEEN

Guatemala City

"Here comes trouble," Kaino muttered.

Bolan watched their contact cross the street. "With a capital *T*." The taverna was just about abandoned. The soldier considered the siesta just about the most civilized idea humanity had ever come up with. To his sadness it was disappearing across much of the world. The siesta was still in heavy effect in Central America. Even here in the bustling capital city, the huge majority of Guatemalans sacked out on the nearest sofa or hammock directly after a gigantic lunch. Bolan, Kaino and Murphy sat around a tile-covered table on the covered front patio, passed around a liter bottle of beer and drank out of little glasses. They watched their contact approach.

"Who is the asshole again?" Kaino asked.

"The Guatemalan asshole version of Murph."

"Aw, man." Murph sighed and grabbed the bottle. "Don't be that guy, Coop."

Bolan had heard the term "lean as a whip." The man approaching was the dictionary picture example. At five-nine he was very tall for a Guatemalan, and by his almost aristocratic Spanish features there wasn't much Mayan in him. "He's a Kaibil."

"What's Kaibil?" Kaino asked.

"Guatemalan Special Operations. They specialize in counterinsurgency."

"Badass, huh?"

Bolan nodded. "They spent decades fighting in the civil war. Utterly loyal to the government. I hear part of their training is to bite the head off a live chicken."

Kaino grinned. "So…he's a geek?"

"Their motto is If I advance, follow me. If I stop, urge me on. If I retreat, kill me."

"That's some hardcore shit," Kaino commented.

"It's part of their field procedure that if they're shot in a nonvital area in battle to cut an *X* over the wound with their knife, pull out the bullet themselves and keep fighting."

Even Murphy was impressed. "Jesus."

"A big part of their success over the years has been that they scare the shit out of their adversaries, in country and abroad. Since the Guatemalan Peace Accords of 1996, they've been tasked with combating drug trafficking, and they've been involved in a number of UN missions."

"What's this guy's name again?" Kaino asked.

"Bang," Murphy answered. "Salcido Bang. And people I know vouch for him huge. He fought in the last and worst two years of the civil war. He was in the Congo in 2005 and 2006, and since he returned he's been a private contractor."

Señor Bang walked straight up to the table and sat. Bolan nodded at the waitress for another glass. *"Por favor."*

The waitress brought a glass and Bolan poured. Bang took the glass solemnly and took a sip. *"Gracias."*

"I have been told that you are a man well worth speaking to, Señor Bang."

Bang was dressed for the Guatemalan highland summer in slacks, huaraches and a white short-sleeved shirt that appeared to be silk. He wore a very expensive diving watch, and a heavy gold chain circled his neck. Except for his coppery skin he looked like Spanish royalty. One lock of his wavy black hair had been artfully arranged into what Bolan suspected was a trademark spit curl. He had a 1970s porn-star-worthy mustache. Kaino and Murphy stared in fascination at the puckered, *x*-shaped scars on top of Bang's left forearm and lower right biceps.

Bang noticed the focus of their scrutiny. "I will admit I am well worth talking to, *señor*. I am a fascinating man with many interesting stories to tell." He suddenly broke into a disarming smile and took another sip of beer. "Some of them are even true."

Kaino and Murphy made noises of amusement. Bolan found himself liking the Guatemalan merc. "Señor Bang, I—"

"Call me Sal. My friends do. Most of the Navy SEALS and Rangers I have worked with call me Banger, but that is a privilege you must earn."

"What makes you think I'm not a Ranger or a SEAL?"

Bang looked around at the men in front of him in turn, Kaino to Murphy to Bolan. "That one is a cop. That one is a soldier. You could be Kaibil, if you applied yourself."

Bolan accepted the backhanded compliment, and noted Bang's discernment. "Sal, have you heard of something called *krokodil?* Or maybe heard of it called *cocodrilo?*"

Bang sipped more beer and shrugged. "I am afraid I have not."

"You've heard of Los Zeta and MS-13?"

Bang tossed back his beer and sighed at the scar on his biceps. "Indeed, I have heard of them."

"*Krokodil* is a Russian designer drug that is making inroads in Florida. From what I've learned, both Los Zeta and MS-13 are fighting over the North American distribution rights. The problem is, it's not being cooked locally, and my investigation took me to Tamaulipas, Mexico, and now to your country."

Bang pushed his glass away and regarded Bolan. "I will speak frankly. I have a friend in El Salvador, who has a friend in San Jose, who knows a very smooth operator from

Texas who is now retired in Tegucigalpa, who says that your friend Murphy is a total idiot 24/7, and is yet—how do you say?—good people."

Murphy rolled his eyes as his reputation preceded him.

"My question is…" Bang narrowed his eyes at Bolan.

"Cooper."

"Señor Cooper, what is it you wish of me?"

Bolan pushed over a banded stack of cash. The Guatemalan quetzl wasn't the strongest currency in the world, but the stack Bolan pushed over was thick and every note had three digits on it. "I'd like to pick your brain, if you don't mind."

Bang smiled again but his eyes were intent. "Toward what intention?"

"I intend to find out why the trail of *krokodil* leads to Guatemala. I intend to wipe out anyone involved with it, and if this is where it's being manufactured, I intend to burn the entire operation to the ground. If I have to destroy all Los Zeta and MS-13 operations in Guatemala to make that happen, so be it."

Bang pushed the stack of money back across the table. "Would you care for a piece of advice, Cooper?"

"Always."

"Convert that stack of money to dollars, and double it. You are going to need the full range of services that I can provide."

BANG TOOK A LONG DRAG on his cigar and slowly blew the smoke out. He held his Brazilian submachine gun with a great deal of familiarity. "I swear, for every five I kill, ten more arrive."

Kaino looked askance at the ex-Kaibil from the backseat. Bolan wouldn't have been surprised if the statement were accurate. Guatemala had survived a vicious, decades-long civil war only to become a war zone in the war on drugs, and it was outsiders who were trying to carve up Bang's homeland.

Guatemala was a very small country with a population that was still split along political, economic and ethnic lines. The Mexican Zetas and the Salvadoran MS-13s were the largest of the invading armies who were trying and succeeding to divide and conquer Guatemala, and if the Guatemalan people were crushed between them, then so be it. Neither one cared so long as the drugs, guns and human traffic flowed, and the return came back in oceans of money.

Bolan could understand Bang's cold anger. He had sacrificed flesh, blood, bone and the best years of his life to see the Guatemalan Peace Accords signed, only to see the paper they were signed on curl up in flames as the drug wars rolled over his country in an unstoppable wave.

"Keep it in your pants, Banger."

"That would be for the best. You do not want to see what I keep in my pants."

Bolan laughed out loud.

Bang glanced out the window and made a disgusted noise at their targets. "Animals."

Bolan sat low and rode shotgun in the ancient bottle-green Chevy Suburban Bang had acquired for them. The Executioner had fought MS-13 before. In the U.S. they were beginning to take a slightly lower street profile to avoid identification and prosecution, but here in Central America, MS-13 street soldiers reveled in their full glory. Three gangsters lounged openly on a stoop. All of them had green tattooing that covered their face like a mask and crawled back over their shaved heads. Tears represented the people they had killed. The number 13 and MS slogans patterned their faces like raccoon masks. Two wore wife beaters, and tattoos covered them from fingertips to shoulders. One gangster sat bare-chested and a tattoo of the Christ as a Mayan priest hung crucified from his collarbones to his belt buckle. A multitude of heavy gold rings, earrings and chains spoke of the wealth they had won as street soldiers. They chatted into their smartphones, leered at passing women and scowled at passing men. Bang's comment wasn't too far off. The MSers sat on the stoop like three wolves that weren't particularly hungry at the moment sitting in a sheepfold.

"So what are you gonna do?" Kaino asked. "Gonna give 'em the hat?"

"I like to save the hat for special occasions." Bolan took out two of Yuri's .45s, removed the safeties and lowered the hammers. "But I think someone needs to have a come to Jesus with those boys."

Kaino cracked his knuckles and made ready. "Here we go…"

Bang looked back and forth between the two men. "What is happening?"

"Coop's about to pull an El Hombre. I've seen this before, Sal. Wait for his go or mine."

"What is an El Hombre?"

"Watch and learn. It's something to see."

Bolan thrust both pistols in the front of his waistband and pulled his guayaberra over it. He slid out of the Suburban and strode across the street. He walked as though he didn't have a care in the world, and he had a friendly smile on his face. The MSers immediately began glowering ferociously at his approach. The bare-chested man with revisionist Christian inclinations tilted his head, exposed the gold and diamond chips of the "grill" covering his teeth and threw Mara Salavatrucha gang signs with both hands.

Bolan smiled brightly and like Superman coming out of a phone booth ripped his shirt open. Buttons popped off right down the placket exposing the two .45s just before the .45s filled his hands. He thrust the weapons forward and the Central American gangbangers screamed and cringed as they were about to get ventilated. The shirtless one put up his hands. "No! No! No—"

The soldier rammed his right-hand .45 directly between

the shaved and tattooed eyebrows, hitting the punk so hard
the .45's slide cycled and chambered a round. Shirtless One
dropped as if Bolan had shot him between the eyes. The MSer
to the Executioner's left produced a knife and lunged. Bolan
slashed his portside .45 across the top of the stabbing hand
and cracked a few metacarpals. He lashed out again with a
backfist strike, but the fist was filled with steel.

The muzzle of his .45 thudded in the gangbanger's eye
socket with a meaty pulp. The guy screamed and rolled down
the stairs clutching his face. The third man bounced up like a
jumping jack and ran up the stoop for the door. Bolan tossed
the .45 in his right hand to grab it by the slide and flung it
like a tomahawk into the fleeing MSer's kidney. The Salvadoran street criminal keened like a rabbit and dropped to
his knees in front of the door to the tenement. Bolan tossed
his remaining pistol into his right hand. He strode up to the
landing, scooped up his fallen weapon and went to work.
The gangster screamed and dropped as Bolan let him have it
across the kidneys again. Bolan gave him the slide of the .45
forehand and back across the face. The gangster's eyes rolled.

Bolan took a knee on the criminal's chest. The gangster
flapped his arms feebly in resistance. The soldier took out
his marker. The indelible black ink stood out against the pale
green tattooing rather well. Bolan gave the name El Hombre
accent marks like it was shining and added a small smiley
face between the eyebrows. He made eye contact with the
fallen-and-signatured street soldier and held it. He spoke a
single phrase in Spanish. It was something he had said before.

"Get out or I will kill you all."

Guatemala City Safehouse

"You are a complete psychopath, *señor*," Bang opined. "But
I like that." The team lounged in the little walled front yard

and strategized. Bolan lolled in his hammock and let it swing. "I never cut myself with a knife and sucked out a bullet."

Bang perked a very dry eyebrow. "What if I said I did not believe you?"

Bolan shrugged.

Savacool sighed. "So you pulled an El Hombre in downtown Guatamela City?"

"Pretty much."

Bang couldn't hide his admiration. "Cooper pistol whipped them, three MS-13 animals, into oblivion."

"Pistol whip, hell." Kaino cracked himself another beer. "It was goddamn Gun-Fu. Black belt division."

"Tell me, Sal," Bolan asked. "What do you think the repercussions will be?"

"Well, you have started a war."

"He did the same thing in Florida," Kaino said.

Donez called down from his sentry position on the balcony. "He did the same thing in Mexico!"

Bang lit a cigarette. "And now?"

"I figure I'll start a war with the Zetas down here while I'm at it."

"I got a question," Kaino announced.

"Shoot."

"We got any read on the Euro-trash hit squad?"

That was a sore point, and the balance of the battle might well depend on it. Bolan had his confidence in his ability and that of his team to give the cartel gangs a run for their money. Team Euro Assassin and who exactly they worked for was the wild card in the mix. "My people are on it, but the answer is no."

Kaino frowned. "What about the Russians?"

All eyes turned to Bolan as the Red Army Choir started singing the Russian national anthem out of his phone. "You are prescient, Master Sergeant."

Kaino leaned close to Savacool. "Is that good?"

Savacool gazed heavenward for strength. "Yes, Kaino. It's good."

Kaino grunted in satisfaction. "I'm prescient."

Bolan answered his phone. "Val."

"Belasko," the Russian major responded.

"I told you, it's Cooper now."

"I much prefer Belasko. Cooper is so American. Belasko is much more Russian sounding."

"Actually it's Basque."

"Belasko is a name I associate with pleasanter times," she responded.

"What can I do for you, Major?"

"Would you consider coming to the Russian embassy?"

"Hell, no. Anything else?"

Svarzkova spent a moment considering her response. "I am hungry."

"I know a great tamale place."

"I prefer meat, on bone," the Russian agent said.

Bolan covered the receiver and glanced at Bang. "You know a good steak house around here?"

"I know the best barbecue in town."

Bolan spoke into the receiver. "I know the best barbecue in town."

CHAPTER EIGHTEEN

Hacienda de los Sanchez Steak House

Russian Military Intelligence Agent Valentina Svarzkova tore into her rack of pork ribs *adobado* like a starving hyena. She stopped just short of snapping the bones between her teeth and tossing her head back like a crocodile to swallow. Svarzkova refused to notice her rice and beans and salad until every bone had been gnawed gleaming and clean. Bolan admired the carnage.

Bolan admired Svarzkova's appearance slightly less.

Actually he admired it a great deal—he just didn't like the math of it. Six-foot, porcelain-complected redheads wearing eye patches were something worth noticing on just about every country on Earth. In Guatemala they were about as rare as unicorns and of equal note. Svarzkova was in Red Witch mode and didn't seem to care what kind of attention it attracted.

Bolan ate steak churrasco and the two of them split a liter of beer. They sat at a corner table. In the opposite corner Kaino and Igor seemed to have reached some kind of détente and shoveled down barbecued goat and chicken respectively. The only point of contention appeared to be the heat. Guatemalans enjoyed their chilies well within a range that could be described as volcanic. Igor seemed to be trying to match Kaino spoon for spoon of hot sauce and by his brick-red complexion and the sweat pouring down his face, he was clearly losing the battle. Bolan had noted both Russians were carrying messenger bags but neither had produced a laptop.

"Igor's going to be on fire all night," Bolan opined.

Svarzkova's eye scanned like a hawk's toward a waiter carrying a tray of flans. "He was warned."

What neither Svarzkova nor Igor had been warned about was Bang. The Guatemalan contractor sat at the corner of the bar. It appeared he and the bartender knew each other and the two of them chatted up a storm. He was dressed in a business suit and his briefcase lay atop the bar beside him. The patio was once again nearly deserted. Most Guatemalans wouldn't consider eating dinner much earlier than nine in the evening. A few Spanish tapas types had started to straggle in for a drink and a snack, but Bolan, Svarzkova, Kaino and Igor were the only real diners.

"You like the food?" Bolan asked.

Svarzkova had prudently stayed with the flavorful rather than fiery. "This is first time I have operated in Central America. It has charms."

"I see you're not exactly in undercover mode."

Svarzkova began shoveling down rice and beans. "Whatever do you mean?"

"You pulled a Red Witch in Florida, didn't you?"

Svarzkova smirked around a wad of fried plantains.

Bolan sighed inwardly. He would contact Aaron Kurtzman to confirm it but he knew he was right. Agent Svarzkova had pulled an El Hombre. She had most likely done some heinous damage to the Zeta or MS-13 or both and let her Red Witch persona be known. Now she was in Guatemala City flaunting it to see who came gunning for her. It was a technique Bolan had been using on this entire mission. The only difference was that Svarzkova had demanded dinner without telling him the battle royal was on. "You should have told me."

"Zeta and Mara trash will only be aware of my presence, much less reacting."

"It's not just the Zeta and MS-13 I'm worried about."

Svarzkova's fork hovered over her plate.

Bolan heard the snarl of multiple, high-power motorcycle engines on the street outside and shook his head. "If you had told me, I would have brought bigger guns."

Three motorcycles screamed to 180-degree spinning stops on the street. The attackers rode two per bike, and the riders on the back faced the wrong way. The tail-gunners jumped off leveling revolving 40 mm grenade launchers. Bolan pulled a .45 from his waistband and put a double tap into each grenadier's chest. They jerked slightly and brought their weapons to bear. They were wearing armor.

Svarzkova and Igor ripped Uzis from their bags as all three discharged their weapons into the patio. Bolan fired again as three flash-bangs turned the outside eating area into a God-slap sonic Armageddon. One just about detonated at Bolan's feet. He felt the concussion rattle his bones, and his eyes and ears were instantly overwhelmed. The soldier closed his eyes, saw the afterimages of the closest bikers behind his eyelids and emptied his pistol. He kicked over the table by memory, grabbed Svarzkova by feel and pulled her behind cover. Bolan pulled his second pistol from behind his back. Svarzkova ripped her shoulder free of Bolan's grasp and rose. She was old school Russian army. They advanced firing on full-auto until their opponents were all dead or they were.

The Executioner opened his eyes to the winking, firefly aftereffects. His ears were deaf and his skull rang. Svarzkova and Igor stumbled forward, spraying the street as they advanced. A biker fired his 40 mm weapon and it went off like a howitzer. Bolan's ears and eyes were compromised, but he smelled the black powder that gave the weapon its concussion blast. Svarzkova staggered as she was hit by a black powder blast wave and painted by tear gas. The Russian stayed on her feet, ejected her spent magazine and slammed in a fresh one. The grenadier fired again. Bolan saw the ribbon-tailed baton round strike Svarzkova in the chest and slam her back across a tabletop.

The bad guys wanted prisoners.

A similar round hit Igor and rocked him back on his heels. It took two more to knock him down. Kaino fired a .45 in each hand. Bang had shown the good sense to jump over the bar. He rose with his Brazilian submachine gun hammering in his hands. Bolan's eyes stung with the CS gas, but he took his spare .45 in both hands and aimed. His target doubled and tripled into three leather-clad, helmet-wearing, grenade-launching attackers in his slewing vision. Bolan put his front sight on the helmet visor of the one in the middle and fired.

The visor shattered and the grenadier fell. The bike rider snapped his head back in consternation. Bolan drilled three rounds between the rider's shoulder blades, and the biker promptly dropped his bike and fell flat to the street. Echoes in the street boomed like a pirate ship firing a broadside as the two surviving grenadiers emptied their weapons. More flash-bangs detonated. A sledgehammer hit Bolan low in the ribs. Every ounce of air blasted out of his lungs and he stopped short of releasing his bladder. The soldier sat against his will, grimacing at the baton round lying between his feet and summoning strength. Bolan's limbs felt like lead, but he took the opportunity to reload both .45s.

Bang had scythed another grenadier's legs out from under him. Bolan rose to one knee, swung up both .45s and emptied them into the remaining grenadier. He dropped his left-hand gun and clawed for his last magazine. The two standing bikes tore away.

The soldier rose to his feet and lurched onto the street. The biker he had shot in the back was crawling away. Most people didn't crawl away with three .45 rounds in their back. That told Bolan that the man had a trauma plate in the front, but soft armor in the back. He lowered his aim and gave the assassin a double tap low on either side of the spine. The killer stiffened and twisted.

The Executioner looked back. Kaino was helping Svarzkova to her feet and weeping from the CS stench she gave off. Bang had reloaded and was covering Bolan, who could barely hear his own voice as he shouted, "Bang! We're taking this guy with us! Get the car! We're out of here!"

Mixco, Guatemala

"THIS SOUNDS MORE LIKE glaring incompetence than a problem."

Remo Haas was an old pro and he let that one slide. "As per our intelligence, the Red Witch was correctly identified in Guatemala City. Her behavior leads me to believe that she was making no attempt to conceal herself or her activities. A loose tail followed her to the Hacienda de los Sanchez Steak House where she met a man and had an early dinner."

"I gather her contact was added to the snatch list."

"Indeed, Director. I ordered the attack to proceed."

"And?"

"The woman and her companion fought back, and were joined by three others in the patio," Haas replied.

"We know the Witch had at least one fellow operative working with her. Did you succeed in identifying the others?"

"The tear gas made things somewhat difficult, but I believe I have a complete picture. Du Bois's helmet camera got a good sweep of the patio during the attack."

The director gazed at a grainy photograph of a Latin American individual spraying an obsolete submachine gun.

"The man with the submachine gun by the bar is Salcido Bang," Haas continued. "He was a Kaibil, and currently operates as a private contractor in Central and South America. I am sending you his file. What is of greatest concern is this."

The director stared at the picture of a big man firing a .45 in either hand. "Master Sergeant Gadiel Kaino."

"Which leads me to deduce that the Witch's contact can be only one man."

Another picture filled the director's screen. Tear gas obscured his face, but he was clearly snarling. His .45 seemed to be belching fire straight into the camera's lens. "El Hombre."

"We must assume they are now working together, if they were not before," Haas said.

"What are our losses?"

"Morris, Felicien, Timo and Zugg. We left one motorcycle in the street."

The director sighed. "How is Goran taking it?"

Goran and Zugg were cousins and thick as thieves. "He's howling for blood. I told you not to hire Serbs. They take everything personally."

"On the other hand, they are not bothered by the sight of blood."

Haas made a noise. "No, Director, they most certainly are not."

"Have you activated tracking?"

"I believed it prudent to contact you first. If the Red Witch and her accomplices are Russian as we suspect, I do not believe they would have the electronic warfare assets in Guatemala to detect our tracking devices, much less take countermeasures. El Hombre disturbs me. He acts like a complete maniac, and yet there is a method to his madness. Except by extraordinary luck, he could not have succeeded thus far without extensive intelligence assets."

"We are in agreement. Activate tracking immediately."

"As you direct," Haas said.

The director watched his screen. Individuals whom he used in a forward deployment capacity were implanted with radio frequency tracking devices. They were fairly simple, but powerful as such devices went. These devices also had a simple sensor that detected whether the individual they were implanted in had a heartbeat. Four windows popped up on the director's screen as a satellite above broadcast a specific signal into Guatemala City and the passively listening radio devices went active. Haas ticked off the names of the assault team. "Morris, no life signs. Felicien, no life signs. Timo, no life signs." The fourth window showed a tiny, regularly blipping line at its bottom edge. "Zugg, heartbeat elevated but steady."

"Give me a location."

The tracking windows turned into dots, one of which was blinking. The computer laid down a GPS grid of Guatemala City. Morris's, Felicien's and Timo's signals formed an unblinking triangular cluster. About eight centimeters away Zugg continued to blink. "Morris, Felicien and Timo are at Guatemalan State Police headquarters. Zugg is in the northern suburbs. What are your orders?"

"Gather your team."

"Prisoners?" Haas asked.

"Of secondary importance. Elimination of threat is of primary importance."

"And Zugg?"

"This is not a rescue mission."

"Understood. Assembling my team now."

Guatemala City Safehouse

BOLAN AWOKE. A SECOND later his watch vibrated in confirmation with his internal clock. Military Intelligence Agent Svarzkova lay naked and spooned against him beneath a Mayan-patterned homespun blanket. She had showered and taken off her red wig but she still smelled vaguely of CS gas. There had been no lovemaking or endearments. Bolan was an American, and when he had first met Svarzkova she had been a Soviet. They had been allies, adversaries, lovers and everything in between. All that mattered in this moment was that they were veterans, battered and bloodied, with a shared mission, who had shared enough experiences that lying together and feeling another body against them was enough. Bolan's face tightened as Svarzkova whimpered in her sleep.

She was a Russian female intelligence agent, and Bolan could only guess how hard the intervening years had been upon her.

Bolan gently disentangled himself. It was in vain. Svarzkova was a field agent and not waking her up was problematic. She turned a gray eye on Bolan. "I smell coffee."

"The master sergeant brews a pretty mean cup."

The Russian agent regarded Bolan frankly. "And? So?"

"Yeah?"

"How do I look?"

Svarzkova looked as if she'd gone ten rounds out of her weight class. Despite the shower, her skin had been violently peppered where unburned black powder had been blasted into her skin. The massive bruise on her chest had literally pushed one of her breasts slightly out of alignment. What hadn't been peppered was red where the CS irritant had been blasted into her at velocity. A blood vessel in her remaining eye was broken and made her resemble one of the living dead. Bolan smiled. "You look good enough to eat, bones and all."

"Americans are a charitable people."

Bolan cocked his head. "And me?"

"You look like you have been on mission with Valentina Svarzkova."

Bolan didn't doubt it. He winced as he rose and limped to the bathroom and considered the man in the mirror and his state of health. His ears still rang, but he could hear at a conversational level. He had no outward signs of a concussion. Bolan flexed his left arm. The *krokodil*-zombie bite on his biceps was pink around the bruising, tender to the touch and worrisome but so far he didn't have a fever. The bite bruises on his neck and leg had faded from black to blues and yellows. Savacool had assured him his floating ribs weren't cracked, but low on the left side the 40 mm baton round had left him blackened as though he had taken a body shot from a super heavyweight. His bruises and trauma from Florida and Mexico seemed to have shaken hands with Guatemala City and said welcome to the fun.

Bolan wrapped a towel around his waist and with effort stood straight and walked into the kitchen. Kaino looked up from brewing coffee and couldn't hide the look of concern that passed across his face. He gave up all pretense. "Coop, you look like shit."

Bolan didn't bother denying it. "How's our boy?"

Kaino grinned. "You got nothing on his blunt trauma. He's still peeing blood. You want me to hang him by his heels and heavy bag him?"

"I think I'll talk to him first. What's our disposition?"

"Cool's on watch on the roof. Donuts and Murph are packing some z's. One of the Russians is watching the street and one is out back watching the river. Don't ask me which is where, I still can't tell them apart."

Bolan took a seat at the dining table. Bang was still red-eyed but otherwise untouched from their steak house encounter. "What's up, Sal?"

"I am doing a little bit of research."

"Learn anything interesting?"

Bang twirled his mustache like a Spanish swordsman. "Well, first of all, given our current situation and what you have told me, it is interesting that there are no pharmaceutical production plants in Guatemala."

"Sort of leaves us at a dead end." Bolan raised an eyebrow. "So why are you smiling, Sal?"

"Oh, well, it is just that Helvetica Marine has a research facility up in the mountains."

Kaino frowned. "I thought that was a type font."

"It is." Bolan sighed. "It comes from the old Latin word Helvetian, which means Swiss."

"Check out the big brain on Coop." Kaino took a seat. "And what are the watchmakers up to in the Guatemalan highlands?"

Bolan smiled. "Yeah, Sal. What are the watchmakers up to up there?"

Bang snorted. "Their website is fascinating. It says they are researching Central American botanicals and studying ancient Mayan herbals to produce the medicines of the future."

Bolan swiftly texted Kurtzman to give him everything on Helvetica Marine.

"Ancient Mayan herbals my Puerto Rican ass," Kaino muttered. "You buying that, Coop?"

"Don't know." Bolan took his coffee and walked toward the bathroom. Bang and Kaino leaped up to follow. The prisoner lay naked and bound in the bathtub. "You speak English?" Bolan asked.

The shower curtain was festively decorated with trees dripping with monkeys and three-toed sloths. The prisoner picked a monkey at his eye level and stared at it fixedly.

"Well, he's not exactly pulling a surly Russian," Kaino opined.

"Maybe he just likes monkeys," Bang offered.

"You hungry?" Bolan tried.

The monkey on the shower curtain didn't blink. Neither did the prisoner.

"So, Helvetica Marine Pharmaceuticals is cooking *krokodil* up in the highlands and smuggling it into the United States."

Every muscle in the prisoner's body locked against his will.

"Oh, he speaks English!" Kaino cried happily.

Bang was pleased with himself. "There is your Euro-trash assassination squad connection."

The prisoner flushed and resumed staring ahead.

"You want me to pull a heavy-bag workout on him now?"

"No, he's given us enough for now."

Bolan went back to the dining room. Files on Helvetica Marine Pharmaceuticals were popping up on his tablet. The director of Helvetica Marine Guatemala was a Swiss national named Emil "Connie" Conz. Bolan took in the perfectly coiffed black hair and the perfectly white teeth in a grinning mouth.

Kaino glanced over Bolan's shoulder. "The guy should run for president."

Bolan glanced at another photo. A blond man built like a refrigerator smiled thinly into the camera. Kaino recognized the man's pedigree immediately. "Who's the muscle?"

"One Remo Haas. He's a sustainable growth adviser."

"Sustainable growth adviser. Yeah, right."

Most of Haas's records were Swiss military and redacted. One part made even Bolan raise an eyebrow. "He was a Papal Guardsman."

Like most Puerto Ricans, Kaino was a good Catholic. "That German-jawed son of a bitch guarded the Pope?"

"So it seems. It's like the French Foreign Legion. If you're a French military officer, taking a post in the Legion is a badge of honor. All Swiss do a stint in the military, but if you do your stint, and then do a bit guarding the Pope and come back into the military?"

"You walk with major wampum."

"Definitely, if I had to bet, looking at all the redacted stuff, he was Swiss Special Forces."

Kaino's face set into a mighty frown. "I thought the Swiss were neutral and didn't fight in wars."

"That's true, but they train like WWIII is tomorrow."

"So he's bad news."

Bolan tapped an app and a satellite focused on a spot nestled in the highlands that gleamed like a white tooth out of the rain forest. Bolan hit zoom on the facility. It didn't tell him much. The facility looked nowhere near large enough to have a major production plant on site. Then again, looks could be deceiving.

"So what's the plan?" Kaino asked.

"I'm going up that hill."

"What about me?"

"You have any jungle or clandestine warfare experience?" Bolan asked.

"Um, no."

"You have any desire to jump out of a moving aircraft?"

"Only if it's on fire."

"That means it going to be me, Sal and Murph. You, the rest of the team and the Russians are going to be the ground team, for extraction or backup depending."

Kaino rose. "I'll call everyone in."

Svarzkova came into the kitchen wearing shorts and one of Bolan's T-shirts. She poured herself a cup of coffee and took a seat. "What is situation?"

Another file popped up on Bolan's screen. "Trouble."

Svarzkova squinted her eye at the file. "Who is this?"

Bolan shrugged. "Mr. Tobias." The man looked be twenty years younger, three shades darker and twenty pounds of solid muscle heavier than Kaino. "Helvetica Marine Guatemala's cultural adviser."

Svarzkova made a derisive noise. "That man is a killer."

"Val, I gather you're operating in cooperation of the GRU liaison at the Russian embassy?"

A single eye as gray as the Baltic Sea narrowed at Bolan. "What is it you are asking?"

"I'm asking for silenced guns and night-vision equipment."

CHAPTER NINETEEN

Mother Russia had provided. Despite the fall of the Soviet Union, Russian embassies still stocked their armories as if the cold war was an ongoing concern and the balloon could go up at any minute.

Bolan and his team did a final equipment check. The Russian PP-93 submachine guns were small, slim, almost dainty, as if a Colt Government Model had gotten drunk and had bad sex with an Uzi. The PP-93s were barely bigger than a handgun. Bolan wasn't a big fan of the 9 mm Russian pistol ammunition they fired. The bullet was small, slow and notorious for not stopping hostiles. The weapon's sheet metal folding stock folded over the top and was almost an afterthought. The strangest thing about the little submachine gun was that it had no cocking handle. A round was chambered by moving a slide in front of the trigger like a tiny pump shotgun. It made for a very clean, compact, snag-free automatic weapon that could be concealed under most normal clothing, and between the low-power, subsonic ammo and nonreciprocating charging slide it was very, very quiet. The PP-93 was an almost ideal weapon for walking up and slaughtering two or three unsuspecting citizens at a bus stop in broad daylight.

Taken as a whole, the weapon screamed "KGB behaving badly."

After getting over her initial displeasure on being excluded from the insertion team, Svarzkova had gone to the embassy and produced the PP-93s along with screw-on suppressors, attached laser pointers and six spare magazines apiece. She had thrown in an assortment of hand grenades and three Russian survival knives. The OH night-vision goggles she had procured were bulky, first-generation Russian technology, but they were the best gear that Bolan was going to get in Guatemala at midnight on a Thursday and he was grateful.

Jack Grimaldi spoke across the cabin intercom. "ETA five minutes to drop zone!"

Bolan, Bang and Murphy checked one another's straps. Murphy didn't look happy in the dim red light inside the cabin. "You down for this jump, Murph?"

"It's been a while, and I never liked it, but yeah, I'm down!"

Bang lit a last cigarette before going out the door and didn't seem to have a care in the world. He was a man who had fought for over a decade, and every battle had been in his own country. For the ex-Kaibil jumping into the forests of Guatemala was old hat.

Grimaldi spoke again. "Coming into range, deploying infrared beacon."

The infrared beacon looked for all the world like a miniature version of a laser-guided bomb. Satellite imaging hadn't given them much choice for an LZ. Most of the real estate around Helvetica Marine was vertical and covered with trees. They had found a tiny clearing about five hundred yards down mountain from the facility, but it still had too many trees and boulders for comfort. Finding the clearing at night with substandard goggles would be hard enough and most of the open real estate in it consisted of a summer scummed-over and rock-strewed pond. It was shaping up to be a real bone-breaker of a landing.

The Stony Man pilto's infrared radar lit up the clearing as bright as day. He guided the beacon down with his joystick and made a victorious noise as it landed. "Beacon down!" He flipped a switch. "Beacon activated and beacon acquired! We are a go!"

The Russian goggles were good only for distinguishing individual objects out to about a hundred meters. The beacon along with their altimeters would give them vital moments to brake their chutes and adjust their descent.

"One minute!" Grimaldi called.

Satellite imaging had shown that a security guard or two sporadically walked the perimeter fence, but didn't seem to be on a high state of alert. They wore cargo pants, vests and ball caps, and Bolan's team was dressed to match just in case they decided to try a walk-in. Bolan pulled his night-vision goggles down over his eyes and powered them up. He viewed the cabin's interior through a grainy, black-and-white TV screen with no peripheral vision. Bolan's team goggled up and gave him the thumbs-up. He spoke into his throat mike. "Team ready!"

"We're over the LZ!" Grimaldi called. A green light winked overhead. The door slid open and cold wind blasted into the cabin. "Go! Go! Go!"

"Murph!" Bolan called. The mercenary braced himself in the door frame, took a deep breath and stepped out into space. "I hate this shit…."

"Bang!"

"See ya!" the man said, then followed Murphy into the night sky.

Bolan stepped into the doorframe and gave himself to gravity. "Team away!"

Grimaldi spoke in Bolan's earpiece. "Copy! *Dragonslayer* going to altitude and orbiting!" Bolan looked up to see the dark, thundering shape of the blacked-out helicopter hammering its way upward into the sky. He turned his attention to the dark mass of planet Earth as it rushed up toward him. The Helvetica Marine facility was an island of light in the ocean of black mountain range and forest. The infrared beacon was a bright, blinking pinprick farther down the mountain. Bolan's phone was attached to his left forearm like a giant wristwatch. He checked the altimeter app and watched the animated dial spin as he plummeted in freefall. Bolan hit his throat mike. "Murph?"

Murphy was clearly responding through clenched teeth. "I hate this shit!"

"Sal?"

"Ready," Bang replied.

"Deploy chutes!" Bolan ordered. Several seconds passed and Bolan's team replied.

"Deployed!" Murphy called.

"Deployed!" Bang called.

Bolan pulled his ripcord and a second later his straps cinched tight as the night sky filled his canopy. He took his toggles in hand and began his spiral descent toward the beacon. Murphy and Bang were little more than smudges in his NVGs. The goggles gave him no perspective on his relation to the LZ. Bolan frequently twisted his wrist and checked his altimeter. "Begin final approach."

Bang and Murphy came back in the affirmative.

Bolan stopped his spiral and began his bank toward the mountainside and the clearing. Murphy snarled across the link. "Oh, this shit sucks!"

The LZ resolved into clarity in Bolan's NVGs. The LZ was a goat screw. Bolan watched Murphy yank his toggles and pull his knees up into his chest to clear a boulder. Bolan winced as the guy promptly hit a tree. Bang came in close on Murphy's heels, but managed to weave between the tree and rock and hit the remnants of the pond. The ex-Kaibil's boots whipped behind him as he skidded in pond scum. He tangled in his lines and the canopy dragged him facedown another six feet through the mud.

Bolan momentarily diverted his attention away from his team as he made his approach. He picked a course between the two disaster landings and flared his chute, grimacing as he came in too fast and too hard. He hit the flat rock running between two stunted pines, but he was still going too fast and felt his feet being run out from underneath him. Bolan fell forward but was saved the face plant into flat rock as his canopy wrapped in a tree behind him. His harness cinched brutally tight as Bolan did a horizontal bungee jump without an ounce of slack. Gravity reasserted itself. The soldier tried to slap out, but every once of air smashed out of his body as he landed flat on his back and the unforgiving rock gave him the mother of all chiropractic adjustments.

For a moment silence reigned in the mountain clearing.

A part of Bolan wanted to give in and just lie stunned and blinking into the night sky, but battle instincts took over. "Sound off!" Bolan rasped. "Murph!"

Murphy groaned. "I fucking hate this jumping shit."

"Sal!"

Bang did a push-up out of the mud. "Here."

Bolan forced himself to his feet. Nothing felt broken. He limped over to Murphy, who sat straddling the tree. He was covered with blood from his upper lip to his sternum. He'd pushed his goggles onto his head and was doing a poor job of trying to push his nose back into place. His lip was split beneath it. Bolan pulled his first-aid kit out of his thigh pocket. Bolan taped Murphy's broken and grotesquely swollen olfactory organ back into place.

"Thanks…" Murphy mumbled.

"You think you have a concussion?"

Murphy hawked and spit out a wad of blood. He looked up and gave Bolan a grin. "Do I have time to have a concussion?"

"No."

"Then I don't." He stuck out his hand and Bolan hauled the soldier to his feet. Bang walked over covered with mud and slime up to his eyebrows. He gave off a scent reminiscent of next day bong water and rotting vegetation. "I suppose passing ourselves off as facility personnel is out of the question?"

Bolan clicked his throat mike. "*Dragonslayer,* this is Striker. Team is down."

"Did you have a happy landing?" the pilot inquired.

"It sucked."

Grimaldi's voice went serious. "Status?"

"Mission is go, *Dragonslayer.* Target status?"

"No movement, Striker."

"Copy that. Continue to orbit on station."

"Copy that, Striker."

Bolan checked his phone and was relieved to find it had survived his involuntary gymnastics. He tapped off the altimeter and hit two recently added apps, examining the facility off feeds from Grimaldi's infrared radar in *Dragonslayer* and the satellite Kurtzman had arranged. The pilot was right—nothing seemed out of the ordinary. Nothing was moving, but then again it was just shy of 3:00 a.m. Bolan took out his PP-93. He screwed on the suppressor, deployed the folding stock and chambered a round.

"Let's move." The team deployed its weapons and limped up the mountainside after him.

It was slow going.

The goggles were less than perfect at depth perception and terrain. Halfway up Bolan called a halt. He was more beat up than he wanted to admit, and he found himself gasping. Murphy was wheezing, spitting and occasionally bubbling. Bang was as fastidious as a cat in town, but once in the field being slimed appeared to be the least of his concerns. His biggest concern seemed to be the holdup. Bolan pushed up his goggles and let his eyes adjust to the moon and starlight.

Their provisions consisted of a single canteen each and two locally manufactured Guatemalan snack bars with jaguars and lightning bolts on the wrapper. Bolan took a few swallows of water and thumbed his throat mike. "Red Leader, report."

Svarzkova came back immediately. "Ground team in position ten kilometers from target, in blacked-out condition, Cooper." Svarzkova had loaded up the Bronco with heavier weapons from the Russian embassy and once up in the mountains had put on a pair of NVGs and driven Kaino, Savacool, Donez and Igor to a position on the road up to the facility they had found by satellite.

"Copy that."

"Ivan, what's your status?"

Ivan was holding down the safehouse and minding the prisoner. He deigned to speak in English. "Safehouse secure, Cooper. Prisoner secure."

"Copy that." Bolan nodded to his team. "Let's move. We lose the NVG for now. Bang, take point."

Bang's teeth flashed out of the mud he was wearing and he began moving up the hillside as though he knew it by memory. The ex-Kaibil was deep into his homeland mission mode. Bolan made a mental note never to be on the Guatemalan's bad side in a forest at night. Whether Bang was navigating with his nose or the Mayan gods of his forefathers were helping him Bolan couldn't be sure, but Bang took them up the mountain as if he were mounting a staircase.

Murphy wheezed from the rear. "Man…he's…good."

Bang held up his fist. The team stopped and they slowly began walking forward as the glow of the facility lights could be discerned through the trees. The three men by silent mutual consent dropped into moving crouches and shouldered their weapons. The facility was a sweeping arc of blinding white building with huge expanses of window. Murphy spit another gob of blood. "It's lovely, but I don't see a major drug manufacturing facility."

Bang smiled. "Would you like to know something about this mountain you are standing on?"

Bolan grasped it immediately. "It's a volcano."

"So it's gonna blow or something?"

Bang gave Bolan a pained look. The soldier sighed. "Caves, Murph."

"Aw, shit!" Murphy was childlike in his happiness. "Goddamn, genuine, underground Bond villain shit!"

"I believe there is a very good chance of it," Bang agreed.

"There are no roads on either side of the mountain. That means if they really are transporting major product their trucks come up out of the caves through the facility and take the only road down."

"Right past Red Leader and the ground team," Murphy enthused. "Gee, I wonder if there's a shipment tonight."

Bolan had to admit that was an interesting thought. Svarzkova had a general-purpose machine gun and two RPGs in the back of the truck. "Let's go in."

Murphy frowned at the fence. "How?"

"Always cut fence," Bolan stated. "Law of the west."

"I didn't bring any bolt cutters. Did you bring any bolt cutters?"

"I did," Bolan assured him. "So did you." He pulled out his Russian survival knife and stabbed it into the ground. He unhooked the throat from the sheath and butterflied the scabbard into two halves. The tip of the sheath opened to form the jaws of a wire cutter.

Bolan called up an app on his phone and extended his arm at the fence. The interior antenna array within the phone stared intently at the wire barrier. The security app told Bolan no current was currently running through the fence. He tapped another app and swept the perimeter with the camera's lens. It told him there were no active infrared or laser motion sensors.

The soldier cut the fence. In the jungles of the lowlands the night was a cacophony of creatures looking for love or marking territory. Up in the mountain fastness the only sound in the night was the wind and the team's breathing. Each snick of snips sounded like a gunshot in the quiet of the mountain night.

Bolan waited for stalag lights, sirens or Claymore mines to go off, but the perimeter stayed quiet. He cut a mouse hole big enough for a man to squirm through. He reassembled his knife and sheath, and passed through. The facility just about hung off the mountainside, so there was only about twenty feet between the fence and the side of the building, but Bolan had no desire to walk across the dead space. He snapped out the folding grapnel Svarzkova had given him and uncoiled his rope. Swinging the grapnel in a short, hard circle, he cast it at a ventilator housing. The hook caught on something solid on the first toss. Bolan climbed the fence until he reached the razor wire and made the rope fast to the support post.

Bolan made a hanging rope traverse to the rooftop of the building. His boots crunched on the gravel. Bolan waited for Armageddon, but it didn't come. He drew his PP-93 and gestured his team to come ahead. Murphy did a Spider-Man routine and Bang brought up the rear. Bolan walked over the helicopter pad and the concrete pylon of the roof access door.

He was very sure breaking through that door would have all sorts of consequences, but Bolan didn't want to break through the door—all he wanted to do was to break through its security. He had Akira Tokaido and the Farm's entire cybernetic team on his side. Bolan pulled a key card from his web gear. He tapped an app on his phone. His phone communicated with the chip in the card. His phone formed a bridge between the card and Stony Man Farm. Bolan swiped the card but left it inside the electronic lock.

A row of blinking red lines resembling a music studio's equalizer pulsed and rapidly turned green as back in Virginia Tokaido and his electronic warfare suite began breaking code. The electronic lock on a roof access door was no match for Stony Man Farm's might. The lights turned green and Bolan finished his swipe.

The roof access door opened beneath his hand.

Bolan had gone down a lot of staircases in his life. This one was thoroughly modern, brightly lit and painted a soothing light green. Soothing, ambient, electronica music played over hidden speakers. Emergency directions were printed on the walls in English, Spanish, French and German. Bolan gazed long and hard at a security camera on a motorized stalk that wasn't currently looking at the landing. Bang shouldered his weapon and lifted his chin at Bolan.

The soldier shook his head.

Bolan took out his hat. It pained him to possibly leave it behind, but the blunt impact mass in the brim gave it calculable end weight. He aimed and threw. His hat spun through the air and pulled a ringer around the camera. The impact mass settled the brim and bill hanging down over the lens.

Murphy grinned. "Dude, you are so going to win me a prize at the fair."

Bolan noted that under the fluorescent lighting Murphy wasn't looking too good. The soldier moved swiftly down the stairs. Shooting the camera might well have set off an alarm, but covered by a hat it required an operator to notice that one of his screens had gone dark. If his machine told him he still had current and feed, the investigation might take some time as he checked his connections and leads. Bolan spoke low as they came to the first landing. "This is the top floor. Ninety-nine times out of a hundred it's the top executive level."

His men nodded and arranged themselves in entry mode. Bolan ran his card and tapped his app. The Farm broke the electronic lock in half the time. He was the least covered in mud or blood, so Bolan held his weapon low along his leg and walked in as though he belonged. He wasn't surprised to find himself in a luxuriously appointed but empty hallway. Murals of Mayan art covered the walls. Evenly spaced, lighted niches in the walls held tasteful pieces of native sculpture. Incredibly expensive doors of lustrously polished native hardwoods lined both walls leading to offices and matched the gleaming hardwood floor.

Murphy hawked in preparation to spit.

Bolan raised an eyebrow.

The man spit a wad of blood into a pocket of his vest and peered up and down the hall. Blood dripped down his chin as he grinned. "Swanky."

Bolan gave him a hard look. The ex-Delta operative had a broken nose and smashed mouth, but they had landed an hour ago and he was still bleeding. It was probably due to the exertion, but despite Murphy's salty attitude Bolan didn't like the man's color at all. "Murph, are you all right?"

"Do I have time not to be?" Murphy asked.

Bolan shook his head. "No."

"There you have it."

The soldier moved down the hall to the head office. The door had a simple brass knob with no apparent lock. He gave the peephole a hard look. There appeared to be multiple lenses around the main fish-eye observation lens.

"What?" Bang asked.

Bolan shook his head. "Retinal scanner."

A vaguely Germanic voice suddenly cut in over the ambient, new-age electronica music. "El Hombre, Sergeant Bang and, how shall I say? Unidentified American."

"That'd be me," Murphy affirmed.

"Drop your weapons. Drop to your knees. Put your hands behind your heads."

"How in the hell?" Murphy asked.

Bolan already knew but he tapped Svarzkova's icon. "Red Leader, sitrep on home base." Bolan heard Svarzkova speak into another line in Russian, and in mounting consternation. She suddenly broke into English. "Cooper! Ivan is not responding! Safehouse must be considered compromised!"

The voice spoke like God on High across the hidden

speakers. "Your safehouse has been compromised. As you can see, you have been expected. GRU Agent Ivan Roltov has succumbed to interrogation. I recommend your immediate surrender."

Svarzkova snarled across the phone. "Ground team assaulting!"

"Negative, Red Leader," Bolan ordered. "Escape and evade."

Bolan heard Kaino start to shout something in the background and Igor roar before Svarzkova cut the line. The door at the opposite end of the hall opened a crack. Both Bang and Murphy put bursts into it but the diminutive subsonic bullets wouldn't penetrate the thick native iron wood. The door opened just wide enough for three metal canisters to bounce onto the carpeting. The grenades didn't explode. Nothing visible came out of them, but they were hissing.

The voice spoke again. "When next we speak you will be under extreme duress." The man's voice took on a sadistic sneer. "Any last words while you still have your free will?"

Bolan took a flattened quarter roll of military tactical duct tape out of the thigh pocket of his pants. Svarzkova had given each team member a small assortment of hand grenades. Bolan ripped tape with his teeth. "Yeah." He stuck a Russian antiarmor grenade shaped-charge shooting end right above the doorknob and taped it in place. "I hope to hell you're behind that door, Connie."

Bolan pulled the pin and stepped back. "Fire in the hole!"

The grenade detonated. The tape kept it in place for the vital second to fire its charge of molten metal and superheated gas through the door, but it was nowhere near enough to stop the grenade from launching down the hall like a rocket-propelled beer can on a stick. Bolan squinted against the searing heat and kicked the door. He sprayed his PP-93 ahead of him like a scythe in the smoke-filled office. The green beam of the laser cut through the smoke as Bolan shouldered his weapon. He touched off a burst just as Helvetica Marine Guatemala's director Emile Conz sprawled into the office safe room and the door pneumatically hissed shut. Bolan's last few bullets splintered wood paneling and sparked against the heavy steel beneath. Bolan's team invaded behind him. His lungs constricted against the smoke. The office consisted of a single leather chair, a small arc of glass desk in front of it and one wall that was all high-definition screen, and another wall that was one huge panoramic window.

Murphy sucked in smoke, put his hands on his knees and coughed, spit blood and kept coughing and spitting. Bang leaned in close. "Murph is fucked up."

"I know."

Murphy deliberately spit blood on the lens above the safe room door. "I say we nuke his ass."

Bolan suspected a safe room door could probably take a direct hit from an RPG. He pointed at another door in the opposite wall. It was gleaming, featureless stainless steel, but it was inset and the wall beside it had a keypad. "That's an elevator."

"Elevator to hell!" Murphy bellowed. "Going down!"

"Finally he talks sense," Bang commented.

Bolan held out his hand. "Give me your antitank."

Bang slapped the weapon into Bolan's hand. The soldier took a long hard look at the door, taped the grenade over the keypad and pulled the pin. "Fire in the hole."

It was a gamble. Blowing a smoking hole the size of a tea saucer in an elevator door wasn't a guarantor of access. Instead Bolan sent molten metal and fire in an obliterating wave through the electronics. The grenade body and handle bottle-rocketed away across the office. He was rewarded as the computer that regulated the elevator decided it had experienced a total failure on the top floor and opened all doors on all levels so that any humans trapped within could escape.

By the same token alarms started going off. The elevator's computer detected that it was still operational, and the car started downward to take any occupants to the safety of the ground floor, and that was exactly what Bolan had hoped for. "Murph, antitank."

Murphy put the last armor-piercing munition in Bolan's hand. The soldier leaned in, taped the antiarmor weapon to the elevator's main cable and pulled the pin. The grenade detonated, and the wrist-thick steel cable snapped.

The elevator car dropped free.

Helvetica Marine was a three-story building. Bolan had bet its executive elevator depended on friction brakes. If there really was an underground complex below, Bolan was wagering the elevator to the lower levels had been a clandestine add-on.

The soldier was rewarded by the sound of screaming metal and failing materials as the elevator car plunged through the facility's adulterated bottom floor and into the cavern beneath. He pulled on gloves and stepped out into the elevator shaft to grab the greased reciprocating cable. "Go!"

Bolan took the ride down, followed by his team. He felt the palms of his gloves heat up with the friction, but it was a short ride and he used his boots as brakes. When his boots hit the roof of the elevator car, he stepped aside and yanked open the emergency access hatch. Murphy hit the car as Bolan pulled a fragmentation grenade and pulled the pin. Bang hit the roof. The grenade's cotter pin pinged away, and all three men crouched as Bolan dropped the grenade down into the open car. The frag cracked and some of the shrapnel shot up the elevator shaft.

The Executioner dropped into the shrapnel-scored and smoke-smeared elevator car. People outside it were screaming. Several bullets shot into the elevator car and richocheted around.

"Frag!" Bolan shouted, catching the grenade Bang

dropped him. He pulled the pin and hurled the bomb out the elevator door. More screaming and more bullets met the grenade's detonation in return. Murphy dropped down and Bang followed. "Cover me!"

Bolan left the elevator car.

He was in a vast open cave. Millennia ago lava had formed a huge molten bubble and created a subterranean dome. The hands of man had leveled the floor, strung lights and turned the cave into a pharmaceutical manufacturing plant. Gleaming stainless-steel vats, pressure chambers and chemical tanks filled much of the space. A loading area lay off to the side, and a one-lane road circled the perimeter so that a truck could roll in from the surface, load up and roll back out. A Kenworth semi was currently parked by stacks of empty pallets along the cave wall on Bolan's right. A gunman fired off a burst and dropped behind a pallet heavily laden with something. The pallet happened to be next to a chemical tank. Bolan couldn't make out what it contained, but it had multiple universal warning labels that it was flammable and toxic. He fired off a burst into the side of the tank, and the hidden gunman screamed as noxious, amber-colored fluid poured forth. The gunman spasmed upward beneath the toxic shower, and the Executioner put a burst in his chest to put him down.

Bolan took in the two dead men his grenades had reaped. He saw some people in lab coats cowering in the back. "We have to get out of here."

Murphy swept the vaulted expanse with his weapon. "Where the hell is everyone?"

"They're upstairs. They thought they had us boxed in the hallway. They never expected us to get down this far."

"So we blow it up?"

"We do that and we go up with it. The bad guys'll be down here any second, and there'll be nothing to stop Conz and the boys from escaping and setting up shop again. If we burn out this cave, they'll just clean it and start again fresh."

"So we run like cowards."

"We beat it for the bushes like bunnies."

Bang looked around. Across the cave an industrial freight elevator door hadn't opened yet. Euro-trash assassins were most likely going to start popping down Conz's private shaft any second. "How?"

Bolan pointed at a loading bay door off to the side. "That door opens due west. It opens on the mountain side."

"For what?" Murphy asked. "There's no road on the western side of the mountain."

"I have no idea, but that's our only way out."

Bolan and his team sprinted for the door. Murphy grabbed the hanging switch box and hit the green button. Nothing happened. "We're in lockdown!"

The freight elevator pinged as the car above began descending.

"Shit!" Murphy swore.

"We're about to get hammered, Coop!" Bang nodded at the chemical tanks. "Last act of defiance?"

"No, we go out the door."

Murphy threw up his hands. "Door's not responding, Coop! We're out of antiarmor grenades, and these Russian squirt guns the Cyclops gave us won't cut us a way out!"

Bolan jerked his head back to the loading circle. "We take the truck."

Bang stared at the heavy clamshell doors behind them that finished the circuit and led to the surface. "Cooper, my first job in the military was driving a truck. This facility is in lockdown. If we ram those doors, that truck will fold like an accordion."

"No." Bolan lifted his chin at the anomalous loading bay door in front of them. "We go that way."

It was the first time Bolan had ever seen Bang dumbstruck. "Cooper, that door opens due west. Like Murphy said, there is no road on the west side of the mountain."

The elevator pinged again. Bolan slapped a fresh magazine into his weapon. The doors opened and armored men with assault rifles and shotguns began sweeping out across the manufacturing floor.

"Sal, we either stay here and pull a Butch and Sundance, or we get in that truck and go see what is behind door number one."

Murphy grinned. "Fuckin' ay, bubba! I say door number one!"

Bolan broke for the truck, immediately attracting bullets and buckshot. He formed the point of a three-man wedge, the team firing as it advanced. Bolan reached the truck and so did Murphy. Bang jerked as something plucked at his arm and blood flew. He skidded into cover beside the truck as Bolan clambered in.

The keys were in the ignition.

The Kenworth semi roared as Bolan started the engine and ground gears. Bullets struck the truck like hail. Murphy and Bang leaped in and lunged into the sleeper cab in the back. There wasn't time to turn around. Bolan slid down in the seat so that he could barely see his side mirror and rammed the truck into Reverse. Literally a dozen men walked forward pouring fire into the truck. The soldier twisted the wheel and the semi went through the bay door rear end first. In exactly one heartbeat the truck went airborne. It was five in the morning and the light on the mountainside was nothing more than a purple smudge. There was nothing to do but hold the wheel straight.

The truck hit the mountainside and miraculously didn't roll or hit any immovable objects. Bolan got the fleeting impression they were in some kind of chute that was mostly a nearly vertical river. Water spewed up on all sides. Metal screamed as the truck ripped against both sides of the chute.

The narrow confines wouldn't allow the truck to jackknife. The chute was a natural part of the landscape rather than man-made, and the truck lurched as if it had taken a body blow as it hit a tree overgrowing the chute.

The vehicle made a noise like a wolverine being killed in the snow amplified a thousand times as it finally hit something. The truck stood for one perilous second, and then the cab did a vertical jackknife that was stopped by a cluster of boulders.

Bolan was mildly surprised to find himself alive and unhurt. The truck ticked and popped and wheezed where it was wedged into place. Bolan cut the engine. "Sound off!"

Bang sounded off. "I'm okay!"

"Fuck…" Murphy wheezed.

Bolan looked at the sky through the cracked windshield. "We have about half an hour until sunrise. We have to move."

CHAPTER TWENTY

Haas was appalled. He glanced at the shattered loading platform. There was no road down the mountain, but the ledge outside the door had formed a natural, volcanic rock platform onto which a helicopter could lower a clandestine pallet. In spring the snowmelt formed a cataract that for aeons had carved a sixty-degree ramp halfway down the mountain. The American commando had apparently driven a semi through the camouflaged door, driven off the cargo platform, the ledge and gone all the way down the cataract. Backward.

Haas had been an infantryman and airborne in the Swiss Army. He had guarded the Pope, and come back to become Swiss special forces. Haas had the best training the Swiss military could provide. He had never fought a battle, but he had killed more men than he had fingers and toes. Haas didn't consider himself a soldier. He was an assassin. He had been examining his opponent's every move since Florida. He knew without doubt that his opponent was a seasoned soldier, but like Haas, that was just part of his résumé. Haas had been a soldier. So had his opponent.

Haas was a Swiss assassin, and he had just locked horns with an American warrior.

He shook his head. "I am appalled."

Emile Conz spit over the edge.

Haas wasn't particularly pleased with his boss. During the attack, Conz had gone from gloating over the intercom to cowering in his safe room. Nevertheless the chain of command was what it was. "What are your orders?"

"Kill them."

Haas grunted and peered past the broken girders of the platform into the darkened tunnel of trees below. "There are several parts of the chute that will require ropes to descend. If the commando and his team still live, the chute will be a killing box for my men. We need to bring in helicopters and trackers. I say let them reach the valley floor and let them run."

Conz ran a hand through his perfect hair. "I defer to you in these matters, Remo. All I will say is that the old men in Bern will want to see heads."

Haas found that profoundly reasonable. "The commando has only a two-man team. One of them was wounded. Satellite imaging shows his ground support team fled down the mountain back to the capital. We still have one of the Russian agents. They will not dare go back to their safehouse, and we have both the Russian and American embassies under surveillance. I believe the American commando is bereft of any immediately available assets. They will reach the valley floor by dawn. I will have marshaled our forces. It will be our killing field."

Emile Conz smiled and sipped coffee. "I defer to you in all these matters, but I require two things."

"Yes, sir?"

"I want information, and then heads."

"WELL?" MURPHY GASPED. "That worked out well. I think we really got their attention."

Bolan stared back up the mountain. Murphy was right about one thing. They had Helvetica Marine's undivided attention. They would be coming and coming hard. The soldier was mildly surprised they hadn't come already. That told him the enemy was taking the time to marshal its forces and do it right. They were probably marshaling some local assets who knew the forest, as well. Fortunately, Bolan had brought along a local asset of his own.

Bolan turned. "Sal, how's your—"

"Shit!" Murphy's jaw dropped. "He's really gonna do it!"

Bang had stripped to his T-shirt. He had torn off the sleeve and held his Russian survival knife while he frowned at the buckshot round he had taken in the shoulder. There was an entrance wound in the meat of his anterior deltoid, but no exit wound in back. Bang took three cigarettes out of the pack in his pocket, bit off the filters and popped the cigarettes in his mouth.

Bang swiftly cut an *X* over his wound while he chewed the cigarettes. Blood spurted as the ex-Kaibil teased out two .36-caliber lead balls with the point of the knife. He spat the small quid of tobacco into his hand and began packing the wound with his thumb.

Murphy was awestruck. "I think I'm gonna puke."

Bolan knew from experience the Guatemalan Kaibils were hardcore, but this was the real deal.

Bang took his own flattened quarter roll of military tactical duct tape out of the thigh pocket of his pants. He tore off a 3x5 inch olive drab rectangle with his teeth and slapped it over the wound and smoothed it down. Bang wiped his knife on his leg with a slightly shaky grin and sheathed it. "Good as new!"

"Fuckin' hardcore, man," Murphy declared, then leaned over and vomited.

"Coop—" Murphy clutched his head as if he had a migraine as the dry heaves finished "—I think I have a concussion."

Bolan nodded. "Yeah." There was nothing to be done. If Murphy had bleeding in the brain, there was an excellent chance that exertion would induce a stroke or kill him. If he didn't, there was a good chance that exertion would start the bruising in his brain to bleed and start the process. The fact was that in the next twenty-four hours Murphy was going to live or he was going to die. The next few hours would likely tell the tale. "Quit your gold-bricking, Murph. Gear up. We have to move."

"You're a real dick, Coop."

"Don't make me order Bang to cut an X and relieve the pressure in your brain."

Murphy stood tall. "Fine, let's walk."

"Try a little water." Murphy slurped some water from the canteen in his vest, then drank thirstily.

Bolan looked at the man as he drank. "You're holding it down?"

"Yeah."

"Think you can hold down food?"

Murphy gave Bolan a queasy look. "Dunno."

Bolan pulled the wallet-size medical kit he had brought with him and zipped it open. It made him leery but the fact was there was no other choice than to survive the next few hours. He broke out two pills in a foil-and-plastic blister pack. "Think you can hold these down?"

"Dunno, what are they?"

Bolan smiled and thought of Calvin James. "My favorite Navy SEAL's personal painkiller and stimulant concoction. For the injured who have to move."

Murphy grinned at the pills. "You got military-grade speedballs?"

"Something like that."

"Ooh! Gimme!" Murphy wolfed the pills and gulped water.

Bolan started walking again. The sun rose over the valley. Monkeys began calling and shrieking in the morning chorus. The soldier nodded to himself. It was going to come soon. He hadn't heard from Svarzkova, so he assumed she had made it out. If they had been engaged she would have messaged. Unless of course an RPG had wiped out the entire team. The enemy had Ivan, and sad to say they had the communications gear Bolan had given him. He didn't think they could do anything with it, but several times in his life Bolan had learned to never underestimate Swiss operatives.

However, like an idiot, Conz had admitted he didn't know who Murphy was. "Murph, give me your phone."

Murphy was already standing taller. "It's yours."

Bolan called a secure number and waited while the phone was thoroughly scanned, its signal digested and routed through cutouts. The phone was picked up on the fifth ring.

"Kurtzman."

"Bear, it's getting pretty bad out here."

"Copy that, Striker. Sitrep?"

"We got hammered. We were expected. Murph got his bell rung and Sal is wounded but not bad. Safehouse is compromised. Ivan is POW or dead. Do you have status on Red Leader?"

"Red Leader and ground team got off the mountain, but they're outdoors. Be warned, once they started moving they received mortar fire. My analysis tells me the enemy didn't know they were there until they moved. I believe the enemy wanted any rescue to be lured in and then hit with heavy weapons at the facility gates."

"Where is Red Leader and ground team now?"

"Parked in the woods and waiting for orders."

A part of Bolan wanted to have Grimaldi fly in, load up with Svarzkova's team and ride in like the cavalry. "Where is Jack?"

"He stood on station as long as he could and then returned to the airport. He has refueled and is awaiting instructions." Kurtzman read Bolan's mind. "You want extraction?"

"It's daylight and Jack'll be a sitting duck trying to winch us up one at a time."

"I don't think that'll bother him too much."

Grimaldi was eternally cheerful. To outside observers it

might fall under the auspices of downright cocky. "You see any kind of decent LZ on satellite?"

"Yeah, but there's something of a walk. Striker, you really have to get out of that valley. It's a killing box."

"Vector me toward the best LZ. See if you can get Red Leader close to it. And how is Akira doing? Tell him I wish I had given him more."

"We'll have to wait and see what kind of window he has. I don't trust the Swiss much for leaving loose ends, electronically or otherwise," Kurtzman replied.

"Me, neither, Bear."

Kurtzman brightened. "Oh, there is some good news."

"I'm about ready for some."

"Your package will arrive within the next forty-eight hours."

Bolan allowed himself a small modicum of joy. "Good to know."

"Mexico to Guatemala is pretty much a straight shot. Morti was very accommodating."

"Morti's a good man."

Bolan could hear Kurtzman's brow furrowing. "Mortimer Morelos is a scumbag, illicit arms dealer of the first order."

"He's lovably loathsome in his own little way."

Kurtzman snorted.

"Useful, too. Fantastic taste in firearms," Bolan continued. "Genuine epicurean. A gun gourmet and a gourmand."

The computer wizard laughed. "I will give him that."

"Is the package stuffed?"

"To the gills. By all accounts your purchases have been lovingly taken care of and will be delivered like new."

"Anything else of note?" Bolan asked.

"Morti wants more money."

"Shocker." Bolan glanced back up the mountain. "If I live to see the coast, he'll get it."

"You know, I think that might just be enough. Our boy Morti really seems to have the love on for you."

Bolan smiled. Morelos was in the trades. He was in the illicit arms trade, but people in the trades lived for a customer who knew his or her trade, treated it with respect, talked the talk, walked the walk and, most importantly had money or knew how to get it.

"Give Morti my warm regards."

"Will do. What are you going to do?"

"Gonna walk for a bit. Heading west. I hate to say it, but I want to see what they've got before Jack steps in it. I have a real bad feeling they're lying in wait for my extraction to come sailing in."

"Copy that. Bear out."

Bolan tapped off. "How you doing, Sal?"

Bang rolled his wounded shoulder gingerly. "I can march. I can fight."

"It's going to be hot today. We're going to need water."

Bang looked around on the forest floor for a moment and dropped to one knee. He pointed at some smudged tracks. "It's dawn. The tapirs will be heading for water. It's that way."

"You're a good man, Sal. Take point."

Bang glanced at the buckshot and bodily fluids littering the ground. "And the mess?"

"Leave it. In fact…" Bolan took out one of his few remaining grenades, unscrewed the butt of his Russian survival knife and took out the roll of fishing line. "Let's see how good these guys are."

"I would suggest ten meters down the tapir trail."

"Great minds think alike."

Bolan turned. "Murph?"

Murphy spoke happily. "Sloth!"

Bolan looked to see a three-toed sloth peering at his team myopically from a branch above.

Bang frowned. "I never cared for them."

"Jesus, Sal, it's like a product of the Children's Television Workshop. What's not to like? Are they supposed to be bad luck or something?"

"No, it is just that you would think that an animal that moved so slowly and so little would be tender, but I find them stringy and rather tasteless."

"Why in the blue hell would you eat a sloth?"

Bang gazed at Murphy frankly. "Because I was hungry." He walked on and continued to muse. "Perhaps if you fed one tamales for six months, and then put it in a tamale, you might have something worth—" Bang's head snapped up. "Rotors."

Bolan had caught the sound a heartbeat ahead of the Kaibil. "I make it two."

Bang nodded. "Yes."

"They'll be watching the water sources. We need to get to the one ahead first. Murph, can you run?"

"Do I have a choice?"

"No. Sal, set the trap and catch up."

Helvetica Marine, security suite

Haas scowled at the file that some well-greased contacts in the Guatemala National Army had sent him. "This one, Bang, he is bad news. A guerrilla fighter, he will be in his element."

Conz lit a cigarette and carelessly blew smoke. "So kill him."

"I have sent Mr. Tobias to do this very thing."

Conz nodded. "And?"

"What are the damages to the facility?"

Haas flipped through another file. "Minor, in the scheme of things. Only one tank of chemicals was shot. Providentially it did not catch fire. We have more in storage. No product was lost. None of the lab staff was injured or killed. The door will be replaced within forty-eight hours, and the ramp is repairable with what we have on hand. Production will not be interrupted."

"Excellent."

"We lost five security men, and two are wounded."

Conz waved his cigarette like it meant nothing.

Haas kept his opinion of Conz off his face but enjoyed the next bit of news. "Your executive office suffered extensive smoke and blast damage. The carpets are ruined. You will be requiring a new personal elevator."

Conz stabbed out his cigarette in a pique.

"What about the meeting?" Haas asked.

"What about it?"

"Given the situation, perhaps a postponement would be prudent."

"Given what situation?" Conz queried.

"That our operation has been attacked in the United States, Mexico and now here at our base of operations in Guatemala."

"And should our Mr. Tobias do the job I pay him for, I believe that should take care of our little problem very nicely. Speaking of which, what has the Russian given up?"

Haas allowed himself a small smile. "Everything. Mr. Tobias was very thorough. He was the number-two man on a Russian GRU team. They came into contact with the American commando. Apparently the leader of his team has had dealings with the American before. She came down to Guatemala with a two-man reconnaissance—"

"She?" Conz perked up.

"Yes. You will find that most intelligence agencies keep a few beautiful women around. This one is also a decorated sniper and has risen to the rank of major."

Conz's mood improved dramatically. "I want her alive if possible."

Haas was well aware of Conz's "playroom" activities. He had wired them for sound and soundproofed them. "Yes, that would be useful. The commando's team air-dropped by helicopter on the eastern slope. I am having some people looking for a foreign helicopter now."

"What is the status of the Russian now?"

Haas snorted. "His status is that he has been thoroughly interrogated by Mr. Tobias. Do you wish him disposed of?"

Conz gave a smile that Haas recognized. "Not just yet."

"What are your orders?"

Conz ignored the question and made a call. Tobias's deep voice answered on the second ring. "Herr Conz?"

"What is your status?"

"I believe I will have them in minutes."

"Very good." Conz stretched out his arms and sighed. "It is dawn. Let us go take coffee and cognac on the terrace and watch the sun rise as Mr. Tobias falls upon the American."

Haas took a cigar out of his humidor. There were worse ways to spend the morning.

CHAPTER TWENTY-ONE

Mr. Tobias caught sight of a pulse of pale yellow fire beneath the forest canopy below. He called to the chopper pilot over the intercom. "Hard around and orbit!" Gray smoke drifted up through the trees. Tobias was a huge man. Rastafarian-worthy black braids had long ago replaced the high and tight haircut he had worn as a United States Army Ranger. Between his chiseled features and his mass of hair he could accurately be described as lionlike. He had done his last stint in Guatemala as a military adviser and had never left. Tobias hadn't exactly gone native, but he had seen the wisdom of being a very big fish in a small pond. He had predicted years earlier that drugs, guns and money rolled through Guatemala in bigger waves every year. He spoke into the com link in Mayan. It was a language he had spent years cultivating. "Mulac? What was that?"

Mulac the tracker came back immediately. "One of your foreigners. He grew impulsive."

"Which one?"

"Goran?"

"Fucking Serbs..." They all wanted payback for their buddy. "The site was a trap?"

"The blood was real, the vomit was real, two of your bullets found flesh. The *Yanqui* chose to find the bright side of the situation."

Tobias smiled. Mayans had a flair for poetry. "And now?"

"There are three of them, as reported, and they have followed a tapir path toward water. One moves unsteadily but without aid. By the bile and the blood, I believe they are no more than fifteen to twenty minutes ahead of us."

"Excellent, Señor Conz would like this finished by nightfall."

Mulac made a noise that expressed what he thought of Señor Conz. "I have relatives whose dead spirits cry for nothing more than the head of Salcido Bang, but to his credit, that is a bigger job than Señor Conz might imagine."

Tobias nodded. He knew all about Salcido Bang. He had been Kaibil, Mulac had been a revolutionary. As far as Mulac was concerned, Bang was a hated Spaniard of the upper class, a weapon of the capitalist oppressors. To Bang, men like Mulac were little more than savages. They represented the absolute opposite poles of Guatemalan society.

Tobias suspected that one of the two Guatemalan men wouldn't live to see sunset. He tapped his link and barked in English. "Otto! Keep your team in line!"

Ottoman "Otto" Ambuhl snarled. "Fucking Serbs!"

"Mulac says the enemy is heading for water. They have probably reached it already. I am going to locate it and drop a fire team ahead of them."

"Copy that."

"WE NEED RIFLES," Bang opined. The ex-Kaibil cut Bolan a fresh slice of tapir liver. The soldier speared it and ate it off his knife. Murphy finished filling their canteens from the little stream.

Bolan listened as the rotors thundered overhead. "Rifles are coming." The rotors continued on a little way but didn't die out into echoes over the valley like the last pass.

Bang wiped his knife and sheathed it. "He's hovering."

"He's inserting." Bolan finished his meal in a single swallow and rose. "Murph! Keep up!" The soldier splashed across the creek and charged for the LZ. He could hear Bang wheezing behind him. After all the beatings Bolan had taken on this mission, if he was the one in the best shape, the team was in trouble. He caught sight of the enemy through the trees. It was a three-man team deploying from fast ropes through a small break in the canopy. Two of the men were dressed in forest-camouflage fatigues and a third much smaller man wore dungarees and khaki shirt. The third man wasn't taking the fast rope very well and was slow coming down. All three were heavily armed. Bolan had an advantage that between his suppressed weapon and the thunder of the rotors his weapon was absolutely silent. He charged, firing on full-auto. The closest man to the ground jerked as he was hit. Bolan kept spraying his opponent. He raised his aim and saw his target jerk as his bullets struck between armored vest and helmet. The target hit the ground wobbling and clawing for his pistol. The Executioner burned the rest of his magazine into the hunter's face.

The second man hit the ground, bringing up his rifle. Bolan slapped in a fresh magazine. Bang emptied half a magazine into the gunman between his chin and his collarbones and toppled him into dirt. The third man hit the ground and dived into the bushes. Bolan racked his weapon's charger on a fresh round and advanced.

The third man was gone.

The fast ropes rose up through the trees as the helicopter clawed for the sky. Bang scanned the perimeter. "We lost one, perhaps the most dangerous."

"Bullshit." Murphy lurched into view dragging the dead third man with him. The man wore civies and had a 5-round burst printed on his unarmored chest. "Couldn't quite keep up with you jackalopes, so I swung wide to flank." Murphy dropped his prize to the forest floor. "Good thing, too."

"Good work, Murph."

Bolan examined their loot. The enemy had inserted a sniper team, and the Executioner took the prize. It was still going to be one long, hard as hell slog out of this valley but a Swiss SG 550 sniper variant rifle could well turn the tide. It was the standard Swiss rifle that started out with precision accuracy anyway and had been given a longer barrel, a tuned action and a telescope. The spotter was armed with the exact opposite. His weapon had a chopped barrel and a folding stock for close-in work. Bang stripped the spotter of his rifle, pistol and magazines.

Murphy shook his head and held up the Uzi he took from the tracker. "What do I have to do to get a big boy gun?"

"Kill someone who has one," Bolan replied. He checked his new weapons' optics, and they seemed to have withstood the battle well. He quickly adjusted the stock to his own dimensions.

Bang walked over and toed the tracker. "He's Poqomam."

"Yeah? Well, for a Pokémon he died just fine." Murphy leaned over the corpse and raised one of the bruises he called an eyebrow. "I choose you, Pikachu! How'd that work out for you?"

Bang gave Murphy a pained look. "The Poqomam are Maya people. He's local. They were rebels during the war, excellent guerrilla fighters, and they've been poachers and drug mules after the peace. They'll know this valley intimately."

Murphy relieved the tracker of his machete. "Whatever."

Bolan checked the rest of the loot. All three had full canteens and a couple of energy bars each. That was going to go a long way toward getting out the valley, as well. Bolan took their communication gear. He knew the main enemy force wasn't far behind them.

Grimaldi's voice came across the link. "Sarge, I'm back on station."

"You safe?"

"I got at least 4,000 feet of ceiling on anything the bad guys got. They'll never even see me."

"Copy that. What do you see?"

"A whole lot of forest. You ought to get out of there."

"That's what I hear."

"Sarge, I'm deploying into LZ 3."

Bolan checked the satellite grid on his phone. LZ 3 was about five hundred yards away and had already been declared nonviable unless they used high explosives to blow the clearing wider, and right now his team was missing the requisite five hundred pounds of HE. "Negative. LZ 3 is too small. *Dragonslayer* cannot land. Winch extraction is too much exposure. Hold on station."

"I'm not landing, and I'm not winching, Sarge." Bolan could hear Grimaldi grinning. "I'm deploying."

Svarzkova spoke across the link and Bolan cold hear the roar of the wind on her end. "Red Leader and Red 1 away."

"I can orbit on station for another couple of hours, Sarge. Then I have to refuel."

"Copy that. Striker out."

Murphy looked at Bolan expectantly. "So what's happening?"

"The Russians are coming, and we're moving for LZ 3, on the double." Bolan broke into a trot. Murphy made a pained noise and followed while Bang hung back on their six. Bolan reached the tiny clearing and looked up. It was a high-altitude low-opening jump. Svarzkova and Igor had jumped from *Dragonslayer's* maximum ceiling and would open their chutes at the last second.

Murphy blinked upward through his bruises. "I don't see anything."

Bolan pointed. "There." Two dots plummeted toward ground.

"Oh, there."

One of the enemy helicopters swept over but they were oblivious to Bolan and his team hidden beneath them, much less the jumpers plunging down from above. All that would change the second Svarzkova and Igor deployed their chutes and went from plunging dots to piñatas. Bolan watched as

Svarzkova and Igor continued to drop like rocks. The Russians were cutting it awfully thin, he thought.

"C'mon…c'mon…" Murphy muttered.

Bolan silently echoed the sentiment.

First one parachute deployed and then the other. Bolan estimated they were at a little over a thousand feet, which was a gutsy move for a high-altitude high-opening jump.

Grimaldi broke across the line. "Red Leader! You have been spotted!"

Murphy gaped. "Ho-lee shit!"

The two divers broke away from their chutes and began freefalling again.

"Russians have balls of steel," Bang observed.

Svarzkova was pulling a base jump without a base. She and Igor had cut free of their main chutes and would low open on their reserves to kill hang time. The main chutes drifted away on the wind like camouflaged ribbons as the two Russians fell. They deployed their reserves at two hundred feet. The team took position around the LZ. The two figures came corkscrewing downward in hard spirals. Bolan could see they were both heavily burdened with weapons and equipment.

The lead jumper came in and his chute caught in the trees. His momentum made him do a carnival ride around the clearing before he smashed into a thicket like a ball and chain of snapping branches. Svarzkova came next. She flared her chute and nailed her landing right in the middle of the clearing. She folded up like a cricket as she hit with a force that made Bolan wince. He charged into the clearing and seized the Russian agent by her straps and began dragging her under the trees. "Covering fire!"

Machine-gun fire stitched the clearing as the chopper thundered into view. Bang and Murphy answered on full-auto and bullets sparked off the chopper's fuselage. The chopper veered from view but the nearby pounding of its rotors told Bolan it wasn't going anywhere. The pilot was circling to show the rest of the enemy where the quarry was.

Bolan bypassed the buckles and cut Svarzkova out of her straps. "Thanks for dropping in."

Svarzkova wheezed. Planet Earth had taken a hefty swipe at her, but she pushed herself to her feet. Bolan heard a second pair of rotors. Svarzkova snapped open the folding stock on her SVD-S Dragunov sniper rifle. "Igor! Take them!"

Igor pushed out of the thicket and snapped together the two halves of his airborne model RPG-7D rocket-propelled grenade launcher. The Russian pulled a rocket from his chest pack and shoved it down the launch tube. Bolan noted that the warhead wasn't the usual flattened football shape of an antiarmor round but shaped more like a beer keg. "Best take cover," Svarzkova advised.

Grimaldi broke in. "Second chopper, coming in hard and low for a gun run!"

Igor stepped out to meet it.

The chopper thundered into view with door gunners leaning out of both sides blazing away. Neither man could fire exactly forward and Igor stood in their blind spot. The Russian shot the chopper in the nose. The aircraft was eclipsed by a ball of fire as the thermobaric warhead detonated.

The blast violently sat Igor on his butt. Bolan felt the heat of the pressure wave shove down on him as if earth's gravity and surface temperature had doubled. He held his breath against the heat and ran out and grabbled Igor as chunks of helicopter began raining from the sky.

Bolan got the Russian under the trees. "You all right?"

Igor yawned and blinked.

Bolan clapped Igor on the shoulder and spoke loud and slow. "Nice shot!"

Igor focused, grinned happily and shot a thumbs-up. Bolan

pulled the Russian to his feet. Grimaldi spoke across the link. "That's a confirmed kill."

The sound of the other chopper's rotors faded into the distance.

CONZ WAS LIVID. "Fuckers!"

"Most unfortunate," Haas concurred. Minutes ago he had been informed that the American commando and his friends had taken a tapir, and with a hearty breakfast under their belts had downed his advanced sniper team before they could even deploy. Now one of his helicopters had been blown out of the sky. Haas picked up his radio. "Mr. Tobias, please tell me that wasn't you."

Tobias's disgusted voice came back. "No, it was Dobro, in the Little Bird. The destruction was total. No survivors."

Conz was turning purple. "Pig fuckers!"

Haas watched the two parachute canopies slowly drift down and disappear into the forest canopy. The HAHO to base jump had been impressive. "The commando has been reinforced." Haas took a pair of binoculars off the table and scanned the sky. It was beginning to become overcast as the daily afternoon deluge made ready to manifest itself. "According to the Russian we captured, they have a helicopter. Neither the FBI agent, the cop nor the Mexican have any airborne training."

"The Russian bitch," Conz controlled himself. "And the other twin, Igor."

"And now they have one of our sniper rifles and an RPG." Haas rose and cracked his knuckles as he looked down into the valley. "It looks like we have a real fight on our hands. I can have two more helicopters here within the hour along with the security force we are maintaining in the capital. We can remove the doors so the men can fire out the sides but they will not be proper gunships."

"Make it so." Conz lit a cigarette. "I have an idea."

"Oh?" Every once in a while Haas had to remind himself that beneath the preening, uber-prick exterior, there was a reason that Conz was head of operations.

"Yes, in fact I have two."

"I should like to hear them."

"One, have Zugg take the Russian to the airport and bring him with the helicopters."

Haas frowned in thought. "The two Russians are brothers, yes, but that will not give us any leverage. I doubt the commando would negotiate for him. As for the Russians, the GRU never makes deals for hostages. They just kill everyone and hope for the best."

Conz nodded. "Have Zugg bring him anyway."

"Very well. And?"

"And contact Gimeno."

Haas frowned again. "The colonel?"

"Yes, he owes us a favor, and if he balks, remind him that he has turned a blind eye to our operation so many times that he is up to his eyeballs in it. Assure him there is more money in it for him."

Haas sighed. "I will admit, Herr Conz, I do not know what you intend to do."

Conz told him.

"Even if it doesn't work," Conz concluded. "It should be interesting."

Haas gazed upon Emile Conz in grudging admiration. "You are without doubt the most evil prick I have ever met."

BOLAN HADN'T BROUGHT ponchos or shelter halves for a 4:00 a.m. raid, and Svarzkova and Igor had stuck to guns and grenades. The team slogged through the daily downpour. Unlike the sweat-warm rain on the coast up in the highlands, the rain went from cooling to cold within minutes. The rain's only benefit was that it was covering the team's tracks as quickly as they made them. Bang was absolutely sure the enemy had another tracker behind them.

The rain stopped as abruptly as it had started, and the sun burst forth onto fresh scrubbed forest.

"Well, that was refreshing." Murphy looked up and gasped into the sudden sunshine. The rain had washed the mud, blood and grime off him and he was as white as a sheet. "Can I have more drugs?"

"In an hour. See if you can eat something."

The team crouched at what was swiftly becoming the hated sound of rotors. Bolan watched a Bell 212 helicopter slide into view at about eight hundred feet. It was a long shot with his rifle, and men in chicken straps stood behind machine guns in each door to return fire. Bolan was sure the enemy didn't know where his team was, but it was disturbing that the helicopter stopped to hover nearly directly overhead.

A voice echoed over the valley through the chopper's public-address system. "Surrender! Or I will kill Agent Ivan Roltov!"

Agent Igor Roltov's face was terrible to behold as he looked up at the helicopter hovering high above them.

Bolan's captured com link crackled. "I know you have stripped several of my men of their communications equipment and are monitoring our broadcasts. Surrender now, or Agent Roltov's death is assured."

Bolan didn't respond. Short of him and his team breaking into the Helvetica Marine facility once more and extracting him, Ivan Roltov's death was already assured. The man on the other side of the line knew this, as well.

"Very, well. Please tell Igor that his brother's last words were that he loved him."

Bolan's blood froze as a figure tumbled from the cabin of the hovering helicopter. The man was stripped to his T-shirt and shorts and even at this distance was obviously covered with blood. GRU Agent Ivan Roltov kicked his legs as he tumbled over seven hundred feet to his death. His hands had been bound behind him. Svarzkova's single eye flew wide and she muttered in Russian that Bolan knew, "God save us all..."

Svarzkova raised her voice. "Igor! *Nyet!*"

Ivan Roltov's body crashed through the canopy a hundred yards away to the north. Igor Roltov roared in rage and pain as he broke cover and leveled his RPG.

Svarzkova's voice cracked in command. *"Starshina Roltov! Nyet! Nyet! Nyet!"*

Roltov wasn't taking no today. The RPG rocket ripped skyward toward the offending helicopter. The pilot saw it and banked away. Bolan grimaced. The pilot had been expecting it. With nothing to explode against, the warhead made a nearly perfect sphere of fire in the air that coalesced into black smoke. Bolan shouldered his rifle. The rocket's smoke trail had drawn a straight line toward the team's position.

"Striker!" Grimaldi shouted across the link. "Fast movers!"

Bolan heard the howl of jet engines screaming in fast and low.

Through a break in the trees, Bolan caught a flash of the fighters, and that one heartbeat told him all he needed to know. They were Guatemalan air force A37 Dragonflies with weapons festooned beneath their wings, and they were making a ground-attack run. In that one eyeblink Bolan caught sight of the Sidewinder missiles on the fighter pair's outer wings. He shouted into his link even as he dived for cover. "Jack! Get out of here! When they're done with us they're coming for you!"

Bolan missed the response as the world went orange and red with rapid-fire explosions. The soldier hugged dirt. The ground vibrated beneath him and he waited for it to stop. Bolan raised his head. Leaves rained down and smoke rose from multiple craters. The sheer number and small size of the detonations told him the jets had used multiple bomblet dispensers.

"Sound off!" Bolan called.

Murphy spoke from behind a large rock. "Can you have two headaches at the same time?"

Bang rose from behind a fallen log. "It has been over a decade since the Peace Accords. I fear the new crop of pilots haven't had much practice. We got lucky."

"Val!" Bolan called. "Val!"

"Over here!"

Bolan moved a few trees over. Svarzkova knelt beside Igor and tightly wrapped a field dressing around his hand. The sergeant's left thumb wasn't currently attached to him and was nowhere in sight.

"How the hell did they get jets?" Murphy asked.

Bang snarled disgustedly. "They own someone in the Guatemalan air force."

"I still don't get how the hell they can get away with calling in an air strike in peacetime!"

Bolan listened to the jet noise fade in the distance. It was punctuated by the tearing sound of miniguns as the jets chased Grimaldi. "They'll say it was a drug interdiction flight. As for the air strike, the only neighbors around here to complain about the noise are the local Poqomams, and it seems they're paid for."

Murphy knocked dirt off his Uzi. "Dicks."

Igor rose and ignored the Russian-issue painkillers Svarzkova offered. He stomped off without orders due north. Svarzkova said nothing. Bolan knew there was no point in trying to stop Igor, and at the moment north was as good a direction as any.

The team caught up with Igor a hundred yards away. He knelt beside his twin brother. Ivan had been extensively tortured and then dropped into the forest from about seven hundred feet. The best Hollywood horror special-effects department would have been stumped to come up with something worse than what was left of the GRU agent. The team stood in silence behind the brothers living and dead. Igor turned and looked at his commanding officer with tears in his eyes.

"This is no place, Major." Igor wept. "No place for good Russian boy to die."

Bang spoke quietly. "This is an excellent place to die."

The Russian slowly turned his gaze upon the Guatemalan.

Bang looked toward the mountain and Helvetica Marine. "That mountain is a volcano. I know the god that lives in it. His name is Buluc Chabtan, and he is a god of war. A god of fire and sudden death. He knows your brother's bravery, and I swear to you, even he will shudder when you paint his mountain red in revenge, and we will help you in this."

Igor made the sign of the cross over Ivan's remains and rose. He nodded at Bang and then gestured to Svarzkova that he was ready. Igor Roltov turned his red-rimmed gaze on Bolan, who nodded in answer.

"We'll kill them all, and burn their operation to the ground."

CHAPTER TWENTY-ONE

Helvetica Marine

"Do we have a casualty count?" Conz asked.

"No bodies found in strike area," Haas replied.

Conz stared out at the smoke still rising from the valley floor. "Those tamale fighters missed? Completely?"

"Mulac reports having found a left thumb."

Conz smirked. "And the American helicopter?"

"The tamale fighters, as it were, report that the American pilot led them through a series of nap-of-the-earth evasive maneuvers. Both pilots fired a missile at him and both times the American's countermeasures foiled them. The Guatemalan pilots broke off the attack when the chase approached the capital. I believe the American pilot is simply beyond their skill set."

Conz started to get angry again. "Beyond their skill set—"

"However," Haas said mollifyingly, "the wingman had the sense to climb to altitude and follow to observe where the American landed. The American set down at the international airport in the private aircraft area, the helicopter hangar."

"Have the police raid the hangar immediately. See if you can get the tower to deny him takeoff privileges."

"I have already ordered it, but it will take time."

"The pilot will undoubtedly expect this course of action," Conz calculated. "He will refuel and take off as quickly as possible."

"Yes, and unfortunately the A37s our friends in the Guatemalan air force are flying have what they call 'short legs' in aircraft terms. They cannot loiter long. However, I have collected a list of all private airstrips within Guatemala. It is proving interesting to arrange, and somewhat expensive, but I will have them all watched within twenty-four hours. I believe refueling will be the American pilot's Achilles' heel. Unless he lands on the roof of the American Embassy or crosses one of the borders, we will have him."

"Good, very good."

Haas watched the sun begin to dip toward late afternoon. "For now, the sun is sinking, and the commando has at least two wounded. If Bang were by himself, he might manage to escape and evade, but saddled with Americans and Russians? Mr. Tobias is relentless, and they cannot evade Mulac."

"Tell Mulac I want another thumb by sunset."

BOLAN FLEXED HIS ARM and winced. There was no getting around it. The zombie bite in his arm was starting to feel hot. He popped more antibiotics and allowed himself half a painkiller. Half of his team was already popping them like candy. Bang's radical field surgery had been a balls-out maneuver, but it was the kind of thing designed to get a man through a firefight, not for extended field duty. Svarzkova had parachuted in with a full Russian medic bag and cleaned and sewn up the wound, but it was clear the ex-Kaibil was starting to feel it. Igor was operating with one arm.

Most worrisome was Murphy.

Twice Bolan had caught the Delta operative staring into the trees as if he was sloth-watching, and it had taken saying Murphy's name several times in an ever-increasingly loud voice to snap him out of it. On top of that, Grimaldi had been chased out of the sky.

They had to break out of the valley now or not at all.

Bolan held up a fist to halt. The team collectively sighed

and drank water. A few minutes passed and Bang came trotting back from shadowing the team's six.

"Sal?"

"I cannot swear to it, believe the enemy is no more than twenty minutes behind us."

Bolan trusted the veteran's instincts. "They're wearing us like underwear. The downpour should have broken our trail and you've been covering our tracks."

"This is true." Bang scowled.

Bolan didn't care for the scowl at all. Bang's in-his-element cockiness was gone. He was clearly troubled. "What are you thinking, Sal?"

"The Mayan that Murph killed. I do not know his name, but I think I remember his face. From a wanted poster, during the war."

"What are you telling me?"

"There was a Mayan guerrlla fighter during the war. No one knew his face. Just his name. Mulac Nahuatl. He was a hunter and poacher by trade before the hostilities began. One of the best. When the war came, as I told you, Mulac's people, the Poqomam, were rebels. Mulac killed our sentries, ghosted our long-range patrols and picked off men one by one. He could track our best snipers to their hides, sneak up on them and kill them without a sound. He killed the man who trained me. The army put a bounty of twenty thousand U.S. dollars on his head. No one ever collected it. The face of the man Murph killed was on the same wanted poster, where Mulac's picture was blank. Mulac was never captured, and part of the Peace Accords was amnesty for the rebels. I do not mean to distress you, but I believe Mulac Nahuatl tracks us now, and I am afraid he is better than me."

"You're saying we can't lose him?"

"No, and we are getting weaker and slower by the hour."

Bolan made his decision. "Screw this. We're counterattacking."

"Fuckin' ay, bubba!" Murphy enthused.

"Val, you and me, sniper team."

"It is about time," the Russian responded.

"The whole situation is FUBAR, so let's keep it simple. Sal, you, Igor and Murph are going to wait for the enemy to show up and make contact. You're in command. Val and I are going to flank them. Igor, how many rockets do we have left?"

Igor made a face. Wasting one of the thermobaric weapons was running a close third to losing his brother and his thumb. "One, antipersonnel fragmentation munition."

"Give it to me."

Bolan took the collapsible RPG and strapped it to his back. Igor handed over the remaining round. The RPG antipersonnel round looked more like a real rocket instead of a football or beer keg on a stick. The warhead consisted of a narrow half-pound rod of high explosive encased in a several hundred steel rings. When the HE detonated, shards of steel ring flew in all directions at just under the speed of sound.

The Executioner nodded at a clump of rocks a few yards down the game trail. It and the huge hardwoods surrounding it formed a natural amphitheater. "That's as good a strongpoint as we're going to find. It's a bit obvious, but what the hell. Let's suck them in and finish this."

Bang led his section toward the redoubt.

Bolan and Svarzkova began backtracking in a wide circle. The soldier chose a fallen log nearly covered with undergrowth and took cover. Svarzkova dropped down beside him as he reassembled the RPG and loaded their last rocket. Bolan cocked the hammer and set the safety. "How you doing, Val?"

"I am good." The GRU agent's eye roved Bolan critically. "You look—" she searched for an English word "—pekid."

"That's a good word."

"I have spent far too much time in American hospitals."

Bolan tore open a power bar and gave Svarzkova half.

They ate and passed a canteen back and forth as they scanned the forest.

"Murphy has a concussion," Svarzkova stated.

"I know."

"Igor will go septic soon."

"I know."

"It has already started with Bang."

"I know."

"You were ill before you ever came to Guatemala."

"I know. Let's hurry up and wipe out Helvetica Marine and then go someplace quiet where we can get the rest we need."

Svarzkova smirked. "I have seen Elvis in *Blue Hawaii* a dozen times. I wish to eat pineapple."

"They grow pineapples in Guatemala."

"I wish to eat pineapple on beach. In blue Hawaii."

"Deal." Bolan peered through the telescopic sight of his commandeered sniper rifle. Bang's shorthairs had been telling him that the enemy had been no more than twenty minutes behind. Bolan's internal clock as well as his spine told him the Swiss foreign legion should be along any moment now. "Get ready."

Bolan laid his rifle to one side at the ready and took up the RPG. He settled back and peered over the optic. He caught movement in a thicket deep in the trees about fifty yards back. It was a thicket Bolan and his team had passed through half an hour before. Bolan heard Svarzkova's intake of breath as she spotted the man. He whispered low. "I've got him. Keep your eye on the forest."

The man emerged from the thicket with professional quiet. He was a big man with grease paint camouflaging his face and blending in with his forest-pattern BDUs and the do-rag covering his head. He scanned the forest long and hard and jerked his head. A second man emerged. Both hunters carried Swiss assault rifles with optic sights. The first man pointed. Just as Bolan had planned the trail they were on gave a line of sight toward the boulders and the stand of towering trees. The second man raised his optic and observed Bang's strongpoint for a few moments. He nodded and put a thumb to the mike on his throat and reported back.

Svarzkova spoke barely above a subvocalization. "They are taking the bait."

Bolan spoke nearly as quietly into his phone. "Sal, they're coming. I have two directly on the trail."

"Copy that, Cooper."

More men came through the thicket, and a pair of two-man fire teams came around from either side of it. The enemy was moving in a squad-strength wedge. It was the best formation when the enemy situation was obscure and terrain and visibility forced dispersion. He counted twelve. It was a heavy squad. Bolan watched them break up the wedge. The center spread out to meet the flanking teams and form a squad line. They were bringing all their firepower in a line for the assault.

A helicopter thundered overhead, but Bolan knew Bang and his fire team were invisible from the air. The helicopter passed on.

Bolan's eyes narrowed.

The enemy assault line began slowly walking forward. They weren't assaulting.

"What is happening?" Svarzkova whispered.

Bolan barely heard the rustling noise in the sky over Svarzkova's whisper. The mortar bomb exploded into a hardwood fifteen yards from Bang's position. The tree groaned and toppled as its trunk was sheared from underneath it. The enemy was firing mortars from the top of the mountain. The altitude greatly extended their range. "Sal!" Bolan snarled into his phone. "Get out of there!"

A second mortar bomb hit right in front of Bang's strongpoint. Only the fact that they were behind boulders might have saved them. The boulders disappeared in fire and smoke as two bombs walked right on target.

The squad leader by the thicket shouted for full assault.

Bolan dropped his eye level with the RPG's aiming reticule. He aimed at the squad leader and the middle of the assault line and squeezed the trigger. The rocket hissed from the launch tube and drew a smoking line through the trees. The closest men on the assault line heard the whoosh over the sound of the mortar bombs and their shouts went unheeded as the rocket-propelled grenade detonated in their midst. There was very little smoke or blast. A pale yellow flash of fire pulsed and men began falling. The lethal radius of the OG-7V grenade was seven meters. Its wounding sphere was triple that. The closest men dropped like they'd been shot, with dozens of bloody tufts sticking out of their clothing. Men farther away screamed and twisted as the metal shards rent their bodies. The thicket behind rippled as the fragmentation sphere moved through it like an invisible wind.

Svarzkova's rifle hammered on rapid semiauto as she shot the few men who remained standing.

Bolan discarded the spent launch tube and took up his rifle. The rocket launch had announced their presence to the world, but the enemy assault team had been annihilated. Svarzkova's Dragunov rifle racked open on a smoking chamber. "Empty!" She dropped down behind cover and reached for a fresh magazine as Bolan scanned for targets.

Svarzkova's single eye flew wide. "Belasko!"

Bolan rolled. He heard no sound other than Svarzkova's voice. He caught a flash of long dark hair and denim clothes as the machete hissed toward his throat. He barely interposed his rifle between himself and the blade. The machete cut into the bottom of his magazine and sank through the stamped sheet steel. Mulac Nahuatl left the blade imbedded in Bolan's weapon and vaulted over Svarzkova as she slammed in a fresh magazine.

The Executioner rolled up and fired, but the machete buried in his magazine threw off his shot and chips flew off a tree just past Mulac's right shoulder. The misaligned rounds in the magazine promptly jammed his rifle for the follow up. Svarzkova rose to follow.

Bolan clapped a hand on Svarzkova's shoulder. "Don't chase him—he's waiting for it. Go straight up the trail and check on the team. He'll be waiting for that, too, but I'll stay between you and him."

Svarzkova broke cover and ran for the strong point.

Bolan slowly moved in parallel. Mulac didn't want a gunfight. He would put distance between himself and his quarry, circle wide one way or the other and resume his stalk.

The helicopters, on the other hand, would be along very shortly.

"Igor!" Svarzkova screamed. "Igor!"

Svarzkova wasn't the screaming type. Bolan ran. He crossed the smoking mortar craters and vaulted over the boulders. Bang and Murphy looked shaken up but all right. Bang looked positively green. Svarzkova waved at them to watch the perimeter. She knelt beside her operative with a panicked look on her face. Her hand hovered over Igor's face indecisively. Her medical pack lay at her knee. Bolan looked down at Igor and winced against his will. The concussion round had apparently slammed Igor against a tree and he had suffered an ocular subluxation.

The tree had slammed Igor's left eye out of his head.

Igor's eyeball hung by the optic nerve and the socket was overflowing with blood. Bolan pushed Svarzkova aside and poured water from his canteen into the wound. The tree had come a millimeter from cracking the Russian's temple and killing him. Instead it had instantly squeezed Igor's eye out of its socket. In the process the tree had also splintered Igor's outer orbital bone and that splinter hadn't done him any favors. The optic nerve was nearly severed, and his eye hung by a thread. There was no way to push the eye back in without shredding it on the protruding bone splinters. Bolan pulled out his knife.

Svarzkova shouted, "No!"

Igor screamed like he was being killed as Bolan severed the optic nerve. The soldier put his knee on Igor's chest as the Russian struggled feebly, packed the wound with antiseptic, then bandaged and bound a field dressing onto Igor's face. The man moaned and twisted beneath Bolan's grip. "Morphine!"

Svarzkova slapped an auto injector into Bolan's hand. Igor made a mewling noise and relaxed as Bolan stabbed him in the thigh and shot him up with twenty miligrams of morphine. Igor's remaining eye rolled and the pupil dialed down to a pinpoint.

Bolan rose. "Murph, Val, get him up between you and walk him. Bang take the lead. I don't care about covering our tracks. We took out about a squad of the enemy. They'll be regrouping. Just do distance, stay out of sight of the helicopters. The sun is going down in an hour and we have your boy Mulac hard on our trail. If we can make it until nightfall, I'm going to risk calling in extraction."

Rotor noise echoed once again and it was getting closer by the second.

Bang nodded. He looked up at the setting sun and looked back the direction Bolan had come. He already knew the answer but he asked anyway. "And you?"

Bolan took the NVGs out of his bag and settled them on the crown of his head. "If I don't link up with you an hour after dark, Mulac won. Call in extraction."

CONZ WASN'T PLEASED. "So the commando and his team escape?"

"We have lost half of our force."

Conz's voice rose. "So they escape?"

Haas looked out over the valley grimly. The previous night had been bad. They had lost a truck and a couple of men, but at least they had driven the intruders from the facility with little in the way of loss to the actual operation. This day had been a complete goat screw. Many men lost, a helicopter shot out of the air and the enemy at large in the dark. Haas was reminded once again that while he had received training as a soldier, he had spent his career guarding the Pope and other important peoples' lives for pay until he had found ending peoples' lives to be far more profitable. Haas was an assassin who engineered death.

He was now locked in a small unit battle with a warrior who dealt it.

Haas sighed as he took in the panorama. The valley below was barely discernable. The sky above had turned purple and stars were coming out. Almost in answer the facility security lights came on, and the glare instantly ruined his night vision and his inky view of what lay below.

"And?" Conz insisted.

"We know the commando and his team have night-vision equipment. We only have a few pair, and some have been lost. Our helicopters do not have infrared radars. I cannot imagine the enemy's jump last night having been managed without one. It puts us at a terrible disadvantage. Most of the men will be reduced to stumbling across the forest floor playing follow the leader. On top of that, unless he somehow blunders close enough to smell them, even Mulac cannot track men in darkness."

Conz regarded Haas in open disgust. "We know they were headed north. Form a skirmishing line. Reconnaissance by fire. Any contact will be met with renewed mortar fire."

Haas controlled his temper. "We also know the enemy has silenced submachine guns. They will be able to pick off our teams at will. Flank and move behind them at will. We would end up killing our own men with friendly fire. I do not even want to contemplate the idea of the enemy helicopter somehow arming itself and returning. The fact is that until I can bring up new equipment, the enemy owns the night. The one advantage we have is that I believe the commando has wounded and is at the limit of his resources. He will wish to escape rather than fight. The enemy's mission is to stop us. I believe they will try again. I believe our best course is to watch the capital, watch the airport and the airstrips and wait for them to surface. I recommend also that we ask the police to monitor the hospitals for any foreigners coming in for treatment of suspicious wounds."

Conz looked at Haas as if he were a small child. "You are head of security for the Americas, are you not?"

Haas's jaw flexed. "I am."

"So you are telling me we have lost over a dozen men, a truck, a helicopter, an elevator, an executive office and a loading dock, and all you have to show for it in return is a left thumb?"

Haas began to let the leash of his anger slip when Tobias spoke into his earpiece. Haas cocked his head and listened. Despite the rage, disappointment and embarrassment fighting within him, he snorted in bemusement.

Conz spoke through clenched teeth. "If there is something funny in this situation, I would dearly love to hear it."

"It is just that Mulac has given Mr. Tobias his report."

"Oh?"

"Both Mulac and Tobias are in complete agreement with my assessment of the current situation."

It was Conz's turn to stiffen with rage. "And I assure you this trifecta of failure will be reflected in my report."

Haas shook his head in bemusement. "However…"

"However what?" Conz snarled.

"Well, it is just that Mulac has expressed his regrets through Tobias that he cannot bring you the right thumb you asked for by nightfall to match the left."

"Why are you smiling, Mr. Haas?"

"Mulac is hoping an enemy eyeball shall be sufficient."

Conz blinked. "An enemy eyeball?"

"So Mulac says. According to Mr. Tobias, Mulac cannot tell if it's a left one or a right one because it is dark."

"You know?" Conz lit a cigarette and offered Haas one. "I did not know you could tell a left eyeball from a right one. I mean, if you found one lying in the forest bereft of the head from whence it came."

"Well—" Haas shrugged philosophically and leaned in to let Conz light him "—if anyone can, I would put my money on Mulac."

Conz grinned delightedly. "Tell Mulac to put it in a jar and bring it to my temporary office. Put it next to the thumb."

CHAPTER TWENTY-THREE

Bolan watched exhaustedly as Igor was lowered limp into Bang's and Murphy's arms. Mulac hadn't come for Bolan in the dark. The soldier had called Kurtzman and given him the situation and told him to find a solution. Bolan had linked back up with his team and called in Grimaldi for extraction. While they waited, Kurtzman came up with a solution. Bolan called Kaino and told him to rendezvous with the strike team on the coast. It had been a nerve-racking fifteen minutes of hovering over the valley, but Grimaldi had winched them up out of the forest in blackout mode without incident. They had flown to the Pacific shore. The pilot hovered over the deserted road and lowered the team one by one. It was going to be a long wait for Kaino and backup to drive out of the highlands.

Grimaldi looked back over his shoulder. "Sarge, I'm on fumes!"

"I know."

"The bad guys know about me, and they're on the lookout. I called a fellow pilot I chatted up at in the capital. The private hangar got raided minutes after I took off. I don't trust these anally retentive Swiss pricks to leave anything to chance. I'm thinking every mud strip with refueling ability has someone watching if not a truckload of gangbangers waiting. On top of that, I'm betting if these guys can call in air strikes they can put money in place with air traffic control. I'm thinking my name is mud in Guatemala. My best bet is to have the Farm fake me a flight plan and cross the border into El Salvador."

"That's a good plan."

"The problem is if I land any place where I can refuel I'll have to clear customs and it's past midnight. On top of that you guys have gotten blood all over the cabin. To be honest I can't guarantee my turnaround time. Frankly I give it fifty-fifty that you'll have to come and bust me out of jail."

Bolan poured some bottled water Grimaldi had brought over his face to keep his eyes open. "Just do your best, Jack."

"Jesus, you look like shit, and I've seen you look like shit." The harness rose into view in front of the cabin door. "Your stop!"

Bolan rose and pulled in the harness. He shrugged into the pack that the pilot had brought and slipped the harness under his armpits. "Winch away!"

The soldier stepped out into the rotor wash. He sagged in the harness and slowly twisted in the breeze. He closed his eyes for a second and opened them as his boots hit the ground. Bang gave him an arm and he didn't object. They moved into the trees by the side of the road. Igor lay unmoving between two emergency blankets. Svarzkova sat behind a tree stump covering the road with her rifle. "How long?"

Bolan tapped the GPS app on his phone and checked Kaino's progress. "Couple of hours."

Murphy tossed the remaining blanket at Bolan. "Why don't you two sleep?"

"I think you should sleep, Murph."

"Me?" Bolan couldn't make out the ex-Delta operative's face but he could hear him grinning in the dark. Murphy shook the packet of pills he had lifted from Bolan at some point when he had closed his eyes during the flight. "I'm hopped up on goofballs, and I hear people with concussions shouldn't go to sleep because they never wake up. Sleep. You should all sleep. I'll watch the road."

Bolan stretched out on the blanket. Closing his eyes was just about the most glorious experience of his life. "One hour." Svarzkova flopped against Bolan like a boned fish.

The soldier never felt it.

BOLAN OPENED HIS EYES to the sound of a car door. It was dawn. Svarzkova drooled contentedly on his chest. He heard voices out on the road and was relieved to hear Kaino's rumble. Bolan disentangled himself and rose. Every muscle in his body ached. He knew there was a pretty good chance that was exactly what was ailing him. Bolan limped over to the group. Savacool nodded. "Cooper, it's good to see you."

"Thanks, good to see you, too, Cool."

Kaino gave Bolan a look of grave concern. "Man, you need to sit down."

"I'll sit in the car."

Donez checked his watch. "We gotta go." He walked over and shook Svarzkova's shoulder gently.

Kaino looked over at Igor's shape beneath the blankets, then gave Bolan a leery look. "Man, his goddamn eye. Really?"

"Yeah, it was rough. Get him in the back."

"And Ivan?"

"He's gone."

Kaino went to help Donez. Murphy was already sitting in the backseat, his head lolling against the window frame. Concussion and exhaustion had finally beaten chemistry. Bolan hoped he woke up. Murphy was a goof, but Bolan had to admit the ex-Delta operative was growing on him.

The team loaded into the truck. Bolan sat shotgun with Kaino driving. Svarzkova sat between them. She immediately put her head on Bolan's shoulder and went back to sleep.

He glanced up the road and looked back at Donez. "You know the drill, Donuts?"

"Yeah, yeah, I know the drill. Pack a *Z* or two. We'll wake you when we get there."

Bolan leaned his head against Svarzkova's, stuck his nose in her hair and closed his eyes.

Kaino spoke in what seemed barely a heartbeat later. "We're here."

Bolan opened his eyes as they drove into the coastal village of Milagro. Kurtzman had picked it. Milagro's claim to fame was that for a coastal town it was in the middle of nowhere, had no airstrip and it had a free clinic run by Christian missionaries that catered to the local fishing villages. Like most villages in Central America, nothing was moving at dawn other than the chickens, and being a fishing village most of the men had already gone out in the their boats before first light. The clinic was a tidy, shiny white single-story building slightly uphill from town. A wooden sign outside proudly proclaimed in both English and Spanish that the clinic had been built two years earlier by volunteers of some denomination from Texas Bolan had never heard of.

Kaino parked the car in back. A little cluster of bungalows housed the missionaries. The clinic windows were up high and small, but Bolan could see that a few lights were on. Bolan and Donez got out. Donez pulled on an old cap from his days on the force and knocked on the side door. Bolan stood to one side of the jamb. A voice called out in Spanish from inside.

"Who is there?"

"Police!" Donez replied.

Donez's cap read Policia in block yellow letters, and he was wearing a tactical vest. The door opened and a thin, acerbic-looking man in a lab coat peered over his spectacles at Donez. "Yes, Officer?"

Donez nodded in Bolan's direction and spoke in English. "My friend needs a doctor."

The doctor eyed Bolan critically and spoke with a deep Texan twang. "I'll say he does."

"So do my friends."

"Son, you don't exactly speak your English with a Guatemalan second language accent. As a matter of fact, you're Mexican."

"That is a fact," Donez averred.

The doctor looked in Bolan's face and didn't like what he saw. "And what's wrong with you?"

"Infected human bite."

The doctor considered that. "Eew. What's wrong with your friends?"

"In the truck I have one multiple concussion, a gunshot wound and an avulsed finger and eye."

"Son, it sounds like you had quite a night."

"I could tell you stories," Bolan said.

"So I suppose if I don't let you in you'll shoot me?" the doctor asked.

"No, but I'll have to tie up you and your staff while we make our getaway."

"Well, how about I treat you and we can discuss the tyin' up part later?"

"Mighty Christian of you," Bolan said.

"We try."

"Doctor...?"

"McCillup, Strickland McCillup."

"Dr. McCillup, I'll have to ask you for your phone."

McCillup sighed and handed over his phone. "I should probably go wake up my intern and my nurses."

"Donez, get everyone inside. Then you and Kaino go get the intern and the nurses. Take their phones," Bolan said.

"On it."

"Well, c'mon in." Dr. McCillup led Bolan inside. It was a small facility, but the equipment was shiny and modern. There didn't appear to be any patients currently taking up any beds. McCillup gestured at a bed. "Have a seat. Let's have a look at you."

"Triage, Doctor."

Donez and Kaino carried unconscious Igor in and put him on one of the two operating tables. Svarzkova walked in with Murphy's arm over her shoulder and mostly carrying him. The doctor expertly cut away the bandages over Igor's face and removed the wadding filling the eye. He looked back and forth between the splintered, empty socket and Bolan several times. He unwrapped Igor's hand and the stump of the Russian's thumb began oozing blood again. "Not that there's anything I could do with them, but I don't suppose you have the eye or the thumb?"

Bolan shook his head.

"Well, I'll be honest. About the only thing I'm equipped to do for this man is prevent infection and make him comfortable."

The back door to the clinic opened and Kaino and Donez ushered in two alarmed nurses and a disheveled intern. One of the nurses was a bubbly blonde. The other nurse and the intern were Guatemalans. All of them were very young. The doctor gestured at Igor. "Clean him up and then I'll have another look at him."

He walked over to Murphy and peered into his face. "I understand you have a concussion?" he said dryly.

Murphy nodded. "Several."

"What happened, if I might ask?"

"Well, I jumped out of a helicopter and smacked into a tree. Then I was in a semi that rolled down a mountain. Then I got blown up, like, two or three times." Murphy paused in thought. "Hey, Doc? How many concussions can you have without keeling over or joining the applesauce on Wednesdays crowd?"

"Son, I believe you are currently bucking for medical miracle status. Why don't you lie back and we'll clean you up in a few minutes," McCillup suggested.

"Right." Murphy lay back and was unconscious just about the second his head hit the pillow.

The doctor examined Bang's shoulder and tsked. "It's nasty-looking, but we can clean that up and sew it just fine. Silvia?"

Nurse Silvia came over and began laying out a tray of forceps, needles and surgical thread. She and Bang began talking in Spanish. Bolan watched as his team got attended to. The doctor raised an eyebrow at Svarzkova, but he clearly liked what he was looking at as he smiled. "And you, young lady?"

"I am fine, Doctor. Only tired."

McCillup looked at Savacool, Kaino and Donez as they stood concernedly over Igor. He smiled at Savacool. "How about you and the boys, Sunshine?"

"I hate to say it, but except for avoiding a mortar attack we had the easy job the other night."

McCillup finally got around to Bolan. The soldier knew he had some spectacular blunt trauma, but it was the bite wounds that really grabbed the doctor's attention as he examined him. "Well, son? That is something I have never seen before."

"Yeah, I get that a lot."

"Well, I'm sure as shootin' you do. The good news for you is that we are just a hop, skip and jump from the rainforest and we occasionally get people with some very weird and wonderful illnesses. I got a few units of broad-spectrum antibiotics that ought to do just the trick. When was your last tetanus shot?"

"Don't know. It must have been—"

"It's today."

"Right."

"You know, son? I was a U.S. Army doctor before I accepted my Lord and Savior, served in the first Gulf War, Operation Desert Shield."

"Thank you for your service, Dr. McCillup."

McCillup made a very Texan noise. "Yes, well, what I'm trying to say is, you and your friends don't smell like cartel to me."

"You've got a good nose. We're not," Bolan said.

The doctor lowered his voice. "Is she Russian?"

Bolan saw no reason to lie. "Yeah, so is the man on the table."

"Are you some kind of black ops or something?"

Bolan really needed Dr. McCillup on his side and decided to level with him, as much as he could. "I don't specifically work for the United States government."

"You'll have to forgive me if I ask what does that specifically mean."

"It means the President of the United States is most likely at least vaguely aware of my current activities, and as long as I don't screw the pooch he generally approves in a way he will never publicly mention."

"You know, son? This is going to sound odd because I've never met you, but if anyone else besides you had walked in here and told me that, I would have called them a liar."

"Yeah, I get that a lot, too."

"Well, of course you do." McCillup looked around at the mauled individuals reposing in his clinic. "Looks like the pooch had a rough night."

"The old dog has taken a beating, but he isn't down yet."

"Well, you've got sand, I'll give you that," McCillup said.

"I'd like to give you your phone back."

The doctor laughed. "Who the hell am I going to call anyway? My congressman? The Russian consulate? The closest thing to central authority around here for miles is the fishermen's guild and they won't be back until dark."

"What about your staff?"

"Well, technically they're volunteers, but I sign off on their living stipends, and if Miguel wants to go to medical school in Texas, well, then he will require my infinite good will."

"You know something, Dr. McCillup? You're okay."

"You just lie back. Sleep the sleep of the righteous. I'm sure your boys Kaino and Donez can keep us in line. I'll have Charlotte start that IV."

CONZ SWIRLED HIS GRISLY trophies in their jar and watched the digit and the orb whirl in the eddy with great satisfaction. Haas and Tobias gave each other sidelong looks. Both soldiers had dished out more pain, disfigurement and death than most men had eaten hot dinners, but even they thought that was excessive. Mulac smiled with childlike delight and spoke rapidly in his dialect of Maya. Neither he nor Conz spoke a common language, but the international criminal and the war criminal seemed to understand each other and in the past twelve hours had become as thick as thieves. Tobias took a healthy slug of brandy and translated. "Mulac says he had the commando beneath his machete. His shadow has fallen across the Yankee. The next time Mulac has him under his blade, he will cut off whatever part of him you wish for your jar."

Conz gave Mulac a dazzling smile. "Of course he will. Mr. Tobias, tell me, didn't you Americans take ears in Vietnam?"

Tobias had a number of very antisocial habits, but taking human trophies wasn't one of them. "Some old-timers will always pull your pud chain if you pour enough beers in them."

"Pull your pud chain..." Conz savored the exotic English slang. Despite a relatively catastrophic past forty-eight hours, he seemed in love with the world.

Haas poured himself another coffee and cognac and eyed his boss. Something was up. Tobias poured the cognac straight into his mug and did the same.

"Well, gentlemen, I have it on very good authority that

a helicopter registered as a Canadian pleasure craft landed in El Salvador."

As head of security in the Americas, Haas was surprised that Conz had learned that first.

Conz smiled with the true smugness of someone who knew something someone else didn't. "The head office has bent their resources to our little problem here in Central America. You will be pleased to know I spoke of both of your bravery and competence despite our setbacks."

Haas was pleased but he kept it off his face. "And so?"

"And so we have men, and guns, a full suite of night-vision equipment and an increased operating budget. The American and his team are still within Guatemala. Their ride home is in El Salvador. We have circulated their descriptions among the Zeta and MS-13. I am in complete agreement with your previous assessment. The American commando has thrown together an ad hoc team to strike at us. We do not need to worry about United States Special Forces or the American government. Our opponents are deniable, expendable and at the end of their resources, and their rope. They must either flee Guatemala, or, if this commando is the kind of American cowboy we believe him to be, he will attempt to continue the mission. Sooner or later he will stick his head up, and we shall lop it off."

CHAPTER TWENTY-FOUR

Bolan awoke. He didn't have any tubes in his arms, so he rose. Other than a momentary light-headedness, Planet Earth stayed in place. The lights were low, and gray light filtered through the high windows. Igor had been moved to a bed. The Russian's wounds had been rebandaged, and he had multiple tubes sticking out of him. Murphy was snoring and appeared to be resting comfortably. Bolan followed the smell of coffee to the clinic's foyer. Kaino appeared to have pulled guard duty and was streaming Puerto Rican baseball on the tablet Bolan had given him. Kaino looked up and pulled the urn from the coffeemaker. "Hey, *muchacho*."

Bolan scooped up a mug and gratefully let the man pour. "How long was I out?"

"A solid twenty-four hours. It's morning again. I think the doc slipped something into your IV. We all agreed to let you sleep. Frankly, you needed it. We all needed it." Kaino sighed. "I mean, it's not like me or the ground team was of any use during the mission, but that doesn't mean any of us had slept in forty-eight hours, either. And it was a long drive over bad road coming down out of the mountains."

"It's okay, Kaino. Where's everyone else?"

"There are only two roads into town, north and south. Donez is watching one end and Bang is watching the other. Val and Cool finished their watch, cleaned all the guns and went and sacked out in one of the bungalows in back."

"What about the doctor and his staff?"

"The doc went home to his place down by the beach. Said

he'd be back this morning. Miguel, Charlotte and Silvia took turns watching you all during the night. All three of you were stable, so I told them I'd mind the store and to go get some sleep. They're all zonked out. I think that was a lot more action than they're used to around here. Silvia checked on you patients about an hour ago and went to scare up some breakfast from the taverna down by the beach."

"How you doing, big man?"

"Tired." Kaino's joints popped as he yawned and stretched. "But I've been on plenty of stakeouts. Figured I'd wait until you were up."

"I'm up. Go get some rack time. Siestas are going to be in short supply come the next seventy-two hours."

"Don't have to tell me twice." Kaino lumbered back into the ward yawning. "Wake me when breakfast gets here."

"Will do." Bolan took the receptionist's chair Kaino had been warming and contacted the Farm. Kurtzman's face popped up on the tablet in a video window. He regarded Bolan's video feed critically. "You no longer look like one of the guys that bit you."

"Thanks."

"How's your safe haven?"

"You really came through, Bear. If you hadn't steered us here, I think I might have scrubbed the mission."

Kurtzman stopped short of blushing. Bolan didn't hand out praise often. "Well, since you're in a grateful mood, let me multiply your blessings."

"Multiply away."

"The good news is that your package has arrived. Bad news? It's in Puerto Barrios on the east coast and you're on the wrong ocean. You've got to cross Guatemala for pickup, or I have to send it on through the Panama Canal. Your choice."

"We'll figure out something."

"The other good news is that our boy Akira is attacking your problem with a will."

"And?"

"And he didn't want to get your hopes up, but when you swiped your electronic skeleton key through the Helvetica Marine roof access door, it was in direct communication with the Farm."

"I was hoping you would say something like that."

"Akira laid down a Trojan Horse in the lock computer, which is attached to the main security suite in the facility. He gave it a fifty-fifty chance of getting in, and about one in ten of getting in undetected."

"But?" Bolan asked.

"But you blew up Conz's office, his personal elevator and his mountainside helicopter dock."

Bolan smiled very wearily. "And they had to install new security."

"And somehow in all the electronic brouhaha, Akira managed to disguise his program as a subroutine. Our boy Akira is a ghost in the system, and not just in the doors."

"Love that man. What does that mean?"

"It means you have choices," Kurtzman said.

"Lay them on me."

"Akira can unlock every door in the place. By the same token he can lock every door in the place, as well. He can also pull a cascade unlocking doors and then locking them behind you. However, if they have a manual override, we can't be sure how long we can play that game."

"Good to know."

"Or Akira can go active, try to sneak into the mainframe, and hopefully start pulling information out of Helvetica Marine's encrypted files, and, uncharacteristically, he seems a little nervous. He says he doesn't trust these Swiss guys at all."

"How so?"

"You know Akira. Russian, Chinese, Iranian, you name an encryption and he's gone waltzing in. He says Helvetica Marine's stuff is a private design, not military. He says it looks subtle, inbred, anal, hostile and very Swiss. He cannot guarantee a clean entry. High risk of detection."

Bolan finished his coffee and poured more. "Are we afraid of retaliation?"

"I can't imagine Helvetica Marine can drop a virus past our firewall, much less break into the Farm mainframe, but Akira thinks if he's detected the counterattack is going to be very interesting and most likely lose us control of the doors and security at the Helvetica Marine facility."

"Tell Akira his Trojan Horse is go."

"You're sure?"

"If worse comes to worst, I can blow open the doors to Helvetica Marine, or drive through them. I want to know their operation, top to bottom, and I'm willing to take the risk."

Kurtzman turned his head and called out across the Computer Room. "Akira! You are go! Time to get sneaky!"

Bolan heard Tokaido whoop and shook his head. "What's the status on Jack?"

"He's still in El Salvador and receiving increasing heat from the local authorities. I'd bet anything that heat is being stoked with Helvetica Marine money. He isn't dead or in jail, and *Dragonslayer* hasn't been impounded, but he says he keeps being denied permission to take off, he keeps getting grilled, and there are Salvadoran soldier types with M-16s standing around the hangar giving him surly looks."

"Well, it beats MS-13 types with Uzis."

"They're most likely waiting in the wings while the fate of Mrs. Grimaldi's favorite son is being decided. The good news is he got refueled before the heat came down. He's willing to pull a breakout on your orders."

"Tell him to take care of himself first. If he has to go, tell him to go. We'll manage on our end."

"I think he knows that, but I'll remind him. What are you going to do?"

"We've all had a nap, and I'm told our guns are clean. After breakfast I'm thinking about loading up the truck and heading east. I need you to work up extraction for Murph and Igor. I'm going to leave them here. They should be safe for the next twenty-four hours, but I want them out of Guatemala and getting the best of care. Actually, assuming Jack can get airborne, make that his first mission priority."

"He won't like it."

"He doesn't have to. He just has to do it."

Silvia came in the front door out of uniform and carrying a gigantic woven basket in both hands. Good smells were coming out of it. "*Buenos dias,* Señor Cooper."

"Buenos dias, señorita, y gracias, muchos gracias."

Silvia blushed at the man's good manners and brought the basket of food into the clinic. Bolan followed her, taking the coffee urn with him. Savacool and Svarzkova had materialized out of nowhere, and the smells seemed to have awoken Kaino and Murphy. The team gathered around a table that Silvia was piling high with foil trays.

"Kaino," Bolan said, "ask her about Sal and Donuts."

Kaino asked. "She says she fed them first, and breakfast is served."

Bolan nodded and the team spent long moments attacking the food. Unlike many Latin countries Guatemalans liked a hearty morning meal. The foil trays from the village's only taverna were full of eggs, tortillas, cheese, black beans and fried plantains. The infection in Bolan's blood had given him unconscious dietary priorities, and he found himself tearing into the aluminum tray of bananas, papayas, mangoes and avocadoes like a scurvy victim from the days of wooden ships. Bolan stopped short of licking the foil clean and moved to wolfing cheese and beans and sausage for the protein.

Savacool smiled. "You know, if you just want to unhinge your jaw and tip the table, Coop, you go right ahead."

Laughter rounded the table. Kaino was only slightly behind Bolan in the gusto department. "Hunger's a good sign."

Silvia checked on Igor, and then took the empty coffee urn up front to make more. Murphy was just starting to look human. The black bruising was turning into spectacular swaths of purple and blue with bits of yellow on the fringes. "So what's the plan?"

"Unless Val can come up with something better, I'm making extraction plans for Igor. You're going to babysit him."

"Well, that sucks."

Svarzkova gave Murphy a frosty look.

He rolled the broken bags of blood vessels he called eyes. "Man, I'm surrounded by Russian cyclopses and none of them like me. Just pick a direction and put me on point."

"Murph, Doc McCillup says you need a week of bedrest, two would be better. And when you get back to the States he recommends you buy yourself a hockey helmet and wear it for the rest of your life. One more hit and you're going to be dead or living in some place with a day room, a big lawn and your biggest concern will be whether you're getting pudding or applesauce with the evening meal, because that's pretty much all you'll have between your ears."

Murphy bristled.

Bolan was relentless. "You read me, Murph? As of right now, you're off mission, and if you're smart you'd retire."

"I'm too young to retire, way too old to start over and now I'm not even good-looking."

"I just might be able to arrange some kind of plush consulting job until you finish your autobiography and sell the rights to Hollywood."

Murphy brightened. "Well, if you put it that way…"

"I am."

"Murph's question stands," Kaino said. "What's the plan?"

"We're heading to Puerto Barrios on the east coast. I have a package I need to pick up. Then we're going to tear Helvetica Marine a new rectum."

Kaino gave Bolan a look. "Yeah, that last assault went real well."

"It went perfectly. The only problem was the enemy was expecting us."

Svarzkova's fork paused over her fried plantains. "You do not believe enemy expects us?"

"Oh, they're expecting us to try something," Bolan confirmed.

Kaino grunted happily. "They just aren't expecting what you're going to try."

"Try hell," Bolan countered. "The enemy just isn't prepared for what we're about to do."

"What are we about to do?" Kaino asked.

"The words *Rolling Thunder* come to mind," Bolan hinted.

Kaino stabbed a thick finger across the table. "I saw that movie!"

Svarzkova nodded seriously. "This was 1980s American exploitation film. I, too, have seen this."

Savacool got it. "No way."

"Way," Bolan affirmed. "We just have to get across the country and make the pickup."

Kaino tapped an atlas icon on his tablet. "It's only about two hundred miles between here and Puerto Barrios, but a lot of that real estate is vertical. We had better be expecting roadblocks, official and otherwise, and we are one motley-looking crew."

"That's why we're going to split up and go civilian. Val and I will be one team. Kaino, you and Savacool the other. We're posing as couples and we'll take different routes. Sal, your face is known around here. Do you think you can escape and evade your way across the country?"

Bang smiled. "It isn't like I have not done so before."

"You have seventy-two hours to reach Puerto Barrios."

"I will be there in forty-eight," the ex-Kaibil boasted.

"What about me?" Donez asked.

"Me and Val and Kaino and Savacool are going to be posing as tourists. Whose cabana boy do you want to be, Donuts?"

"I got a better idea," Donez said. "No one in Guatemala knows my face and I'm a Mexican citizen. The guy who runs the taverna has a motorcycle. I'll buy it from him and head straight up the coast. I'll cross the Mexican border and jump on a plane at Tapachula International. Bet you dollars to donuts I reach Puerto Barrios first."

"Donuts, you're on. Take one of the PP-93s. Go buy a motorcycle and get out of here."

Donez pounded the rest of his coffee and rose. "I'm gone. *Suerte, amigos, amigas.*"

Bang rose, as well. "Take me on the back as far as Iztapa. I'll break north from there."

The soldier and the cop went bike shopping. Bolan nodded at Kaino. "You're posing as a married couple. Kaino, you do all the talking and do it all in Spanish. Cool, don't talk unless you have to."

Savacool regarded Bolan drolly. "You're telling a black girl from West Miami to keep her mouth shut in the car for seventy-two hours?"

"Just do your best, I know you will. You guys can have the truck."

Svarzkova reloaded her plate. "And us? We are married couple?"

"No way, you're smoking-hot surf-wax slave."

"Oh?"

"Yeah, and we're both going blond," Bolan answered.

CHAPTER TWENTY-FIVE

Amatitlán, the highlands

They had made good time. Bolan and Svarzkova were about fifteen miles outside the capital and already a quarter of the way to Puerto Barrios. They had exhausted Nurse Charlotte's supply of sunless tanning solution, and Bolan and Svarzkova were bronzed like confirmed sun-and-surf worshippers. A bottle of peroxide had bleached Bolan blond. He had borrowed a pair of cargo shorts and an old Aloha shirt from Dr. McCillup and gone casual. Svarzkova wore nothing but a bikini with a sarong over her hips and was immensely popular in the few places they stopped to buy fuel and eat. In the village they had acquired an ancient yellow convertible VW Beetle and put a couple of surfboards sticking up in the backseat as window dressing. No one asked them for their IDs or passports. Guatemalans eagerly took Bolan's dollars, ogled Svarzkova's body and in between times the old VW slowly but steadily put miles behind them.

They sat at a picnic table outside a gas station that had a kitchen shack on the side and ate cheesy rice and plantains and drank some vaguely yellowish-green, saccharine-sweet form of Guatemalan juice. Bolan looked up at the sun as it began to fall toward Lake Amatitlán. It had been a good day of driving. It was going to be a long hard night of more of it on poorly maintained mountain roads.

"How you doing?"

Svarzkova took a deep breath. "I like Guatemala."

"Me, too."

"It could be Garden of Eden, but too many serpents."

That described far too many places Bolan had been. "You miss Russia."

"Russians love heat and sun, but Mother Russia calls to me. I should not be here. Many battles to be fought at home."

Bolan took a long hard look at his counterpart. Bolan's War Everlasting had taken its toll on him inside and out, but he had absolute faith in his mission, and absolute faith that whatever happened to him, the light in the darkness he fought for would continue to burn. Major Svarzkova was Russian. If one read about Russia's levels of endemic corruption, alcoholism, drug addiction, murder, suicide and rates of AIDs infection you might think they were an African country on the brink. Now it had spawned *krokodil* in desperate anesthetic horror-need. In the major's life there had never been any good times. Her mission was the same as Bolan's, only she expected to lose. In her experience the light she fought for was an idea rather than anything real enshrined in a constitution or a living ethos. If that light existed anywhere in Russia's vast expanse or in any Russian heart, she expected that light to go out on her watch. She expected to die and fail. The saving grace of her life of brutal service to one corrupt regime after another was that when the final, blackest darkness ever known fell across Russia, the muzzle-flashes of her guns would light that night until she fell.

Bolan watched Svarzkova tuck cheesey rice and plantains into a tortilla. "You're smoking hot."

"You always know right thing to say."

Bolan's tablet peeped at him. He took it out of his knapsack and enabled Kurtzman. "What's up?"

"Where are you?" Kurtzman asked.

Bolan enabled the Farm GPS tracking. "We're in the Lake Country, about a kilometer outside Amatitlán, about forty-five minutes out from Guatemala City. Why, what's up?"

"Akira has something."

"What?"

"Russians."

"Got one right here and she's a jim-dandy."

Svarzkova smirked over her fruit punch.

"No," Kurtzman countered. "Akira thinks we have Russians flying into the capital tonight."

"He's broken the Swiss encryption?"

"Not exactly."

"Last I heard 'not exactly' usually means no."

"He hasn't broken into the Helvetica mainframe, or into Conz's personal files. But Akira did manage to ghost into Haas's personal laptop the last time he synced it with the mainframe. We are currently monitoring Mr. Haas's nonencrypted activities."

Bolan felt like some luck just might have come his way. "Haas is keeping tabs on a flight."

"Originating from Russia?"

"Their flight originated in Moscow, flew to New York, then Miami and is currently inbound to La Aurora International in Guatemala City. Haas's laptop has checked their flight status several times in the past twenty-four hours. The information was sent to someone else in encrypted form, under the file name CHEF."

Svarzkova nodded. "In Russia 'chef' is individual who cooks drugs. It usually implies chemist with certain level of expertise. Above street level and not using product. A professional."

"Bear, tell me Akira broke into the airline's passenger registry."

"That was the easiest part," Kurtzman reported. "Two individuals, booked as husband and wife. Grigory and Masha Shalimov."

Svarzkova rapidly began texting Moscow. Bolan calculated. Despite the recent battle at the facility, Helvetica Marine was expecting two "chefs," arriving tonight in La Aurora International Airport. Bolan gazed northward past the volcanoes toward the capital beyond. "What's their ETA?"

"Ten o'clock in the p.m. You have a little time if you want greet them."

"You say Haas's laptop is tracking their flight and ETA?"

"Unless the Swiss have absolutely bamboozled Akira, the answer is yes. Why?"

"What's the chance that Akira can tell Haas's laptop that the flight has been delayed an hour?"

Kurtzman saw it instantly. "On it."

Svarzkova went back to smirking as she texted.

Bolan enabled tracking on the rest of his team. Kaino and Savacool had already passed the capital and were moving at a steady clip for the Atlantic. Bang had gone dark, and true to his promise Donez was close to the Mexican border. No one was in range to be of any help. "Bear, Val and I are going to burn for the capital. I need you to find me a tailor's shop. I need you to communicate to them they have wealthy clients coming into the capital who need work done for an event tonight, and we're going to need a new car. Something slick."

Kurtzman turned his head and shouted across the Computer Room at his team. "You got that?"

"Got it! On it! Consider Haas late to the party!" Tokaido returned.

Carmen Delahunt called out happily. "Consider the couture arranged!"

Kurtzman nodded across the link. "Done."

"So what is plan?" Svarzkova asked.

"We're going to pull a dirty trick on the Swiss."

"Dirty trick is fifth favorite thing in Russia."

Bolan had suspicions but he asked anyway. "What are the first four?"

"Food, vodka, sex and revenge." Svarzkova gave Bolan a sleepy smile. "Best if dirty trick involves all four."

"I can guarantee you at least two and you get to keep the clothes."

"I demand three and keep clothes."

Bolan nodded. "Done."

He polished off his juice and rose. "Let's do some distance."

La Aurora International Airport

"You look smoking hot," Bolan admitted.

Svarzkova peered at Bolan over her mirrored sunglasses and from beneath her dress cap. "We should go into private business."

Bolan could think of a worse Gal Friday to go into business with. Svarzkova did indeed looking smoking hot. Pepe the twenty-four-hour tailor had exceeded himself. There were no twenty-four-hour tailors in Guatemala, but a phone call and a huge amount of money opened the shop doors in the tailor district. Bolan was almost ready to believe Pepe had painted the chauffeur's uniform onto Svarzkova's body rather than sewn it. The Russian intelligence agent looked like the superhot assistant of some supervillain out of a comic book. Bolan's gray tropical wool suit was far from Savile Row, but given the time window, the off-the-rack outfit had been altered to his frame and he looked like very serious, overpriced private contract security. The few bruises that were visible just made Bolan look even more mad, bad and dangerous to know.

Carmen Delahunt had gotten hold of a BMW armored limousine. Once again no one asked for passports or IDs. Despite Moscow, Mexico and several Middle East and African hotspots, Guatemala still held the title of the most violent place on Earth. A beautiful chauffeur and her hard guy security goon didn't raise any eyebrows, and the money made sure they entertained only various levels of idle interest.

Svarzkova had come through on her end. The Russian drug chefs were a genuine husband-and-wife team named Boris and Nedezdha Fominov. "Woman is dangerous one," Svarzkova remarked. Bolan nodded. She looked it. Except that she was missing bolts in her neck, she could have passed for Frankenstein in a red wig and housecoat. According to the file Svarzkova had shared, Fominov's nickname was "Mama Neddi," and she had a very bad reputation in Moscow police circles. Though she did have a degree in chemical engineering, she was the brains and the willpower of the operation. Her husband was scrawny, bearded, bespectacled and balding. All he needed was a pair of bongos and a beret to look like a 1950s beat poet from San Francisco. The file implied he did most of the chemistry. They were rumored to have some very powerful patrons in the Moscow mafya.

Bolan checked his tablet. Flight 913 out of Miami was on final approach. "Let's go take delivery."

He snapped a PP-93 into the Russian consulate concealment rig and slid out of the limo. He knew Svarzkova had brought some personal weapons along and had to be armed but how she was hiding them in Pepe's sex-chauffer outfit was an intriguing line of speculation. They walked through Aurora International as though they owned the place. They stopped outside the international flight security gate, and Svarzkova raised a sign she had handwritten in Cyrillic that read Shalimov.

Flight 913 out of Miami began debarking.

Svarzkova flashed her sign as weary vacationers and professionals walked through the gate. A person didn't need a Geiger counter to pick out the Russian "chefs." They were rumpled, exhausted and Russian-looking. Mama Neddi's photo hadn't done her justice. She was built like a refrigerator. Svarzkova called out in the mother tongue. Bolan arranged a grim look on his face as both chemists' heads snapped around.

Svarzkova rapid-fired congenial Russian chatter. She nodded at Bolan, smirked at the surroundings. Boris looked at Bolan with weary gratitude. Neddi gave Bolan the fish-eye and returned to looking upon Svarzkova with grave disdain. The agent blithely ignored the scorn and rattled on happily. Bolan didn't understand much, but he knew exactly what Svarzkova was saying. The theme of the night was "let's get you home and safe," and to various degrees the Russian drug cooks seemed willing. Svarzkova led the way to the limo. Bolan hung back on their six. Several times the Russians looked back at him, and he let them observe him constantly scanning the surroundings.

Svarzkova led them to the curb and opened the limo's door. The Russians slid in, and Bolan took the seat facing them. The Russian agent started the engine and aimed the limo toward the capital.

"You speak English?" Bolan asked.

The Russian nodded.

"There's bottled water and sandwiches in the minibar."

Neddi turned her dishwater eyes on Bolan. "You are American?"

Bolan snorted. "Canadian."

"Ah. Do you speak Russian?"

Bolan jerked his head back at the driver's seat. "That's her job."

"Ah."

Neddi's permanent scowl was a near perfect poker face. Her body language told Bolan something was wrong. A cue had been missed, or deliberately exposed. Neddi sighed and whispered to her husband.

Boris lunged. He snapped his wrist and the black wedge of a plastic push dagger that had beaten Guatemalan customs punched toward Bolan's face. The Executioner raised his forearm and deflected the blow. The fiberglass-reinforced point sank through the limo's upholstery. The soldier seized his adversary's wrist in his left hand. He gave the Russian a right palm strike straight to the face. The soldier was seated and it wasn't his most powerful blow, but Boris's septum snapped and tears squirted out of his eyes. Bolan rose slightly in his seat and rammed his right heel low into Boris's floating ribs with one hell of a lot more power. Ribs snapped and Boris bounced back into his seat.

Bolan slapped leather for his PP-93.

Neddi seized Svarzkova's hair from behind and brutally yanked her head down between the headrest and window. Svarzkova desperately tried to drive. Neddi's second yank savagely jammed her victim's head between the seat and the door frame. The limo swerved off the road and promptly rammed into a power pole. It came to a violent halt and the airbags deployed, smothering everyone's attempt at violence, effluent dust turning the limo's interior into a snow globe.

Boris awkwardly stabbed for Bolan again, but this time his fore and middle fingers stabbed for his eyes. The soldier caught the fingers as they snaked over the deflating safety cushion. He made a fist and Boris gasped as Bolan snapped both digits at the first knuckle. Neddi bailed out of the limo.

Bolan pumped his fist into the side of Boris's head like he was chopping wood, and the Russian chemist collapsed to the floor of the limo.

Svarzkova flung open her door and pulled a spectacular limbo maneuver that unwedged her head and ejected her out of the driver's seat. She limboed again and just barely ducked beneath a right hook from Neddi that would have taken her head off. Svarzkova hurled herself into a shoulder roll across the sidewalk to give herself room and bounced up in a fighting stance. Neddi was on Svarzkova like salted cod on gruel and the Russian catfight was on.

Svarzkova stepped in, her spinning back-kick a joy to behold. The knife edge of her foot collided against the side of Neddi's jaw with apocalyptic force. Bolan had seen Svarzkova drop grown men to the ground. Neddi ate the round kick like a superheavyweight eating the jab of a bantam. Svarzkova's problem in close-quarters combat was that she didn't have a left eye and when an opponent closed she had a blind spot. Mama Neddi stepped up and her right hand cracked across the side of Svarzkova's face with the sound of a firecracker going off, only it was flesh meeting flesh.

Svarzkova's ocular implant squirted out of her head, and she dropped to the pavement like she'd been shot.

Neddi didn't bat an eye as she began kicking Svarzkova.

"Hey." Bolan spoke quietly as he extended his machine pistol. "Knock that shit off."

Mama Neddi gave Svarzkova one more boot for good measure and backed up a step. Her huge chest heaved, and lank strands of her dyed hair straggled out of her bun. Her huge, man hands creaked into fists. Her Russian accent was thicker than Svarzkova's and 100 percent less charming. "You will not shoot, Yankee pussy-boy."

Svarzkova shoved herself up to hands and knees. "Shoot the bitch!"

"I don't shoot unarmed women."

Neddi leered.

Svarzkova found her eye. She wiped it on her jacket, spit on it and shoved it back in her head. Even Mama Neddi seemed vaguely impressed. The Russian agent levered herself onto to her feet radiating rage. Bolan tossed her the PP-93. Svarzkova caught it happily and quite deliberately aimed it at Neddi's knees.

"But she'd shoot you." Bolan cracked his knuckles as he continued.

He could see the sociopath within the mono-block of woman known as Mama Neddi raise her dukes. "You cannot make me talk."

"I don't have the time. I'm not even going to try. But you have to ask yourself three questions, *babushka*."

"What questions?" Neddi asked.

"Do you love your husband?"

Bolan might as well have waded in with a right-hand hay-maker.

He watched Mama Neddi's facade crack slightly. He glanced at Svarzkova. "Do you believe this woman is willing to shoot your husband in the stomach, lock the two of you in a basement and let you listen to him scream for days until he dies or you beg to tell us everything we want to know?"

The look on Svarzkova's rapidly swelling face said it all. Neddi shook.

Bolan's cobalt-blue gaze was arctic with cold. "Do you believe I'm willing to wash my hands of you and let her do it? In U.S. Intelligence circles this is known as extraordinary rendition. I swear to you, I will let this woman rendite you in extraordinary fashion in a subbasement in Guate while I walk away."

Bolan knew he'd hit pay dirt. All sociopaths cared about something. He didn't want to imagine how complicated and quite possibly dangerous the Fominov love life might be, but sociopaths had a movie in their head, and messing with the plot, much less the cast, threw them careening into a bizarro zone that many of them would do anything to make right again.

Neddi's hands fell open at her sides as she began to cry.

"Now get in the car, facedown, beside your husband, and don't move."

Mama Neddi shuffled toward the limo weeping and snuffling and assumed the position behind her unconscious husband. Bolan eyed Svarzkova. The left side of her face was rising like yeast and turning colors that Murphy could empathize with. "Are you okay to drive? We gotta go."

"I will drive out of here."

Bolan slid back into the passenger side. Neddi was weeping and stroking her husband's unconscious head. The soldier bellowed, "I said don't move!"

Mama Neddi hugged the floor and whimpered in Russian. Svarzkova ground gears and Bolan was relieved as the limo backed up and onto the street. He checked his watch. They'd lost time. It was going to be a long hard drive to Puerto Barrios, and a sleepless night watching some ultraviolent Russian drug cooks with severe psychological issues.

Bolan put a boot on the back of Neddi's neck and tapped an app on his phone. He texted the Farm.

Package Received.

CHAPTER TWENTY-SIX

Mariscos, Guatemala

Bolan handed Svarkzova a steak. It was the best cold pack he could manage at the hour. "How you doing, Slappy?"

"Slappy..." Svarzkova flopped the cold blanket of flank on the side of her head. Bolan had pulled over in Mariscos to grab a few minutes of down time. Neddi and Boris were fed, watered and resting comfortably in the limo's capacious trunk. Bolan had the car alarm set. If they tried a break out, the soldier would know it. The beach bungalow he had rented overlooked Lake Izabal. Svarzkova sighed as the cold air from the refrigerator flowed into her face. "I am prepared to surrender title of 'Red Witch' to Mama Neddi."

"Oh, cheer up." Bolan handed her a cold grape Fanta and cracked himself an orange. "You've usually been shot, stabbed, hurled from a moving vehicle or impaled with farming implements by this point."

"I know." Svarzkova smiled beneath her meat compress and sipped soda. "Do not jinx me."

"Never."

"What is plan?" she asked.

"Got a couple."

"Name one."

"You haven't seen my new ride," Bolan stated.

"Yankee men and their rides..."

"No, I really think you'll like it."

"I like VW Bug."

"Oh, yeah?" he queried.

"I had dream while you let me sleep in limo. I dreamed we took Bug. We took surfboards. We left guns behind. We drove to Costa Rica. We never looked back, and we were happy."

"That's a good dream."

"I am tired, Belasko."

"We're all tired, and the next forty-two to seventy-four hours will decide this, one way or the other."

"No, you do not understand. I am weary, in my bones."

Bolan took a long hard look at the battered, one-eyed Russian agent sitting with a steak on her face and a decimated team in a bungalow in Guatemala. "I know. I've been there."

"Did you know I was shot since last time we met?" Svarzkova asked.

"No, I didn't know that."

"I laid in snow for forty-five minutes. Backup never showed. Finally bystander took me to hospital. There have been three attempts on my life in past four years. At least one inside job." Svarzkova closed her eye and sagged back into the couch. "More and more, I dream of dying someplace, without gun in hand. But like saying, too young to quit, too old to start over."

"You could always settle down, find a man and get married."

Svarzkova took the meat off her face. Bolan stared at the bruised socket of her left eye. The horrific bruising was temporary, but the soldier knew Svarzkova saw her mutilations and body-wide scars every day. The GRU agent stared at Bolan steadily. "Could you love this face?"

"I so want a skull-job right now," Bolan said gravely.

Svarzkova blew soda out her nose.

"That was ladylike."

Svarzkova clutched her face and made a very obscene Russian gesture.

"I'll make you a promise. If we live through this, you and I will go surfing in Costa Rica," Bolan said.

Svarzkova smiled.

"You feel better?"

"I do. I am sorry. Self-pity is disgusting," the Russian agent replied.

"A girl's allowed to have a pity party once in a while." Bolan shrugged. "But like any party, a beautiful woman should show up late and leave early."

"You know right thing to say."

"I'm going to go say some stuff to Neddi now. Drink your Fanta and grab a nap. We leave in an hour." Bolan grabbed another couple of sodas out of the ice bucket and went outside.

He heard Svarzkova mutter in bemused disgust. "Skull job…"

Bolan walked out to the limo and set down the sodas. He drew his PP-93 and knocked on the hood. "Mrs. Fominov. We need to talk now. I'm going to open the trunk. You try anything, and your husband is the first one I shoot."

Mama Neddi's voice sounded small and muffled. "I try nothing."

Bolan opened the trunk and jerked his machine pistol meaningfully. "Get out."

Mama Neddi crawled out stiffly. Bolan had given Boris a heady cocktail of painkillers, and he slept peacefully between a pair of Mayan blankets the soldier had bought by the side of the road. He pointed his pistol at the pavement. "Sit."

Mama Neddi sat.

Bolan nodded at the plastic bottles of Fanta. "You want pineapple or peach?"

"I prefer pineapple."

"Knock yourself out."

Mama Neddi stuck the entire mouth of the bottle between her lips and sucked soda like a child. Bolan waited while she downed half the bottle and pulled it out gasping, then said, "Let's talk."

"About what?"

"I'm interested in why you're here. You're interested in the possibility of you and your husband leaving Guatemala alive, maybe even free. I'm sure we can meet somewhere in the middle."

"My husband requires medical attention. He has internal injury where you kicked him."

Bolan considered Dr. McCillup. "I'll make you a deal. You tell me everything, and if I believe you, I'll have a doctor and a nurse helicoptered in, and your husband taken to a private clinic. Upon the success of my mission I'll release your passports, money and credit cards and you can arrange your own departure from Guatemala."

"That is all? No repercussions?"

"None with me."

"And Cyclops?"

Bolan smiled. "I understand you have pull with the federal and Moscow police, and probably connections with the Russian Foreign Intelligence Service. I'll promise you that there'll be no repercussions for your actions in Guatemala. But I'll tell you this for nothing. The second you step onto the tarmac in the Russian Federation, the GRU will be watching you, and Cyclops wants nothing more than to see you and Boris gut shot and dying in the snow."

Mama Neddi digested that. Corruption in Russia was endemic. The GRU was riddled with corruption as much as anyone else but it was mostly internal. Russian Military Intelligence still considered itself Mother Russia's last, holding line. It was very difficult to buy off.

Bolan cracked the peach Fanta and wiped the sweating bottle across his brow. "Talk, now or not at all."

"What are your questions?"

"Don't make me ask you questions, Neddi. You won't like it. Your husband will like it less. Tell me everything, now."

Mama Neddi finished off her soda, then eyes gazing into middle distance, she began speaking robotically. "*Krokodil* has problem."

"What kind of problem?"

"Problem with *krokodil* is junkies."

"And?" Bolan probed.

"They steal their supplies. Kill for ingredients. Junkies cook their fix."

Bolan knew the answer but he wanted to keep Mama Neddi rolling. "And?"

"Key to profit is to make product American junkies will steal and kill to buy, instead of steal and kill to make."

"And so?"

"We have recipe. *Krokodil* successful in Russia because several strong opiates are available as over-counter drugs. This is not case in United States. Helvetica Marine in cooperation with gangs successfully created demand."

Without a serious opiate supply, Bolan knew that the new rock-bottom need that had created the *krokodil* junkies couldn't be sustained. Helvetica Marine had created an insatiable need, but it was a need that chewed up and spit out the consumers. Bolan considered his battles in Florida with Cocosino and the *krokodil* zombie siege at Savacool's place. For a drug cartel, financially it was a dead end.

What they really needed was the old bait and switch.

And that was where Neddi and Boris came in. "You've got your opiate substitute."

"You Americans invented it. You have three painkillers far more powerful than anything available by prescription, but your politicians fight over it, afraid it will be the new OxyContin, the new prescription drug that crosses state lines and becomes the new heroin."

"And you have the new heroin."

"*Krokodil* is horrible, disgusting."

Bolan could tell that despite her insanity, Mama Neddi considered *krokodil* an affront to her criminal nature.

"Most drugs end up destroying user or sending them into rehab. This is nature of business. It is known, and predictable. But *krokodil?* It destroys too quickly. For proper, profitable, pusher-consumer relationship, user must consume drug rather than drug consuming user. My husband and I had a good corner on heroin in Moscow, but then *krokodil* came. It ate profits. It ate junkies. We bent minds to task. Through research we found chemicals derived by Helvetica Marine in Guatemalan highlands, combined with opiate derivative that nearly any chemist could make, would create clean *krokodil*. No rot or cook-and-die zombies. Helvetica Marine is already involved in illegal banking, black market arms and drug trade. I tell you, life in drug trade is short and brutal. You always end up betrayed. Most end up dead. Consider need for laundering money, secure international brokering and discretion. Could you ask for any better partner than Swiss?"

"No."

"So you understand."

Bolan gazed upon Mama Neddi like the filth she was. "I understand you completely."

"And, so?"

Bolan stared down at Mama Neddi implacably.

"I have told you."

"You've told me nothing, and I asked you a question," Bolan said.

"What question—"

"Why are you here?"

"I told you—"

"Why are you and your husband here, tonight?"

"We have come to cook the first shipment."

"How much?"

"Cannot be sure until we see equipment and quality of ingredients," Neddi replied.

"Give me an estimate."

"At least two metric tons."

Bolan kept the revilement off his face. Two thousand kilograms of product-improved *krokodil* hitting the streets was a pharmaceutical Armageddon. The number was absurd and in fact obscene. But he knew from very recent and bloody experience Helvetica Marine didn't deal in absurdity, and they had both Los Zeta and MS-13 lined up to be their sales and foot soldier manpower. Two thousand kilos would be enough to spread a tidal wave of addiction from Florida to California, and that tsunami would continue north.

"Who were you supposed to meet?" Bolan asked.

"I do not know. We were told we would be picked up at airport."

"Who were you supposed to contact if you ran into any trouble?"

"Man called Mr. Tobias."

Bolan held out Mama Neddi's phone. It was connected to his and Bolan pushed in his earbud. "Call him, tell him you and your husband never got out of Miami and that the DEA has you in a holding room in the airport. You are lawyered up, and this is the first phone call you have been allowed to make."

Neddi typed in the number. It answered on the first ring, and the Farm was already tracking it. "Where the hell are you?"

"Florida. We have experienced difficulties in customs. Somehow we have been recognized, or suspected."

"I stood in La Aurora Airport with my dick in my hand for an hour, and I've been calling in favors, having men combing the streets and sending out feelers in all directions."

"This is second phone call I am allowed to make," Neddi said.

"What was the first?"

"Lawyer."

"Is he there?"

Bolan nodded.

"Yes, he is in room."

"Put him on." Tobias ordered.

Bolan spoke. "Hello?"

"Who the fuck are you?"

"I am Mr. and Mrs. Fominov's legal representative. Forgive me when I say I don't even want to know who the fuck you are."

Tobias was silent for a moment. "What is the situation?"

"The situation is you have the DEA and some other types flashing badges and talking fire and brimstone. My read? Someone put Mr. and Mrs. Fominov on a list, but I don't think these junior G-men have diddly-squat. I predict I can have them on a plane in twenty-four to forty-eight, tops."

"I see."

"Our next move is to contact the Russian consulate and raise holy hell with—"

"You will shit-can that idea, stat," Tobias rumbled.

Bolan allowed some surprise to come into his voice. "Well, if you say so, but—"

"I say so, and what is your name, pal?"

"Bueller, J. C. Bueller, of Bueller and Bueller." In the past hour Akira Tokaido had built a website with a phone number and email, and Carmen Delahunt had been briefed to answer the phone. "Listen, do you want me to call you when—"

"From this point on I wish to deal directly with your client. If I feel the need to speak to you again, I will."

"Oh…kay."

"Put Mrs. Fominov back on."

"I am here."

"Call me as soon as you are on a plane."

Tobias's end went dead. Bolan disconnected the phones and spoke into his. "You get all that?"

"Oh, indeed," Aaron Kurtzman confirmed. "That Tobias guy sounds like a real hard-ass."

"He is. Can you track him?"

"Anytime he uses his phone. Assuming he uses it again. I bet he goes through a lot of them. However, we did successfully download a virus, and if he sends anyone anything on that phone, they'll be infected, Farm style."

"Good to know."

Mama Neddi glared up at Bolan with renewed gall. "And, so?"

"A deal is a deal. I'll get Boris medical attention, and when my mission is over, you're free."

"I don't believe you."

"I don't care."

Mama Neddi's eyes focused on Bolan. "I believe you."

"I don't care. Now get back in the trunk."

Mama Neddi hoisted her huge frame up and crawled into the trunk. She went back to spooning her husband as Bolan slammed the lid shut and reset the alarm. "Bear, I need you to get Dr. McCillup and one of his nurses to Puerto Barrios. I had to put some hurt on Boris Fominov during pickup, and I promised medical attention for him as part of the co-operation deal."

"I've spoken with him once while I checked on Murphy and Igor. He seems like a real salt-of-the-earth kind of guy. I don't think it should be hard to convince him."

"I think you're right."

"What are you going to do now?" Kurtzman asked.

"I promised Val a nap. I think I'm going to grab one myself while the getting is good. Any word on the team?"

"Donez is in Mexico and we're arranging his flight. Kaino and Savacool have a big jump on you and should be pulling into Puerto Barrios around daybreak. God only knows where

Bang is. However, we have a safehouse arranged. As soon as he makes contact, we'll vector him in. I've downloaded the locale to you."

"Copy that, Bear. And thanks, out." Bolan walked back into the bungalow. Svarzkova was fast asleep and wearing her eye patch. The steak sat in a pan on top of the stove, and he took that as a hint she expected to be fed when she woke up. Bolan took a hint from Mama Neddi and spooned in behind Svarzkova.

Marine Helvetica

"THE RUSSIANS ARE being detained?" Conz asked. He watched laborers working at restoring his office to its former Euro chic glory as he spoke into his phone.

"That's the story," Tobias reported. "The lawyer thinks their names got put on a watch list."

"And how might that have happened?"

"I have no idea. My fellow American is running around with that one-eyed Russian bitch. If she's GRU and operating in the Americas, she's got to have some kind of pull. The Fominovs are known organized-crime participants in Moscow. Maybe the bitch put two and two together, or maybe she just made a shopping list of usual suspects and mailed it marked urgent to Homeland Security. Either way our cooks got red flagged."

"Their status?"

"The lawyer thinks he can have them out today or tomorrow at the latest. He says the Feds don't have shit except their names."

"Who is this lawyer?"

"I texted the info to Haas."

Haas nodded. "I am having some people from the North American division look into it. At first glance they seem legitimate, or at least as legitimate as the kind of lawyers who would represent the Fominovs can be."

"What have you found out about Svarzkova?"

"Nothing much more than what her man Ivan gave up under torture. She's a woman, and she rose to the rank of major in the GRU, through fieldwork both at home and abroad. That says a great deal. We know she is a trained sniper. Her spreading a net and catching the Fominovs at the airport is certainly not out of the realm of possibility, particularly if the American is receiving at least tacit assistance from the United States government."

"But you do not like it."

"I do not like it at all, Herr Conz. Even if everything is exactly as it seems, I believe we should postpone until we have the Russians in hand and have fully debriefed them. Waiting until we have eliminated the American and his team would be equally if not even more prudent, as well."

"That is not going to happen. We have a schedule to keep."

"I suspected you would say as much." Haas sighed. He sensed he was quickly getting pushed into the "You get paid to worry" category.

"Do you think we can produce the product?"

"We have the machinery and the materials, and our chemists have produced the Fominov recipe in small batches. However, to produce it on such a large scale so quickly without the Russians overseeing operations? I fear we may have to deal with quality control and safety issues."

"I have absolute faith in our chemists."

"I am sure they will be gratified to hear that."

Conz made up his mind. "The Zeta and MS-13 are prepared to accept delivery?"

"They are. Their chiefs in Guatemala want to see the money and sample the product."

"Then I say we go into full production immediately. By all means, let us impress the Guatemalans."

CHAPTER TWENTY-SEVEN

Puerto Barrios

Bolan and Svarzkova drove into town. According to directions, the safehouse was just slightly up on the western side of the hills ringing town. The vantage was only five minutes from downtown but gave them a view of the port and the airport. Bolan rolled the battered limo down the one-lane road. It was early, and while the port and the airport were busy below them, the hills were nearly silent. A lone man in a poncho and traditional Mayan hat rode a donkey in the middle of the road and smoked a cigar in the morning sun. Svarzkova took up her weapon as Bolan gave the horn a tap. The man on the donkey turned and waved.

It was Bang.

Bolan slowed and Svarzkova rolled down the window. The Russian agent called out happily, "I admire your mule, Señor Bang!"

"*Gracias.* But it is not a mule! It is a jackass! I have named him Cooper."

Svarzkova giggled. Bolan flipped off the ex-Kaibil and drove on toward the safehouse. Bolan turned left a half klick along and took a short private road up to a small and faded-looking pink Spanish colonial. The house had a wall and a gate, and within a tiny circular drive girded a fountain overgrown with reeds and algae. The Bronco Kaino had been driving and a shiny-looking motorcycle Bolan suspected Donez had rented sat parked beside a bottle-green rental

Jeep. Bolan pulled in and he and Svarzkova slid out. Sava-cool was armed and waved from the roof. "Looks like the gang's all here!"

Svarzkova snuffed the air. "I hope Kaino is cooking something."

"Me, too."

Kaino came out on cue followed by Dr. McCillup and Donez. Bolan noticed the good doctor had a battered-looking Colt 1911 Government Model pistol tucked into the front of his cargo shorts. "You got here quick, Doc."

"Well, a very intriguing man named Bear called me and told me I had a patient. He arranged a private flight from a private airstrip at a very odd hour. He mentioned cracked ribs and possible internal injuries?"

Bolan went to the trunk. "How are Igor and Murph?"

"I stand by my statement. Our Mr. Murphy is a medical miracle."

"In more ways than one."

McCillup laughed. "He does exhibit many weird and wonderful qualities, but he is fresh out of miracles. He admitted he's had past concussions. That man should retire posthaste."

Bolan nodded. "And Igor?"

"Unlike Murphy, who seems to get stronger the more brain cells of his you kill?" McCillup nodded at Svarzkova. "Or this one who gets prettier with every trauma?"

Svarzkova beamed.

McCillup stopped smiling. "Our young Russian friend is facing issues. I suspect he has brain damage. I x-rayed him twenty-four hours ago. His neck is a mess. He's lucky he's not paralyzed. The loss of his twin brother, the loss of his eye, knowing his career is over. He's nosing over into some pretty severe depression."

"Well, I got more for you, Doc." Bolan knocked on the trunk and spoke loudly as he popped it. "No sudden moves!"

Mama Neddi blinked and covered her face at the sudden light. Boris mewled and tunneled into his blanket.

"How are we on a secure room, Kaino?"

"The place has a cellar. It's pretty medieval but it fits the bill."

"Take the lady downstairs and I want her handcuffed and hobbled. Donuts, go with him. Watch her. She knows how to hurt a guy."

Mama Neddi had spent the night in a trunk and her stiffness had already hobbled her to a great extent. Kaino and Donez hauled her massive frame out and escorted her inside. Svarzkova withdrew her PP-93 and followed. McCillup prodded Boris a few times where he lay. Boris moaned. "His abdomen is as stiff as board. He's bleeding inside."

"I need him alive."

"Oh, he won't die for days."

"I need the Bride of Frankenstein to believe he's going to be okay. In fact, I need him okay, I'm kind of a stickler for a deal being a deal," Bolan said.

"Well, I can dope him up to the moon and put a smile on his face if that would help."

"You're a fascinating medical professional, Dr. McCillup."

"Before I found God? I got stories."

"I'd like to hear them sometime," Bolan said.

"I bet yours are better. Meantime, let's get him in a room and comfortable." Bang and the donkey clopped into the drive. McCillup waved. "How is the shoulder, young man?"

"Much better for your ministrations!" Bang slid off the donkey and hitched him to wrought-iron bench. He ambled up and peered at the battered Russian. "You want help with the patient?"

"Much appreciated."

Bolan watched McCillup and Bang half walk, half carry Boris inside. He took a deep breath and realized he needed more sleep.

"How you doing, Coop?"

Bolan looked up to see Savacool looking down from the eaves with a submachine gun in hand. "How are you, Cool?"

"I seem to be spending a lot of time on rooftops."

"Sorry."

"No, actually I'm really short and I kind of like it." Savacool looked down from the roof judgingly. "Coop, you looked better when we left you on the coast. You're starting to look like a dog's dinner again."

Bolan heaved a very weary sigh of amusement. "A dog's dinner?"

"That would be you."

"Is that a Florida thing?" Bolan asked.

"It's my thing, and this is the third time in a week I've watched my favorite white man start going septic green. McCillup brought you another IV just in case. I'm saying the case is in point. Go lie down. We'll wake you for dinner."

Bolan didn't have to be told twice. He stuffed inside and realized he was stumbling. Kaino jerked his head at a door and Bolan went through it and ensconced himself in the hammock strung inside. He closed his eyes and stayed awake just long enough to note Svarzkova arranging her body around his without tipping the hammock. She murmured soothing endearments in Russian.

Bolan gave himself over to oblivion.

Bolan awoke.

His eyes were gummy with matter and he had a tube in his arm. His head felt hot and light. His body felt as though it were two dead bodies, every part of him ached and he felt like his joints were full of sand. He was sick again, sick down to his blood and bones, and he knew it. Svarzkova had stopped spooning and now stood over him looking severely concerned. McCillup had pulled up a chair next to the hammock. "Son, you need to—"

"I don't have the time."

"You got time for a blood infection and going into compete renal shutdown?"

"I need you to do whatever you have to do to keep me going another forty-eight hours."

"Son, this isn't my first trip to the rodeo."

"Thank God."

"Don't take the Lord's name in vain. I need to put you on some very powerful medications regardless. They will knock your ass out. So if you really are this stupid or the situation really is this desperate, I'll have to put you on some very powerful stimulants to keep you sharp. I can't guarantee a happy marriage. You could drop unconscious or just drop dead."

"Do it."

"You don't know what you're asking," McCillup said.

Bolan gave McCillup a very shaky smile. "Would you believe me if I said I did?"

"Well, son, I guess I would. I'll have to go into town and I'll need your friend the Bear to arrange—"

Bolan shoved out his phone. "Hit the last number called."

"Right. You should eat if you can."

Food sounded utterly revolting. "Tell Kaino I want steak and a soft drink and to keep it coming."

McCillup switched out Bolan's IV for another. "Here it comes, and it won't stop coming until we can get you to a hospital. Unless you drop dead, you're going for a ride."

Svarzkova looked down at Bolan and looked like she might start crying.

"Hey," Bolan said.

"What?"

"Spoon me."

"You smell like death."

"Spoon me anyway."

Svarzkova curled herself into Bolan's embrace and managed a happy sigh. She had showered while he was unconscious. Her hair smelled like jasmine. Bolan shoved his face into it and went back to sleep.

"You awake?"

Bolan awoke. The world was a strange, jangly place. "Yeah, I'm awake."

Kaino held out a platter of chopped meat, beans and rice and a bottle of grapefruit Fanta. "Well, you look and sound better. How do you feel?"

Bolan considered. "Hungry."

"That's a good sign."

Bolan eased himself up to a sitting position in the hammock. The pretty colors tried to pull him down in a one-hundred-color Crayola crayon undertow. Bolan rode it and his vision returned to normal. He resisted throwing up and started eating instead. Bolan checked his internal clock and found it was offline. "What time is it?"

"Around seven in the p.m. The doc hit you with the heavy stuff to kill your infection and then slowly started adding the stimulants. Don't know what kind of shit and didn't ask."

Bolan gulped grapefruit soda like mother's milk and didn't stop until the bottle was empty. "I need another."

Kaino took a bottle off the floor and opened it. "Way ahead of you."

The strawberry was even better. Bolan inhaled half and went back to attacking his food. "What's new?"

"Everyone is worried about you," Kaino said.

"What else is new?"

Kaino managed a smile. "Your buddy the Bear really needs to get hold of you."

"What's up?"

"Well, I told him you were knocked out, and maybe it's because I'm a cop rather than a Fed, or a mercenary or a spy, but he confided in me."

"You're a confidable kind of guy, Kaino. You know sometimes even I feel like I can confide in you."

"That's sweet. The upshot is we're in."

"In?"

"Like Flynn. Tobias made a call. His phone spoke with Haas and Conz's phone. The Bear told me to tell you the virus you put in the system when you attacked is Trojan Horse ready, and the crap you pulled with that Russian she-moose's phone, it's in. He said they most likely have countermeasures, but we have an opportunity for a perfect cyberstorm."

"The Bear is the best of the best."

"I can see why. Well, so far it's all been passive, but your people have been listening. Helvetica Marine has decided the best defense is a good offense. They're going to produce the product on schedule and with or without the Russians. The Zetas and MSers are going to take delivery. It's on. Sounds like there's going to be a great big bad-guy sausage party on the side of that volcano." The big man waggled his eyebrows. "Tell me we're going to crash it."

"I told you, Kaino. In *Rolling Thunder* style."

"It's not like I can ever doubt you about anything again, but I'll believe it when I see it."

"I saw it on the drive up here. I saw the container vessel with the correct number," Bolan said.

"Oh, Coop! Tell me it is fully loaded!"

"Loaded like Dr. McCillup having a Korean War flashback. The Mexico war has officially moved south."

"Awww shit!" Kaino enthused. "We're pulling a goddamn *Guns of Navarone!*"

"Something like that," Bolan admitted. He pushed his empty plate aside. "Help me up."

Kaino gave Bolan an arm. The dizziness was gone, but Bolan had nothing solid in his knees and he gratefully let Kaino take a big chunk of his walking weight. Kaino walked him down the hall. "Got a war council going on."

"Lead on."

Bolan's team rose from the dinner table and gave him a standing ovation. The seat at the head of the table had been left empty for him. Kaino roared. "Check out the big balls on this gringo!"

Savacool shook her head as she applauded. "We thought you were dead."

McCillup shrugged helplessly. "I gave it fifty-fifty."

Bolan winced as Donez pounded him on the back. "Big iron balls on El Hombre! Blue-eyed conquistador son of a bitch!"

"Coop?" Bang grinned. "I have a donkey outside named Cooper. But your balls? They are bigger than his."

McCillup grinned at his patient. "I made him turn his head and cough. It's all true."

The table broke out into a storm of obscene commentary. Bolan's team laughed and he laughed with them. In the face of heavy-duty pharmaceuticals and infection, laughter was welcome medicine. Each member of the team had made hell runs across Guatemala to be on time for a suicide mission, and the team was ready. Bolan eased himself into a chair. "I thank you all for your testimonials and support."

Kaino slapped a huge hand down on Bolan's shoulder. "Yo, just lead us to victory, man. We've come too far to fail. This shit goes down."

Bang nodded. "What he said."

Savacool shot her gleaming smile. "Coop, I'm in so deep I can't go home without a win."

"Then let's finish this." Bolan tapped an app and put Kurtzman on speaker. "The team is assembled. Tell me the good news."

The computer expert's voice came across the tablet's speaker. He was clearly pleased with himself. "Our boy has been busy."

Bolan knew he meant Akira Tokaido. "What has he done?"

"You know how he infected Tobias's phone?"

"Yeah?"

"Well, the infection is spreading. Tobias did some texting, and those he texted received the gift that keeps on giving."

"Who has Tobias been trading texts with?" Bolan asked.

"Yony Trigueño, who happens to be the number one MS-13 man in Guatemala."

"Anyone else of interest?"

"Only Erwinito Iboy."

"I'm guessing he's a Zeta?" Bolan queried.

"He's the man leading the Zeta charge into Guatemala."

"And their phones are infected?"

"And infecting everything they communicate with."

Smiles broke out across the table. They were finally catching a break.

"What has Tobias been telling Trigueño and Iboy?" the soldier said.

"One simple message, and that is everything is on schedule."

Bolan considered what he had learned from Neddi Fominov. "That means they went ahead with production without the Russians."

"That seems to be the size of it."

Savacool sighed. "The Zeta and MS-13 have to know Helvetica Marine is selling to both of them."

"I'm sure they do," Bolan agreed. "But Conz is selling them a ton apiece. That's one hell of a lot of product to move, and new product at that. Both the Zeta and MS-13 will want to see how the product sells through distribution channels they already have before they start the war for exclusive rights."

Kaino grunted. "I still can't imagine Conz is dumb enough to schedule both gangs for pickup at the same time."

"No," Kurtzman answered. "From what we have gleaned, Iboy and some of his boys are taking delivery tomorrow night, and Trigueño and some likely lads from the Zetas are taking delivery the day after."

Bolan pondered out loud. "I wonder if we could make Conz stupid enough to invite them both at the same time, and without him knowing."

Bang laughed. "You are an evil man."

"Bear," Bolan asked, "do you think Señor Trigueño might receive a message saying that he is taking delivery tomorrow night?"

"Oh, I think something to that effect can be arranged."

"I admire a tidy package as much as the next girl," Savacool commented. "But there's only six of us, and you're inviting a bunch of hardcore criminals to an already crowded party."

"You have a point, Cool." Bolan looked around the table. "Anyone want to leave the MS-13 out of this?"

"I for one would like to leave them dead with fruit bats nesting in their bones," Bang stated.

Savacool was appalled. "Fruit bats nesting in their bones?"

Kaino laughed. "Now, that is some fucked-up Mayan death shit."

"Death to them," Svarzkova agreed. "And fruit bats."

Bolan nodded. "So we're all in. Cool?"

It was clearly violating the FBI agent's better judgment. Savacool heaved a sigh. "We're all in."

McCillup raised his hand. "I'd like to volunteer."

The team all looked at the good doctor.

McCillup shrugged. "I fired a bazooka in basic, back in the day. How much different can it be? And speaking of basic, I knew my way around a Garand back in the day, as well."

"You want to do this?" Bolan asked.

McCillup's face set in some very hard lines. "I spent some time on the internet since we parted ways on the coast. I researched this *krokodil*. So no, I don't want to do this, but this just has to be done. Someone needs to say no, and I happen to think I need to be in the back of a Mexican narco tank with a fine bunch of like-minded folk."

Murmurs of agreement and respect rounded the cabin. Bolan already admired the man, but this was close to a suicide mission, nonsanctioned, and McCillup was a missionary and a civilian. "Did you see real combat?"

"I was usually busy patching people up, but this wouldn't be the first time I've been shot at."

"How old are you again?" Bolan asked.

"I run two miles on the beach every morning and do a hundred push-ups every night before I go to bed, Junior. And between the two of us? Given your condition, you want to bet which one of us drops first?"

Bolan knew defeat when he saw it. "No."

Kaino openly approved. "Shit, I wouldn't mind having a doctor along on this one. I'm pretty sure someone is going to get shot. Plus we're out Murph and Igor, and we need every volunteer who has a set on this one."

"Every volunteer who has a set?" Savacool gazed scathingly at the master sergeant.

Kaino cringed.

Savacool shook her head. "Sets are fragile things, Kaino. They shrink from the cold, and one light love tap leaves their owners on the ground puking. In my experience, most sets are good for one tussle and then they need eight hours sleep and pancakes and coffee before they're any good for anything again."

Svarzkova concurred. "This is overwhelmingly true in my experience."

"Girly parts, on the other hand," Savacool continued, "can get pounded all night long and—"

"La-la-la-la-la!" Kaino covered his ears. "I am *not* listening to Cool!"

McCillup laughed and nodded at Savacool and Svarzkova.

"Worse comes to worst, I can pull an old man and sit in the car while the girls go shopping."

Bolan gave himself to fate. "You're hired."

"Thanks, I guess. It'll be interesting to see the elephant again at this point in life."

"Doc, the elephant has gotten a lot nastier in the intervening years."

McCillup looked Bolan in the eye. "I was in Korea, son. You ever experienced a human wave attack?"

"Would you believe me if I said I had?"

"You know, I believe I would."

Bolan spoke to his tablet. "Bear, we got a satellite?"

"You'll have a good six-hour window," Kurtzman replied. "With the proposed pickup time right square in the middle of it."

Bolan nodded. It was starting to have the makings of a real mission. "We're going in hot and hard in the Hombre Anvil. We're going straight down their throats and see if they have the stomach for it. I suggest everyone get as much rest as you can. Kaino, Cool, if you don't mind I'd like to make a Last Supper worthy last supper for tonight. I want a weapons and equipment check of everything we have here tomorrow morning and then split into our scatter teams and meet up down in the port. We'll do a second check of everything Morti sent. With any luck Morti did us right."

Savacool snorted. "Oh, he has a serious man-crush on you. There might just be a dozen roses in it."

"Assuming Morti's love for me is pure, we head out just after sunset."

Kaino leaned back in his chair. "And that is our Achilles' heel. You want me to drive that monster over 120 miles from the port to the highlands without attracting attention?"

"Would I do that to you, Kaino?"

Kaino blinked. "Does your pilot pal have a C-130 tucked away someplace we don't know about?"

"Well, that's never outside the realm of possibility," Bolan admitted.

Bang saw it. "Morti sent us the trunk in a container vessel. That container will be loaded onto a train."

Bolan nodded. "Kaino, you are going to ride in style straight into the train yard in Guate and roll out hot. We take the same route you took up the mountain. Last time you got cheated. This time you're going to unleash hell."

Kaino raised a hand to his ear. "I'm sorry, Coop. I can't seem to hear you over the sound of my erection."

More laughs broke out.

"Just see if you can keep it out of the food, Kaino. You still got KP duty tonight."

Kaino cracked his huge knuckles. "With pleasure. Cool and I went shopping while you were asleep. I'll rattle some pans for you."

Bolan rose and felt another wave of light-headedness. Mc-Cillup put a steadying hand on his shoulder. "Son, this was the most exciting conversation I have ever been privy to, but you have had just about enough excitement for the night." He put his hand to his head like a mentalist making a prediction. "I see an IV and a nap." The doctor leered at Svarzkova. "And a spooning, in your future. Particularly the future before dinner."

Svarzkova folded her arms across her chest affirmatively. "Only spooning has saved him."

"Ma'am, you won't get any arguments from me."

Bolan took a deep breath as the room stopped spinning. "Me, neither."

Svarzkova gave Bolan an arm and he gratefully took it and leaned on her as they went back to his hammock. Bolan sank into the Mayan cotton, another grateful sigh escaping him. Svarzkova smiled down at him out of her mangled face. "So tomorrow we die."

"It's likely," Bolan replied.

"Any last request?"

"An act of oral outrage, and a grape Fanta."

Svarzkova's single eye narrowed. "You realize my jaw hurts."

"Assuming survival, I'll take a rain check."

Svarzkova made a very Russian noise. "You may have rain check." The GRU agent turned and went back down the hall. "I shall fetch Fanta."

CHAPTER TWENTY-EIGHT

Helvetica Marine

Remo Haas tried desperately to keep war from breaking out. Erwinito Iboy and his Zetas had shown up on time. The problem was Yony Trigueño had shown the incredibly bad taste of showing up ten minutes later and insisting it was the right day and the right time. Guns had stopped just short of being drawn in the lobby. Haas and Tobias had managed to get them separated to opposite sides of the room, but the MS-13 boys shot the Zetas suicide smiles and threw gang signs. The Zetas silently glared stone-cold murder. Iboy was tall, thin, and could have passed for a matador. Trigueño was pure Maya and could have passed for Mulac's brother. The Mexican and the Salvadoran continued to argue in ever louder and ever faster Spanish.

Conz debarked the elevator flanked by two of Haas's men, with Mulac following him close as a shadow. Conz's smile turned up to game-show-host wattage as he spoke happily in Spanish. "Erwinito! Yony! Come! Let us not argue in the hall. Each of you pick a man and follow me into my office. I have cognac and cigars. Mr. Tobias! Why don't you take the rest of the men into the commissary and get them beers and something to eat!"

The Zeta and MS-13 muscle glowered at Conz and looked to their leaders. Conz took it in stride. "I will thank you not to kill one another until you have left this building as millionaires."

That went a long way to curbing the glaring and gang signing.

"Besides!" Conz smiled and took in the surroundings. "We just remodeled."

A few of the thugs smirked or rolled their eyes. Haas was again reminded why Conz was in charge. Iboy and Trigueño each nodded at his right-hand man. Conz turned and led the way to the elevator. With his back to the cartel members he shot Haas and Tobias a look of pure, unadulterated rage. Haas brought up the rear as Tobias began ushering armed killers toward the commissary.

The elevator ride to the third floor was as quiet and mordant as a grave. The two security men stayed outside. Everyone took seats on the new furniture while Conz himself poured brandy in fishbowl-size snifters and lit Cuban cigars all around. Conz finally sat, blew a smoke ring and managed to get everyone to toast. The snifters chinged and Conz went behind his desk. Haas stood by the door with his hand on the butt of the Heckler & Koch Personal Defense Weapon beneath his jacket. Mulac stood by the window behind Conz, ready to make his own mayhem.

Conz sighed. "Gentlemen, I know you are competitors. I know there has been bloodshed between your factions, and most likely will be more. I wish to be no part of it. I simply produce a product. I am currently sitting on two tons of it, far more of a quantity than either of you can move alone. I would strongly suggest you keep the peace, make more money than God, and once the pipelines have been established you can then resume killing each other over them."

He gazed at the Salvadoran and chose his words carefully. "Yony, everyone knows the balls you have, the foresight you have. Your business acumen. When my superiors said find the man who can make this happen? You will remember I came to you first."

Trigueño nodded and puffed his cigar. "I do not deny this."

"Then why?" Conz spread his hands to encompass the room, the people in it and the facility. "We have a good thing here. Can we not make half a billion dollars first before starting a fight?"

Trigueño examined his cigar with great care. "What the fuck are you talking about?"

Conz made a pleading gesture. "Yony, why are you here? You were to take delivery tomorrow. I am flying in Salvadoran cooks to prepare a feast for you. Now your men are eating Erwinito's. I flew in Mexican cooks for him."

"Señor? I came here tonight because your man told me to. He said it was urgent, and we must reschedule, for tonight." Trigueño contemplated Iboy over his cigar. "I had no idea the Mexican would be here."

Conz's face went flat. He shot a look at Haas, who got on the phone. "Mr. Tobias, you are required in the executive suite immediately." Haas only half listened to Tobias's angry response. Mulac was looking out the window intently. He slowly raised his finger and pointed out toward the road.

Conz stood and peered. Haas pulled his weapon and was to the window in three strides. He squinted into the darkness. The road was little more than a twisting line of darkness between the trees as night genuinely fell.

Mulac pointed again.

Haas caught movement. It was a flash of motion in the gloom, but something was on the road and moving fast. The vehicle hit the short straightaway to the facility and lights suddenly blazed on. An apocalyptic fortress thundered toward Helvetica Marine borne on a Kenworth Class 8 chassis.

Haas called up an application on his phone and tapped the general alarm. His eyes widened as nothing happened. He shouted in Swiss. "Herr Conz! We must move belowground!" Haas went to the door and bounced off as it didn't open beneath his hand. He tried the handle a second and a third time. He swiped his universal card and the lock peeped at him and blinked red.

Outside the gate guards began firing.

MORTI HAD COME THROUGH in spades. Every square inch of the narco tank had been scrubbed of black powder and smoke residue. All their weapons from Mexico had been lovingly cleaned. Best of all, he had welded a ring mount around the top hatch and a pintle for whoever was driving shotgun. Kaino was driving. Bang was blasting away in the passenger seat through the armored slats with a Russian PKM machine gun. Bolan and Svarzkova stood in the top hatch on the slanted iron ladder. Svarzkova touched off short bursts as the narco tank barreled for the front gate. Donez and Savacool manned the forward firing slits. McCillup stood at the bottom of the hatch ladder with an armful of rocket-propelled grenades.

Svarzkova's brass flew past Bolan's face as he leveled the RPG.

Bolan put his optical on Conz's panoramic office window and fired. The RPG rocketed across the mountainside and impacted the bulletproof glass. The window disappeared in a flash of orange fire and smoke.

"Rocket!" Bolan called. McCillup handed him a reload. The soldier shoved the tube between his knees and slid in a fresh projectile.

Kaino boomed over the sound of gunfire and the thunder of the Anvil's engine. "Going through!"

Bang blasted down the last gate guard and the gate itself sheared away from the force of the Anvil's cowcatcher prow striking it. Riflemen were congregating at the front entrance of the facility and blasting away. Bullets whined off the Anvil's armored hull like hail. Kaino ignored the gunmen and took the Anvil around the road flanking the buildings. Bolan gave the riflemen a rocket for their trouble. The Anvil dipped as it went down an incline. Beneath the trees and the camouflage netting Bolan knew the doors to the underground factory lay behind the facade of foliage.

Kaino's voice rose. "Brace for impact!"

Bolan and Svarzkova dropped down and grabbed the iron ladder to the hatch for dear life. The Anvil hit the clamshell doors. The soldier caught the Russian agent as she went flying, and her momentum nearly ripped him off the ladder. Donez lost his perch at the firing slit and went tumbling in the Anvil's iron belly. Savacool yipped as her feet went out from under her, but she held on. McCillup went sliding across the iron flooring. The Anvil was inside and careening out of control.

"Shit!" Kaino cried.

The Anvil hit something heavier than the doors and bucked like a bronco. Metal screamed. Kaino screamed, too. "Tanks! Tanks! Tanks!"

Kaino wasn't howling about armored vehicles. The master sergeant slammed his steel shutters closed against the spraying fire and chemicals. The Anvil rocked as a tank full of something volatile exploded against her side. Flames roared in a wave over the open top hatch and searing heat washed inside. "Kaino! Reverse!" Bolan let Svarzkova go and readied his launcher. Kaino ground gears, and the Anvil reversed out of the inferno. Bolan clambered up the ladder and stuck his head out in a fog of smoke and burning chemicals. Kaino had kamikazed straight into the main chemical tanks and had generated his own genuine toxic inferno. "Hard left! Hard left!"

Kaino cranked the wheel as he stepped on it in Reverse. Anvil was a giant iron pig and moaned and squealed in protest. She wasn't exactly on fire, but her nose up to the cab was covered in flame. Bolan beheld the mother lode. Two tons of synthetic *krokodil* lay piled and palleted off to one side. Crystalline aqua-blue product was neatly packaged in clear plastic kilo bricks. Bolan pulled the pins on the two remaining Russian white-phosphorus grenades and tossed them. The weapons thudded, and burning particulate flew into the air. Inside the streamers of smoke the bricks of *krokodil* blackened and burned. Bolan didn't know whether junkies smoked *krokodil,* but he suspected breathing in the two tons of burning improved product might prove fatal.

Bolan dropped down and slammed the hatch. "Kaino, take us around to the aerial loading pad!"

Kaino shoved the Anvil into gear and took it around the truck loading and off-loading loop girding the burning factory. Bolan spoke into his phone. "Bear! Open the outer door to the helicopter loading pad!"

"Opening!" Kurtzman responded.

More explosions shoved against the Anvil's hull. The vehicle lurched to a halt. "Anyone who is getting out, let's go!" Kaino called.

Bolan snapped his knife open and cut the straps tying down Donez's rental motorcycle. It was a 2008 Honda Nighthawk. He heaved it up and threw a leg over the saddle, then slung a Garand and a bandolier of clips over his shoulder. Svarzkova jumped onto the seat behind him. "I am with you!"

Bolan didn't argue. "Kaino! Drop the door!"

The hydraulic unit whined and Bolan held his breath as smoke rolled into the Anvil's cabin. The interior of the drug factory was a burning and exploding hell. The burning chemicals stung Bolan's face as he kicked the Nighthawk into life and rolled down the ramp. Relief was in sight as the new outer door to the mountainside rolled upward at Kurtzman's command. The enemy was expecting them to come up the elevators or to exit the way they had come.

Bolan rolled out onto the newly rebuilt platform. It clung to the side of the hill, and a narrow footpath led back up to the facility. Bolan pulled down his NVGs and gunned the Nighthawk's engine. "Hold on!"

The motorcycle flew up the mountainside. Svarzkova held Bolan tightly with one arm while she filled her hand with a PP-93 and aimed it forward low past his shoulder. A guard had run to the perimeter to look at the fire blooming out of the mountainside. He looked down too late and took a long burst from Svarzkova in the chest. Bolan reached the lawn and spun the bike to a halt.

The front entrance was littered with bodies from Bolan's RPG blast. "Bear, do we have security cameras?"

"At the moment we own the facility."

"Sitrep."

Security screens flashed across Bolan's phone. "The enemy is moving all forces to the elevators and to the outer doors you crashed. So far we still have lockdown in the facility."

"How's the board meeting going?" Bolan asked.

"No clue. You knocked out the security cameras in Conz's office."

"How you doing down there, Kaino?"

"It's getting hot!"

Bolan unslung his Garand and flipped off the safety. He nodded to Svarzkova. "Let's go." They ran at a crouch to the front entrance. The RPG had shattered the glass and left four men dead. Four more men were angrily punching the elevator button and swiping at doors that peeped and blinked red at their card keys at the back of the lobby.

One gunman noticed Bolan and Svarzkova and shouted the alarm. The Executioner shot him down. The other three clawed for weapons and dived for cover, but there was nothing in the lobby that provided any kind of barrier to a full-metal-jacketed 30-06 rifle bullet. Bolan's M-1 spit out its spring magazine and Svarzkova's pinged away a second later. Blood pooled from behind the sofas and the reception desk.

The soldier thumbed another magazine into the breach and

the bolt shot home. "Bear, lock out all doors to the stairs. I want a bad-guy-free walk to the top floor."

"Done."

The lock on the stairwell door peeped and blinked green. Bolan and Svarzkova went upstairs. At the second level a security man shouted and pointed at them through the narrow window in the security door. His face disappeared and the door dimpled slightly as he tried to fire through it. The needlelike bullets of his German PDW were not up to the task of penetrating security doors. Svarzkova snapped her Garand to her shoulder and rapid-fired eight rounds. The big WWII battle rifle was up to the task, and she was rewarded by a muffled scream. They went on to the third floor. Bolan paused before reaching the landing. He suspected someone would be watching the landing through the window. "I need third-floor security cameras, Bear."

"Negative, Striker. We have lost feed on the third floor except for several empty offices."

"Is the enemy regaining operational control of the security suite?"

"No, I'm betting they shot them out. "You sure the two of you want to walk into that hallway?"

"We empty Garands through the door, throw grenades and go in submachine guns on full-auto. Full assault."

Bolan smiled. Svarzkova was a door-kicker born and raised. "Let's do that, right after Bear opens the elevator doors." He had never seen Svarzkova so happy.

"This is good plan."

"We assault on my go. Bear, open the elevator doors," Bolan ordered.

"Opening!"

Gunfire broke out above.

"Now!"

Bolan and Svarzkova charged to the landing, firing their Garands through the door as fast as they could pull the triggers. They dropped their spent rifles and drew grenades and submachine guns. "Third-floor stairs!" Bolan ordered.

The lock on the cratered door peeped and Bolan kicked it. Cotter pins flew and two fragmentation grenades followed. Bolan and Svarzkova held back as the grenades detonated and then went into full assault on the third floor. Smoke filled the air, shrapnel scored the walls and bodies littered the floor.

Kurtzman spoke rapidly over the link. "I have a helicopter, inbound!"

"Give me visual on the roof!" Bolan requested.

"Negative on roof feed!" Kurtzman replied.

Svarzkova snarled. "How?"

Bolan stared down the hall at the door to Conz's office. "We blasted out the window. Someone inside survived and they went out and up to the roof. The helicopter was probably called in when MS-13 showed up unannounced."

Grimaldi spoke across the line. "Did someone say helicopter?"

Bolan smiled. "Where are you, Jack?"

"There was no love in El Salvador. So I busted out, headed straight out over the Pacific, crossed the three mile international line and broke north. Did you know Helvetica Marine lies exactly on the fifteenth parallel? So I just made a hard right. Oh, and that was after I picked up Murphy and Igor. Murph is hanging by a chicken strap with rifle in hand. Igor claims that despite his injuries he can pull the pin on a grenade and drop it out the door, and I believe him."

"How far out are you, Jack?"

"I can see that inbound chopper on my radar, and I'm in blackout mode. He just isn't going to reach that roof."

"Copy that, Jack." Bolan and Svarzkova took up their rifles and reloaded.

The enemy burst out of one of the darkened offices. It was a three-man wedge. They had taken the intervening moments since the attack to suit up. They wore ballistic helmets and full Threat Level III body armor. They came out PDWs blazing, and the beams of red laser sights sought out Bolan and Svarzkova's lives. In the heartbeat separating them Bolan saw Haas's face beneath his helmet in the lead. The Swiss mercenary was depending on his armor to save him in close quarters combat with Bolan. The big Garand bucked against the Executioner's shoulder as he fired all eight rounds in the magazine.

Haas should have been wearing Threat Level IV armor.

Bolan put four rounds into Haas, center body mass and gave the other four to the man on his right flank. Svarzkova gave the third man all eight. The armored men fell as their trauma plates failed to deflect the steel-cored bullets and the projectiles bored through Kevlar and the flesh and bone beneath.

Svarzkova groaned.

The soldier looked back as the Russian sagged against the wall. Her left hand looked as though three PDW projectiles had torn through it. Shattered bones and fingers stuck out in different directions as she clutched it. She gave Bolan a very weary look. "The Belasko curse."

Bolan swiftly wrapped the hand in a field dressing. He snapped the sling off her bloodied Garand and strapped her left arm to her chest. Svarzkova groaned and took her PP-93 from its holster. "I will go upstairs. Draw fire. You go out window. Climb and flank."

"All right." Bolan spoke into his phone. "Bear, give Val doors as requested."

"Copy that."

Bolan reloaded his Garand as Svarzkova walked in a slightly unsteady fashion back to the stairs. "Give me the door to Conz's office."

"Copy that."

The lock peeped and blinked green. Bolan drew the PP-93 like a handgun and kicked the door. The suppressed weapon *click-clicked-clicked* as he swept the room in an arc in front of him. No one was home. The RPG round had done its damage. Bolan counted three dead men on the floor. One of them was the MS-13 leader Yony Trigueño. By Bolan's estimate that left at least Conz and the Zeta leader Iboy up top. Bolan slapped in his last magazine for the Russian weapon. "Give me the door to the safe room."

"Copy that."

Bolan stood to one side and aimed. The heavy steel door slid open and the light came on, but the well-appointed cubicle was empty. The party was on the roof. Bolan went to the window. Smoke roiled up out of the facility from multiple points. Down the mountainside the aerial loading door glowed orange and belched black smoke as if the volcano had gone active again.

A black nylon weapon sling hung outside the shattered window. Bolan glanced up. Someone had tied four of them together to make a rope, thrown it over the railing up top and buckled the two ends together below to make a sling. Svarzkova's voice spoke in Bolan's earbud but she was talking to Kurtzman. "Roof access door."

"Copy that," Kurtzman replied.

Bolan heard the door slam open. Svarzkova had managed to unscrew her suppressor to draw even more attention to herself and she blazed away. Bolan put a foot in the stirrup and hauled himself upward. He got one hand on the railing and then another, and kicked a leg up. The soldier drew his PP-93. Svarzkova crouched behind the concrete block of roof access. Conz was firing at her while Iboy flanked. Bolan shoved out his submachine gun like a pistol and fired. Iboy staggered. The soldier held down the trigger until the gangster fell. Iboy dropped to the roof and Bolan swung his muzzle on Conz.

Bullets sparked off the railing by the Executioner's head and Conz threw himself behind a ventilator housing. The

PP-93 clicked empty and Bolan tossed the spent weapon away. He rolled onto the roof and came up with the Garand in hand. Bolan put a round high through the top of the ventilator to let Conz know he could take him any time.

The night lit up above the valley as *Dragonslayer* painted the incoming helicopter with her spotlight. Murphy's rifle stuttered fire as he emptied his weapon into the offending chopper's cockpit.

Bolan put another round high through the ventilator and called out, "You just lost your ticket out of here!"

"Fuck you!" Conz shouted.

Bolan put two more rounds through the beleaguered ventilation unit. "Conz! Come out! I'm willing to let you live because I want to know what else your company is up to."

That was met with silence.

"I have a pretty good idea where most of your body is positioned! Last chance!"

Bolan didn't like the silence. "Val! Covering fire and flank his ass!"

Svarzkova opened up. Bolan put two more rounds through the ventilator's center. He dropped to one knee as the Garand pinged away its magazine and grabbed a new one. Bolan caught motion out of the darkness to his left.

Mulac loped out from behind another ventilator unit, machete in hand. Bolan raised his rifle and the machete chopped into the stock. The soldier spit in Mulac's eyes, and that gave him two heartbeats to leap out of machete range. Mulac snarled and came on. It was clear the Guatemalan was a master of the machete and Bolan had an empty rifle.

But Bolan had an M-1 Garand.

He didn't have a bayonet mounted, but the weapon was over three and a half feet long, and nine and a half pounds of wood and steel. Bolan ignored the sound of Conz and Svarzkova exchanging fire. Mulac came in, deliberately slicing for the fingers of Bolan's left hand. Bolan snapped his hand out of range. At the same time he swung the butt around with all his might.

Mulac's jaw shattered beneath the Garand's steel butt plate. Bolan pulled back and rammed the butt directly between his adversary eyes. The tracker fell dead to the roof.

"Tell the bitch to lay down her weapon, or you're dead!" Conz called out.

Bolan turned to find the man aiming a gun at him over the ventilator. The ruby beam of its laser sight lay squarely against Bolan's chest. "Val! Shoot him!"

"If that Cyclops bitch sticks her head up, no matter what happens I will put ten rounds through your chest! Then I will gouge out her other eye with my thumb! Now the bitch puts down her gun! Your buddy in the helicopter puts his people down on the ground, then he lands on the roof and we go for a little ride!"

Conz had Bolan dead to rights. Svarzkova was in bad shape and had to stick her head out around the roof access to fire.

"I'm going to count to three!" Conz snarled.

The man was so intent on Bolan that he didn't notice a small dark object lob over the roof access. He didn't notice Svarzkova's grenade until it literally clanked to the top of the ventilator unit in front of his face.

Bolan hit the deck.

The Russian high-explosive grenade went off in a small but spectacular pulse of orange fire and Bolan felt the force and heat roll across the roof. He did a push-up and reloaded the Garand and took in the carnage with ringing ears. "Clear!"

Bolan walked over. The ventilator housing had been crushed like a beer can. Conz had been thrown four feet and mostly didn't have a head. The soldier spoke into his phone. "Jack, the LZ is clear."

"Roger that."

Gunfire rang out below. Bolan strode to the edge of the roof. Tobias ran across the front lawn firing behind him and leaped into one of the SUVs parked out front. Bolan raised his rifle.

The Anvil rolled around from the side of the facility trailing smoke and fire like Satan's own semi. The SUV roared to life; the Anvil hit it broadside. The fender crumpled as Kaino kept the pedal down. He pushed the SUV through the perimeter fence. The Anvil told Tobias goodbye as Kaino pushed him right off the mountainside.

Bolan spoke into his phone to Kurtzman. "Do we have any civilians in the building?"

"Some cooks in the commissary is all I see."

"Are they sealed in?"

"All the rooms are sealed," Kurtzman replied.

"Do you have climate control?"

"I do. Why?"

"Seal off the commissary ventilation, then open all other vents," Bolan directed him.

"You want me to flood the facility with chemical smoke and burning *krokodil?*"

"Kaino, break out the windows in the commissary and get the people out. Bear, fumigate the place."

Dragonslayer, over the Pacific

BOLAN LET THE HUM OF the rotors relax him. Nearly every member of the team was passed out. Svarzkova lay in his arms loaded with morphine for her hand. Bolan could feel the infection within him using his exhaustion as leverage to reassert itself. Kurtzman had sent an anonymous message to police and fire resources in the capital that the Helvetica Marine facility was on fire and responders should be aware of extreme chemical danger. They had left the commissary workers the keys to two of the remaining SUVs.

The mission was an unqualified success. They had taken losses, but the *krokodil* operation was smashed. The supply in the United States would quickly dry up. Los Zetas' and MS-13's operations in Guatemala and Mexico had taken some serious blows. Bolan glanced out over the dark Pacific. Helvetica Marine was an international operation. Bolan wondered what else they might be up to.

He was going to have to look into that.

* * * * *

The Don Pendleton's
Executioner®
HOSTILE FORCE

Government agents become targets of an international crime ring.

When two U.S. agents are executed and a third goes missing, the government can no longer deny that one of its units has been compromised. To plug the leak and rescue the missing operative, Mack Bolan is called in. But Mack's not the only one looking for the missing man. But the Executioner has his own plans for cleaning up the organization, and he's going to start at the top of the chain.

Available January 2, 2013, wherever books are sold.

GOLD EAGLE®

www.readgoldeagle.blogspot.com

TAKE 'EM FREE

2 action-packed novels plus a mystery bonus

NO RISK

NO OBLIGATION TO BUY

Don Pendleton
PERILOUS SKIES

Asia is ground zero when stealth planes fall into the wrong hands.

When billion-dollar stealth technology drops to bargain prices, governments and drug cartels around the world want in on the action. Suddenly, hot spots are cropping up everywhere, and even the United States can feel its military security slipping away. No country is safe unless Stony Man's command can find a way to destroy the technology. And the clock is already counting down.

STONY MAN®

*Available February 5, 2013,
wherever books are sold.*